Marilyn

Jeremy Wilson

A SWORD & SHIELD BOOKS PUBLICATION
DALLAS

MARILYN

Published by Sword & Shield Books, LLC

5473 Blair Rd Ste 100 #385616

Dallas, TX 75231-4227

WWW.SWORDANDSHIELDBOOKS.COM

Map by Betty Smith

Interior illustrations by author or by Dall-E with author guidance

ISBN 979-8-9918045-0-9

First Edition: October 2024

Printed in the United States of America

Dedication

To God first, without whom nothing is possible.

Then to the women who are a part of my life and color my world:

To my wife, Julie: without your love, support, and encouragement, this story would never have been written.

To my mother, Debra, and my Aunt Donna: without your support and aid, this story would not have been written nearly as well.

To my mother-in-law, Marilyn: your very name was the spark that inspired me. Thank you for loving me like one of your own.

To my daughters and daughter-in-law: Betty, Shanna, and Navia. You are all so very different from each other, and I love each of you for that.

You all mean more to me than I can truly express in a short dedication. So, I will simply say thank you. I love you all.

Sea Cave
Solva
Afonffordd
Moridu
Tintagel

num

Glouvum

Abona

Bearda Market

Glestinga

Mêlotir

Execaer

Southwest

Britannia

CONTENTS

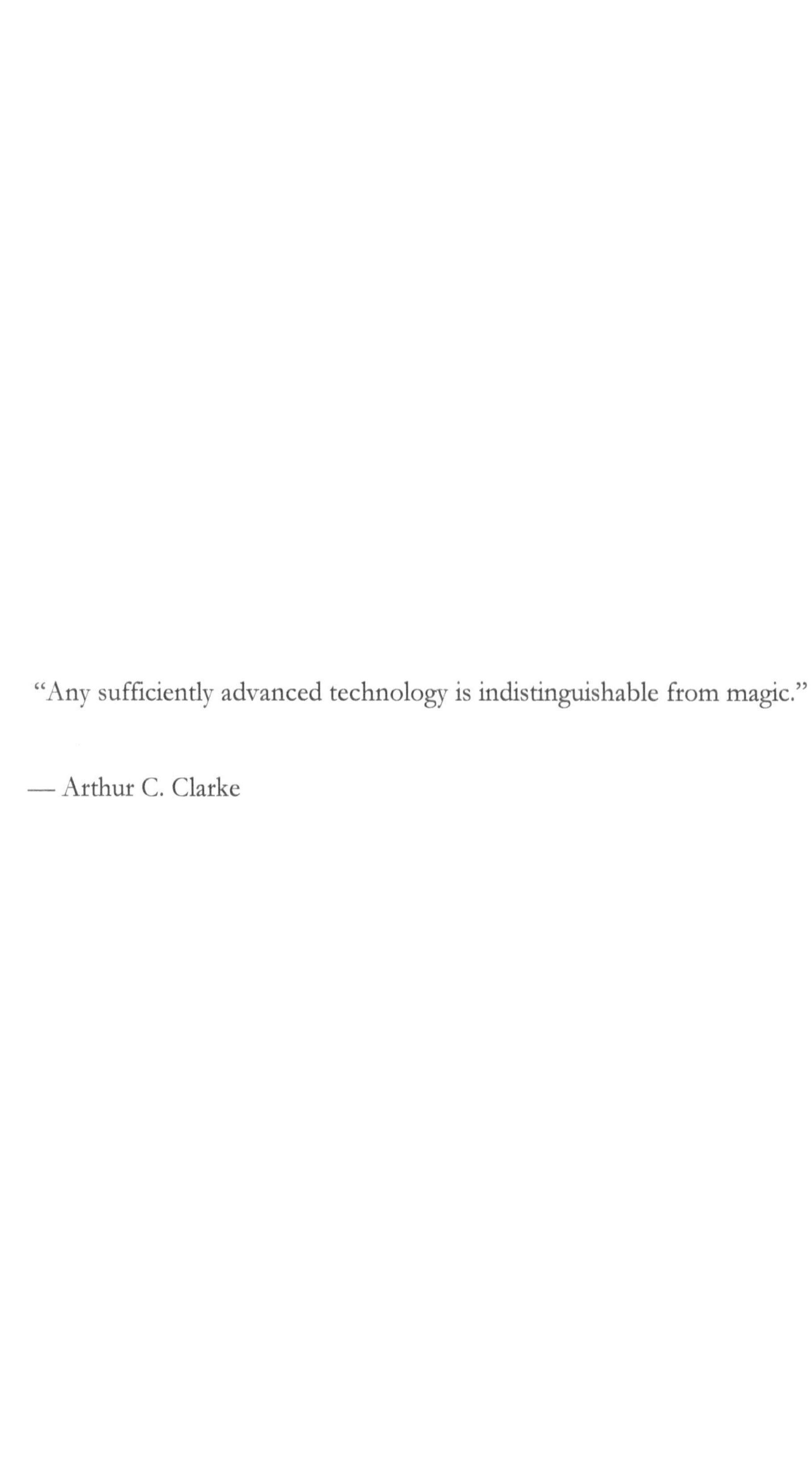

"Any sufficiently advanced technology is indistinguishable from magic."

— Arthur C. Clarke

MARILYN

PROLOGUE

Event Horizon

Her fingers clung desperately to the cold metal of the catwalk's railing, her knuckles white with the effort. Time seemed to stand still as a cable supporting the catwalk snapped, the sound echoing through the cavern like a death knell. The catwalk jerked violently, yanking her arms and a grunting yelp from her throat. Though she fought to hold onto the railing, it seemed determined to shake her off.

Time suspended in an eternal instant as her grip finally gave way, her breath caught in her throat, and her heart began to hammer from a reactive spike of adrenaline. Her eyes darted to the control room window where a familiar figure stood pressed against the glass, his face frozen in a mask of horror and disbelief. Their eyes locked, and in that brief moment, she understood the adage that your life flashes before your eyes. Surely, the speed of thought was faster than even light!

The eternal instant passed as gravity asserted its dominance, pulling her down toward the glowing portal below. As her foot breached the shimmering surface, a jolt of electricity hit her like a live wire, the shock seizing her leg with the intensity of an electric cattle fence. Fiery pain flared, replaced almost instantly by an icy, numbing sensation, coupled with an unexpected pressure – a feeling of being stretched and compressed all at once, as though she were being violently pulled up from a great sea depth.

The pain drew her gaze downward, where the image of a cave loomed large and vivid through the portal's surface, beckoning her into its depths – a surreal experience that, in that absurd instant, carried a flash of levity. She barked a laugh at the fleeting thought of herself as Alice, tumbling through the looking glass.

The electric storm traveled up her body as she passed through the portal. When her head breached the threshold, swallowing her primal scream, reality itself seemed to unravel. She was everything and nothing, all at once – a being whose awareness expanded across the cosmos, touching the stars and the voids between them. She was an insignificant speck. She was a god, omnipotent and eternal. Time stretched and bent, compressing her entire existence into a single, overwhelming moment. She glimpsed the darkness at the end of the universe and, overwhelmed, surrendered to it, embracing oblivion.

CHAPTER 1

Secrets

Inside a starkly lit military locker room, a figure stood before a mirror, adjusting the collar of a crisp uniform. Marilyn, her reflection silently judged, still looked more like a boy trying to play soldier rather than a distinguished military officer. It was a fact not lost on her. Her lean, fit build, combined with her above–average height for a woman – though still falling short of the average man – and a military–mandated short haircut, gave her a tomboyish appeal. The feminine curves of her figure were easily overlooked unless deliberately sought out. She could be feminine when she wanted, but in a male-dominated environment, it was easier to be treated as 'one of the boys,' even if not always perceived as such.

She spent a moment more in quiet introspection, studying her reflection. "Look at you now," she said to herself quietly, her dulcet accent still carrying a hint of Wales and the Welsh language of her grandparents, despite the number of years she had been in the states now. To say she was unconventional only highlighted the unconventional path that brought her here. Marilyn was a unique fixture here – a U.S. citizen born on foreign soil. The moment of reflection, both in the mirror and in her thoughts, brought with it a flood of memories that started with her upbringing around her grandparents, and followed a trail of circumstances and choices that led to this mirror, this moment.

She thought of her father – a U.S. diplomat stationed at the embassy in London, and her mother – a local resident of Wales. The two met there while her father was on holiday on the Pembrokeshire coast. They fell in love, wed, and gave birth to her a year later. Her father's continued work as a diplomat in London encouraged a life ruled by his partial presence, tearful trips to the train station, and a deep-seated need to prove herself and make him proud.

His persistent absence in her youth made her think of her grandmother, who stepped up to fill the void. A key influence in Marilyn's formative years outside Cardiff, her grandmother insisted she learn both French and Welsh, often poking fun at her father's American English. "That is not proper English, Robert," her mother had once chided playfully. Marilyn could still see her grandmother, even more serious-minded than her mother, echoing the sentiment: "Teach the girl to speak correctly, and she will go far!"

The memory pulled in her grandfather's laugh – a carefree spirit whose boisterous personality balanced her grandmother's seriousness, always replying with a cheerful chuckle, 'Let the girl be, Gran!' From him, Marilyn learned a sense of adventure. The two often spent a great deal of time exploring the charming coastlines and treading the historic sites of the Welsh countryside.

Her thoughts drifted back to the day they left for the States, a solemn journey marked by the loss of her mother to breast cancer and a poignant reminder of the fragility of life. Though her father blamed his demanding career, Marilyn always suspected it was the heartbreak that prompted the move. Her resolve had hardened during those years, driving her to excel in school.

Her mind flitted through the last decade, hitting touchstones. She could still see herself, a determined teenager, devouring textbooks on science and chemistry, delving for the secrets that might save another mother from a dire fate. The acceptance letter to West Point arrived, a ticket to a future she eagerly embraced. Every challenge, every sleepless night studying post-graduate work at MIT, every accolade and rank gained in the Air Force, wove a complex tapestry of experiences, each thread contributing to the woman staring back in the mirror.

She glanced around, the empty locker room providing a much–needed moment of solitude. Her hand trailed down to her abdomen, fingers lightly tracing the area above her navel. She tightened her abdominal muscles, scrutinizing the reflection that stared back at her. 'Not going to show for another three months, doc said', she mused, patting her stomach gently before straightening her uniform. 'I have time…'

Exiting the locker room, she moved down a nondescript corridor with only numerical designations marking the doors until she reached one, unremarkable except for the memory of its significance: Room 423. No nameplate adorned this door. Instead, a plain, unassuming card reader waited next to it, the only indication of the secured space beyond. Sliding her ID card, the door unlocked with a muted click, and she stepped into her private office.

Her office was orderly and tidy, a testament to her disciplined military background. A photo of her parents hung on the far wall behind her desk, next to her matted and framed University degree, proclaiming her academic achievements: dual doctorates in Chemistry and Materials Science. Her desk, with its high–tech flat–screen monitor and computer, was the only area that bore any semblance of clutter. It was littered with a small collection of trinkets – a Rubik's cube, a Newton's Cradle, and other knickknacks that piqued her interest – interspersed amongst neatly stacked papers and reports.

Sitting prominently on her desk was a polished brass placard, the engraving catching the sparse light filtering in from the overhead fluorescents. "Lt. Colonel Marilyn Morgan" it read, her full title and name clearly inscribed. A quiet sense of pride welled up in her each time she read those words, a constant reminder of her achievements. The rank inscribed on the placard was more than just a symbol of her achievements. It was a testament to her dual roles as the base's lead scientist and the head of special operations. Balancing these responsibilities came with a cost: her innate desire to share scientific discoveries often clashed with the burden of preserving national security. With a wry smile, she acknowledged the weight of her duties. Just another day at the office in a job that was anything but ordinary.

Nerdy knickknacks strewn about her desk lent the office an air of whimsy that contrasted sharply with the imposing military base housing it. Bobble-headed figures of famous scientists stood among items reflecting another of Marilyn's passions: the magical world of Harry Potter. Books from the series nestled lovingly among thick tomes of scientific literature on the bookshelves, while replica wands from the movie franchise proudly shared a wall mount.

She let the door close behind her, then stepped over to a coat rack in the corner and hung her uniform jacket, draping it casually over a vibrant Gryffindor scarf. Close by, on a side table, a replica of a Golden Snitch – the chief prize in the fictional game of Quidditch – hovered above its base as if by magic, basking in the blue glow of its neon lights. To the initiated, it was simple magnetic levitation, but to the unversed, it added a delightful hint of magic to an otherwise mundane world. Marilyn tended to be a private person. So, the gifting of such trinkets having to do with the book series or movies had become a commonplace occurrence with her staff.

A Mova Globe of the Earth, another delightful trinket that appeared to rotate on its own as if by magic, sat atop a filing cabinet in the corner. Its rotation lent a feeling of quiet motion to the room. While working, she often paused to watch it, the spinning sphere within offering a reminder that the world, indeed the cosmos, still held mysteries to be discovered.

The corridor, her office, the locker room – they all reminded her of the hidden depths of this place. This had once been the site of the ambitious Superconducting Super Collider project in Waxahachie, Texas. It was supposed to be a beacon of scientific progress, a symbol of human achievement. Instead, it became the façade for something far more secretive.

Marilyn glanced at a calendar on the wall next to the wand replicas where the month of October 2023 was prominently displayed. The accompanying image displayed a breathtaking Hubble image, paired with a stirring quote from Albert Einstein: "The important thing is not to stop questioning. Curiosity has its own reason for existing." A date – Monday, October 30th – was circled in bold red marker, adorned with the words 'B–Day Party.'

She stared at the date on the calendar a moment longer, smirking at the amusing coincidence that the collider project had been decommissioned the day after her birth, 30 years ago. It was a conspicuous irony, as if her life and the secret project were somehow intrinsically linked.

She recalled the mission briefing, detailing the stories of how, in 1993, a crashed alien spacecraft was discovered deep beneath Texas soil during the initial stages of excavation on the super collider tunnels. Officially, budget overruns had shut down the project, but Marilyn knew that was when the real work had begun.

Behind the scenes, the operation continued in earnest, now a clandestine military site housing operation "Glass Table." It had taken three decades of secretive construction and technological advancement for humans to catch up to the type of research they were now performing on the unearthed artifact.

'I need to call Dad,' she thought, pulling herself from the moment of reverie, knowing that communications security at the base prevented him from being able to call her. 'He'll want to wish me a happy birthday.'

Marilyn settled into her chair and logged onto her computer, where a myriad of unread emails awaited her attention. One message in particular caught her eye, marked with the unassuming yet significant tag: "TS–SCI," an abbreviation known to those in the intelligence community as Top Secret/Sensitive Compartmented Information. It was a common sight in her inbox, a stark reminder of the covert nature of her work.

"Subject: Glass Table – Energy Consumption Study," the title read. She clicked on the message. The email detailed the latest results from the energy consumption studies on the artifact, usually referred to as the 'disc' by her team because of its shape. Scanning through the technical jargon and encoded phrases, Marilyn effortlessly deciphered the missive, her mind processing the information as easily as others might read the morning paper. The studies were an ongoing effort to understand the function of the artifact – the only intact remnant of the alien ship found at the crash site.

Findings thus far suggested possibilities pulled from the pages of science fiction – gravity manipulation, Alcubierre drives, concepts that were purely theoretical until now. However, one thing was clear: these tests required immense energy. The email made it clear that further testing should occur at night, when demand on the local power grid was lowest, until onsite generators were online.

Marilyn immersed herself in her work, looking for patterns and connections among the deluge of data, reports, and scientific papers, some even written in other language – task made easier by her natural affinity for picking up new languages. Out of sheer academic curiosity, she had even picked up some Latin, allowing her to peruse Newton's "Philosophiæ Naturalis Principia Mathematica," a prized possession on her bookcase.

Though sometimes tedious, she found a certain joy in the task, a sense of fulfillment akin to solving a complex puzzle where each piece was a snippet of coded information. As she delved deeper into her work, time began to distort and stretch in the peculiar way it does when one is completely absorbed in a task.

The muffled sounds of a familiar voice echoing from the hallway outside her office finally pulled Marilyn's attention away from her work. As she glanced up, her gaze was drawn to the silhouette of a figure striding past her office door, engaged in an animated conversation with a colleague. Her eyes followed the two men, then landed on the large wall clock. The hands now accusingly pointed to 1:06 PM. She had worked straight through lunch again. An almost imperceptible sigh escaped her lips. It was time for a break, and perhaps some sustenance beyond the confines of her office.

Rising to her feet, she stretched, protesting muscles singing their relief after the long hours of sitting. Grabbing her coat, she stepped out of her office, hearing the familiar click of the magnetic lock engaging behind her. With that, she turned and headed toward the base's mess hall.

Marilyn was greeted by the muted hum of lunchtime conversation as she entered the base's mess hall. A blend of familiar voices and strangers filled the air – personnel from various parts of the base, engrossed in their private conversations.

She moved toward the counter to begin the familiar ceremony of making a cup of hot tea, then scanned the room for the source of the familiar voice she'd heard earlier outside her office. Finally spotting him, a smile played on her lips as she secured her steaming cup and weaved her way through the tables toward him.

Absorbed in a report, Philip Lawton, or "Flip" as the team affectionately referred to him due to Marilyn's distinctive Welsh pronunciation of his name, sat at a table near the back. As she approached the table, the aroma of freshly brewed coffee wafting from his cup was as familiar as the man himself.

He was so engrossed in his reading, he didn't notice her approach at first. When he finally looked up, their eyes met, and a warm smile that melted her like butter in the sun spread across his face. "Hey, Mare. D'ja eat yet?" His Texan drawl rolled off his tongue, a sound that, over time, Marilyn had come to find oddly charming – a contrasting rhythm to the rapid–fire technical discussions that filled their days.

Marilyn hesitated for a fraction of a second, the question hitting closer to home than he realized. Her stomach churned, not just from hunger, but from the weight of the secret she carried. How long could she keep it from him? Not much longer, she suspected, but today wasn't the day.

"Afternoon, Flip," Marilyn returned the greeting, her Welsh accent giving the nickname an even more affectionate lilt. She settled into the seat across from him and said, "Just popped in for a cup of tea." A playfully sour look crossed her face as she eyed his coffee mug. "How you Americans drink coffee, I'll never understand. Nasty stuff that," she confided, her accent still as lilting as ever, even after her years spent in America.

"Hey now…you're American too, you know," Philip replied, continuing their gentle banter. He took a sip of his coffee, holding Marilyn's gaze over the rim of his mug. "Coffee's not that bad. Why don't you give me a kiss and see for yourself?" He drawled 'coffee' in a way she was certain only a Texan could. He flashed her a teasing grin, the challenge evident in his eyes.

Marilyn gasped in mock scandal, her eyes darting around the mess hall. "Philip! Hush, you." Her admonishment was more playful than serious, yet she was still mindful of the need for discretion. The pair had been working together for over a year now, their initial professional respect borne of a shared dedication to the alien technology they were attempting to decipher. Over time, that respect deepened, threading through their interactions until it blossomed into intimacy – a profound depth of love and respect she had never felt before. Now lovers, their relationship was a secret shared only by the shadows that witnessed their stolen moments, while carefully maintaining a professional façade in public. Philip, however, seemed to delight in skirting the boundaries, his demeanor remaining cavalier in the face of her concern.

"We're on track for the test at twenty hundred hours. We don't want to cause any brownouts in the local grid," Philip said, his joviality fading into the stern professional focus that marked their discussions about work.

Marilyn nodded, mentally converting the time to 8 PM as she took a sip of her tea. "I know – I read the report this morning. I'm looking forward to it."

The two sat there for a time, each sipping their beverage of choice as they discussed the project and upcoming test. Their conversation ebbed and flowed, touching on technical details and shared anecdotes. Marilyn loved moments like this, working with Philip. Beneath the disarming drawl of his Texas accent lay a sharp mind that had attracted her to him even more than his good looks.

Time lost all meaning in these shared moments, a fact not lost on her as she looked up and saw the mess hall begin to empty, the clamor of the lunchtime crowd gradually giving way to a subdued hum. Philip's stern professional focus softened. His eyes, usually sharp with concentration, now held a gentle concern. "You okay, Mare? You seem a bit…distracted."

Marilyn's heart fluttered uneasily. His keen observation was one of the many things she admired about him that made it difficult for her to hide anything from him as well. She met his gaze, her mind racing with the enormity of the secret she carried, tumbling over the countless potential repercussions of her truth. Revealing her pregnancy could upend her career and threaten her position on the project. Yet, more than the professional implications, she feared what this could mean for their relationship.

She knew Philip loved her and that he'd want to play the hero. His southern–bred chivalry would undoubtedly lead him to want to protect her, to rescue her from any perceived danger. But Marilyn didn't need rescuing; she was a strong, independent woman who had made her way in a field dominated by men. What she needed was understanding and support, not a white knight charging in for the rescue.

"Just thinking about the test, that's all," she lied, wrapping her secret around her like a protective cloak. For now, she would keep it to herself, sheltering them both from the potential storm of change that was to come.

Just as the serious tone of their conversation began to ebb, Philip's attention was drawn to a quiet rumble, followed by a sheepish look crossing Marilyn's face. "That your stomach or an underground seismic event?" he quipped, his eyes twinkling with amusement. "You haven't eaten yet, have you?"

She shifted uncomfortably, caught between her growing hunger and the nausea that often accompanied her pregnancy. Not divulging her condition to Philip was a fact that made sharing a meal with him slightly nerve–wracking. "Perhaps…" she conceded reluctantly.

"Well then, Lieutenant Colonel! How about a burger and fries to go with your tea?" he offered, rising from his seat before she had a chance to protest.

A short time later, Philip returned and sat the tray of food before her. While Philip busied himself with his report, stealing glances at her every now and then, she lost herself in her meal. The absurdity of craving such a meal, one that would likely have her rushing for the restroom under different circumstances, was not lost on her. Yet the thought of a juicy burger, crispy fries, and a cold milkshake was suddenly irresistible. The food was gone in a flash, and she sat back, her hunger momentarily silenced.

With her meal devoured, Marilyn leaned back in her chair, a satisfied smile on her face. Suddenly, an un–ladylike belch escaped her, her hand flying to cover her mouth in surprise. A blush crept up her cheeks, but Philip merely chuckled, his eyes sparkling with amusement.

"Well now, you sure know how to charm a guy, Mare," he teased, shaking his head with a grin.

Rolling her eyes, she shot back, "If I were trying to fit in with you boys, I'd need a lot more flatulence." Then she added with a haughty tone, arching an eyebrow, "I have higher standards."

Suggesting the moment of levity had passed, she met Philip's gaze evenly. "We should both rest before the test, don't you think? It's likely to be a late night again." The practical suggestion hung in the air for a moment before she added, "And perhaps we could share dinner in your quarters?" Her voice was soft, hinting at the intimate possibilities the evening might hold.

He seemed about to respond when she continued, her tone light, a twinkle in her eyes. "And if you're a good soldier, I might just let you inspect my barracks… thoroughly, before we report to the lab."

Philip's eyebrows shot up, a bark of laughter escaping him before he rose to his feet, standing tall and straight. He saluted her with exaggerated formality, somehow keeping a straight face despite the glint of mischief in his eyes. "Yes, ma'am. I'll be on my best behavior, ma'am."

He turned, striding out of the mess hall, leaving Marilyn to stare at his retreating back, her lips twitching with suppressed mirth. As the door closed behind him, she shook her head, chuckling to herself. "Idiot," she muttered, an amused smile dancing on her lips as she imagined the rest of her day.

Marilyn stood before the sealed doors of the cavernous chamber, turning off the reminder alarm on her cell phone set for 7:45 PM. She punched in a security code and stooped slightly for the required biometric eye scan. The heavy doors gave way to an impressive sight.

Before her stretched a catwalk that extended some thirty meters from the entrance before bisecting another circular catwalk encompassing a five-meter diameter, within which lay the artifact. Tethers extended upward towards the cavern roof, supporting the significant weight of the assembly as it hung suspended mere feet above the artifact.

The central walkway, suspended over the middle of the artifact, led to a round platform housing a workstation and a complex array of additional equipment, carefully calibrated to redirect and focus a high-energy beam of protons crucial to the imminent experiment. Ayesha had once remarked that it all looked like a Pokémon ball from the observational control room overlooking the cavern and its contents.

As Marilyn approached the workstation, she took in the awe-inspiring scene. The chamber was a monstrous gash in the earth's crust, the impact of a non-terrestrial craft leaving a deep hole, more like a bullet's entry into soft clay than a crater. Time and geological processes had eventually concealed the entrance, leaving the underground cavern to protect its hidden treasure until its chance rediscovery by the collider project excavation crew.

At the heart of the cavern, centered beneath the suspended catwalks, lay the 'Glass Table' – an enormous disc the team believed to be the core of the alien craft's engine. With a supernaturally smooth surface on its top side and edges, it measured just under sixteen feet across. Its exact diameter only gained significance once Avery pointed out that whoever had built it was surely aware of both the speed of light and the golden ratio.

She recalled him standing at the whiteboard, scribbling diagrams and numbers with the excitement of a child on Christmas morning. "Light travels just under three meters in ten nanoseconds," Avery had said excitedly. "Multiply that by the golden ratio and you get the precise diameter of the thing!" His excitement at the discovery was warranted; it had opened a path of speculation and exploration that led to significant advancements in the project. It was clear that whoever had built it was obviously aware of these fundamental constants. There could be no other explanation for the correlation between them and the artifact's size, perhaps even basing their units of measure on them in some way.

Unlike its smooth surface, the underside of the nearly foot-thick platter consisted of a seemingly chaotic jumble of crystalline protrusions of varying lengths, sizes, and directions. At first glance, the jumble appeared random, but careful observation looking through the translucent disc revealed a complex pattern not unlike a fractal pattern, hinting at an unseen order within the chaos.

Made entirely of crystalline material, the team still hadn't determined what it was. Harder than diamond, it resisted all attempts at sampling, yet weighed far less than an equivalent structure of quartz or glass.

As she stood at the workstation, checking her controls and measurements, Marilyn felt the familiar rhythm of the collider operations pulsing under her feet. A multitude of computers, machinery, and technical equipment gradually powered up, the technological behemoth coming to life. The almost electric hum of anticipation in the air signaled the team's readiness for the experiment.

She glanced up at the bay window of the control room built into the nearby cavern wall overhead. Philip was there, settling into his station. She made some final adjustments, donned her earpiece, and initiated the routine communication check.

"Comm's check, Control," she uttered and awaited a response.

"Reading you loud and clear, Site," Philip's voice echoed through her earpiece.

With the communication test complete, Marilyn went through similar checks with the rest of the team. "Power flow nominal," "Data acquisition system is operational," "Cryogenic systems are optimal," "Magnetic field stable." Each report came in, confirming the readiness of various systems.

"Control is green, Site. What's your status?" Philip inquired, initiating the final check.

"EM Deflector is standing by," Marilyn responded, her gaze fixed on her own screens.

"All systems are go. Ready to begin the countdown on your mark, Lieutenant Colonel," Philip finally confirmed, turning to look at Marilyn through the control room glass. There was a brief silence as everyone held their breath, awaiting the start of the experiment.

Marilyn could almost feel Philip's grin from where she was standing, his playful demeanor always bubbling up in these high-stakes moments.

"You ready to make history, Mare?" Philip asked through the earpiece, breaking the silence.

"Well, Flip…" she began, exaggerating the nickname and clearing her throat intentionally, smirking. The sound of suppressed chuckles from other team members came through the comms, lightening the air. "Now that we've dropped the formalities… we're always ready to make history. Or, you know, cause an impressive light show. Either one." Her light-hearted response veiled the undercurrent of uncertainty that always accompanied these moments.

"Ten-second countdown on my mark." She paused, waiting for the clock on her display to zero out the seconds.

"Mark!" she finally commanded, the thrill of the moment electrifying the air around her.

Anticipation buzzed in the air as the countdown began. At her workstation, Marilyn made the final adjustments to the proton beam's alignment, her fingers moving with practiced precision.

The beam fired when the countdown hit zero. At first, nothing appeared to change, but then, as she watched, a soft light began to pulse within the crystalline structure. Its rhythm, seemingly random at first, began to exhibit a definite pattern.

"Flip!" she exclaimed, her voice trembling with excitement over the comms. "The disc! It's resonating. The energy pattern - it's like it's alive!" What had once been a translucent mass of alien minerals turned into a spectacular light show of rhythmic pulsing.

As the pattern stabilized, Marilyn turned to her controls, "Increasing emitter frequency… three point six… point seven… point eight…" With each increase, the pattern in the crystalline artifact followed suit, increasing in tempo and complexity.

A sheen of energy, akin to the force fields of her favorite sci-fi movies and TV shows, began to cover the crystalline surface of the disc.

As she continued to increase the frequency, the entire team watched in astonishment as the crystalline light show began to cohere into an image of a dimly lit cave, incredibly detailed and astonishingly real. The effect reminded Marilyn of adjusting the antenna on an old-fashioned glass

TV with the same eerie, phosphorescent glow – a high-tech display on a grand scale.

Without warning, the glowing sheen evaporated, leaving the crystal-clear image of the cave even more vivid than before. Suddenly, a wave of vertigo seized Marilyn as an energetic pulse exploded outward from the disc. Like an expanding soap bubble, the wave passed through her, shifting gravity itself and throwing her off balance.

Just as suddenly as it had begun, the expanding bubble reversed direction and collapsed back toward the disc surface. Already disoriented, the passing wave seemed to reach out and grab her, tossing her like a ragdoll and yanking her over the side of the platform's railing. With reflexes borne of adrenaline, she managed to grab hold of the platform's railing. As she hung from the railing, feet dangling over the edge, realization dawned as her cellphone slid off the workstation and passed through the image into the world beyond rather than crashing into the artifact's surface. It was no projection or display, but a portal – an actual, tangible gateway to that other place.

The platform itself suddenly shifted, a victim of the violent pulse the disc had emitted. A support cable snapped, and Marilyn lost her grip. Time froze in that sudden moment of realization that she was falling. She could hear the horrified gasps of her team echo through her earpiece as she was pulled into the portal. The last thing she saw was Philip's shocked face pressed against the control room glass. Then everything went black.

CHAPTER 2

Support

Philip was the first to react. His gaze was glued to the screen, where Marilyn lay unconscious on the other side of the portal. "Damn it!" he muttered, yanking off his headset. He pressed against the glass of the control room window trying to get a better view of her directly, then tossed the headset onto the console and turned to his communications officer. "Naomi, get me an earpiece. And get Dr. Bennett down here! Now!"

"Yessir!" Naomi nodded, quickly pulling out an earpiece and tossing it to him. He waited impatiently as she grabbed the handset and dialed. "Dr. Bennett, please…" she exclaimed when someone answered. "I don't care – just get him! It's an emergency!" he heard her bark to whoever had answered. After moments that felt like an eternity, she continued. "Dr. Bennett? This is Naomi Higgins down in the main lab. We need you here right away," she said calmly. "Look, I can't explain. You just…need to see for yourself. Yessir. See you soon."

With that, Philip shot out the control room door. He slipped on the earpiece as he hurried down the stairs and through the security door into the cavernous lab. "Status update!" he demanded as he arrived at the edge of the platform. His order resulting in only silence, he turned to look up at the control room's bay window to see Naomi pantomiming instructions to turn his earpiece on – something he'd forgotten to do in his haste. "Idiot," he muttered, removing it switch on the power.

"Doctor Bennett will be here any moment now, Flip," Naomi said encouragingly over the comms.

"Can you see anything?" Takashi added, worriedly. Philip glanced up to see the entire team gathered at the control room's bay window, peering down into the lab.

"Back to your stations!" he barked, looking up sternly. "If this thing goes belly up while she's in there…" He left the rest unsaid as the team disbursed back to their respective stations. Satisfied, Philip turned back to the platform at the end of the catwalk.

"To answer your question, Tak: not at this angle," he replied into his comms as he tested his footing on the broken central platform. He stepped gingerly onto it and heard Naomi gasp, mimicking his own reaction as he stumbled. Tilting from the broken support cable, the platform groaned, but held under his weight as he made his way to the railing from which Marilyn fell. He took stock of his surroundings and didn't see any other damage. Though askew, the proton emitter was still shooting a steady beam at the portal.

Looking up at the control room, he spoke into his earpiece, "Simms, can you shut down the proton emitter remotely if needed? It's still going full bore. But the platform is unstable. Last thing I want is radiation poisoning, so keep an eye on things. Otherwise, leave it running. I don't want to mess with the status quo until I take stock of things."

"Yessir, I can shut it down if needed," Avery shot back. Philip watched the control room for a moment as Avery turned to the other team members. Ayesha gave Avery a thumbs up as she consulted her console, but Takashi held his hand out flat hand and wobbled it back and forth.

Philip's worry grew until Avery chimed in over the headset. "Flip, the cryogenic systems are holding steady, but Tak's worried about maintaining the power at this level for an extended time. It might hold up, but things will go sideways if there's a brown out," Avery reported.

'Worries for later,' he thought as he looked over the edge of the platform's railing and through the surface of the artifact to see a dark, earthy abode, perhaps a cave. Relief washed over him as he spotted Marilyn in the dim light from the lab, like a window into a darkened room. She was lying unconscious, but clearly breathing.

"I have eyes on," Philip reported as he shifted his position to get a better view. "The lieutenant colonel is alive, but unconscious. Tak, keep a close eye out for power fluctuations and let me know if anything changes. The experiment opened some kind of portal and she's on the other side. If it shuts down, there's no guarantee we can get it back again!"

Orders given, Philip turned his attention to once again Marilyn, still lying unconscious on the other side, and waited for the doctor to arrive. Moments later, the sound of a familiar buzz drew Philip's attention to the exterior camera focused on the lab's entrance door. Dr. Bennett was standing there, a figure of calm urgency. "Doc's here, Simms. Let him through," he ordered unnecessarily as the familiar buzz and click of the lab door's magnetic lock deactivated as he was speaking. "Careful making your way onto the platform, Monty," he called to the man as he approached along the catwalk. "One of the cable's snapped."

Moments later, the doctor was standing beside him. Philip watched the doctor's expression shift from shock to horror, then grave concern. "I need more light," he finally responded, looking around the cavern. Though well-lit nearby, the brightness quickly fell off into the dark recesses of the giant cavern. As for the place into which Marilyn had fallen, the light was even more muted, perhaps as an effect of the portal.

"I got it," Philip replied and made his way over to an emergency box mounted on the wall beside the lab door. Opening it, he grabbed the flashlight, battery-powered lamp, and first aid kit within, grateful that they'd had it installed after a previous power loss had left some of the crew trapped in lightless cavern for half the night. There was even a gallon bottle of water and some protein bars just in case a longer stay warranted.

Philip made his way back to the railing, handing Doctor Bennett the flashlight while he held onto the first aid kit and lamp. The beam from the flashlight split into a chaotic kaleidoscope, more fully illuminating the space beyond than Philip had expected as the doctor shone the beam down through the portal. She did indeed appear to be in some sort of cave.

His scrutiny of Marilyn's still, motionless form from the platform was interrupted moments later by Avery rapping sharply on the control room's glass to snag Philip's attention. The man gestured to his ear and shrugged in confusion. Looking down, Philip realized he had involuntarily removed his earpiece when the doctor arrived, cutting the team off from communication. Despite his earlier warning, every member of the team was once again pressed to the control room's bay window, wondering and worrying.

Shaking his head in exasperation, Philip redonned the earpiece. "Sorry about that," he drawled, dropping formalities, the Texan lilt in his voice evident as he clicked his headset back on. They were all as concerned, obviously. "I'm not used to being on this end o' things. We can see her breathing steadily. But the doc says there's not a lot else he can tell from here. She's out cold."

It was evident Naomi had switched the comms, piping the conversation to the control room channel, as Ayesha's voice interjected. "Maybe try tossing a bucket of water on her?" she suggested.

Philip glanced at the portal, thinking. He flicked on the lamp and tossed it over the railing toward the center of artifact. The lamp sailed through the shimmering surface where it arced and fell at Marilyn's feet, acting as if it had been thrown through an open window. "Maybe you can just go get her?" the doctor suggested.

"I would love to," Philip replied. "But we don't know where she is, nor why she's unconscious. Could be an environmental factor – gas or low oxygen maybe."

"Get some men down here then? We could use that broken cable there," the doctor persisted, nodding to the length of cable that had snapped and lay loosely splayed on the platform. "Tie it around you and lower you down? If you pass out, we could just lift you back out again."

"If I were more confident in the stability of this thing Monty, I'd risk it!" Philip responded in frustration. "But this is new to all of us. We don't know what we're dealing with here."

The doctor shook his head. "I knew you guys were up to some pretty secret stuff down here, but I thought it was weapons tech. But this is straight out of a sci-fi movie!"

"Yeah," Philip nodded, adding "And top secret. What you now know goes on behind that lab door stays behind it. We clear?"

Doctor Bennett nodded seriously, then pretended to zip his lips.

"So, what are we going to do about her?" he asked the doctor.

"Under the circumstances, your teammate probably had the best idea. Splash her with some water," the doctor replied.

"Simms, can we rig up a hose down here?" Philip said into the comms.

"Already on it," Avery replied, confirming that the team had been quietly listening the whole time. Soon enough, hose at the ready, Philip took a deep breath. "Guys, keep an eye on your monitors," he ordered into the comms. "Watter and electricity don't usually mix well. I'm going to try a short blast."

He tightened his grip and squeezed for a two count. Water jetted out, surging towards the portal. He missed Marilyn by a few feet, his aim thrown off by the uncanny gravitational shift. By the look of it though, he may as well have been spraying water out of an open window. "Anything weird?" he asked the team.

"Negative, Captain," Avery came back a moment later. "Readings are nominal across the board. Tak said there was an uptick in the power, but nothing extreme and nothing he didn't expect."

Philip fine-tuned his aim and let another stream fly, adjusting until the water hit Marilyn's face. The sudden impact jolted her back to consciousness, her body convulsing as she gasped for breath.

"Bloody Hell!" Marilyn exclaimed as she shot upright, the cold, hard ground beneath her leaching the warmth from her body. Her surroundings swam into focus as her vision cleared: a dimly lit cave, stalagmites and stalactites encrusted around an all–too–familiar artifact. Just like the one in the lab, except this one was nestled in the cave wall, its smooth side concealed. Its jagged, crystalline side faced her, radiating a soft glow. The ambient light danced upon the cave walls, casting long, eerie shadows that twisted into the deeper recesses of the cave.

Dazed, she rose unsteadily to her feet, the dull throb in her head serving as a harsh reminder of her recent fall. A sudden movement caught the corner of her eye. Looking up, she recognized Philip through the jagged facets of the crystal, standing in a distorted version of the lab, his gaze fixed on her through the fractured reality. Beside him, she made out the figure of Dr. Bennett, her own recognition dawning as she viewed them through the fractured visage.

Her breath caught in her throat; it was like looking at her world through a shattered mirror. 'Well, Alice… you've really done it now,' she mused to herself, her feeble attempt at humor doing little to suppress the rising panic.

Still reeling from the impact of her fall, a low-pitched, almost buzzing noise interrupted her thoughts. The sound, reminiscent of a beehive, set her heart pounding. Her eyes darted to the source, finding her dislodged earpiece on the ground. A moment of dizziness washed over her as she bent to retrieve it, turning her relief into disorientation. Once her surroundings steadied, she listened to the earpiece, now emitting a series of strange, low–pitched noises, like a tape being played at too slow a speed. Amid the uncertainty, an unexpected voice emerged, distorted but unmistakably familiar – Philip's Texas accent, transformed into a deep, ominous sounding, elongated hum of words.

Fumbling to insert the earpiece, her trembling fingers struggled to steady it. "Hello? Can anyone hear me?" she called out, her voice bouncing off the cavernous walls. She was unsure whether her messages could be heard on the other side, even though she was receiving theirs.

Her panic eased as Philip's voice broke through, though it sounded unnaturally slow. "Marilyn! Can you hear me? Are you okay?!" Philip's asked, his voice slow and drawn out.

"I think so, Flip…nothing broken but my pride…and I'm sopping wet! Thanks for that by the way," she said, her tone dripping with sarcasm as she dripped with water.

Through a shard of the artifact, she saw relief wash over Philip's face. "Flip, there's something wrong with the comms. I think the water affected the earpiece. You sound like a recording being played in slow motion!" Dusting herself off and regaining her composure, she added, "I can barely understand you. I think the water affected the earpiece."

"Funny, you're coming across like a chipmunk," he retorted, obviously attempting to mitigate the affect by speaking as quickly and in as high a pitch as he could. She picked up a garbled utterance from someone else on their side, which she couldn't decipher. Then, Philip, responding to the indecipherable interjection, advised, "Hold on, Mare, we're gonna try something," speaking as quickly as possible. After a moment of silence, his voice returned to its familiar pitch. "How's this? Better?"

"Much better, thank you." she replied. "What did you do?"

"You can thank Avery. He figured the weird effect was some sort of Doppler shift caused by the portal. It's slowing down signals from our side and speeding up ones from yours. Naomi just ran the comms through a signal processor to correct it," he explained.

Marilyn ran her fingers tentatively over the jagged, crystalline side of the artifact – sharp and unyielding. A knot formed in her stomach at the realization – she was trapped.

"Flip…" she began, her voice trembling.

"Well, would'ja look't that! The dial is set to four point two…" he interrupted, his voice drawling through the earpiece. She could see him through the fractured reality. He had moved to the workstation on the platform above his side of the portal.

"And? Why is that significant?" she asked, her tone tinged with annoyance.

"I guess the answer to life, the universe, and everything really is forty–two!" He chuckled.

"Flip, this is serious!" Her voice came out sharper than she intended, the lingering fear causing her to bristle. Recognizing the worry in her tone, he inquired seriously, "What's wrong?"

Taking a deep breath, she attempted to regain her composure. "I don't think I can get back through the portal. There's another artifact here, just like the one in the lab. But it's embedded in the cave wall, bottom–side out. I can see into the lab, but it's like looking through the shards of a broken mirror or something." As she provided further details, she began searching for her cell phone, which she remembered falling through the portal. She spotted metal in the dim light, but upon closer examination, discovered it was an electric torch that Philip must've thrown into the cave when she was unconscious. No longer functioning, it appeared that water had seeped in through a crack in the lens and shorted it out. She tossed it aside and kept looking.

"Lookin' for somethin'?" Philip's voice echoed in the cave, his familiar drawl easing her tension. She could see him through the fractured facets of the artifact, studying her every move. "We can see you clearly like we're watching you on a video screen."

"I'm searching for my cell phone," she said, her gaze sweeping the rocky cave floor. "I saw it tumble through the portal in the chaos. If I'm still on Earth, I can use it to check my location or make a call."

When she found it, half covered in dirt but otherwise unharmed, she quickly pulled up her phone's screen – but the 'No Signal' icon stared back at her. "It must be the cave blocking the signal," she said to herself, unconsciously speaking out loud.

Before she could dwell on it, a deep, resonant rumble echoed from the depths of the cave, a low, continuous sound – not unlike the snoring of a large animal – sent a shiver down her spine. Her heart pounded as she scanned the darkness, listening intently, when a wave of realization washed over her. The sound was rhythmic, familiar. It wasn't snoring – it was the echo of ocean waves crashing against rocks. She was in a sea cave. A blush of embarrassment warmed her cheeks as relief flooded through her.

As her tension subsided, she spoke into her earpiece, "Naomi, it sounds like I'm in a sea cave. I can hear the ocean, but I don't see the entrance and I don't think my signal will reach much further. Can you rig something up to extend the range of the comms, just in case?"

"I'll rig a battery pack to a signal booster, ma'am, but you might still lose signal if you move too far," Naomi warned.

"Well, let's hope it doesn't come to that," Marilyn responded more confidently, holding onto her cell phone tightly. "My cell phone should pick up a signal once I get outside the cave, if I'm still on Earth, that is."

"You sure you're okay to explore on your own, Marilyn?" Philip asked, his voice betraying a hint of concern.

"As okay as I can be, given the circumstances," she replied, her eyes narrowing as she surveyed the cave. "I'll be careful, Flip. Wherever I am, I'm likely to be stuck here at least overnight. And for what it's worth, the air is breathable wherever I am. While I'm gone, could you…"

"We're way ahead of you, Mare," Philip interrupted. He turned away from the portal in her view and began to relay instructions to the team. "We need a survival pack – warm clothes, food rations, a first aid kit, and a compact sleeping bag."

"Wait, Flip." She held up a hand. "Add a long coat and a beanie. I don't know how cold it's going to get here. Also, grab my fatigues and boots from my quarters. I won't get very far in these dress heels. If I am still on Earth, I have no idea where this blasted portal dropped me. I could be in hostile territory."

"Anything else?" he asked.

She smiled at him, realizing she had been barking orders, over-compensating for the insecurity she felt in her uncertain situation. "And perhaps a tricorder and a phaser too, in case I run into a pointy–eared alien who wants to take me to his leader," she said to add levity to the moment.

Philip laughed, but there was a touch of relief in his voice. "Right, Mare. One long coat, beanie, fatigues, boots, and imaginary Star Trek equipment coming right up. We're on it."

Marilyn turned on the LED light on her cell phone, but it quickly became evident that it was insufficient for her needs. As she moved deeper into the cave, away from the ambient light of the crystals, the dark crevices grew more menacing. She had two pressing needs: a better light source and a restroom.

Turning back towards the portal, she called out, "This cell phone light won't cut it," then stopped herself. As much as she could wish it were so, he wasn't in the room next door. Shaking her head, she spoke calmly into the comms, "I need another torch before I break an ankle." The Welsh lilt in her voice growing stronger, she added, "And some toilet paper too."

Philip raised his eyebrows, "What's a torch?"

"Don't be daft! A… erm… what do you Americans call it – a flashlight!" Marilyn shot back. "Although I don't see anything all that 'flash' about it…"

Philip grinned. "Hang on a sec. There's a flashlight in the emergency supply locker. I think there's some paper towels in there too. Will those do?"

When she affirmed, he disappeared from view for a moment, then reappeared holding a flashlight stuck through a roll of toilet paper. He lobbed it through the portal, where it tumbled to the ground nearby.

Marilyn blinked in surprise, then grinned as she picked up the impromptu care package. On the other end, Naomi chimed in with a laugh, "TP is important!"

Philip chuckled. "She practically sprinted to the latrine to nab it for you!"

"Thank you again, Naomi. I'll be back soon everyone," she said and headed off into the cave, flashlight in hand.

Venturing out of the cave, Marilyn felt her world shift from the eerie calmness within to an environment pulsing with vitality. The passage from the chamber was large enough to walk upright, its uneven, downward slope dotted with jagged rocks that obstructed her view to the outside. Drawn onward by the growing ambient light and the increasingly audible crash of waves, she felt the world around her becoming more tangible with each step.

Rounding a final bend in the passage, she stepped into the open and gasped at the spectacle before her eyes – the sight of a rocky shore, wet stones glowing with the reflection of a setting sun. A brilliant red fingernail of sunlight hung at the edge of the ocean, casting vibrant hues that were fading into the serenity of the approaching evening. Above, an all too familiar moon suspended itself in the deepening sky, its tranquil glow dispelling any doubts. She was still on Earth. But her relief at seeing the moon was swiftly punctuated by frustration as she glanced down at her phone, the stubborn lack of signal a stark reminder of her isolation.

Turning her attention to her immediate needs, she found a secluded spot to relieve herself, then surveyed her surroundings. The cave was carved into a bluff by the sea, the beach below more a shingle of pebbles and small stones than a stretch of sand, and driftwood was notably scarce. Resolving to search for deadwood on the plateau above, she began her climb.

Ascending the bluff, she noted the tell–tale signs of the tide's cyclical reach. While not prohibiting access to the cave, it would certainly deter the curiosity of a casual explorer.

With the afternoon light waning, Marilyn made her way along the plateau, collecting deadwood from small stands of trees that dotted the landscape. Eventually, a large bundle of wood strapped to her backpack holster, she made her way back to her original point of egress.

As she began the climb down and the afternoon gave way to approaching dusk, she paused to survey the untouched coastline and the open sea. The absence of civilization was glaring. No distant city lights stained the horizon, no ships or oil platforms punctuated the coastal view, and the sky was free of the silver streaks of passing aircraft.

In one sense, the view and landscape seemed oddly familiar – a memory from childhood she couldn't quite place. But it also reminded her of articles she'd read about remote isles in the Pacific Ocean, like the Kermadec Islands. She'd never been there, but she'd seen images – subtropical islands, hundreds of kilometers away from civilization, their natural beauty preserved by their isolation. Could that be where she was? This absence of any sign of human presence made her conclusion feel right. The isolation would explain why the sea cave and the artifact on this end of the portal hadn't been discovered yet, she reasoned.

As twilight approached, a chill settled over the landscape. A damp mist began to rise from the sea, slowly shrouding the moon in a ghostly veil. Knowing the descending darkness would soon make the bluff too dangerous to traverse, Marilyn quickly descended the remaining distance to the stony beach and cave entrance. The looming danger of the growing shadows made her feel even more isolated.

Back at the portal, the first supplies had arrived: the fatigues and boots she had requested, along with the coat and beanie hat, a backpack of food rations, a compact sleeping bag, and a first aid kit. Marilyn added the collected wood to the pile and started a fire, its warmth chasing away the creeping shadows of the cave.

Re–engaging her earpiece, Marilyn spoke into the mic, "Flip, when we talked about this, I thought I was in for a rugged camping trip. But this… this is glamping!" Marilyn let out a short laugh, "Thank you so much for this. It's more than I could've asked for. But can I make just one more request?"

Philip's voice crackled in her ear. "Sure thing, Mare. What'cha need?"

"I need a portable GPS locator. I still have no cell service, wherever this place is. But the Moon and Sun are the same – I'm still on Earth. With that, I should be able to figure out where I am so I can be rescued. All I can tell for now is that this place is a sea cave on a beach somewhere. Given the lack of any sign of human habitation though, I think I might be on an uninhabited island somewhere in the South Pacific."

After a pause, the earpiece came alive with a chorus of relieved voices. Philip's voice broke through the chatter, "Copy that, Mare. We'll get it to you as soon as we can. Everyone's glad to hear you're still on home turf and not some distant planet in a galaxy far, far away."

"Hey, we dug a hole to China!" Avery chuckled.

Ayesha chimed in, "Ma'am, I know he's joking around, but Avery may have something there. Maybe this thing is a portal straight through the middle of the Earth or something. From where we are, that would put you somewhere in the middle of the Indian Ocean between South Africa and Australia. Mostly nothing out there but a lot of ocean."

Amidst the chatter and speculation, Marilyn moved to a discreet spot out of view of the portal to change into the requested dry clothes and boots. Once dressed, she methodically began to unpack her supplies, carefully arranging her makeshift home. Setting her sleeping bag aside for last, she stowed the backpack of food rations and the first aid kit away. Then, she spread her damp clothes and former shoes out to dry and hung the long coat and beanie hat on a protrusion in the cave wall. Bit by bit, the cave began to feel less alien, a touch of normalcy seeping into her extraordinary circumstances.

As she was arranging her sleeping bag near the fire, Philip's voice abruptly sliced through the silence. "Listen, Mare. We've got a problem."

"What?" she responded, her alarm complementing the tension in his voice.

"Tak says the power draw from the proton emitter is too high," Philip relayed, his words heavy with implication. "Once the world starts to wake up and the power grid sees the morning demand surge, we won't be able to maintain it. If we don't recalibrate, we risk a brownout, which could cause a cascade failure. We might lose the portal… and you."

A chill coursed down Marilyn's spine at his words. "So, what does that mean?" she asked, her voice reduced to a near whisper.

Philip hesitated before admitting, "While you were away, I… didn't change the frequency, but I backed off the power just a bit."

"Flip! That was foolish!" Marilyn protested, her heart pounding. "I might've come back to find the portal gone and not know what happened!"

"I know, Mare," Flip replied, his voice tight with regret. "But we were running outta time, and I didn't know how long you'd be gone!"

Resolute, he continued, "Listen, when I made the adjustment, from this side at least, it just reduced the size of the portal a little. We think we can draw down the power to an acceptable level and keep the portal active. Naomi said comms shouldn't be affected, but the portal's gonna shrink to about the size of a football. We've got about fifteen minutes before we have to dial it back. Is there anything else you need before then?"

Her face softened, accepting the circumstances for what they were. "You're right, of course Flip. Sorry," she sighed. Her brow furrowed as she grappled with their new reality and looked around at her gear, then glanced back at the portal. "Power. I'll need a way to keep my earpiece and cell charged just in case I get a signal or we lose the portal."

"You got it, Mare," he replied. "We have a portable solar charging kit that was being evaluated for field operations. It's not part of the standard gear, but Tak should be able to adapt it for your needs. We'll get it to you when we can power up again tomorrow night. Hopefully, we'll find you and get you back sooner than that. But… just in case…"

At Philip's words, Marilyn could feel the worry creeping into his voice, tangled with a thread of hope. She found herself wanting to alleviate his concern, despite her own predicament. "I'm doing okay, Flip," she reassured him, her voice steady. "You and the team are doing everything you can, and I couldn't ask for more. Please, tell everyone thank you for me."

"I will," he replied, his voice thick with relief. "In the meantime, the backpack we sent over has the LED Lantern from the emergency supply locker in it. It's power pack has a built–in USB outlet. I had already thought ahead and added a charge station for the headset, but I'll get your phone charge cable from your quarters. The power pack won't last that long, but hopefully you won't need it that long. It's only meant to last a couple of days at most."

"That's a smart addition," Marilyn responded, a small smile forming. "I appreciate your foresight, Flip. That could make a world of difference." Philip's silent nod indicated his appreciation of her gratitude.

He handed his headset to Dr. Bennett, who had been a silent observer up to now. "Marilyn," the doctor began, "the first aid kit you have is extensive enough to deal with minor emergency needs – but it's not exactly a modern pharmacy in there. Do you have any prescription needs or anything?"

Aware that Philip was still within earshot, Marilyn paused, her heart racing as she considered how to reply. She was all too aware of her pregnancy and the prenatal vitamins she should be taking, but she didn't want Philip to know yet. "Not unless you think I need something?" she ventured.

Dr. Bennett seemed to understand her subtle hint. "Well, given the basic rations you'll be on, it couldn't hurt to supplement a bit. We don't want you to come down with scurvy or something equally archaic. I'll send over some vitamin packs to make sure that doesn't happen." His light tone suggested it was a casual suggestion, rather than a medical necessity. Satisfied, he handed the earpiece back to Philip.

As Philip put the headset back on, he informed her, "Takashi is about to start drawing the power down. Report any issues immediately, okay? When he reaches the 50% mark, I'm going to attempt redirecting the beam, aiming to retarget the portal's location on the surface. Be prepared for that."

Marilyn acknowledged, then selected a ration pack and stationed herself to vigilantly monitor the portal from her end. One by one, the crystals outlining the disc ceased to glow. Without transition, they shifted from projecting fractured images of the world beyond to utter darkness.

The glow receded in a gradual circular pattern before halting momentarily. Then, the now significantly smaller illuminated area shifted positions, mimicking a projector being adjusted on a screen. This pattern – reducing size, redirecting position – continued until the portal had shrunk to an ethereal stained–glass window, showing a tantalizing glimpse of her home lab, just inches above the ground.

"Mare, we're keeping the comms open," Philip's voice came through the earpiece, clear yet subdued. "Try to get some rest. We're on this."

She sighed, momentarily forgetting that Philip couldn't see her, and nodded. "Thanks, Flip. Goodnight."

"Goodnight, Mare."

As the darkness of the cave enveloped her, Marilyn found herself accompanied only by the artifact's soft glow, the distant sound of waves, and her thoughts. Alone. Lost. Yet, not devoid of hope. Tomorrow promised new possibilities. A day for answers. A day for discoveries.

Embracing this thought, she tightened the coat around herself and allowed sleep to claim her. The gentle murmurs from the team in her earpiece served as a comforting lullaby, a tangible link to her home, her era, and her reality.

Standing next to Philip, Dr. Bennett glanced up at the control room window, then silently tapped his ear and made a cutting gesture with his hand. Catching the message – 'kill comms' – Philip disengaged his earpiece and quipped, 'Eh, what's up, doc?" attempting a Bugs Bunny impression that bore only a passing resemblance.

"Has she told you yet?" concern was etched on Dr. Bennett's face.

"No," Philip sighed. He knew about Marilyn's pregnancy but hadn't let her know he was aware. The information had come to him inadvertently; he had overheard a message Dr. Bennett had left on Marilyn's answering machine about rescheduling her prenatal appointment. His shock morphed into dismay, leading to a heart–to–heart with Dr. Bennett where he confessed his accidental discovery.

Though the doctor had dutifully cited HIPAA regulations and base medical policies, their longstanding friendship and mutual trust had spoken louder. Unspoken gestures and knowing glances had confirmed Philip's concerns. He even had a fairly good idea of when and how it had happened – a night involving too much alcohol and careless decisions.

"She hasn't said anything, but I'm sure she has her reasons," Philip confided. 'And hopefully, we can get her home safe before it becomes an issue,' he thought privately.

They watched silently as Marilyn left the cave and, after a moment of hesitation, Philip spoke, seeking reassurance. "She seemed fine. The way she described falling through the portal though… You think the baby's alright, Monty?" he asked, his voice filled with concern.

"I'm sure that is the case, Philip," the doctor responded, reassuring him in a deep, resonant voice that Philip had come to associate with age and wisdom even though they were only a few years apart in age. "She didn't appear to be bleeding. And she's young and strong, and in the very early stages of pregnancy," he added. His reassurance gave Philip some relief. He had faith in the doctor. He had to, given Monty's inability to physically examine Marilyn. But with the impotence he felt at the moment, faith was all he had.

Friendship since their college days had taken them through shared beers at local sports bars and weekend golf games. Philip had liked the man from the start, calling him 'Monty' until the man earned his doctorate. After that, 'Doc' felt like a more fitting mix of respect and friendly affection. "Hmm… 'Montgomery' – Nope, just too big o' mouthful for this Texas boy, Doc," he remembered saying with a grin when the man had once asked why Philip never used his real name. They were out for an afternoon of golf at time. Monty just grinned and shook his head at Philip's simple explanation.

But in those moments when he needed his friend and not "Doctor Bennett," when moments of gravity struck, Philip found himself slipping back to 'Monty' in earnest conversation. By contrast, the doctor had maintained a professional approach. He always addressed Philip by his first name, never adopting the casual nickname 'Flip' used by the rest of his friends.

That shared love and respect between friends though was the primary reason why the two of them were standing there now. Philip had been instrumental in bringing Monty his post on the base as one of its only civilian residents. And right now, Philip was glad of it.

"Listen, the rest of the team doesn't know anything about the pregnancy, so…you know…discretion would be appreciated," Philip said.

"You haven't told them anything?" Monty asked, his surprise evident. "Philip, you know I can't share medical information except in strict circumstances. Regardless," he paused, turning back to stare at the artifact. "Not the biggest secret you've asked me to keep," he quipped, grinning.

His grin faded into a serious expression as he glanced at the portal. "But I think it would be wise for me to join your team down here for the time being to keep an eye on Marilyn and be available if she needs me," he added. "Most days, nothing of consequence happens at the base clinic. And what does happen, my PA can most likely handle."

"That's a good idea," Philip said gratefully. "Let's get up to the control room and get you a monitoring station set up."

CHAPTER 3

Discoveries

Marilyn awoke to the sound of trickling water; it must have rained during the night. Water drizzled down the cave wall, forming a puddle near the smoldering remains of her fire. As the puddle drained, the runoff joined with other rivulets from deeper within the cave, forming a tiny stream that coursed steadily towards the cave's entrance.

Marilyn pulled herself from the cocoon of her sleeping bag and made her way to the cache of supplies she stashed in a pile nearby. She pulled out her canteen for a sip, then rummaged through her gear. 'No toothbrush or paste,' she thought, disappointed, making a mental note to ask for them. Making do with what she had, Marilyn used some water from her canteen to rinse her mouth as best as she could and freshen her face. A bemused smile formed as she realized something else was missing. 'No hairbrush either,' she thought. 'So much for glamorous camping…'

With her morning ritual complete, she retrieved her earpiece, slipped it on, and engaged it. Clearing her throat, she announced, "Lieutenant Colonel Marilyn Morgan reporting in."

"Afternoon ma'am," came Naomi Higgins' voice, crisp and professional. "Flip went to the mess hall for a moment – said he'd be right back. How did you sleep?"

"About as well as can be expected, given the circumstances," Marilyn said stretching the aches from her body. "And it's morning here. Or at least it should be," she added, her tone laced with confusion.

"Something wrong, ma'am?" Naomi probed, picking up on Marilyn's uncertainty.

"My internal clock may be a bit skewed, but I don't normally oversleep. Years in the military drills that out of you," Marilyn explained, her voice reflecting a hint of self–surprise.

"I understand, ma'am," Naomi empathized, her tone soothing. "Every fall, when we push the clock back, I wake up an hour early for a couple of weeks. When you signed off last night, it was just after eleven in the lab. It's just past noon now – about thirteen hours," she reasoned, her voice holding a note of reassurance. "Given the ordeal you had last night, it's completely understandable." Pondering what Naomi said for a moment, Marilyn pushed it from her mind as a familiar voice chimed in on the channel.

"Maybe this'll help!" Flip's voice broke in, his familiar timbre laced with mischief. Concurrently, a thermos came hurtling through the soccer ball–sized portal, landing on the cave floor amidst parcels she hadn't noticed before. 'The team was busy while I slept,' she thought, staring at the pile of newly arrived goods. In the dim light, she hadn't noticed them earlier.

"I thought you might need some coffee," he continued, his voice carrying a teasing note.

"Flip, you know I don't drink coffee! Yuck!" Marilyn protested, her face scrunching in distaste.

"I know," he admitted with a chuckle. "It's Earl Grey. Just keeping you on your toes."

Muffled chuckles and a chorus of greetings echoed in her earpiece from the rest of the team. She unscrewed the thermos, the aroma of the tea instantly soothing. She took a tentative sip.

"Thank you, Flip," she said, a hint of gratitude in her voice. "You even remembered the honey!"

"With the portal powered down, we can't see much from this end right now, ma'am," Naomi's voice cut in. "But the GPS locator you requested should be nearby. So, you should be able to power it up and find where you are."

"And Doctor Bennett sent over a care package. He said to take one a day," Chip chimed in, his voice steady and reassuring. "Also, Tak wired up a solar array to a rechargeable power pack in case your battery pack runs out. But it's too large to fit through the portal right now. We'll have to send it tonight when we can power back up."

"Excellent! Thanks, everyone!" Marilyn's voice rose with excitement as she rushed to retrieve the GPS locator. "Flip, I've got to go outside to use this locator. It won't work in the cave. The sooner I find out where I am, the sooner we can get me home. I'll be right back."

Marilyn unpacked the GPS locator from its protective wrap and, grabbing her flashlight, rushed toward the cave exit. As she emerged into the open, she was greeted by a clear sky, the rivulets of water running down the cliff face the only remnants of the rainstorm from the night before. A sense of surprise washed over her when she realized it was early morning, but she quickly brushed it off. Perhaps the time difference between the lab and her current location was more substantial than she'd assumed.

Once outside, she powered on the locator, eagerly watching the display for a sign of her location. However, all that appeared was the disheartening message of "GPS Signal Failure," accompanied by the line "Relocate Device" blinking on the small LED screen.

Frustrated, Marilyn trudged back to her camp by the portal and tossed the uncooperative locator aside. Re–engaging her earpiece, she relayed the unfortunate news. "Flip, this GPS locator is broken. It isn't picking up any satellite signals."

Before Philip could respond, Naomi interjected, disbelief coloring her tone. "That's not possible, ma'am. I calibrated it just before we packed it up and sent it over."

"Maybe passing it through the portal affected it somehow," Philip speculated. "If that's the case, sending over a replacement won't do us any good."

"Well, then I suppose I should explore the vicinity – see if I can find any clues to where I am," Marilyn proposed. A small blinking light on her earpiece caught her eye. "Listen Flip, my earpiece is blinking. That usually means it has about 20 minutes before it dies completely. I'd better leave it here to charge while I'm gone."

"I get it, Mare. I'm not thrilled, but I understand," Philip conceded, his tone begrudgingly accepting. "Just promise to be careful, okay?"

"I will, Flip." Marilyn paused, then addressed another member of her team. "Listen, Naomi, while I'm out, could you do me a favor?"

"Of course, ma'am! What do you need?" Naomi chimed in, eager to assist.

A touch of embarrassment colored Marilyn's voice as she made her request. "Could you make sure a toothbrush and some toothpaste are here when I get back?" At the same time, she started unpacking the vitamin supplements Dr. Bennett had sent over.

A chuckle sounded from Naomi's end. "Absolutely, ma'am!" Her voice was thick with suppressed amusement.

"I can't believe we didn't think of that! Sorry, Mare!" Philip interjected, embarrassment evident in his voice.

"Don't worry about it, Flip. It's impossible to think of everything," she reassured him. As she swallowed a vitamin with a swig from her canteen, she added, "Oh, and if you could add a hairbrush to that list, I'd appreciate it."

"Sure thing, ma'am," Naomi replied. Then Ayesha interjected, "If you're willing to wait a bit, I could run down to the PX and grab everything for you."

Marilyn shook her head, even though they couldn't see her. "No need, Naomi, but thank you. I need to start exploring and figuring out where I am. The sooner I do that, the sooner you guys can send out a rescue party."

Marilyn found the bluff near the cave much easier to navigate in her sturdy boots compared to the ill–suited footwear she had worn the evening before. As she reached the top of the bluff and stood, the morning sun was just cresting over the forested land that spread across the plateau. Preoccupied with gathering firewood in the dwindling daylight the night before, she hadn't had a chance to explore more than a short span beyond the cave.

Away from the cliff's edge, the terrain transformed into a verdant expanse of wilderness. A lush canopy of towering trees draped over a forest floor, their broad leaves filtering the morning light into a dappled dance on the forest floor. The undergrowth beneath was moderate, a mix of wildflowers, shrubs, and ferns that bloomed in sporadic clusters, lending soft contrast to the surrounding foliage.

Before making her way inland, she decided that she needed to mark her location somehow so she could find the cave again more easily when she returned. She stacked stones into a cairn near the cliff edge, making sure it was visible from both the shore and the woods. Not having a knife to carve an arrow, she used smaller stones to indicate the direction she intended to follow.

Once done, she referenced her compass and started a mental map, aiming to keep the sea on her left as she travelled north–east along the cliffside, scanning for an opening in the trees – a rabbit trail or deer run she could follow to higher ground where she might gain a vantage and see the lay of the land.

As she went, she marked her trail, occasionally creating small stacks of stones or breaking branches at eye–level where trees encroached upon her path. These signs would be almost invisible to the untrained eye but would serve as a beacon for her on her return journey.

Walking along the edge of the plateau, she was struck by how familiar the coast seemed. It reminded her of the Pembrokeshire Coast in Wales – a place she and her family had visited many times in her childhood. But the forested plateau above was completely foreign – like an undisturbed scene from an ancient time, the virginal landscape untouched by human hands.

Uneventful and barren of any other signs of life, it was mid–day before anything of interest caught her attention. Having trekked perhaps ten miles along the top of the bluffs in a north easterly direction, she spotted a group of large birds – maybe ravens or rooks – circling in the distance above the tree line. Their distinct cawing led her gaze to an elevated area that promised a panoramic view.

Building a small rock pier to mark the path of her departure from the coastal locale, she set off in their direction, leaving the comfort of the coastline and delving deeper inland. As she moved further from the shore, the forest canopy suddenly thinned, and she spotted a peculiar structure standing starkly in a natural clearing, against the backdrop of the forest. As she approached, she realized it was man–made, a prehistoric structure that, despite its crude form, possessed a sort of imposing elegance. Consisting of three standing stones and a capstone laid on top, it looked like a crude, stone stool built for a giant.

An unsettling sense of familiarity washed over Marilyn as she continued to examine the structure. If not for the earth concealing most of the standing stones, and the capstone bearing fewer signs of weathering, the structure could be twin to Carreg Samson – an ancient burial mound she had seen many times while hiking through the Pembrokeshire countryside of Wales in her youth.

Her unease was quickly replaced by worry though as realization dawned on her. The structure seemed almost Neolithic – a remnant possibly left by a tribe of indigenous people. And they could still be in the area. Mental images of a cannibalistic tribe lowering her into a cookpot or turning her on a spit over an open fire prompted her to forget the site and move to a more concealed location under cover of the surrounding forest.

Once she reached the edge of the clearing, she quickly crafted another clear marker, a conspicuous arrangement of stones pointing in the direction she had entered the clearing from. She had no idea how far she had ventured, but with each step, the unease grew, gnawing at her composure. However, she couldn't afford to lose track of her route back to the cave.

She decided to alter her course, veering southeast. With the compass as her guide, she followed the contour of the land, seeking higher ground. Her pathway was marked by small, regular disturbances: a branch snapped here, a pile of stones there. She navigated her way through the landscape, avoiding brambles and briar patches that threatened to snag her clothing and impede her progress.

As she rounded a rocky outcrop, she froze. Ahead, a figure was stooped at a small pool fed by a trickling natural spring. He was quietly filling what appeared to be a leather bladder with water when the sound of her foot crunching among the forest floor's dead twigs drew his attention.

His eyes widened, mirroring the shock that rippled through her own body, rendering her momentarily breathless. He fell prone, words spilling from his mouth in a torrent she couldn't comprehend, his voice spiked with fear. His dialect was strange, guttural, and yet… familiar. Words she thought she recognized fluttered at the edge of her understanding. This "hermit" – for she could think of no other word to describe him – was terrified of her.

His dialect bore an uncanny resemblance to Welsh, but was different, foreign. 'Coedwig' and 'ysbryd' – forest and spirit – stood out amongst the garbled speech. Other words were close enough to Welsh to tease her understanding, reminding her of how Romance languages such as Italian, Portuguese, and Spanish share similar words. Forest… spirit… forgive… no hunt… no kill…. Suddenly, the frantic rambling of the hermit made sense: He mistook her for a forest spirit, pleading for his life, promising not to hunt in her domain.

Amused by his superstitious terror, and no longer frightened, she wondered at his origin. 'Could he be a shipwreck survivor, or a descendant of survivors?' she pondered. The island – if it was an island – was large enough to support life. Yet, how such a place could remain so secluded in today's world was beyond her comprehension.

Setting aside her curiosity for the moment, she reached out to comfort him. He recoiled with a whimper of fear. So, drawing back, she instead spoke softly, making soothing gestures to show she meant no harm. "It's okay…I won't harm you!" She knelt and waited for him to meet her gaze, then tried to emulate his language as best she could. "{No kill}," she reassured, smiling. She followed with a familiar Welsh word, palming her chest, "Ffrind."

Hesitant, he parroted her words, "{No kill}?" Seeing her calm demeanor, he slowly rose, the tension visibly lessening in his posture. Then, as he repeated her Welsh phrase, his confusion gave way to understanding. He translated her word into his own language. "{Friend}!" he exclaimed, a triumphant smile illuminating his face.

Curiosity supplanted their initial fear as they studied each other. The boy was about 15 years old. Long, wavy hair framed a face that held telltale signs of adolescence – spots, and the beginnings of facial hair. He was dressed in a basic, yet well–fitting tunic that reached his knees, covering woolen trousers held up by a thick leather belt. High leather boots laced up to his mid–calf. A spear and a belt knife tucked into a sheath at his waste completed the picture of a seasoned woodsman. Apart from his pale skin and lack of headdress, he reminded her eerily of the sepia–toned photographs of Native Americans she'd seen in secondary school history class.

Finally, he touched her face and gazed into her eyes, looking from one to the other for a moment, and stroked a bit of her short hair between his fingers. Satisfied that Marilyn was indeed mortal, he stepped back and rested his spear against a tree.

Standing tall and proud as a peacock proclaiming its domain, he palmed his chest and announced "Uthyr," then gestured toward her expectantly. She understood – he was telling her his name, which to her ears, sounded a lot like he was saying "Tooth Ear" but without the 'T.' He was expecting her to introduce herself in return.

"Marilyn," she said, pointing at herself. "Ma'erlyn," he repeated in his guttural accent. As Uthyr spoke her name, Marilyn was struck by the way he pronounced it, his tongue catching briefly between the syllables, turning it into something unfamiliar yet strangely beautiful.

'Ma'erlyn,' she thought. "Close enough," she muttered and nodded acknowledgement. Satisfied, he picked up his spear, turned and stalked away.

He walked no more than a couple of paces before he glanced back, an expression of mild surprise on his face when he saw she wasn't following him. Rather than asking or encouraging her to come, he simply raised an eyebrow and turned around, resuming his journey with an air of self–assured expectation. He seemed to take for granted that she would follow, as if it was the only logical course of action.

Shrugging, Marilyn decided to play along, curiosity piqued by this audacious young man. With nothing else to go by, she followed him towards his destination. They hadn't gone far though – perhaps 30 yards when the forest canopy opened up into a clearing encircling a small hill.

Emerging into the clearing, Uthyr's encampment came into view, dominated by a wild boar trussed by its hind legs from a low branch at the clearing's edge. Covered in protective linen, the gutted carcass swayed gently in the breeze, its throat expertly slit. Blood drained from it, collected in a small hole beneath, ensuring the scent didn't spread and attract unwanted predators. A distance away, discarded innards were being pecked at by a flock of carrion birds, their raucous caws echoing through the woods. Marilyn recognized them as the same birds that had drawn her attention and led her inland earlier.

Various elements of a successful hunting trip were scattered around the site. A rabbit carcass, hidden under a hefty rock, rested nearby. A bedroll of furs was laid atop a fallen log. A pack filled with essentials – a tinder box, rations, and other miscellaneous items, hinted at the boy's resourcefulness and skills as a huntsman.

Marilyn watched as Uthyr lay his spear and waterskin near the log and went about gathering firewood. After a few moments of observation, she joined in. As they worked at setting up his campsite, she decided to try and learn more of his language. Pointing at her head, then gesturing in a manner she hoped he would interpret as speaking, and finally pointing to him, she tried as best she could to indicate she wanted to learn words from him. She then pointed at a tree and said "tree" in Welsh, then pointed at him, repeating the process for "bird" and "boar."

Uthyr just looked at her, confusion etched across his features. Marilyn's gestures became more insistent, her brows furrowed, lips set in a tight line. Her gestures took on an edge of desperation, the soft swishing sounds of her hand cutting through the air growing sharper with each failed attempt. 'Is this boy simple–minded?' she thought. 'What else can I do to get him to understand?'

As her frustration grew, a twinkle appeared in Uthyr's eyes. He echoed her words slowly, with seeming confusion, as if struggling to understand her attempts at communication. But his eyes and a sudden mischievous grin spoke otherwise. Marilyn's brows knitted together, suspicion creeping in. Was he teasing her?

Eyes dancing with mirth, Uthyr observed the peculiar, nearly hairless individual – this "Ma'erlyn" – engage in a comedic spectacle of name–giving. 'What a strange little man,' Uthyr mused, then reconsidered. 'Or perhaps not a man,' he thought, noting the creature's smaller stature beneath the odd clothing. 'Perhaps he is one of the fae from gran gran's tales?'

Nodding to himself, satisfied that he had reached the correct conclusion, Uthyr focused once more on the conversation. He had grasped the essence of Ma'erlyn's intent – to exchange words from their respective languages. Yet, the sheer delight he derived from the fae's sincere, if slightly flustered efforts, compelled him to maintain his pretense of bewilderment. His amusement brimmed over when Ma'erlyn, frustrated, mirrored a gesture his little sister often displayed when teased – fists clenched and a tight-lipped growl.

Unable to contain himself any longer, Uthyr guffawed loudly. "{Okay, okay, okay}!" Uthyr finally conceded in his own tongue, hoping his jovial tone would cross the language barrier. He extended placating gestures, pressing his palms downward, a lingering gleam of mirth in his eyes. "{Settle down}," he advised, still chuckling softly. In response, a grin spread across Ma'erlyn's face, his blush and returned composure serving as a silent acceptance of the shared jest.

Uthyr marveled at the man's peculiar garb, a mix of awe and envy stirring as he studied it. The cloth was tough and woven better than anything he'd seen before, its colors expertly dyed to blend in with the surrounding forest. This patchwork of greens and browns would offer a significant advantage in remaining unseen – 'A useful trick, especially when those Saxon dogs come prowling,' he mused thoughtfully.

His curiosity then shifted to Ma'erlyn's pack, constructed of a similar cloth but reinforced with an alien metal. It was lighter than any iron he knew, yet seemed to possess a strength that defied its weight. Amid his silent admiration, Uthyr wondered if his new acquaintance would share with him the secrets of its making.

As the sun made its way to the pinnacle of the day, Uthyr realized he hadn't eaten since dawn with all the excitement of meeting this stranger. He was hungry. 'Perhaps he is hungry too,' Uthyr thought. He spread a couple of furs on the fallen log – a convenient seat – gesturing to the spot beside him. As Ma'erlyn sat beside him, he reached into his belongings and brought out a leather pouch. The scent of dried fruits and nuts filled the air as he opened the pouch and presented it as a snack the two could share while he was preparing the rabbit for roasting.

In response, Ma'erlyn dug into his own pack and produced a flat white object about the length of his hand with strange symbols on it. He watched in stunned amazement as Ma'erlyn peeled away the outer layer of the object to reveal a hardened, compressed rectangle of similarly mixed dried fruits and nuts combined with oats and barley.

Ma'erlyn tore the mixture in half and offered him a share in exchange. Uthyr took it and sniffed. It smelled of honey and an acrid spice he did not recognize. 'This man possesses the wisdom of the gods!' Uthyr marveled. 'Who would think to mix honey and grains into a brick?' He took a bite, filling his mouth with delight. 'Truly, I must discover the origin of this spice! Strange clothes? Exotic food? From where does this Ma'erlyn come?'

His thoughts turned to preparing a meal from the rabbit he'd caught earlier, his practiced hands gathering wood for a fire. However, as he placed the kindling and was about to strike his flint, Ma'erlyn's hand shot forward. A small metal box flickered to life in her hand, producing a flame as if by magic.

The sight of Ma'erlyn controlling fire so effortlessly left Uthyr in awe. Uthyr pointed at the metal box, both delighted and curious. His new friend was full of surprises. 'Surely such a creature wielding such magics is no mere mortal!' he thought. His fascination piqued, Uthyr indicated his desire to examine the magical device.

Reading his intent, Ma'erlyn teased him, snapping the flame out with an abrupt movement. The loud click startled him, sending a ripple of laughter through Ma'erlyn. The laughter was infectious, but he thought to himself, 'I know not from where he hails, nor his customs. Perhaps what I did is considered rude and I should wait for it to be offered.' This spurred an additional thought. 'Maybe Ma'erlyn will trade with me for the magic box!'

Surveying his possessions quickly, he saw nothing of great value except his spear and knife. Quickly pulling it from its sheath, he held it out – his most prized possession. His intent to offer a trade misunderstood at first, Ma'erlyn recoiled slightly, apprehension clouding his face. Realizing his eager mistake, he flipped the knife handle out and offered it to Ma'erlyn, gesturing toward the magic fire box. "{A gift for a gift}?" he quickly asked, gesturing to the strange man. Understanding replaced the worried expression and the man smiled and nodded. Uthyr thought he was surely the winner in this trade. Though it was his favorite knife, he wasn't sure it was truly equal to such sorcery.

As the brilliance of the day gave way to the gentle chorus of crickets in the late afternoon, Uthyr began to feel a sense of familiarity with his companion as they shared the campsite. Through a day marked by broken sentences and gestured explanations, Ma'erlyn seemed to gather a rudimentary understanding of Uthyr's tongue. Uthyr was impressed with the man's intelligence and the quickness with which he was learning to hold a conversation.

Uthyr noted Ma'erlyn's curiosity about his life, his family, and his homeland. Sensing his curiosity, Uthyr grabbed a stick and sketched a rough map on the earth.

"{This is the land I know…}" he drew a jagged line and pointed to the area it enclosed. "{Land…and sea…}," he gestured to either side of the line. "{We are here}," he marked a spot on the map, "{My village, Moridunum, is here, two day's walk from this place. My people are Briton}."

Uthyr noted the intensity of Ma'erlyn's gaze as she studied the map. Something was wrong. The inquisitiveness he saw before was being replaced by another emotion. Apprehension? Confusion? Ma'erlyn looked ill, like a man who is sick from the sea.

Suddenly, Ma'erlyn snatched the stick from his hand, the stranger's grip trembling slightly. Uthyr watched, puzzled, as Ma'erlyn continued to sketch the rest of the island, the stranger's strokes frantic, the lines haphazard. From what Uthyr could see, Ma'erlyn had just drawn a map not dissimilar to a map his father had from his father's father – one engraved into a wood panel that had been pillaged when the Roman conquerors left the island.

Ma'erlyn pointed to another location on the map and, voice almost frantic, asked "Lun–dun?" Looking down, Uthyr recognized the location. "{Ah…Yes, Lundenwic…}," Uthyr said, confusion beginning to furrow his own brow. The man scratched several lines into the dirt from the sea cutting inland and asked "Saxons?" almost demanding. Uthyr spit on that spot of the map. "{Saxons}," he acknowledged with disgust.

Ma'erlyn muttered something Uthyr couldn't understand, then corrected himself, speaking in Uthyr's language. "{We are here?}" Ma'erlyn demanded, the tone shaking, filled with fear. "{This place… We are here?!}"

Uthyr could only nod in confirmation. But before he could utter a word, Ma'erlyn was on his feet, hastily gathering his belongings.

"{I must go}," Ma'erlyn blurted out, and without another word, he was off. Like a startled hare, he vanished into the nearby woods, leaving Uthyr stunned and alone in their once–shared campsite.

Uthyr sat in the growing twilight as campfire light replaced daylight, his mind reeling from the abrupt departure. The intense fear he'd seen in Ma'erlyn's eyes puzzled him, and he couldn't help but wonder what had compelled the stranger to flee so suddenly.

Uthyr glanced down at the map, his thoughts racing. 'Ma'erlyn never mentioned where he was from,' he mused. A flicker of worry crossed his face. 'Could he be a castaway, lost at sea, perhaps?' The thought of the man lost and alone gnawed at him.

Shaking his head, he surveyed their now–empty campsite. Another thought struck him, darkening his features. 'Or maybe he saw the map and realized he was deep within the land of his enemies.'

"{By the spirits!}" Uthyr muttered to himself, "{I hope that is not the case! His clothes…his magic…I have never seen its like! We would do well not to invoke the wrath of such a man…}" His eyes returned to the map, tracing the lines of his homeland. 'I must tell my father of all this,' he thought with conviction.

As he went over the event in his mind, he realized it smacked of a fairy tale. If one of his friends had returned from hunting bearing such tales, he would have laughed and accused his friend of making up stories. He needed evidence to bring to his father as proof of the encounter with the stranger and his magic.

With determination, Uthyr stood and cast his gaze around the campsite. He knew what he could present! Searching, his eyes finally caught a glint of metal near a fallen log – the magic metal fire box – exactly what he was looking for. Picking it up, he handled it with a gentleness born of lingering awe and reverence for its strange, enchanting magic.

Removing the small lambskin pouch of medicinal herbs from around his neck, he emptied the pouch of its contents and placed the magical object inside. Securing the pouch around his neck once more, his gaze fell on the knife he had traded with Ma'erlyn. It lay in the dirt, abandoned in the stranger's hasty departure. He picked it up, weighing it in his hand for a moment before sheathing it.

With one last look around the campsite, Uthyr lay back down for the night. Underneath the celestial tapestry of the night sky however, sleep remained elusive for hours. Despite the peace and serenity around him, his mind still buzzed with unanswered questions.

Fleeing from the campsite, Marilyn tore through the underbrush, panic driving her every step. Her mind spun with the implications of her discovery, propelling her frantic dash through the dense forest. Brambles snagged at her legs and branches slapped against her arms, but she was heedless, her mind a whirlwind of terror and confusion. Her only focus was reaching the shore, reaching the cave, reaching for some echo of the world that was her own.

She tore through the woods, the sound of the sea growing louder, focusing on the setting sun, using it as a beacon, a light that she prayed would lead her back to sanity, the trail she had left for herself utterly forgotten. She just ran, driven by a need to escape, to deny the reality that had been thrust upon her.

Suddenly, the forest gave way to the open sky. With reckless abandon, Marilyn had been so eager to reach it, she almost tumbled over the edge of a seaside cliff. Skidding to a halt near the edge, she overbalanced and she fell hard on her backside. Her heart was pounding, her breath coming in ragged gasps. Teetering at the edge, she envisioned her body, broken and mangled on the rocks below, taken by the sea. 'They would never know what happened to me!' The thought sent a wave of nausea crashing over her, and she retched, emptying her stomach over the cliff's edge.

She lay there for a moment, drained, before forcing herself to her feet. "This can't be happening," she muttered, her words almost lost in a gust of howling wind. But the looming cliff and the yawning sea below were real. As real as the fear that gripped her.

With shaking legs, she stumbled along the bluff, looking for the cairn that marked the location of her cave. 'Maybe I'm dreaming all this? Maybe the lab accident put me in a coma?' Denial tried to worm its way into her thoughts, a lifeline to sanity in a world that had suddenly turned upside down.

But she knew better – these cliffs, rocky beaches, and bluffs that had once seemed eerily familiar now held a darker meaning. The sea stacks along the water line stood accusing. "You know where you are," they seemed to whisper. She closed her eyes, wishing this really was a dream.

When she finally spotted the cairn, a spark of hope ignited within her. 'The team must have figured it how to get her home by now! They will know what to do,' she thought desperation. "God, let it be so," she said quietly, a small prayer to a divinity about whose existence she had doubts.

Marilyn scrambled down the cliff towards the rocky shore below, carelessly jumping the last couple of feet and running to the mouth of the sea cave. The sight of the familiar entrance renewed her panic. 'No wonder the ruddy GPS locator didn't work!' she thought bitterly. 'There're no goddamn satellites!' With the sun gone and darkness creeping in, Marilyn could barely see a few feet into the cave. She tore off her pack, fumbled for her flashlight, and rushed inside, her eyes locking on the basketball-sized aperture of the portal.

Fear, desperation, panic all surged within her. She grabbed a rock and slammed it against the jagged crystals surrounding the portal, screaming, "Philip! Philip, help me!" In her panic, she had forgotten they couldn't hear her. She was alone, trapped in a time not her own. The realization hit her like a blow, and all her pent–up fear and despair erupted in a primal scream that echoed off the walls of the cave.

CHAPTER 4

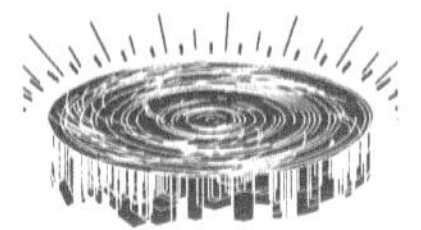

Revelation and Commitment

Philip strolled into the control room with Doctor Bennett at his side, where he found everyone too engrossed in their duties to notice. So, he announced to no one in particular, "Doctor Bennett's gonna be joining us 'til we get Mare home, y'all."

Amid the unsolicited welcomes and Monty's gracious thank you, Philip's gaze caught movement on his workstation monitor. His heart pounded as he witnessed Marilyn frantically striking the surface of the portal with a rock. Her terror was evident. He could only make out her face and shoulders through the basketball-sized aperture.

"What the hell?" Philip muttered, swiftly re–engaging his earpiece before rushing out of the control room. The exclamation drew everyone's attention, and they scrambled to their station's with looks of concern as Philip shot out the control room door.

On the comms, Philip's urgent voice broke through, "Tak, we need to open the portal wider. I can't see a damn thing through this small gap!"

"But sir, we need to…" Takashi started, only to be interrupted.

"I don't care, damn it! Give me as much of a view as you can!"

"I will, sir!" Takashi responded. "But you need to recenter the targeting on the emitter from down there. We have no clue what might happen if we attempt to expand the aperture, and it intersects with the artifact's edge. And neither of us wants to discover that it could have disastrous consequences at this point."

"I'm sorry, Tak," Philip said as he reached the platform. He took a deep breath, seeking to still his racing heart. "I appreciate you staying clear headed. Recentering the emitter now."

He watched as the aperture size gradually increased. Once the aperture was large enough for him and Marilyn to see each other, Philip gestured for her to insert her earpiece. He knew her view of him was fractured and disjointed, turning his desperate gestures into a kaleidoscope of urgent movements she was failing to comprehend. Regardless, he patiently continued to gesture, trying to communicate despite the difficulty.

Finally, understanding dawned on her, and he watched as she scrambled to the charge station, fumbling with the earpiece, nearly dropping it in her desperate haste. "Flip? Flip! Oh God! Flip?! Can you hear me?" Her Welsh accent, usually so charming, was now thick with fear.

Philip responded urgently, "I'm reading you, Mare! Loud and clear! What's wrong? What happened?"

The panic in her voice was palpable as she cried out, "Flip, it's just horrible! I can't… we can't…" Marilyn's voice broke, overcome by sobs. "We've got to make this blasted thing let me back! You've got to help me!"

Doing his best to project calm and reassurance, he said, "Marilyn, it's going to be okay. Listen, even if we can't get this artifact to cooperate, we'll figure out where you are, and we'll come to get you. I swear it, I'll be on the chopper myself to pick you up!"

There was a pause as Marilyn took a deep breath, then started again. She spoke quietly at first, but her voice rose in volume and anxiety with each statement. "Flip, you don't understand! This…portal…" she said as she gestured angrily at the artifact. "…didn't just put me in some other place! It put me in another time! Like I'm bloody Doctor Who or something!" Her words came tumbling out, barely a breath between them, "I'm in Wales in the middle of the goddamn dark ages for Chrissake! You've got to fix this thing! You must get me home! I can't be stuck here!"

"Mare, please listen. I need you to try your best to be calm and rational. You aren't making any sense! You've been gone what? Five minutes maybe? How could you possibly think you're in another century?!" Philip urged, his voice a blend of concern and disbelief.

"Five minutes?! Flip, I've been gone more than twelve hours! Now you're the one not making any sense!" Marilyn retorted, her fear mixing with frustration.

Simms cleared his throat, cutting into the conversation. "If I might interject... you're probably both right."

"I'm sorry Avery, what?" Philip responded, taken aback. At the same time, Marilyn echoed, "Come again?"

Avery explained, "We've pretty much been neck deep in our own little sci-fi movie since we accidentally turned this thing on – at least for our current level of technology. But we have all sorts of theories about what could be possible. One of those possibilities is called a wormhole – a bridge between two points in space and time like walking through a door between two rooms."

"So that's what this artifact is? A wormhole?" Philip inquired, trying to grasp the concept.

Avery responded, "This is all speculation of course, sir. But I believe so, yes. People like Stephen Hawking and Kip Thorne have speculated about the possibility of such things using words like 'exotic material' to describe…well…the door frame, for lack of a better analogy. I'd say our artifact here qualifies as that."

Impatient and on edge, Marilyn snapped, "Fine, it's a wormhole. How does that make both Flip and me right?"

Avery continued, "Well…this door – we've never experienced anything like it before. It's possible that there is some sort of time dilation effect happening."

Naomi added, "That would explain the Doppler effect on the comms that we had to correct."

"Exactly. While the Lieutenant Colonel is near the portal, time passes at almost the same rate as here in the lab. But the further she gets away from it, the slower time appears to go for us from her perspective – and from our perspective, the further away she gets the more it would seem the universe is zipping by," Avery elaborated.

"Then why do I not see something like that? I went outside the cave yesterday to collect fire wood and the world wasn't spinning like crazy or anything," Marilyn questioned, a hint of panic still lingering in her voice.

Ayesha chimed in, "I remember this old movie called 'The Time Machine'. The inventor sits in it, pulls a lever, and goes nowhere while the whole world is zipping by around him."

"I remember that movie!" Takashi exclaimed. "Shouldn't the Lieutenant Colonel be seeing something like that?"

Avery dismissed the comparison, "First of all, that's Hollywood, not reality. And secondly, H.G. Wells was imaginative, but he wasn't Einstein."

Philip further explained, "By Einstein's rules, Mare, your experience is relative to you – wherever you are, you experience time the same. Whenever you come near the portal, time just speeds up right along with you, and when you get further away, it slows down right along with you too."

"Exactly. Standing still, you don't even think about it, but you're moving through space as the Earth spins, which rotates around the Sun, and so on. From your perspective, though, you're standing still. Time behaves the same way," Avery added, lending support to Philip's explanation.

"So, what can we do? How do we make this door work both ways?" Marilyn asked, her voice tinged with desperation.

Philip's eyes darted around the platform, an idea forming in his mind. He was searching for the end of the broken cable when movement caught his eye. Dr. Bennett was approaching, coming up the catwalk toward the platform.

"Monty? What's up?" Philip asked, momentarily distracted by the newcomer.

"I came to talk face-to-face with the Lieutenant Colonel," Dr. Bennett replied. Turning to face the portal and Marilyn, he said, "Marilyn, high degrees of stress can alter our perceptions a great deal. The mind can play some pretty nasty tricks on itself trying to deal with a situation – especially one over which that person feels they have no control."

Interrupting him, Marilyn blurted out, "I'm not going crazy Doctor Bennett!" Philip watched her take a deep breath before continuing. "I really am in Wales and it really is the dark ages here! I barely remember more than a few footnotes from my history class in secondary school to say exactly when but…"

This time Doctor Bennett interrupted her. "Marilyn, what makes you believe your circumstances are as you describe?" he asked analytically. "How do you know where…or when…you are?"

"That's not a short story," Marilyn replied. "For anyone that doesn't know, I'm American born, but I spent my childhood in Wales. My father was a diplomat…" She paused, collecting her thoughts.

She launched into a quick recounting of the events that transpired during her journey beyond the confines of her cave – the eerie familiarity of the region, the ancient ruins at Carreg Samson that she could almost recognize, and her meeting with Uthyr and the conversation that transpired. Her descriptions were so vivid and detailed that the room filled with gasps, incredulous whistles, and murmurs of disbelief, as if her tale transported them all back in time with her.

"But the dark ages? How do you know that?" Philip asked, his brow furrowed in confusion.

Marilyn's eyes blazed. "The boy I met – Uthyr – called London 'Lundenwic,' Flip! It hasn't been called that since before the Vikings invaded, probably in the seventh century. And before that, it was Londinium, back when the Romans left in the 400s!" The fact that he's 'Briton'… Saxon invasions… his clothes… the language sounding like some prehistoric ancestor of Welsh… everything pointed to that era! I'm in the goddamn dark ages I tell you!"

Philip absorbed her words for a moment, his mind racing with the implications of her experience. As much as he was drawn into the details of Marilyn's adventure, he knew he had to keep his focus on the present challenge. As he searched for other possibilities in his mind, Naomi's voice over the comms broke his train of thought. "Google says she's right sir. I just did some quick searches from what she said and she's definitely in the dark ages – probably sometime in the fifth or early sixth century. Not like folks were writing diaries and history books though, so…hard to say for sure."

Now more certain than ever, Philip came to a decision. The portal was their only option and they still had work to do. "Naomi, are we still monitoring on the DARTS?" he inquired, shifting back to his professional tone.

"DARTS?" Dr. Bennett raised an eyebrow.

"Data Acquisition, Recording, and Telemetry System. DARTS," Philip clarified.

"Ah…" Dr. Bennett nodded in understanding.

Turning his attention back to the task at hand, he addressed the team, "Everybody, monitor your stations and keep a close eye on your readings. I wanna try somethin' out," he said, his Southern drawl slipping in.

Acknowledging the responses, Philip grabbed the end of the broken suspension cable still attached to the platform. Holding his breath, he dropped it through the portal. As he fed more through, the weight on the other side pulled it to one edge, gravity shifting from down to side–ways betwixt the two worlds.

Marilyn's voice came over the comms, curious but worried. "What are you doing, Philip?"

The reaction was immediate. "Flip, power draw is rising," Takashi warned through the comms.

"Alright, just keep an eye on it, Tak." Philip said as he continued feeding the cable slowly into the portal.

"Sir, what I mean to say is, you need to stop now! Energy spikes are hitting critical levels!" Takashi's urgent voice echoed in his earpiece once again.

Philip's attempts to pull the cable back were met with resistance as though it had become rooted on the other side of the portal. Amidst Takashi's urgent demands to cease, the portal began to hum, the intensity increasing the harder Philip yanked on the cable.

Marilyn's voice came over the comms again, now tinged with panic. "Philip, something's wrong! Stop, please!"

In a wave of panic, and with no means at hand to sever the cable, Philip pulled with all his might. Suddenly, the portal let out a sharp electrical crack. The luminescent sheen that had first stretched across the smooth surface of the portal when the experiment began now flashed back into existence, slicing the cable with a guillotine's precision. A moment later, it was gone.

Philip stumbled backward and landed hard on the platform. "Ow, fuck!" He grunted.

"You okay, sir? What happened?" Avery Simms's concerned voice broke through the comms.

"Dollar in the swear jar! Thar's what!" Ayesha chimed in, attempting to add levity to the tense moment.

"The power draw is nominal again," Takashi's relieved voice informed him. "What were you doing anyway?"

"Something apparently very stupid," Philip replied, wincing as Dr. Bennett helped him up.

"What were you trying to do?" Marilyn's voice came through the comms, concern and curiosity mixed in her tone, as Philip watched her pick up the severed piece of cable on her end, examining it with confusion.

"I was hoping that as long as something was in the middle of passing through, the portal might somehow allow it to travel both ways. If it had worked, we could've just tied you up and reeled you back in," Philip explained, a touch of frustration in his voice.

"Now what do we do?" Marilyn asked, desperation creeping back into her voice.

The room was filled with a tense silence, the team members exchanging worried glances. No one had an immediate answer, and the atmosphere became thick with uncertainty.

"I don't know, Mare. Give us a moment to think, okay? We'll figure something out, I promise," Philip finally responded, but his voice lacked the confidence he had hoped to convey.

Marilyn's breath caught in her throat, and her panic began to grow. The silence on the other end of the comms was almost worse than any rejection of her plea.

"Could she reach the artifact from the other side? The smooth part?" Ayesha ventured, the question filling the air with tentative hope.

The hope they all felt resonated in Marilyn's voice as she quickly scanned the cave around her, focusing on the place where the portal's artifact was embedded. Her voice cracked as she responded, "There's… there's no way. The artifact's encased in stalactites and stalagmites. It would take a mining crew days to get it out with power tools. Me with a mining pick? Months to never! I can't… I can't wait that long."

Philip glanced around the room, his team's faces reflecting the same helplessness he felt. The brief spark of hope had been extinguished as quickly as it had appeared. His entire world, the woman he loved, was right there – mere feet away and yet as unreachable as if she were on another planet. Philip's heart ached at her words. He yearned to leap through the portal, to hold her, comfort her, promise her everything would be okay. But he knew better. He couldn't help her by joining her.

"Mare, we'll figure this out. We have a game plan even if it takes a while to dig out the artifact. You just need to be patient! We just need time…." he pleaded, trying to keep the desperation out of his voice.

"GODAMMIT PHILIP! I CANNOT STAY HERE! I CANNOT! YOU DON'T UNDERSTAND! I'M PREGNANT!" Marilyn screamed into the earpiece. The comms fell into a stunned silence, all chatter, muted though it was, coming to a halt. The team was in shock. Philip, who had known her secret, was taken aback by her outburst. Marilyn was left panting and sobbing, having revealed her secret in the most terrifying way possible.

"Guys, give us a moment?" Philip's voice broke the silence, and he heard Naomi respond, "Cutting team comms now, sir." Dr. Bennett patted him on the shoulder consolingly before making his way quietly to the lab exit.

Philip's heart was heavy as he watched Marilyn through the portal. To her, he was a fractured image, but he could see her clearly – alone, defeated, and silently crying as the adrenaline faded. His heart ached for her in her desolation. The irony that she looked more broken and fractured emotionally at this moment than her broken view of him was not lost on him.

Marilyn couldn't believe what she'd just done, the shock of her revelation dousing the flames of her hysteria. Wiping her nose on her sleeve and palming the moisture from her cheeks and eyes, she tried to regain some semblance of composure.

"I am so sorry, Flip," she sniffled. "You didn't deserve to find out that way. God, what must the team be thinking right now?"

"Don't worry about them, Mare," Philip said gently. "As for me," he paused, then shrugged. "I already knew." Marilyn blinked in surprise, her mind scrambling. 'He already knew?'

His voice broke the silence. "Marilyn…," he whispered. Through the fragmented view, she looked up to see him standing there, strong and steady – a lighthouse on a stormy night. "Listen to me… We will figure this out. I promise you… I will not leave you there, especially not now. We… will… bring… you… home…," he vowed, emphatic promise in each word.

Through time and space, through this fractured view, Marilyn felt a wave of his deep and abiding love wash over her. A small sob escaped her lips as she wiped fresh tears from her face. "Promise?" she asked, her voice small, vulnerable.

"Promise," Philip replied firmly.

As her sanity reasserted dominance, questions began filling her mind, "How long have you known…? How did you find out…? Was it Dr. Bennett?"

Not giving him a chance to respond, she said accusingly, "He told you, didn't he? Thick as thieves, you two! He's not supposed to do that!"

"It wasn't him, Mare!" Philip finally interjected. "Doc didn't say anything! Well…at least not directly anyway. Remember last week when you asked me to drop by your quarters on my way to the PX and nab your grocery list off the fridge so I could pick a few things up for you?" he said.

"Yes, I remember," she recalled tersely. "So?"

"Well…I overheard Doc leaving a message on your answering machine to confirm your prenatal care appointment," Philip admitted. "I asked him about it, but he was tight as a clam. I promise. We've known each other a long time though like you said. But like my gramma used to say, 'Sayin' nothin' says loads!'."

Marilyn considered his words, her heart swelling with emotion. She'd always thought herself good at keeping secrets, but this man she loved had quietly borne hers for over a week, acting as if nothing were wrong. His strength, his silent support, and the trust he'd shown in her made her love him all the more. "Why didn't you say anything, Flip?" she asked, her voice filled with both wonder and gratitude.

"I didn't say anything because I figured you had your reasons, and you'd tell me when you were ready," he replied simply.

Takashi's voice suddenly cut through the comms. "Flip, sorry for interrupting. But I asked Naomi to open the comms to let you know.... We can't sustain this level of power. If we don't reduce power soon, we'll brown out and lose the portal."

"Copy that, Tak. I just need a few more minutes, then we can reduce the power. Listen, keep comms open for a sec," Philip replied.

Marilyn watched as, like a Cubist painting in motion, pieces of Philip broke apart and reformed in the facets of the crystalline surface. He was fishing around in his coat pockets. "I was waiting ...," he said nervously, "...for when you finally told me about the pregnancy."

"Congrats by the way Mare!" Avery suddenly chimed in, followed quickly by similar sentiments from the rest of the team and Dr. Bennett.

"Guys!" Philip interjected, then waited for the apologies to die down. Taking a deep breath, he continued, "I imagined this happening under very different circumstances but...."

Having fished it successfully from his pocket, she saw him drop something through the portal. It came sailing through to her side and landed at her feet.

Marilyn picked it up – a small, hinged box covered in a rich, red velvet. She opened it delicately, presenting it to herself with the same care she knew Philip would have taken if he were able. A one–carat, Marquise–cut diamond set in platinum lay nestled inside.

"Oh, Philip!" she gasped, holding her free hand up in front of her mouth, fresh tears filling her eyes.

"Marilyn Fiona Morgan, will you do me the honor of sharing your life with me?" Philip asked earnestly. She looked up from the beautiful ring to the fragmented image of the man she loved – he was kneeling on one knee.

In that moment, all her fears, doubts, and worries washed away. She knew this man would move heaven and earth to bring her home to him. She looked up and smiled at Philip with pure joy. "Yes, Philip," she exclaimed with all the love she could muster, returned across time and space. "I will marry you."

Cheers and congratulations erupted over the comms as fresh tears of joy coursed down Marilyn's cheeks that she had no desire to wipe away. Her heartbeat echoed in her ears, filled with new hope and determination.

She took a moment to slip the ring onto her finger and was elated to see it was a perfect fit. Admiring her hand sporting her new ring, she pondered, 'I wonder how Philip knew my ring size?' But the moment was short lived as Takashi's gentle reminder pulled her from her reverie.

"Yes, of course, Tak. Go ahead," she acknowledged, and watched as the aperture began to diminish, shrinking like the flame of a lantern being turned down. Marilyn couldn't help but feel a pang of separation, as if the distance between her and her team had somehow grown. The portal was once again a small stained–glass window, a fading connection to her time, her world, and the man she loved.

While the team worked to make sure the portal was stable, she built a fire. Settling into her sleeping bag, she continued to admire the sparkling ring that graced her finger as the fire's dance reflected in the diamond, splashing brilliant rainbow sparkles across her hand. Surprisingly, the act of focusing on the sparkling ring had a calming effect, allowing rational thoughts to return.

"I just want to apologize to everyone," Marilyn said, her voice carrying a hint of embarrassment. "I know I acted irrationally earlier. Thank you for understanding."

The responses were immediate and empathetic. "It's totally understandable," said one team member. "I'd probably behave worse," said another, followed by a general murmur of agreement and reassurances like, "Completely forgotten."

"Philip's gone topside," Naomi's voice informed her. "He's working on getting a construction crew to fix the broken suspension cable. He said he'd be back as soon as possible."

"Okay," Marilyn responded, trying not to let her loneliness show.

She lay back, her thoughts turning to practical matters. "You know, with the portal like this, we really need to get a range extender working for the earpiece. We can't risk losing communication."

Naomi responded quickly, her tone regretful. "Avery and I were just discussing that, ma'am. We don't think it's going to work."

"Why not?" Marilyn asked, curiosity piqued.

"Lt. Colonel, pretend for a moment that the portal is like…a black hole," Avery interjected, his voice filled with both excitement and reverence. "While you're next to the portal, you're inside the hole, and the radio signal is not changed much – we can talk to each other with a little adjustment for the Doppler Effect. But leave the cave and you're outside the black hole – what comes in looks like the noise of the universe, and nothing goes out."

Marilyn was intrigued. "Avery, how do you know all this stuff?"

He chuckled, a hint of pride in his voice. "Mostly educated guess, ma'am. Flip's an engineer – he focuses on applied physics. My passion has always been theoretical physics. I wrote my graduate thesis in college on the consequences of folding space–time."

"You mean like time travel? In Hollywood movies, that's always a bad thing," she teased.

Avery was eager to debunk that notion. "Again, pay no attention to Hollywood sci–fi films – they're all wrong because they need a plot to create drama. Remember that movie from the 80s where that kid goes back in time and accidentally gets in the middle of his parents' meeting? That's called a paradox, and the universe just won't allow it. You can't go back in time and kill your great grandmother because doing so would prevent your birth, thus preventing you from going back in time in the first place."

Takashi couldn't help but join in. "But she's there, Avery. I mean, sure it's fifteen hundred years in the past, but she could do something that changes the present, couldn't she?"

Avery's tone was firm. "Tak, you aren't understanding. The present we are in – here…now – exists because, from our perspective, the Lt. Colonel has already done whatever she is going to do from her perspective. Call it fate…serendipity…pre–ordinance…whatever…the fact is, this whole thing – the lab accident, the Lt. Colonel going back in time, all of it, happened because it was supposed to happen."

His words struck a nerve with Marilyn. "You make it sound like my fate isn't in my own hands, Avery. I refuse to accept that."

Naomi's voice, calm and reassuring, intervened. "I don't think he's saying that at all, ma'am. You have the freedom to make whatever choices you like. He's just saying that the present we have now exists because you already made those choices from the perspective of history."

"Exactly," Avery confirmed.

"You guys are making my head spin," Marilyn finally admitted, feeling a mixture of fascination and exhaustion. "It's late, and I need to get some rest."

A few moments of silence followed Marilyn's words, the crackling fire the only sound breaking the thoughtful quiet. The conversation had traversed through physics, fate, and the perplexing nature of time, leaving a sense of wonderment and contemplation lingering in the air.

Just then, the familiar voice of Philip came through the earpiece. "Mare, I'm back. I've got a crew on the way to fix the platform. How are you holding up?"

She looked down at her new engagement ring, the fire's glow reflecting in its facets, and smiled. "Better, thanks to the team here. They've been incredible."

"We're just doing our job, ma'am," Naomi chimed in warmly, the others echoing her sentiments with gentle reassurances.

"I'll be working through the night, but I wanted to check in before you tried to get some sleep," Philip continued, his voice softening.

Marilyn felt a longing to say something more, to express the emotions swelling in her heart, but she knew the team was listening. "Thank you, Flip. Good luck with everything there. I'll… I'll talk to you in the morning."

"Goodnight, Mare. Sleep well."

A brief silence hung heavy, filled with unspoken feelings, before she finally whispered, "Goodnight."

As she settled into her sleeping bag, Marilyn felt a complex mix of emotions. Fear, uncertainty, and the theoretical possibilities they'd discussed all swirled in her mind, but at the core of it all was a sense of determination and love that anchored her. As the fire slowly crackled, Marilyn was lulled by the dance of light and shadow against the cave wall and drifted into a fitful sleep.

Naomi paused outside her barracks, Captain Lawton's instructions still echoing in her mind. Tonight's events had rattled everyone, but she suspected they had shaken him most of all. "Probably him more than anyone," she muttered. Though both he and the lieutenant colonel tried to hide it, Naomi and Ayesha had both long suspected there was something more between those two. Of course, tonight's events had revealed the truth of that speculation. Insisting on taking the first watch, he sent the others to get some R&R. 'Was it any wonder?' Naomi thought, shaking her head.

Still, the reprieve was welcome. She had four hours before taking the next watch, but even with the fatigue weighing on her, she doubted she'd be able to sleep under the circumstances. Lost in her own thoughts as she fumbled for her security badge, she was pulled back to the present by a familiar voice calling down the hall.

"Hey, Naomi! Wait up!" Ayesha jogged toward her, her eyes lighting up with excitement. "It came?!"

Naomi blinked in confusion, following Ayesha's gaze down to the floor beside her door where a parcel she hadn't noticed before lay.

"Is that what we've been waiting for?!" Ayesha grinned.

Naomi felt a thrill of excitement as she picked up the package, her fingers brushing against the tape. "I bet so," she grinned, pushing the door open and inviting Ayesha inside. These barracks were a far cry from Bagram Airfield – larger, quieter, and with perks; small luxuries Naomi appreciated that made underground life more bearable.

Naomi tossed the parcel on her bed and headed straight for the bathroom.

"You pick now to go pee?!" Ayesha asked, impatiently. "Get back in here and open it already!"

Naomi emerged holding a pair of nail scissors, smirking. "Hold your horses! I was just grabbing something to cut the tape with. We don't want to destroy the box if this is it. We still have to wrap it!"

Sitting on the edge of the bed, Naomi began meticulously cutting the tape, careful not to damage the packaging. Ayesha stood watching, an excited gleam in her eye.

"You think we'll get her back by her birthday?" Ayesha asked, worry creeping into her voice. Naomi caught the expression on her face and grinned.

"We will," Naomi said, though her voice carried a confidence she didn't quite feel. She pulled the sword from the box, its gleaming blade catching the light.

Ayesha's eyes widened. "Wow," she breathed.

Naomi turned the sword over, admiring the craftsmanship. "It's even more impressive than I imagined. The lieutenant colonel is going to flip when she sees it."

Ayesha stepped closer, running a finger along the intricate cross guard. "He did a fantastic job with my sketches," she said, admiring the filigree.

"I'll say," Naomi agreed. "She'll be surprised, right? You didn't blab to anyone did you?"

Ayesha smirked. "I've kept bigger secrets than a birthday present, Naomi," she chided. "She doesn't know a thing. I promise. Way you're staring at the thing though, you look like you're tempted to keep it."

Naomi blushed but continued to admire the blade. Though a real weapon, it was crafted as a replica of a prop from one of the Harry Potter movies the lieutenant colonel loved. They had commissioned the sword together after visiting a local renaissance fair last April, where they stumbled upon a skilled weaponsmith. "I am tempted!" Naomi teased.

"Do that and me, Tak, and Avery will all kick your ass!" Ayesha teased back. "Besides," she added, her tone becoming serious. "Given what's going on, maybe she could actually use it now."

Naomi frowned. "So far as I know, swordplay isn't part of military training in any branch," she replied. "And I don't think she's had fencing lessons. So, it wouldn't be of any use to her even if it is a real sword."

"Yeah, maybe you're right. But still... that story she told," Ayesha said, trailing off, leaving the rest unspoken.

"It was pretty incredible," Naomi nodded. "I can't shake this feeling though. Like déjà vu or something. I swear I've heard the names Marylin and Uthyr spoken together before." She shook her head as though trying to dust the cobwebs off a memory that just wouldn't surface. "I just can't remember where...." She looked up to see a distant expression on Ayesha's face, lost in thought herself.

"Me too," Ayesha finally replied. "But not quite. It's more like...like hearing a story about two people named Romero and Julia, instead of Romeo and Juliet."

Finally, unable to recall any specific memory, Naomi stood. "It'll come to one of us eventually," she said. "Let me wrap this up again. Glad you got to see it before we give it to her though – whenever that ends up being."

Naomi carefully repackaged the sword, wrapping it snugly in its original packaging. She dug through her utility drawer, pulling out a roll of packing tape and securing the box shut. While she worked, Ayesha continued, "Flip said he wants eyes on the portal at all times until we figure this thing out. So, I'll be taking post after you in eight hours." Her tone softened. "You should get some sleep if you have to report in less than four."

Naomi chuckled, shaking her head. "I'll try, but I doubt sleep won't come easy tonight."

Ayesha nodded in understanding. "Yeah, I get that. Still, you'll be useless if you're falling asleep at the console."

Satisfied with her wrapping job, Naomi stood, stretching her tired muscles. "True enough," she admitted. "I'll see you in the morning, Ayesha."

"Take care," Ayesha said with a half-smile as she headed for the door, leaving Naomi alone with her thoughts - and the weight of the night's events pressing down on her.

Naomi glanced back at the box holding the sword, lying on her desk. “Let’s hope she’s back by her birthday,” she whispered, before turning off the light and slipping into the quiet darkness of her room.

CHAPTER 5

Technology and Magic

Marilyn savored a bite of scrambled egg, her taste buds waking to the unexpected luxury. The warmth of the food was a comforting contrast to the cave's damp chill, and she smiled in contentment as she chewed. A bagel, generously slathered with cream cheese and jam, awaited her next, a taste of home that felt both familiar and out of place in this ancient setting.

As she ate, she glanced at the portal, its steady glow a reminder of the connection to her team and the world she'd left behind. She recalled eagerly retrieving her earpiece from its charger when she awoke, seeking that connection. The sound of construction had buzzed in the background of their greetings, a subtle reminder of the ongoing work on the other side.

Naomi's voice had been a cheerful surprise, and Marilyn remembered her words with gratitude. "I brought breakfast," Naomi had announced, her tone warm with concern. "Dr. Bennett says you need to eat properly." Moments later, a cardboard box had come sailing through the portal, filled with the delightful assortment that now lay spread before her.

She'd been surprised and touched by the team's thoughtfulness. They'd thought of everything: bagels and cream cheese, jam in a small jar, scrambled eggs wrapped in foil, salt, pepper, and even utensils. They were looking out for her, even from centuries away.

Philip had been absent from their morning conversation, fast asleep after staying up all night. His dedication had kept the construction crew working through the night, fixing the broken suspension cable, and installing backup generators to stabilize the portal's power – her lifeline to the present. She'd felt a pang of guilt at his exhaustion, but his efforts had bolstered her confidence in their success.

As Marilyn continued to enjoy her meal, conversation flowed easily through her earpiece, the sounds of the lab a constant background hum. The connection to her team, the familiar taste of home, and the progress they were making filled her with new hope. The realization brought a new sense of determination.

With a new day and fresh perspective, she decided she wouldn't wait passively to be rescued. There was work she could do – like finding help to mine the artifact from the cave wall. Brief discussions with the team had come to the consensus that their best chance at getting Marilyn home would be to gain access to the flat side of the artifact embedded in the cave wall. They were assuming a lot - that the artifact would likely work both ways. But no one saw any other options or choices. So, it was decided. She was going out beyond the cave, ready to face whatever awaited her in that Dark Age world, to find help. She would start with Uthyr.

As Marilyn bit into her bagel, relishing the taste of butter and jam, her eyes were drawn to the portal, now noticeably larger and casting a brighter glow across the cave's interior. The difference was remarkable enough that it made her curious. "Tak, has the portal gotten bigger?" she asked, her curiosity piqued.

"Yeah, about that! I've been crunching the numbers on our power consumption data for the last twenty-four hours. The good news is, with the onsite generators up, we can safely keep the portal fully open at all times if needed." Takashi's voice buzzed with excitement. "Oh, and Flip had crews working through the night while you slept. He stayed up with them and kept the proton beam focused on it while he had it done, but the artifact is standing on its edge now, next to the platform, rather than lying beneath it."

Marilyn's brow rose. That was certainly a welcome development, allowing more flexibility and access to supplies. But it also triggered something else, a question she had meant to ask but had slipped her mind. "Wait, that reminds me," she said, her tone turning serious. "I meant to ask last night, but it slipped my mind. Do we know if increasing the portal size has any impact on the time dilation effect?"

Takashi's enthusiasm dimmed slightly. "I had the same thought. Avery said we would need to do experiments on your end to know anything more. Put timers at different distances and monitor the rate of time flow; stuff like that. He said it doesn't really matter though. The time dilation effect is still largely a mystery to us, but at any appreciable distance by his calculations, about three days goes by for every minute in the cave."

With her eyes still fixed on the portal, Marilyn nodded to herself. It was both a marvel and a puzzle, a gateway that linked her to her time, but also held secrets that they were only beginning to uncover. The connection between the aperture size and time dilation was yet another riddle, but perhaps one they need not solve under the circumstances.

Silence on the other end of the earpiece lingered for a moment, when Avery's voice finally broke through, his tone thoughtful. "Ma'am, the nature of the time dilation effect is still beyond our understanding. We're not sure whether increasing the aperture size would amplify the effect. Nor are we sure if the effect follows a uniform boundary – like some invisible bubble – or tapers off with distance. I suspect the latter is true, but just can't say for certain. For now, it's safest to keep the aperture at a minimum size unless necessary to increase it in order to mitigate any effects we aren't aware of."

"I agree," Marilyn said, a frown creasing her forehead. The implications of the time dilation were far–reaching and unsettling. "I'll power it down then when you're ready to leave for the day ma'am," Takashi interjected. "Let's make sure you have what you need first."

Naomi's voice chimed in, sounding a bit more cheerful. "I checked the logs of when you left the cave yesterday morning versus the moment Flip noticed your return. How early was it when you left, and how late was it when you got back?"

Marilyn thought back, her memory clear. "When I left the cave, the sun was just coming up, and it was full dark but right after dusk when I returned. I was gone perhaps twelve hours."

"Lieutenant Colonel, did you take your cell phone with you when you left yesterday?" Avery suddenly interjected.

"Yes!" Marilyn replied, catching on. Pulling it from her pack, she told them the date and time it displayed. 'At least this useless thing could do that for me,' she thought.

She heard Avery mumbling for a moment. "Assuming its fairly uniform at any appreciable distance, three days go by over there for every minute that passes here. On a larger scale, six months per hour," he informed her.

The revelation landed with a gentle but profound weight. Marilyn's mind struggled to comprehend and accept the idea. If what she was told was true, then over four years had passed while she slept – another 6 months while she ate breakfast! It was surreal, believable, but at the same time not, and yet…

"Is that truly possible?" she asked, her voice tinged with wonder rather than disbelief. "I need to see this for myself."

Her voice trailed off as she grabbed a flashlight and began to traverse the jagged passage that led from the cave chamber to the entrance. The passage's crooked descent obscured her view, heightening her anticipation. As she rounded the last bend and stepped outside the cave, the biting chill of winter air took her breath away. The once soft, damp beach was now rigid, patches of ice and snow lodged between the jagged rocks. The waves rolled in more sluggishly, the sea itself seeming to feel the grip of winter. Even the air smelled different, filled with the crispness that only comes with the cold season.

A wave of astonishment washed over her as she stood, frozen by the sight. The reality of the time dilation effect was undeniable, its evidence stark against the white landscape. "It's real," she managed to say as she made her way back to the cave chamber, her voice imbued with a sense of wonder and acceptance. "It's winter outside."

"Is it always wet in there?" Avery's question cut through her thoughts.

She looked around the cave, suddenly noticing the constant wetness, the trickle of water down the walls. It had been that way since she first noticed it the morning after her arrival, never changing, always present.

"Yes," she replied, her voice still unsteady. "Always. The water is always trickling down the walls."

"If my calculations are correct then," Avery mused, "a year of precipitation seeps into the ground and flows through the cave every two hours."

His words hung in the air, heavy with implication and awe. Time was a river, flowing and twisting in ways they could never have imagined. The cave was a unique intersection of nature and technology, a nexus where time itself bent and reshaped. Marilyn's mind whirred, thoughts tumbling over each other as she tried to grasp the enormity of what they were dealing with. The artifact, the portal, the time dilation – each piece was part of a puzzle that was only growing more complex. But one thing was clear: she was trapped in a world that moved at a pace all its own, and every moment inside the cave was precious.

Ayesha's voice broke the contemplative silence, her tone thoughtful. "Ma'am, when you were recounting your story last night, something about it just kept nagging at me – like a memory I just couldn't recall. And with Avery's talk last night about you already having done what you're still going to do, I wondered if there would be some evidence of you being there."

"So," she continued, "I've been researching the time you're in, and it's a mishmash of myths, legends, and scarce historical records. In fact, just about all of it comes from scholars and historians who wrote about the history of the British Isles hundreds of years after the fact. But one name kept coming up that you mentioned: Uther. And he called you... Merlin.... Right?"

Ayesha's implication struck like lightning. Marilyn scoffed, interrupting her. "I am not 'Merlin'! Some robe–wearing kook with a pointy hat?! Running around waving wands and chanting spells? Next, you'll be saying I'm Gandalf! ...Or Dumbledore!" Chuckling erupted across the comms from the entire team.

When the laughter died down, Ayesha persisted, not deterred by Marilyn's disbelief. "Hear me out," she urged. "What if the legends about Merlin were true, but as seen through the eyes of others in that time? It's entirely possible that Merlin wasn't a wizard in the traditional sense. What if he – or she in this case – simply had access to technology far beyond that era? Think about it."

"Any sufficiently advanced technology is indistinguishable from magic," Avery chimed in, sounding pensive.

"Come again?" Marilyn inquired. It sounded familiar, a saying she'd heard before.

"Something a well-known sci–fi writer named Arthur C. Clarke once said," Avery replied, adding "He was pointing out that stuff we take for granted today – TVs, phones, the radio, airplanes, and so on – would seem like magic in a time where they rely on torches and horse–drawn carts."

Marilyn frowned, the playful dismissal fading. "So, what are you trying to say? That I am Merlin? Or that I should play at being Merlin?"

Ayesha's voice softened but remained determined. "I can't tell you that one way or another. Your choices are your own. But I am saying that where and when you are is probably pretty brutal and uncivilized. You might want to use your technological advantage to help you survive. And playing at Merlin provides the right context to do that. You could play into their superstitions and beliefs in magic, especially since you're a woman and pregnant. It could protect you, especially to conceal those facts."

"I see your point," Marilyn responded, contemplating Ayesha's words.

Ayesha continued, "You said Uthyr believed you were a man. It's probably best to continue the ruse, even if you don't pretend to be Merlin. In many societies back then, women were treated very poorly – second class members of society, little more than property… And if it turns out that the legends making up part of the stories and history we know are based on the exploits of one Marilyn, whose name was mispronounced and mangled by history, then so what? It just proves Avery's point!"

Marilyn's eyes widened, her mind racing with new possibilities, new fears. The idea was outlandish, but it held a certain logic. If she was going to survive – indeed, thrive – in this world, she would need to use every advantage at her disposal, including the use of knowledge and technology that would indeed seem like magic to the people of that era. And the notion of being perceived as a magical being? It was as unsettling as it was empowering.

"I don't know anything about Merlin though," she conceded. "My inner nerd was fed by science growing up, not fantasy. My love of Harry Potter is about as close to fantasy as I come!"

"That's actually better," Avery interjected. "The less you know, the more your choices are your own. Otherwise, you end up sort of stuck; like playing a part in a movie script with a lot of missing lines. You would be trying to make things happen based on some vague idea of what you think should happen. And most of what you think you know would probably be wrong and mislead you anyway!"

She shook her head slowly, smiling wryly, coming to a decision. "So, my choices are still my own; I understand I think. Alright I'll do it, but no pointy hats or wands, okay?"

"How about the Harry Potter wand mounted in your office?" interjected Philip suddenly. The team snickered all across the comms as Philip yawned loudly. "Good morning, Mare. I figured you wouldn't stay holed up in that cave, so I came to see you off."

Marilyn felt a surge of gladness at his unexpected presence, along with a pang of missing him. She masked her emotion with a simple thanks. "I appreciate it, Flip, but no – no wand, thank you. But yes, I will be venturing out…as 'Merlin,' apparently."

"How about the Gryffindor scarf?" Philip teased. "Those striped colors could help you pop! Really stand out!"

More snickering, louder this time, flowed in from the team over the comms.

"Flip, please…," Marilyn pleaded.

Philip interrupted, "Mare, 'Please' isn't the magic word today! It's Abracadabra!"

Outright chuckling and guffawing erupted over the comms.

"Are you done, mister?" Marilyn asked seriously but trying ineffectively to hide an amused smirk.

"Yup! Done!" Philip said as the chuckling died down. "Seriously though, Mare, be careful out there. You might want to hide the ring I gave you too. Flash that, and every brigand and thief in the land will slit your throat."

"Good advice. I hadn't thought of that. I'll do something with it, Flip. Thank you for reminding me."

"Annnyyyway…" Ayesha interrupted, rolling her eyes. "You've got a deal, ma'am," she said, her voice filled with satisfaction. "No pointy hats."

"Ok, folks, she said 'no' to the wand too!" Philip's voice broke through the lingering amusement, injecting a sense of urgency into the conversation. "But she's going to need other things if she's going to survive out there. She's got the beanie and the long coat, but she'll need more to bring Merlin to life. Let's get to work!"

With that, the team was galvanized into action. Over the next hour or two, they put their heads together, brainstorming, discussing, arguing, and assembling a collection of items that would not only serve practical purposes but also play up the role of Merlin in a world unprepared for modern wonders.

Grabbing her pack, she began stuffing it with essentials she already had – the compact sleeping bag, the replacement Zippo lighter she procured to light her fire the night before, her eating utensils, and her vitamins. Soon she was adding other things as they were tossed through the portal – sometimes carefully packaged, and sometimes not. As she packed the lighter, she was reminded to request additional flints and a canister of butane, which soon arrived and were added to the pack.

A rugged survival knife equipped with a serrated edge in a belt holster came sailing though, halting her packing. A whetstone to keep it sharp landed on top of the knife a second later. She put the whetstone in her bag. But rather than put the knife in her bag, she decided to stop and work its holster onto her belt loop. A compass was built into the knife's handle – a feature that might prove handy. Yet it was the lethal edge of the blade that drew her attention, a sobering reminder that she might have to use force to defend herself.

Conscientious about killing, she requested a unique defense: a quarterstaff with an integrated shock baton. Designed to incapacitate rather than kill, the staff's sleek metal tip could deliver a jolt strong enough to deter any threat. It was her chosen defense against potential threats – both animal and human. 'And let's face it,' she thought to herself, amused. 'What is a wizard without their staff?'

Soon she had the backpack filled, having added a host of additional items she might need. Doctor Bennett had provided antibiotics and other non-emergency pharmaceuticals to supplement her first aid kit. Along with it, she packed a tactical flashlight, a pair of walkie-talkies, a hand-held mirror, a spyglass, and a magnifying glass. A laminated physical map was folded and stuffed into a side pouch.

A bivouac tent was also added to the list of essentials. Lightweight yet sturdy, it would offer her the protection she might need from wind and rain without burdening her with unnecessary weight. The compact design was perfect for her solo journey, providing a place of refuge without the complexity of a full–sized tent.

The team also thought of her need for clean water. They included water purification tablets, simple to use and effective in making any freshwater source safe to drink. Additionally, they packed a small portable water filter, capable of removing impurities and providing her with safe drinking water from streams or rivers. It was another essential tool that could make her journey as 'Merlin' more sustainable and less perilous.

Finally, convincing herself that she would be coming home and knowing that she was going to need to put some sort of proof into her report, she requested an instant camera with a pack of film to complete her arsenal of modern–day magic.

As Marilyn looked over the assembled gear, she could feel the weight of the task ahead. These items were a bridge between two worlds, and she was about to walk that bridge alone. But with Uthyr as a potential ally and a mining crew to be assembled, her mission was taking shape.

"Alright, everyone," she said, her voice a blend of determination and apprehension. "I think we've thought of everything we can." She added her canteen and some spare ration packs and energy bars to the top of the pack and zipped it closed, her hands momentarily pausing as reality set in.

"Once I step out of this cave, I may not be coming back for a while – well…at least not for me anyway." Marilyn's smile was brave but tinged with sadness. Philip had come down to the platform, ostensibly to inspect the repairs. But she knew he had come to say goodbye, and his eyes, filled with concern, confirmed it.

"What's wrong, Flip?" Marilyn asked cautiously.

"Guys, can you give us a moment," Philip's voice trembled slightly, betraying his emotions. Moments later, after the team had expressed their well wishes and left the channel, she and Philip stood alone, facing each other across the barrier of the portal. Silence lingered between them, heavy with unsaid words.

"I love you, Mare," Philip finally said, his voice choked. "Be safe out there and don't hesitate to come back here for any reason. I couldn't bear…" He trailed off, his eyes glistening, unable to finish.

"I love you too, Philip," Marilyn responded, her eyes moistening. "Don't worry. I'll be okay! I'll be careful, I promise!" Her words were laced with both hope and uncertainty, and she reached out, wishing she could touch him through the barrier.

With a final glance around the cave and then at Philip, she said, "See you in ten or fifteen minutes!" His soft chuckle and smirk letting her know that her attempt at ironic levity succeeded, she set her earpiece back on the charger, turned, and exited the cave, her role as Merlin just beginning.

CHAPTER 6

Rumors and Reputation

As she exited the cave and ascended the bluff to the plateau above, the familiar landscape brought an odd comfort despite the unsettling knowledge of 'when' she was. The bitter winter briefly experienced earlier was gone, replaced by a bright day in early spring. Even so, a chill lingered in the air, making the long coat and beanie cap comfortable rather than stifling. Sparse patches of ice and snow still lay about the trees where shadows persisted.

Standing atop the bluff by the cairn she'd built the day before, Marilyn extracted the laminated map and a Sharpie from her pack. It was a physical map of the southern half of the main British island that used a color scale to portray the landscape and elevation, capturing the coastlines, rivers, lakes, and contour of land in the 21st century. Geologic changes over the past fifteen centuries were likely minimal, though roads would have been pointless to include. The map lacked any indication of terrain – whether a spot was dense forest, swampy bog, or open field remained a mystery. 'Still…' she thought, 'a bird in the hand….'

Although the map lacked roads, it did contain something else significant. Jagged polygons could be found at various locations – some of the largest cities on the island in modern times – labeled with their modern-day names. There was no guarantee of their existence though during the century in which she found herself. But she mused, thinking that the team must have marked the rough locations of these larger metropolitan areas assuming these population centers would still exist, albeit smaller and under different names, even in the 6th century. She was pleased to see that Carmarthen – her ultimate destination in her search for Uthyr – was among the places included.

In addition, someone had also had the foresight to mark various well-known neolithic ruins. Given Ayesha's support for this insane idea that Marilyn step into the role of a mythical magician, she had little doubt as to the culprit. Using the Welsh coastline and Carreg Samson as reference points, she marked the approximate location of her cave on the coast.

Based on her current location, Haverfordwest, the closest town, was a half–day hike in good terrain. While not necessarily a major metropolitan town by modern standards, Marilyn figured someone had chosen to include the largest and most likely to exist town near where Marilyn thought she was when she discussed her location with the team in more detail the night before.

Next, she wrote 'Moridunum' above Carmarthen – its current name in this century, as she had learned from Uthyr. This was her ultimate destination – the last known residence the young man had shared with her.

As she capped the marker, her hand brushed against her engagement ring, and she was struck by its incongruity in this era. She recalled her promise to Philip to keep it concealed or find some place to stow it for later retrieval. More than a symbol of love and commitment, the ring was now the only tangible connection she had to her time and the man she loved – a connection she couldn't bear the thought of losing.

Considering the surrounding landscape for a hiding place that could endure a millennium, she found no spot suitable. Each potential location was either too exposed or likely to be disturbed over the centuries.

Frustrated but undeterred, she slipped the ring off her finger and threaded it onto the chain around her neck, tucking it securely into her shirt. The cool metal against her skin was a reassuring presence, and she promised herself that she would find the perfect spot for it later. It was a challenge, but one she would meet in due course.

With a determined nod, she packed away her map and set out toward Haverfordwest – or whatever the town or village was called – assuming it existed now as it did in her time. Using her compass as a guide, she focused her mind on the journey ahead and set out. It began in solitude, the path stretching out before her, unmarked and untrodden. The land was wild and rugged, a blend of sprawling moor-like heathland, broken up by dense forests, and jagged, rocky hills. Her compass guided her, a steadfast partner in a landscape that almost seemed untouched by human hands were it not for the occasional clump of standing stones, laid out in patterns too regular to have occurred naturally.

But as the miles passed beneath her feet, signs of life began to appear. At first, it was only a faint column of smoke on the horizon, a subtle hint of humanity's presence. It was a sight that brought both relief and trepidation, knowing that the challenges of human interaction in this era were not far ahead.

Soon after, she encountered her first water obstacle – a lively stream that danced and churned through a rocky bed. Carefully picking her way across small stone islands breaking the shallow stream's path, it was here that she encountered civilization for the first time. Along the stream was a modest monastic site nestled against the shallow stream's bank, with simple wooden structures surrounded by well–tended gardens. It was a place of quiet reflection where a few monks in plain robes moved silently among the plants, their hands busy with the tasks of the day.

Marilyn paused to watch them, struck by the serenity of the scene. This humble settlement was a reminder of the spiritual undercurrents that flowed through the fabric of this time, shaping the beliefs and lives of its people. With a sense of reverence, she continued on, leaving the monks to their sacred duties.

As she journeyed beyond the settlement, following an oft–treaded cart path, the landscape changed, giving way to patches of cultivated land. So, putting away her compass and allowing the path to guide her journey eastward, she took time to observe the environment and people as she walked along.

Shepherds tended to their flocks, their weathered faces turning in her direction, eyes narrowed with curiosity. They watched her pass, staff in hand, their dogs wary and watchful. Farmers toiled in their fields, often no more than a small patch of land near their abode, fenced off by wood or stacked stones to keep rabbits out or livestock from grazing there.

A few larger plots of land seemed to be common farmland. In one part of the field, women and children picked crops, filling straw baskets with the spoils of their labor, while in another, a farmer guided an ox, tilling the ground. Boys trailed behind, digging up and tossing rocks that had been unearthed to the side.

Occasionally, she would be noticed. Mothers would pause their toiling to watch her pass, faces marked by both interest and caution, as their children silently gawked. Marilyn was sure she looked quite strange to them in her long coat and beanie cap. Every now and then, a man would casually display a weapon, a subtle sign that her presence was noted and assessed. She understood their caution and met their gaze with a respectful nod, keeping her distance and continuing on her path.

The cart path eventually led to a small hamlet that surrounded a small wood and stone bridge, spanning a river deeper than the one she had encountered before at the monastery. A water mill stood off to the side, its horizontal wheel turned by the river's flow. The wooden paddles creaked rhythmically, and the sound of grinding stones told of the miller's diligent labor within. Nearby, children played, and women bustled about with their daily tasks, glancing up occasionally to watch the stranger pass.

She hadn't quite known what to expect upon leaving the cave that morning. In her mind's eye, she had envisioned some quintessential provincial village of stone and wood and cobble–stone streets. The reality, though, was a great deal more rustic. Hovels and cottages sporadically lined the dirt–packed cart path as it meandered through the village, built using little more than wood timbers or wattle–and–daub with thatch covered roofs.

As she walked through the village, goodwives gathered their children from playing in the street, their faces reflecting the same mix of curiosity and apprehension she had seen in others along her path. A couple of farmers, leading asses laden with goods, gave Marilyn curious looks as they passed, but said nothing.

A farrier paused in shoeing a horse to stare at her with an appraising eye. It occurred to Marilyn that her strange clothing might appear more refined to one such as he. He likely wondered why she wasn't riding a horse if she could afford such exotic garments.

Marilyn was wondering how she might get a horse when a young girl, perhaps eight or nine, burst from the doorway of the cottage attached to the farrier's workshop. Her clothes were thread–bare and dirty, her hair the color of wheat and sun–kissed skin. Bright and fearless, the young girl ran up to Marilyn and stood before her.

The farrier stood watching them warily, his hammer poised, making Marilyn aware that he was ready to defend his family. Looking up at Marilyn, her blue eyes shining, the girl asked, "Are you the iachydd?"

Marilyn's brief time with Uthyr had shown her that the language spoken in this century shared a common ancestry with the Welsh she knew. There were some hurdles, but not insurmountable. Uthyr had taught her enough to hold a conversation and learn as she went. For unfamiliar words, she knew how to signal her confusion and ask for their meaning.

Fully aware of the man's watchful eye, Marilyn slowly squatted down to eye level with the young girl and smiled at her, laying her quarterstaff on the ground, adopting as non–threatening a pose as she could. "I am from another land," Marilyn told the girl, making sure to speak loudly enough for the man to hear as well. "I do not understand. What is 'iachydd'?" she asked.

Glancing over her shoulder at the man, suddenly uncertain, the little girl took a step back from Marilyn. To put the girl at ease and, thinking quickly, Marilyn picked up a small, flattened pebble and presented it to the girl, smiling. Using a slight–of–hand trick learned as a child, Marilyn made the pebble vanish feigning surprise, then reappear from the girl's ear to much delight.

The girl's eyes rounded with amazement, and she squealed enthusiastically, snatching the pebble from Marilyn's hand, and running over to the farrier. The child's delight was infectious, forcing a grin from his face as Marilyn collected her quarterstaff and stood. "Papa! The man in black is hud!" the little girl exclaimed, presenting him with the pebble.

'Magic,' Marilyn mentally translated based on context, as she suspected she often would for a long time to come.

As Marilyn stood smiling, the farrier approached. "I am Bryn," he said simply. "Are you the 'iachydd'? My wife cut her leg and is ill." Marilyn understood. He was hoping she was a physician or healer of some sort.

"I am Maril…," she began, then cleared her throat attempting to smooth over her own self–interruption. If she was going to play this part, she decided she may as well dive in. "I am Merlin," she replied, trying the name on for the first time.

"My wife is sick. Can you help?" he asked, his eyes hopeful, his voice edged with worry.

"I help. Take to her," Marilyn stuttered, feeling rather ineloquent with the language she was still learning. But the man seemed to understand despite her accent and stumbling speech.

"Come," he said gesturing and turned toward the cottage.

Marilyn followed Bryn through the low doorway, her eyes adjusting to the subdued ambiance. The modest cottage had wattle-and-daub walls that showed signs of many seasons. Years of foot traffic had hardened the dirt floor, but woven straw mats and animal skins provided spots of warmth and comfort. A small window, more a cut in the wall draped with gossamer cloth, spilled the muted hues of the early afternoon into the room. Central to the space was a hearth, its flame casting a gentle glow and radiating a comforting warmth, over which a kettle hung, humming softly.

Marilyn's gaze was immediately drawn to a corner of the cottage, where a bed, modestly raised on a wooden frame, beckoned her attention. The bed's straw foundation was surprisingly topped with a layer of goose feathers, subtly hinting that, despite their humble abode, the family had small luxuries. Upon it rested a woman, every rise and fall of her chest seeming labored, her skin gleaming with the sheen of fevered sweat.

In the muted light, the young girl lingered at the doorway, the weight of worry evident in her eyes. Marilyn's heart went out to her as she noticed the bucket by the bed, its water and cloth a testament to the child's poignant efforts to soothe her ailing mother.

Bryn hesitated, then murmured something, gesturing toward the woman. Marilyn caught the word, "Eira," and realized he was introducing his wife. His eyes were clouded with worry. Gently, he pulled back a soiled cloth bandage from her leg, revealing a deep, jagged cut. He began to explain in halting words, using gestures to convey his meaning. Though she struggled to understand his words at first, a combination of his motions and the tone of his voice allowed her to piece together the story. Eira had tripped in the fields and fallen onto a sickle, resulting in the grievous injury.

Marilyn felt a pang of sympathy, recognizing the danger of such a wound in an era without proper medical care. The leg looked inflamed, and from the restless way Eira was moving, Marilyn surmised the wound was causing the woman a lot of pain.

Taking a deep breath, Marilyn gestured towards the hearth and the bucket, then mimicked pouring. Bryn quickly understood, pouring the water into the kettle already hanging over the fire. Once done, Marilyn pointed to the empty bucket and combined the few words she knew, saying, "Water… river?" hoping Bryn would catch her meaning.

Bryn turned to the young girl and spoke in a mixture of command and desperation, "Brya, {…something…} water {…something…} river." With a nod, Brya grabbed the bucket and darted out the doorway. Marilyn smiled slightly, mentally noting down the new phrases she'd picked up. 'Fetch or get,' she thought, 'and maybe… from?' Marilyn was amazed at how quickly the words were beginning to make sense to her, even in the midst of such a dire situation.

Kneeling beside Eira, Marilyn unzipped her backpack, the sound strangely loud in the humble cottage. As she revealed her comprehensive medical kit, the metallic glint of the instruments and the sterile wrappings caught the flickering firelight, drawing Bryn's gaze. His expression wavered between awe and uncertainty, a silent question forming in the furrow of his brow.

With slow, deliberate movements meant to communicate her intentions, Marilyn held up a small water purification tablet. Her gestures – mimicking dropping something into the water and then taking a sip – were an attempt to bridge the linguistic divide. The tablet met the boiling water with a soft plop, its subsequent effervescence casting dancing reflections on the walls. Bryn's eyes widened, the magic of the moment not lost on him.

Cleaning the wound felt like a sacred ritual, the cottage a quiet shrine to this act of healing. The antiseptic wipes glided over inflamed skin, the sharp intake of Eira's breath punctuating the stillness each time the cloth met tender flesh. Marilyn's hands were steady, her touch a whisper of comfort in a chorus of pain. She locked eyes with Bryn, finding within his gaze a dawning trust, a silent understanding passing between them in the shared language of humanity.

The needle and thread seemed out of place in the rustic setting, yet Marilyn's hands moved with practiced grace. She was acutely aware of the stark contrast between her methods and the expectations of this era. Each pull of the thread closed not just flesh, but also a chasm between past and future, an almost tangible link between her world and theirs.

As she applied the antibiotic ointment, it struck Marilyn how her ministrations were both an anachronism and a blessing – the sterile bandage unfurling as a banner of hope in a time shadowed by the relentless uncertainty of survival. These were not just medical supplies from her time; they were symbols of a future where pain could be managed, infections warded off, and lives saved with a certainty that bordered on the miraculous.

The process complete, she began repacking her kit just as Brya burst through the doorway, a whirlwind of youthful energy. She wasn't alone; a young man trailed behind her, the weight of the full bucket evident in the strain of his muscles. Bryn expressed his gratitude to the newcomer with an intensity that filled the room, the relief in his voice transcending the language barrier.

As Bryn and the young man conversed, the newcomer's eyes darted curiously between Eira's bandaged leg and Marilyn, lingering on the remnants of her medical kit. Words exchanged between Bryn and the young man were mostly lost on Marilyn, but the names 'Merlin' and 'healer' punctuated the conversation. Marilyn suspected that news of her presence, nor indeed her efforts here, would not remain within the confines of the cottage much longer.

The young man soon said his farewells, mentioning 'father' as he did so, a clear indication of familial duty calling him away. His departure, with Bryn following close behind, left a quieter space, the atmosphere in the cottage one of subdued reflection. Outside, the rhythmic sound of Bryn's tools against metal spoke of a world persisting in its routine, while inside, Marilyn found herself in a tableau of care and recovery. Brya stayed close, her young form a shadow of worry and hope, while her mother rested fitfully. And Marilyn, amidst it all, felt a profound sense of connection, a solitary traveler who'd become an integral thread in the fabric of this family's life, if only for a fleeting moment in time.

The two sat there for a time while the workshop next to them echoed with rhythmic hammering. Eventually, Brya's worried gaze shifted from her mother to Marilyn, her urge to ask questions hampered by uncertainty. Trying to express her fear, she managed, "Mother… {byw}?" Then, seeing Marilyn's confusion, Brya mimicked choking and added with a saddened tone, "{marw}?"

Marilyn, understanding the depth of the girl's fear, grinned reassuringly. Having deciphered that 'byw' meant 'live' and 'marw' meant 'die', Marilyn shook her head emphatically and gestured with vitality and announced cheerfully "byw" – live! Brya's relief was palpable as she wrapped Marilyn in a spontaneous embrace.

Drawing back, she gave Brya a few directives using her limited vocabulary and hand movements, emphasizing the importance of keeping Eira cool and hydrated to stave off the fever, hoping her message came through to the young girl. Brya, still holding onto the hope Marilyn had given her, nodded in understanding, ready to take on the responsibility of caring for her mother.

As the shadows grew longer outside, signaling the transition to evening, the sounds from the workshop ceased, replaced by muffled greetings. A moment later, Bryn re–entered the cottage, accompanying an older man, who bore a crate filled with fresh produce and a dressed bird. At his entrance, Marilyn rose out of respect.

Bryn's introduction was brief but clear, the words 'Merlin' and 'healer' recurring. The older man's resemblance to the young man hinted at a familial connection, likely that of a father and son. Their exchange was brief, punctuated with gestures towards the dressed bird and the produce. As the older man took his leave, Marilyn noted him leading the freshly shoed horse away, and the pieces clicked – Bryn's craftsmanship had been bartered for food.

Now alone with Bryn and Brya, Marilyn watched as Bryn approached with a hesitant, hopeful look. "Will my wife live, Merlin?" he asked, the weight of his worries evident in his voice. Marilyn was pleased with herself that she understood him clearly, given the similar exchange she'd had with Brya earlier and the words she had picked up there. Offering a reassuring smile, she nodded and confirmed confidently, "Your wife will live."

After a moment's pause, Marilyn held up her hand, signaling the importance of her next instruction. She then handed Bryn six pills, pointing to them and then to her eyes to emphasize their significance. Gradually, Marilyn mimicked the act of eating and showed two fingers, suggesting two pills after meals, and then used gestures to indicate the rising and setting sun, hinting at dawn and dusk. Her stern gaze and the repeated act of pointing from the pills to Eira left no room for misunderstanding. "She needs these to fully recover," Marilyn conveyed through her gestures.

Like storm clouds dispersing to reveal the sun, the atmosphere in the room lifted and hope illuminated the faces of both Bryn and Brya. Their gratitude shone brightly, and in a gesture of hospitality, Bryn pointed to the dressed bird and vegetables, making a sweeping gesture around the cottage to signal Marilyn's welcome to stay the night and share dinner. The warmth of the hearth, combined with their gratitude, promised a comfortable respite for Marilyn.

Making herself comfortable, Marilyn watched Bryn prepare the meal in a roasting pot using salt and aromatic herbs from earthen crocks, while Brya tended to Eira. As he and Brya busied themselves, the trio engaged in animated conversation, with Marilyn using a blend of gestures and her growing vocabulary. Shared curiosity encouraged overcoming the linguistic divide as each exchange both sated their fascination and deepened Marilyn's understanding of the rhythm and rules of the Old Welsh they spoke as she learned new words and phrases.

As twilight transitioned to darkness, Bryn lit lanterns, augmenting the firelight cast by the hearth as they shared the evening meal. Conversation continued, allowing Marilyn to immerse herself deeper into the intricacies of the ancient language, maintaining the use of body language, echoing phrases, and language previously learned to expand her knowledge. Every gesture, shared laugh, and parroted phrase tied her closer to this ancient cadence which echoed in the modern Welsh from her own past.

Conversation eventually succumbed to the deepening nighttime and the exhaustions of the day. But as the hearth fire slowly dwindled, Marilyn found her comfort and confidence growing. Finally, as they bid each other goodnight, Marilyn's last thoughts, as sleep took her, were to marvel at the connections being forged, one word and gesture at a time.

Cicadas sawed through the nearby forest in the late afternoon sun as Padrig stood under the shade of an oak, methodically sharpening his mother's precious scissors. The cicadas' chorus and the spring's warmth mingled with the soft breeze and rhythm of his work, lulling him into a languid stupor. As he stood there methodically whetting the stone, stroking the blades, and stropping them against a leather strip, lost in daydreams, Meical's excited and unexpected greeting startled him, pulling him from his reverie, clumsily cutting his finger as reward.

"Ow!" he said, dropping the scissors and jamming his finger into his mouth. "Hey Meical," he muffled around the finger, annoyed – with himself or with Meical he wasn't sure. "What has you so excited?"

Meical, catching his breath, relayed, "I've just been to Bryn's!"

The two were close in age, though Meical was a couple of years younger, and neither was old enough to take part in the spring hunting rite that marked the beginning of manhood. Padrig's father said he would be allowed to participate next spring, a day which Padrig eagerly awaited to prove his right to be called a man – if he brought home a worthy kill that is.

Removing his finger from his mouth, he smirked at the younger boy. "You know Meical, Brya will not be of marrying age for many years. You should set your sights elsewhere."

Ignoring the jibe, Meical bubbled over with news, "Bryn has a guest! A stranger came to town today dressed in strange clothes – calls himself Merlin! Brya said he knows magic!" He took a breath, as though realizing he'd skipped crucial details, "Eira cut her leg badly and caught a fever. Merlin is healing her with his magic!" Meical's eyes flicked to Padrig's bleeding finger. "Maybe he can fix that for you!"

Padrig stood and motioned for the boy to follow him as he headed inside to wash his hand and find something to wrap his finger. The cut was worse than he expected. Surprised, he glanced at the younger boy. "Magic, eh? In our village? So where did he come from?" he asked curiously.

"Brya told me," Meical said, his voice hushed, as if sharing a secret. "Merlin is not Briton, nor Saxon! Brya said she doesn't know where he came from. He just appeared!"

Overhearing the two boys talk from her perch near the window, Padrig's mother, Gwyneth, with strands of grey weaving through her once–black hair, chimed in, her needlework momentarily forgotten. "What's this talk of magic and healers? What are you boys on about?"

Before Padrig could respond, Meical interrupted excitedly, sharing the news. "I think my mother will want to hear about him." he added, talking more to himself than to Padrig's mother. "Well, I am off! I must go let father know Bryn said the horse will be shoed before sunset." As Meical darted out the door, Padrig's father came in, dodging the energetic boy.

Padrig's father stepped inside and set aside his tools. "What has gotten into that boy?" the older man asked, glancing back out the doorway before closing the door behind him.

His father listened intently as Padrig relayed Meical's story. Then he added, "I cut my finger sharpening mum's scissors. Nasty cut too…I thought I might go in the morning and see if this Merlin might heal me."

A thoughtful look spread across his father's face. "Healer, eh? And magic?" he said skeptically. "I would like to see this Merlin's skills firsthand. The crops on the eastern field have been suffering; maybe he has a trick or two to help. It's getting late though. It'll wait for the morning."

Nodding in agreement, Padrig's mother rose, "And I want to check in on Eira myself, husband. She's been a good friend," she said. Through the window, her gaze landed on the discarded scissors in the yard. "Padrig, when you have cleaned that cut, fetch my scissors. It is nearly time for supper, and I have more sewing to do."

The next morning, as the sun cast a soft golden glow over the village, Padrig and his parents approached Bryn's cottage. The scent of dew–soaked grass hung in the air, mingling with the chatter and murmurs of villagers. There were already a number of their neighbors gathered, including a gaggle of women clucking over Eira, who seemed much healthier than Padrig expected given Meical's prognosis the night before.

A path had been cleared through the crowd to the door of the cottage. From this vantage, Padrig could spot the mysterious guest. Merlin was a tall figure, his attire dark and unusual compared to the earthy tones worn by the villagers. His eyes, keen and observing, seemed to take in everything and everyone. At his side was a satchel, its contents a secret to all.

Brya was speaking to an elder when she noticed Padrig. The young girl paused to wave, a light–hearted smile lighting up her face. Sparing a glance for her mother who stood nearby, in apparently high spirits and looking lively, Padrig understood Brya's happiness.

"Is this the healer?" Padrig's father asked, nodding towards Merlin.

"Seems to be," replied a neighboring farmer, Arwel. "Heard he uses herbs and potions. Some even say incantations."

Gwyneth leaned in closer, curiosity evident in her eyes. "Well, I for one am grateful. Eira looks worlds better. We could use a healer in these parts."

"I just hope his skills are not limited to people," Padrig's father murmured, his thoughts on the ailing crops, as the three of them approached closer.

Padrig, intrigued, decided to introduce himself. "Greetings," he began, approaching Merlin cautiously. "My name is Padrig. Can you…," he started uncertainly. Then, blurting out quickly before he lost his nerve, "Can you heal me too?" Padrig showed Merlin his still bandaged finger, the wound not looking as dire as it felt, but discomfort still nagged at him.

The strange man in black grinned at him encouragingly, then took his hand and removed the bandage, examining the cut with gentle yet firm fingers. "You will need to clean this regularly, but I possess a remedy that might hasten its mending," he intoned, his voice low and soothing. From his pack, Merlin produced a bottle and a small fluffy white ball.

"This has properties similar to mead," Merlin explained. "You should clean cuts like this with mead. It will burn a little, but it cleans the cut and helps prevent flesh rot and fever." After cleaning the cut, Merlin applied an ointment from another tube that felt soothing in contrast to the burning fire of the liquid he had used to clean it. Finally, the man applied an odd type of bandage that stuck to the skin as he wrapped it about Padrig's finger.

Padrig's father, who had watched the entire exchange quietly, then spoke. "I am Owain, father to Padrig. And that is my wife, Gwyneth." He pointed to Padrig's mother standing over by Eira. Merlin stood and bowed slightly. "It is my pleasure to meet you, Owain. How may I assist you?" he asked politely.

Padrig listened as Owain relayed his troubles with the crops in the eastern field, then stood with his mouth hanging open as Merlin relayed a remedy for the problem. The last part of Merlin's solution sounded disgusting, but as Owain nodded speculatively, Padrig knew the coming days would be filled with distasteful work.

"You must do three things, Owain. First, a field often farmed produces…tired earth," Merlin explained. "Much as you must rest overnight, the earth too must be allowed to rest. Divide your field into three sections and each season, leave one of those sections unplanted to rejuvenate."

His father nodded as Merlin continued, "Second, the land can become...bored, in much the same way you might tire of repeating the same task."

"Oy! That's what happened to me!" Padrig interjected, holding up his injured hand, grinning. Merlin smirked in response, "I did not say the land loses focus on its duties, Padrig." Laughter erupted from the nearby listeners, including Owain. Padrig, a little embarrassed, decided it best to remain quiet.

Merlin then refocused his attention on Owain, "As I was saying, the land craves variety. Rotate your crops. Plant a different type in each of the other two sections every season. The soil will appreciate the change, and in turn, it will yield more bountiful harvests."

Whispers of agreement and understanding buzzed around them, but Merlin, eager to continue, raised his voice slightly for emphasis, "Lastly..." The murmuring ceased, and he went on, "Lastly – and this is most important – you already know the land thirsts, but it also hungers. Each season you must nourish it and feed it with the chaff of your crop and, more importantly, dung – from horses, cows, sheep, your own chamber pots – the source does not matter. Till that into the earth and wait a few weeks for the smell to subside. Then plant your crop."

As Merlin continued, more villagers were drawn in by his words. Padrig caught bits and pieces of whispers around him. "Ah, my grandfather told me about the dung trick," an older man claimed, trying to look wise. A woman nearby, not to be outdone, chimed in, "A cousin of mine, over from the next village, he said the same thing years ago. Just never had the need to mention it, did I?" Another piped up, "Had a neighbor once, moved away since, but he used to swear by such remedies." Padrig couldn't help but grin. Some folks always wanted to act like they knew it all. Still, whether they really knew or just wanted to show off, it made Merlin's advice feel even more special, wiser in some way. The buzz of chatter grew, a mix of excitement and people trying to outdo each other.

Padrig's parents spent a little more time mingling with their neighbors while he sat watching Merlin give aid or offer advice to those that approached. Eventually, done with a conversation he'd been having with Bryn, Owain stretched his back and sighed. "Well…the work of the day will not do itself!" he announced, shooting a playful glance at his son. "Come on, Padrig." He started walking, beckoning for Padrig to follow, then looking to his wife.

Gwyneth, her face animated with excitement, waved them off. "I'll be along shortly," she promised, already deep in conversation with a group of women, their voices a flurry of gossip and speculation. Padrig spared an amused glance for Eira thinking to himself, 'Mother hens all coddling the same chick' as he followed his father back toward their farm.

The sun dipped low by the time Padrig sat down to dinner with his parents. The warm glow of candles illuminated their faces, creating an intimate setting as they spoke about the day's events.

Gwyneth recounted how well Eira had looked, her eyes softening. "Bryn is so relieved. We are all fortunate Merlin came when he did."

Owain raised an eyebrow, "Yes, I spoke with Bryn for a moment before Padrig and I left. He did indeed look relieved and happy." He paused to take a bite of his meal, then continued, "He also mentioned Merlin was on a journey to Moridunum and was looking for a horse."

Gwyneth nodded, sipping her drink thoughtfully. "It is as you said. But who in this village, or the next for that matter, can spare a horse? Merlin was told as much, so Dafydd offered to let Merlin ride along with him in the cart on his way to sell crops and pay tithes to the prefect in Afonffordd. He and his son Kei left soon after you and Padrig returned home."

Padrig's ears perked up at the mention of Kei. He always enjoyed their visits to Afonffordd and secretly wished he could tag along, not only for the trip but for the tales Kei would surely share on their return. "So, Merlin's gone then?" he asked. "He went with them?"

"No," his mother replied. "Merlin declined. He wanted to wait another day to ensure Eira's recovered fully." She paused, a hint of mischief in her eyes, "Those two, they delight in gossip and the tales they tell grow larger with each telling. I expect by the time they are done, when Merlin arrives there, all of Afonffordd will be buzzing with news of him."

Chuckling, Padrig retorted, "So true, mother! The last story Kei told, by the time he was finished, the fish he and his Da' caught last week was as big as the boat and took three days to haul in!"

The comment earned a snort and grin from his father as Gwyneth took a drink from her cup, then continued. "Just as well though. Alderman Ecder spoke up then and offered the same, but in the morning. Merlin thanked him and accepted. So, he will be leaving in the morning with Alderman Ecder."

Padrig, curious, asked, "Why is Alderman Ecder journeying to Afonffordd?"

His mother was chewing her food, so his father jumped in with an explanation, "To pay tithes to the prefect for the rest of the village. In his youth, Ecder trained and fought with the Romans, becoming a skilled fighter, well–equipped to protect our village's contributions from any bandits or thieves as he brings them to Afonffordd."

Gwyneth nodded in agreement. "Before he left, Ecder tried to persuade Dafydd to let him handle the tithes, or at least wait for the morning so they could travel together. But Dafydd? He thinks more with the hair on his chest than with his head." She let out an exasperated pshaw and took a sip from her drink before continuing, "And for what? To save a little extra tithing? Ecder is fair and honest. He does not take more than his due that I have ever known!"

The room grew silent for a moment as Owain became pensive. As he broke off a piece of bread, he said "We should have offered something for Merlin's assistance. After all, a man must earn his living," then dipped the bread in his drink and stuffed it in his mouth.

Gwyneth considered this, "Perhaps we can send something with Padrig in the morning. Some bread, cheese, maybe a bit of our cured meat?"

Owain nodded in agreement. "It is decided then. Padrig, you will go to Bryn's with the provisions first thing."

When Padrig returned to Bryn's early the next morning, a small basket of provisions in tow, he glimpsed Merlin seated upon the back of Ecder's cart, already headed east down the cart path. A thin veil of mist clung to the ground, lending a surreal quality to the scene. Merlin, spotting him, raised a hand in acknowledgment. Padrig waved back, feeling an odd mix of admiration and curiosity for the mysterious man.

Leaving the provisions by Bryn's doorstep, he noticed other baskets, some filled with bread and others with fresh fruits or herbs. The village, it seemed, was united in its gratitude. As the cart became a speck in the distance, Padrig couldn't help but wonder about the stories Merlin would gather on his journey. With a last glance at the receding figure, he mused, "I wonder if we will ever see him again. I wish I knew magic!"

CHAPTER 7

Justice

"Looks to be trouble ahead," Ecder muttered as the cart came to an abrupt halt.

The sudden cessation of the cart's monotonous creak had jolted Marilyn from her reverie. She'd been lying in the back of the cart for the past hour, letting her imagination play with the shapes of passing clouds. Though she had tried to initiate conversation with Ecder earlier in their journey, he had proven reticent. Whether wary of strangers or merely stoic, he replied her attempts at conversation with brief, unembellished responses. She had eventually given up and decided to quit trying, lie back in the cart, and enjoy the scenery.

Marilyn sat up and followed Ecder's pointing finger. The path, having turned a corner, stretched straight for several hundred yards ahead. The foreboding forest to either side, with its dense undergrowth, had been their constant companion since leaving the village earlier that morning. Now, ahead and about a hundred yards away, the woodland gave way to a swampy moor where, blocking their path, stood three men. Two were mounted on horses, while the third – a massive, intimidating figure – stood out front, leaning casually on what looked to be a halberd.

She rummaged through her pack and pulled out a spyglass. "Perhaps they're just travelers," she suggested, extending the instrument.

Ecder shook his head, eyes never leaving the trio. "Travelers don't just stand still in the middle of a path, waiting. Those men are…" He muttered a couple of terms in his language that Marilyn didn't understand. When she expressed her confusion, he elaborated, "Both are mean spirited. But one might rob you and leave you bruised, while the other… the other would kill as soon as look at you." Marilyn understood, committing the unfamiliar words for brigand and cutthroat to memory.

Peering through her spyglass, Marilyn saw the men clearly: unwashed, unkempt, and undeniably menacing. The largest man sported a vicious scar across his face that pulled one corner of his mouth into a permanent sneer, rendering him even more terrifying. Marilyn suspected that size and a more gruesome visage made him the leader of this gang. The three men were simply watching and waiting – they knew their quarry had nowhere to go but forward or back the way they came. And with those horses, any attempt to run away and avoid confrontation would be pointless. Likely it would simply embolden the men to pursue.

"What is that you hold, Merlin?" Ecder asked, drawing Marilyn's attention – especially considering he'd barely strung ten words together the entire trip up to now. He was pointing at her spy glass.

"Here, look through this end," she replied, passing him the spyglass. Ecder took the spy glass gingerly, then mimicked her actions uncertainly, following her instructions. Having achieved focus, she heard him exclaim in surprise, "By the gods! What magic is this, Merlin?!"

A smirk danced on Marilyn's lips as she watched Ecder's astonishment. Objects she took for granted in her time could evoke awe, even fear, in this ancient world. It was moments like these that starkly reminded her of the temporal chasm between them. Meeting Ecder's gaze, she playfully coined a term for her device. "This is… my 'stick of far sight'," she declared. Though she sought a term akin to 'wand' or 'scepter', her limited vocabulary fell short. However, a swift exchange with Ecder enriched her with the word for 'scepter'. Accepting the spyglass back, Ecder's deep respect for the tool was evident.

Hopping down from the cart, Ecder's eyes darted around cautiously. "Such men are why I never bring my wife or daughter on my travels," he whispered, voice laced with tension. "Had Dafydd been patient and traveled with us, together we may have discouraged such men." He paused, a shadow crossing his features. "I hope he and Kei are alright."

Ecder discreetly retrieved a hand axe from the concealed compartment beneath his cart seat. Taking position on one side of his horse, leading it by the reins, he addressed Marilyn. "I've brought extra crops with me and tucked some coins under the bench. We can use them to negotiate if these men are mere brigands."

After Ecder positioned himself, Marilyn methodically stored her spyglass and took up her quarterstaff. Her military training had honed her into an adept, and if pressed, lethal adversary. Though her movements were deliberate, her eyes carried the weight of one who understands the gravity and consequences of their own capabilities. Meeting Ecder's gaze with a look of steady resolve, she said, "I will act only if necessary, but if it comes to it, I can handle myself."

Their approach was met by the echo of jeering laughter. As Ecder and she came closer, details Marilyn missed through the spy glass became more apparent. One of the men on horseback held a bow casually with arrow nocked, waiting to be drawn. The other man on horseback had a short sword and dagger stuck through a rope belt on either hip.

Unexpectedly, it was not the man on foot, whom Marilyn had pegged as the leader, who addressed them. Instead, the archer on horseback sneered downward, a taunting challenge in his voice. "It looks like we have travelers who haven't paid the toll, eh, Cadoc?"

Cadoc, eager to assert his sycophantic support, chimed in, his voice dripping with feigned innocence. "Sure does, Rhys! Not paid at all! If they had, you'd be the first to know. Yes, you would!"

Rhys continued, his tone authoritative, "This path across the moor? We patrol it. We keep it safe for folk like you… but there's a toll, of course."

Almost gleefully, Cadoc added, unsheathing his dagger with an exaggerated flourish, "That's right, Rhys! A toll! Shall I collect it?"

Marilyn's training taught her to assess a situation quickly. Realizing the danger, she opted for a direct approach. She carefully pieced together her response in Old Welsh, hoping her phrasing carried the right weight. "I am this man's… 'sell sword'. Tread carefully, for crossing us might exact a price you're ill–prepared to pay yourself."

Before the tension could escalate further, Ecder, protective and diplomatic, intervened, "We've food enough for a meal and some coin too. Let us pass in peace, and it's yours."

Rhys, far from satisfied, shifted his gaze to the burly man on foot, a smirk playing on his lips. "That is a start. But Efan here," he said, indicating the man with a nod, "is in dire need of a horse. And it just so happens, you have one."

Marilyn, ever the pragmatist, countered, "Without the horse, this man cannot get his goods to market. You are robbing him of his livelihood."

Rhys chuckled, feigning sympathy, "A sad tale indeed. I suppose then you will have to leave the cart as well. But look on the bright side – at least you can walk away with your lives." Cadoc burst into sycophantic laughter, clearly relishing their predicament and his leader's wit.

Efan's grin broadened, revealing a set of stained teeth. Taking a menacing step towards Marilyn, he taunted, "What will you do, little man?"

When thinking back on what happened next, Marilyn would later recall the ensuing moments happening with the suddenness of a car crash. But in those moments that followed, time seemed to stretch and bend, each detail amplified, each second expanded as if reality itself hesitated.

In a fluid, well–practiced motion, Marilyn swiftly and mercilessly jammed the end of her quarterstaff upwards, directly into Efan's groin. A guttural sound, a mix between a groan and scream, escaped his throat as he doubled over and collapsed to the ground, gasping for air, his eyes watering from the intense pain.

Rhys, eyes wide with shock, swiftly went to draw his nocked arrow. But Ecder was quicker and, with an almost primal scream, he threw his hand axe at the man. But the farmer was no warrior, and the hand axe was not balanced for throwing. Rather than striking Rhys, the axe missed but bluntly connected instead with the bow, knocking it from the archer's hands.

While Rhys turned his horse to search for his bow, Ecder sprinted around it to retrieve his axe. Distracted by concern for Ecder, Marylin was suddenly tackled to the ground by Cadoc who had apparently leapt at her from the back of his horse, knocking her staff from her hand.

Marilyn was still grappling with the man, trying not to be pierced by the dagger he wielded, when she heard a meaty thunk and his eyes went wide. Blood seeped forth from his mouth as he tried to speak, then collapsed atop her, wide eyes already drooping and glazing over in death. Ecder had apparently managed to retrieve his hand axe and drive it into Cadoc's back.

As Ecder yanked his axe free, a sudden yell escaped him when an arrow sprouted from his arm, splattering blood on Cadoc's back and Marilyn's face. Apparently, Rhys had dismounted and found his bow. Ecder, having dropped his axe, ran to take cover from arrow fire behind his cart while Marilyn pulled herself out from under the now dead Cadoc.

Just as Marilyn managed to sit up and grab her staff, she felt the solid kick of a heavy foot drive her back to the ground. Efan, though still reeling, was not down for the count. His face twisted in rage, had staggered towards Marilyn, clearly intending to make her pay for the pain she'd inflicted. He now stood over her with a menacing sneer, foot planted on her chest, pinning her down.

Reacting almost by instinct, Marilyn swiftly triggered the shock feature on her staff, jabbing it into the hind quarters of Rhys's horse. The animal, panicked and in pain, violently bucked – its powerful hind leg striking out and connecting brutally with Efan's face. The sickening crunch that followed left no doubt – his face was a ruined mess, and he dropped lifelessly to the ground.

Marilyn rose to her feet, locking eyes with Rhys, who stared in shock at the chaos and the fall of his comrades. As realization dawned and he moved to nock another arrow, Marilyn acted swiftly. She closed the distance between them and thrust her stun baton into his chest. Electricity sparked and crackled as Rhys sunk to his knees, momentarily incapacitated as he involuntarily wet himself. Marilyn swiftly swung the other end of her staff around, connecting solidly with the side of Rhys's head. He fell to the ground, unconscious.

Ecder sat on the ground, his back pressed against the wheel of his cart, trying to steady his breathing. Occasionally, a sharp sting made him wince as Merlin stitched the arrow wound. Trying to take his mind off the pain of having his flesh sewn up, Ecder looked around him at the handiwork of the ill–fated events that brought him here.

Nearby, the rogue that went by the name Rhys lay bound and unconscious, tied with the rope that the one called Cadoc had used as a belt. That one lay dead where he fell, his blood staining Ecder's hand axe, abandoned next to the body in Ecder's flight for cover. The third and most imposing ruffian also lay lifeless where he fell, a pool of blood forming near the mangled remains of his face, the consequence of a forceful horse's kick.

At the thought, his gaze shifted to the two horses the cutthroats had owned, now grazing beside the cart path, their reins tied to a tree branch. Before tending to his wound, Merlin had acted with efficiency in collecting them, tying off their reins to ensure the horses did not wander off.

People often mistook Ecder's quiet demeanor for timidity, or perhaps naivety or slowness of mind. But he was neither. Often given to observation and introspection, in the solitude of his thoughts, he clung to a childhood lesson: to listen more than he spoke, ensuring that when he did break his silence, it was with words of weight and meaning. Recent events with Merlin had left him with a torrent of emotions and reflections, all yearning for expression.

As Ecder observed Merlin's precise movements, a sudden realization struck: the delicate touch, soft hands, and smooth face, with no hint of a beard, all pointed to a shocking truth. "You are… a woman!" he blurted out, his voice a blend of disbelief and wonder.

Merlin's eyes darted up, meeting his gaze with an intensity that momentarily silenced the world around them. "That is very dangerous knowledge, Ecder," she cautioned, her voice a soft whisper carrying the weight of countless secrets. "It is knowledge I would prefer remain hidden. Are we clear?"

He swallowed hard, nodding his acquiescence. 'What might she do if I betray her?' he pondered, a chill running down his spine.

Satisfied with Ecder's silent nod, Merlin continued, "In many lands, women are little more than slaves, viewed as property to be owned. A woman's life is not her own, dictated by the whims of a man, forced to satisfy his desires, bear his children, and raise them. In my homeland, women are treated differently – not quite equal, but far better. There, a woman can choose her path in life."

Having finished suturing the wound, Merlin applied a gentle salve and began wrapping it with deliberate care. With a playful smirk, she raised an eyebrow and posed a question, "Surely you take me for a witch?"

Ecder hesitated, torn between awe and fear, his gaze darting to Rhys, who groaned and shifted. "I… I do not know, Merlin," he managed. "Do you hail from a land of witches?" Gathering a shaky courage, he motioned towards Rhys and added, "Your staff – it commands lightning!"

Merlin chuckled softly, shaking her head. "Ecder, imagine you introduced fire to a man who has never seen it. What must it be like to be that man? To him, the flame and its heat are magic! You, oh great wizard, have captured a piece of the sun!" Merlin's eyes shifted toward the quarterstaff leaned against the cart as she continued, "My staff, and its abilities, come from knowledge, not magic."

Her explanation lifted the oppressive weight of superstition from Ecder's mind. Merlin, though enigmatic, knowledgeable, and indeed powerful, was – overall – very human. Ecder realized suddenly that Merlin's words had transformed his initial fear into awe and profound respect. Looking up at her, he vowed, "I will keep your secrets, Merlin. I owe you a life debt; the least I can give you in exchange is my silence."

Merlin grinned at him, her eyes twinkling with mischief. "For someone like you, I imagine silence is not too great a sacrifice." Extending her hand, Merlin helped him to his feet. Ecder could not help but grin back. "But some day, I may call on you again to aid me with something requiring a strong arm," she continued. "Nothing dangerous mind you, just…help that will allow me to return home to my own land."

Ecder nodded firmly. "When the time comes, Merlin, call on me; on my honor, my arm and aid are yours."

Ecder watched Merlin retrieve her quarterstaff, then walk over and rummage through a saddle bag on Rhys's horse. She soon returned with a flask in hand. "I think it is too late to continue our journey. Do you agree?" Merlin inquired, glancing over her shoulder at Ecder. Following her gaze to the low–hanging sun, he nodded. With too little daylight left to cross the moor, traveling by night would be treacherous.

Seeing Ecder's nod, Merlin proceeded to upend the flask in Rhys's face. The ruffian groaned, blinking awake. As his reality set in, awareness of his predicament only fueled his defiance. He spat a venomous word at her, foreign to her ears. Turning to Ecder, she asked its meaning.

Ecder grinned. "He called you a fatherless child, born of an unwed mother," he relayed.

Turning back to Rhys, Merlin manipulated her quarterstaff to produce its crackling lightning and held its lightning end near his face. "I warned you not to cross us, did I not? Do you really wish to tempt me further?" Her voice held a calm menace, chilling even Ecder.

Rhys, looking absolutely petrified, shook his head vigorously. Satisfied, Merlin said, "Ecder, collect the horses and secure their reins to the back of your cart." As she spoke, she began hoisting Rhys to his feet.

As Ecder headed to the horses, his amusement vanished abruptly. 'Merlin! This piebald belongs to Dafydd,' he exclaimed. Suddenly worried that Dafydd and Kei had met with misfortune by these men, he added, "I have seen Dafydd leading this very horse many times through the village."

Merlin's expression darkened. "Take us to your encampment. Now!" she demanded of Rhys. "Ecder, follow us in the cart."

Guided by Rhys, they traveled a short distance off the main path down a dry strip of land that ran between the dense forest and the moor. After a brief trek, Rhys cut through a break in the trees, not easily seen from the cart path. As they ventured deeper, the break widened into a clandestine clearing. Haphazardly pitched amidst the trees was a forlorn tent, the fabric aged and fraying. From within, soft, heart–wrenching sobs echoed, instantly capturing their attention.

Without hesitation, Merlin shoved Rhys to the ground with surprising force. "Watch him, Ecder," she snapped. "If he moves, break his knees." As Ecder casually walked over, the terror was evident on Rhys's face. Ecder kicked Rhys onto hist stomach and stood over him, foot firmly planted in the brigand's back.

Ecder watched as Merlin violently yanked aside the heavy tent flap, revealing the dark interior. A heart–rending cry, raw and pain–filled, echoed out, followed by the cruel jingle of metal chains. With tenderness unexpected in the charged atmosphere, Merlin leaned in, her voice soft and comforting, like a mother soothing her frightened child. "Kei?" she whispered, the name almost a sigh. "Oh, you brave, dear boy. Look at me, Kei. I won't let anyone hurt you anymore. I'm here with Ecder. You know Ecder, right? From your village? You're safe now."

She carefully reached in, the movements slow and deliberate, pulling a blanket from her pack. "I'm Merlin, Kei. Here, sweet boy, cover yourself with this," she murmured, draping the blanket around his trembling form. "Now, let's get those shackles off you."

Merlin looked sharply at Rhys, still pinned by Ecder. "The key," she demanded, her tone sharp. Ecder grabbed a handful of Rhys' greasy hair and wrenched his head back. The trapped man winced in pain. "Pocket… left side," he managed to gasp out through gritted teeth. Without releasing him, Ecder reached into the indicated pocket, pulling out a small iron key. Merlin took it with a flash of disdain and quickly unlocked the shackles. They fell away with a clank, the cold metal finally off Kei's tender wrists.

A moment later, Merlin emerged from the tent with the boy nestled in the crook of her arm, wrapped in her blanket. His appearance was disturbing: torn clothing barely covering his battered frame, evidence of inhumane treatment marred his skin, every bruise and cut a testament to his torment.

Spotting Rhys on the ground, the terror in Kei's eyes flared. Without a word, Ecder grabbed the man's hair again and ground his face in the dirt, ensuring the boy wouldn't have to see the face of his tormentor. "He's finished, lad. This vermin will not hurt you anymore. I promise you," he assured, his voice low and dangerous.

Merlin covered Kei's ears hugging him to her chest, muffling what she said quietly next, seething. "They had the poor boy shackled to a stump in there. He's been bruised and beaten at the least…and from what I could see of his injuries…worse things," she said, seething with anger and staring daggers at Rhys accusingly. Relinquishing her hold, she let Kei hold her and she stroked his hair as he began to sob quietly, relief at being rescued consuming him.

Rhys, his eyes and voice both filled with terror, quickly protested. "That was not me! I never!" Trying his best to shake his head in denial, Rhys continued, "Efan! He was the twisted one, not me! I swear on my mother's soul!"

Ecder's face darkened, and with a voice cold as ice, he pressed his foot down harder on Rhys' back, extracting a choked gasp from the man beneath him. "You cannot take oath on your own worthless soul, you motherless cur."

In the midst of this, a stricken Kei burst out in righteous anger. "They…they killed my da'!" he cried out between gut–wrenching sobs. With a sudden, unexpected force, he lunged at Rhys, his small feet kicking furiously. Rhys yelped in pain and squirmed with each blow landed, but neither Ecder nor Merlin moved to halt the boy's actions. It was only when Kei's outburst began to wane, exhaustion taking over, that Merlin stepped in. She gently pulled the young boy into her arms, holding him close as he sobbed into her chest, his cries slowly softening into quiet whimpers.

Merlin locked eyes with the trembling Rhys, her gaze unyielding. "Ecder, in these lands, what is the fate of a common thief?"

"It varies with the severity of the theft," Ecder began cautiously. "But for one such as him, the punishment would likely be the removal of his sword hand, signifying the theft of another man's means."

Her expression darkening further, she pressed, "And for murder?"

"For that, he would be set against a wall, and archers would send their arrows into him," Ecder replied, the weight of the judgment evident in his voice.

Merlin's face contorted with anger as she continued, "And the punishment for what was done to this boy?"

"A monster committing such deeds would be tied to a stake in the village square and burned alive," Ecder said, his voice laden with disgust.

For a moment, a chilling silence enveloped them. Then, Merlin spoke, her voice firm yet controlled, "While your fate remains undecided, there is one immediate justice we can serve. Strip him of his clothes, Ecder. Kei needs better to wear than the rags these men have left him."

A while later, Kei, dressed in much better attire, stood next to Merlin and Ecder, observing a stripped Rhys shackled to a tree at the forest's edge, facing the east moor. A chain hung from a low branch, just reaching his shoulder. Below, a sharpened limb stump protruded menacingly upward from the tree trunk, directly between Rhys's legs. Ropes bound each of his ankles, taut against the tree. The immediate danger of the stump was not evident, but the implication was chilling. Even Ecder, accustomed to harsh justice, felt a shiver of acknowledgement at Merlin's dark creativity.

Merlin's gaze bore into Rhys, who, realizing he wasn't to be immediately killed, let a flicker of defiance return to his eyes. Ecder spoke, voice heavy with warning, "I would not be too smug if I were you," and nodded toward Merlin.

"Time and fatigue will be your enemies here," Merlin stated coldly, motioning towards the sharpened stump. "Should you tire, that will serve as retribution for what was done to Kei."

Rhys's face went ashen, the weight of his fate settling in. "But it wasn't me! Efan was the monster, ask the boy!" His eyes darted to Kei, pleading.

Kei only looked away, the shadows of recent trauma still fresh in his eyes. Merlin's voice cut through the tense silence. "That may be. But neither did you prevent it," she said accusingly, acid on her tongue. "If exhaustion does not settle your fate, a few days blistering in the sun will do just as well as being burned at the stake – only more slowly," she spat out with disdain. Without another word, she beckoned Ecder and Kei to follow. As Rhys's screams filled the air, Ecder threw one last comment over his shoulder, "I would save your energy if I were you."

As Merlin and Kei settled on the newly acquired horses, Ecder ensured his cart was properly stowed and ready for travel. They had intended to rest at the rogue's campsite, but the events had shifted their priorities. Instead, they chose to journey onward despite the encroaching dusk. As they moved deeper into the moor, Rhys' chilling wails continued to reach them, each cry fainter than the last but nonetheless haunting. Ecder looked over the vast expanse and thought to himself, 'Sound sure does carry a long way in these moors.'

CHAPTER 8

A New Faith

The small vessel navigated the River Sabrina's gentle current, while Cadfan sat engrossed in scriptures from his treasured book - a rare and prized possession. His journey across the sea from Gaul had been a trial of tumultuous waves and fierce storms, often confining him below deck, pale and seasick.

'Travel by sea is a pursuit for the young,' he mused, a wry smile deepening the lines on his face. The tranquil final leg of the journey, aboard this modest river vessel, felt like a blessing as it quietly sailed towards its destination.

"Glouvum dock ahead!" the boatman called, jolting Cadfan from his thoughts. Cadfan closed his book, securing it in his leather pack as thoughts of his old friend surfaced. 'It will be good to see Dubric again. I hope he has done well with my teachings and spreading the Gospel in this land,' he thought, his heart a mix of anticipation and concern. The message in Dubric's letter had been urgent, but maddeningly vague as to why urgency was called for.

As the boat bumped gently against the dock, Cadfan dug deeper into the pack and pulled out a small pouch that clinked with coins. After giving his greying beard a thoughtful stroke, pondering the fare for the journey, he retrieved a couple of small copper coins, and he handed them to the boatman, their mutual nods conveying unspoken respect.

The boatman tied off the mooring line as Cadfan stood and adjusted his woolen tunic, which had ridden up slightly. The air around the docks was rich with mingled scents of fresh fish, livestock, and the earthy aroma of wood. Anglers busied themselves with their nets, hoisting shimmering fish onto the pier, while further upriver, boats laden with goods plied their trade over the river's gentle ripples. The river's significance was unmistakably clear – it was Glouvum's vital vein, infusing life and commerce into the town and surrounding lands.

Cadfan momentarily swayed as he stepped onto solid ground, the phantom rock of the boat lingering beneath his feet after so long at sea. Deciding that walking would help, he let his surroundings guide his steps. As he ambled along, growing more confident with each step, the town's layout unfolded before him, a familiar scene that echoed the many riverside settlements he had visited in his travels.

Along the riverside stood smaller, aging wooden buildings, gradually sprawling outwards. Further afield, atop a modest rise overlooking the town, a large, imposing stone structure stood out, clearly a remnant of Roman architecture. Though time had worn its edges and vines crept up its walls, it still commanded respect and showed signs of recent repairs and modifications, marking it as the residence of the town's current ruler.

With the main thoroughfare's packed lime and shale crunching beneath his sandals, Cadfan's thoughts returned to his reason for coming as he entered the riverside market square. The ambient noise was a cacophony of hawkers calling out, children's playful shouts, and snippets of conversations that floated to his ears. The wooden structures that lined the streets spoke of the town's growth from a humble outpost to a bustling trade hub. There were no grandiose stone monuments here; instead, the buildings, practical and unassuming, were clearly made to serve a purpose.

The streets, rather than following a straight, Roman–inspired grid, meandered organically. They wound around and branched off into smaller alleys, from which an unpleasant odor occasionally wafted. The main path was well-kept, though he still had to side-step pools of sewage that sometimes seeped onto it from the disused alleyways where residents flung refuse water.

He made his way through the crowd, taking in the variety of stalls: fresh vegetables here, the tempting aroma of freshly baked bread there, and the meticulous handiwork of local craftspeople displayed proudly. The townsfolk seemed robust, their attire and demeanor telling of hard work and a straightforward approach to life.

Dubric's instructions had been clear about what to look for in this bustling environment: a post with the sign of the fish – a discreet symbol of his faith that was not out of place here, seamlessly blending with the riverside's milieu, echoing the livelihood of the local fishermen and the vibrant marketplace they anchored.

Guided by Dubric's letter, Cadfan kept an eye out for the designated post amidst the fishmongers' stalls. Once found, he took a simple wooden token from his pouch and twiddled it between his fingers, a rhythmic motion meant to catch the attention of the one he sought. The token distinctively bore the same fish symbol on one side and a cross on the other. He walked casually among the fishmonger's stalls until his efforts were rewarded, catching the attention of a fishmonger – an old man with a distinctively long gray beard – who signaled to him with a knowing grin.

Cadfan approached and displayed the token. The fishmonger's keen eyes shifted from the token to Cadfan's face, a slight smile curling on his lips. "Ah, Brother Dubric has been expecting you," the elderly fishmonger said, studying Cadfan for a brief moment. "I am Aled. Wait a tick." He leaned back slightly, peering into the tented stall behind him and murmured something softly. A moment later, a kindly looking older lady with lines of age and wisdom etched on her face stepped out, her eyes bright and friendly. "This is my wife, Mair," Aled introduced, as she gave a gentle nod and smile to Cadfan. "She can watch over things here while I take you to Brother Dubric."

As they walked further into town, Cadfan noticed a recurring symbol: a vivid red X painted on the door lintels. "What does this mark signify?" he asked, a sense of unease settling in.

"A mark of the sickness," Aled whispered, guiding Cadfan's gaze to a scene unfolding not too far off. A wagon stood still, and as Cadfan watched, a sheet–wrapped form was gently carried from a house bearing the red X. From within, the muted sounds of crying and soft weeping could be heard, a testament to the sorrowful impact of the affliction.

"Some recover," Aled said, his voice hushed. "And some do not."

The scene highlighted the severity of the sickness's hold on Glouvum, and as they continued, Cadfan noted the number of marked doorways just within his view. 'How many more do I not see?' he pondered worriedly. His realization was alarming; every few homes bore the haunting red X. This was no mere passing ailment. Glouvum was on the brink – a town teetering on the edge of a burgeoning plague.

"Has it been long?" Cadfan asked, nodding toward a marked house where sounds of grief emerged.

Aled sighed, "Too long. Brother Dubric does what he can, but the heavenly host remains silent."

Cadfan's concern deepened. This was more than he anticipated, and the weight of the responsibility began to press on him. The townspeople needed more than words; they needed hope, and soon.

With the afternoon nearly gone and dinnertime approaching, Dubric decided to wrap up. "Before we part my friends, let me share with you a few last words of hope from the prophet Isaiah," Dubric said.

Looking down at the scroll before him, he read, "Be not afraid, for I am with you. Be not dismayed, for I am your God."

A deep, sonorous voice, instantly recognizable, interrupted Dubric and brought a broad smile to his face. "I will strengthen you and help you; I will uphold you with my righteous right hand," he heard Cadfan orate from the back of the room as he looked up.

Surprised and delighted, Dubric's exclaimed, "Friends! This day we are truly blessed! We are honored to be visited by my friend and teacher! Well met, Father Cadfan! It is good to see you again."

The room filled with warm greetings and welcomes from the small congregation, and Dubric's heart swelled with pride. Though modest in size, the group embraced his teachings of love, hope, and kindness.

Cadfan quieted the gathering, offering apologies for the interruption, and urged Dubric to continue.

"So, my friends…Let us remember the afflicted in our prayers and help our neighbors in need where we can," Dubric continued. "And let us thank our most gracious host, Aurelius, for such wonderful accommodation!" Dubric gestured toward Aurelius, introducing him to Cadfan and the congregation. Aurelius smiled and nodded silently in acceptance of the praise. "Without whom we would all still be meeting on the hill outside of town!" Dubric said jovially, grinning widely.

After a final announcement that the gathering would assemble again in a week to renew their faith and sustain each other, Dubric dismissed the gathering. A light–hearted murmur arose as people stood and began shuffling out, nodding to Cadfan as they left.

With the congregation gone, Dubric approached Aurelius to thank him again for hosting and to facilitate a more intimate introduction to his esteemed friend and mentor. As Dubric gathered his belongings from the table, his gaze fell on Aled, patiently standing beside Cadfan. It occurred to Dubric that Aled was likely anticipating a more tangible token of appreciation for the watchful vigil he had kept. Fishing a copper from his purse, he walked over and discreetly palmed the coin into Aled's hand as he shook it.

"Thank you for keeping such a vigilant watch for my friend Aled. Now if you will excuse us, it has been long since we last spoke and Father Cadfan and I have weighty matters to discuss," Dubric informed him. With that, Aled nodded graciously and left the three of them standing alone.

They exchanged introductions and pleasantries, the reunion striking a chord of nostalgia. "It seems you have indeed found a gracious host in Aurelius," Cadfan remarked, his eyes twinkling, acknowledging Aurelius who beamed back a smile.

Dubric chuckled, "Certainly better than the hill and tent where I started."

The banter continued, light and teasing, yet with an undercurrent of mutual respect and camaraderie. "That's what you get for coming to Britannia alone," Cadfan teased.

"I have missed you, Father Cadfan," Dubric admitted, embracing him in a heartfelt hug. Turning to Aurelius, Dubric asked, "May Father Cadfan and I speak alone for a time, please, Aurelius?"

"Yes, of course!" Aurelius replied. "If you will excuse me…" he added, then walked out of the room to another part of the house.

As the door closed behind Aurelius, leaving Dubric and Cadfan alone, a comfortable silence settled between them. Dubric's gaze traveled over the room, the warmth of the gathering still lingering in the air. The simple yet hospitable surroundings spoke volumes of Aurelius' generosity.

Finally, Cadfan broke the silence, his voice resonating with the warmth of old friendship, "You've done well here, Dubric. Your teachings have truly touched their hearts."

Dubric smiled modestly, "It is the Lord who touches hearts, I am merely His vessel."

"And what of the king of this land? Have you touched his heart as well?" Cadfan inquired, a teasing gleam in his eyes.

Dubric's expression turned more somber at the mention of King Uthyr. "I have sought an audience, but he has been difficult to reach. The affairs of state and his campaign to unite the surrounding lands and tribes under his rule keep him exceedingly occupied."

Cadfan nodded, understanding the practical difficulties Dubric faced. "The burdens of leadership can be heavy, and the king must prioritize the immediate needs of his realm. But we must find a way to help him see that the spiritual well–being of his people is intertwined with the prosperity of his land."

Cadfan paused, allowing the weight of his words to settle before he continued, a gravity in his tone that matched the seriousness of the situation they had witnessed earlier. "The land is sick, Dubric. The people are suffering. The health of the land and its people reflect the faith of its leader. Uthyr needs to open his heart for the sake of his kingdom."

The mention of sickness reminded Dubric of the rumors circulating around town. "There have been stories of a healer named Merlin coming in by ship and the West Road. He was last seen headed to Moridunum, or perhaps he is there already."

Cadfan's brows furrowed in skepticism, "Be cautious of such tales, Dubric. Many who claim to heal are but deceivers, leaving the people with nothing but false hope and lighter purses."

Dubric acknowledged the warning with a nod. "The tales are quite extraordinary though," Dubric conceded. "So much so, that I find it difficult to dismiss their claims outright. But then, perhaps I too am simply seeking a glimmer of hope in these desperate times."

Cadfan placed a reassuring hand on Dubric's shoulder, his eyes showing understanding and concern. "Hope is a strong comfort, Dubric, something to be desired in challenging times. But we must be watchful, separating truth from the deceit of those who would take advantage of desperation. Our task is to lead the people with wisdom and the true light of the Lord, so they aren't misled by empty promises and lies."

Dubric nodded thoughtfully in response to Cadfan's earnest words, his gaze fixed on the flickering flame of a nearby candle. "Then our path is clear. We must approach King Uthyr, offer our counsel and aid in this time of need."

Cadfan's eyes gleamed with determination. "Indeed. We must endeavor to gain an audience at King Uthyr's stronghold come morning then. The lessons of Constantine have shown that a land's faith often begins at its helm," he admonished, patting Dubric on the shoulder.

Dubric shook his head in exasperation. "I've tried, Father, believe me!" he remarked with a hint of frustration.

Cadfan smiled and consoled him though. "Ah, but by your own admission, we must be shrewd," he replied. "This king needs a more pragmatic reason to grant us an audience and we shall provide it!"

"And what reason is that?" Dubric asked.

"Just before my departure from Gaul, news reached me of King Clovis' death. Now, his sons squabble over the fragments of his dominion. While Uthyr may not have to fear a coordinated assault from them, leaderless warriors often resort to piracy, raiding unsuspecting coastal settlements. Such men often turn to banditry with no leader to keep them in line. It's a warning King Uthyr should heed."

Dubric just smiled and shook his head in acknowledgement. 'Of course, he has a solution,' Dubric thought to himself. 'I hope I am nearly so wise when I am as old as he.'

As the first light of dawn brushed the sky with hues of pink and gold, Dubric and Cadfan made their way towards the imposing stone stronghold of King Uthyr. The morning air was crisp, a light mist swirling around their feet as they walked the cobbled path leading up the modest rise. The stronghold, a relic of Roman grandeur, loomed above them, its worn edges and creeping vines giving it a sense of ancient authority.

They approached the main entrance, a heavy wooden gate fortified with iron bands, where a pair of guards clad in chainmail and bearing spears stood watch. Cadfan stepped forward, his stature straight and his voice steady. "We seek an audience with King Uthyr. We bring news from Gaul and offer counsel in these trying times."

The guards exchanged glances, their expressions unreadable, before one of them disappeared within the stronghold. After a brief wait that seemed to stretch, he returned, nodding to his companion. "You may enter. King Uthyr will see you."

With a grateful nod, Cadfan and Dubric stepped through the gate and into the inner courtyard. The sounds of daily life within the stronghold met their ears – the clanging of metal, the chatter of servants, the neighing of horses. They were led through the stronghold, the ambiance austere and the stone walls cool and damp. Quickly, they found themselves in the heart of the fortress – a large, rectangular Great Hall.

The room buzzed with activity, a central hub of discourse and decision–making within the stronghold's protective walls, the air charged with the clinking of metal and the heady mix of debate and strategic discourse. At the far end, King Uthyr stood at the head of a lengthy, well–worn table, encircled by a diverse assembly of advisors engrossed in fervent discussion. He stood tall, with a commanding presence that would have named him king even without the simple brass band, adorned with a single ruby, that rested upon his brow. His demeanor was more indicative of raw strength and power than regal finesse. His intense, watchful eyes scoured the room, absorbing every detail, missing nothing.

As Dubric and Cadfan approached, the murmur of conversation diminished, and all eyes turned towards them. The weight of the attention was palpable, yet they maintained their composure, walking forward with measured steps, their resolve to present their message and offer aid, unswayed by the attentive gazes around them.

King Uthyr's gaze settled on Cadfan and Dubric as they halted before the long table, a flicker of recognition in his eyes. "Ah, the holy men from the village, I've heard of your endeavors." His tone was nonchalant but his eyes sharp, assessing.

Cadfan bowed respectfully, "King Uthyr, we bring news from Gaul. Clovis, King of the Franks, has passed, leaving his sons to quarrel over his kingdom. This may lead to increased banditry and raids along your southern coast."

Uthyr listened attentively, his brow furrowing. "This is concerning indeed," he mused, a hint of sternness in his tone. "The little princes will likely be too busy nipping at each other to be of any trouble. But the king's dogs have been cut loose to hound my shores." A smirk played on his lips, appreciating his own pun, and a few of his advisors snickered and agreed. "I shall have my men heighten their watch," he added decisively. Attempting to dismiss them without further ado, he added, "Now if that is all? Good."

Uthyr's dismissive gesture paused in the air as he appeared to reconsider, his hand slowly returning to the table. "This is indeed troubling news," he finally conceded, his gaze sharpening with a strategic glint. He turned to one of his advisors, a grizzled man bearing the scars of many battles. "Do we have men to patrol the southern road? Have we any reports of raids?"

The advisor, his posture rigid as if perpetually ready for conflict, shook his head. "We patrol only from Execaer to Clausafon, sire. We have received no pigeons regarding raids."

Uthyr nodded slowly, his lips pursed in contemplation. "Surprising news. The Jutes already control Wight Isle and have been pecking at our shores of late. Maybe these Franks will keep them busy enough to stop raiding our shores for a while, or they already do so."

Another advisor, younger and with an air of keen intelligence, interjected, "What of Cornwall, sire?"

Uthyr's gaze darkened, a frown creasing his brow. "Yes, Gorloys could pose a different kind of problem. Most of my strength has been committed to protecting our Eastern border from the encroachment of the Saxon dogs. I dream of a day we have reclaimed Londinium. So, I have paid little heed to the south."

Cadfan, sensing an opening in the conversation and an opportunity for inquiry, interjected respectfully, "Sire, forgive me, as I come new to these lands. What is Cornwall? Who is Gorloys?"

Uthyr looked at Cadfan, assessing the missionary before him, before he replied, "The Cornish people inhabit the western half of the southern peninsula. Gorloys is ruler of the land there."

Uthyr's expression turned distant for a moment. "I know naught of him beyond what little I learned from my father – a man who's been dead more than five years now. My father attended his wedding, a political match with some young girl from Dumnonia named Ygraine. I remember my father being particularly incensed about it."

"Why would that anger your father?" Cadfan asked, curiosity evident in his tone. "Such political marriages are common in these lands, are they not?"

Grinning, Uthyr replied, "Yes, because my father sought the same prize, but for she and I to wed. Gorloys was quicker in his dealings." He paused, the humor fading from his eyes. "But as we say, 'the die is cast.' There's no reworking what's already been shaped in the forge."

His gaze refocused on the present concerns. "I've long seen the wisdom in securing his allegiance or, at the very least, an alliance with him. But I have had no time to see that endeavor through. My efforts to repel the Saxons from our lands have consumed all my attention. Now, it seems I must make the time."

Pausing for a moment as if forming a resolution, Uthyr then motioned to one of his scribes. "Send a missive to Gorloys, requesting parley on neutral ground. He may define the terms. Let it be known we seek discussion, not conflict."

Uthyr then turned his attention back to Cadfan, a calculating look in his eyes. "You – the bearer of ill tidings – what is your name?"

"I am Father Cadfan, sire," he replied, offering a deferential nod, and motioning to his companion. "This is Brother Dubric."

Uthyr's eyebrow quirked up as a sardonic smile tugged at the corner of his lips. "Father?" he echoed, a trace of irony lacing his voice. "Cadfan, is it? Very well. You will attend this parley as well. I have no rapport with Gorloys, and he has no reason to trust my word. But he may take the word of a wise man who bears the news directly from the land of its birth."

Cadfan, seeing the opportunity for both diplomacy and spreading his faith, bowed his head in agreement. "I am at your service, King Uthyr. It would be my honor to accompany you."

Uthyr nodded, satisfied. "It's settled, then. Prepare for travel in…," glancing at his advisor who held up a hand, he continued, "…four days' time. Be here at dawn ready to travel."

Feeling ignored and keen to press his own concerns, Dubric stepped forward. "King Uthyr, there is another matter that weighs heavily upon us. The people in the town are falling ill, and we fear it is a manifestation of the spiritual ailment plaguing this land. Many have not known the grace of God, turning instead to the worship of false idols. If you, as their king, accept the Holy Trinity, the people will follow, and I believe their spiritual and physical well–being will improve."

Cadfan, stepping beside Dubric, added in a voice layered with years of wisdom and experience, "In my many years, I have seen the land and its people flourish when they embrace the light of God. The physical health of the people is inextricably tied to their spiritual vitality, which can only be found in the grace of God."

"I've heard enough," Uthyr replied sharply, after a tense silence. "Men such as you demand that we must give allegiance to their god, promising prosperity in exchange. I say no! If your god wants my allegiance, then let him prove he is deserving of it and heal my people! Then come see me."

"Faith is not some magic spell, my king," Dubric replied earnestly. "It is…"

Uthyr raised a hand, cutting him off, as his gaze hardened. "Magic? I've seen real magic!" He pulled out a metal box from a pouch around his neck and snapped it open. "Once, this could produce fire with a mere snap. The magic within has since diminished but show me your god has such power to heal the afflicted with a snap of a finger, and maybe I shall believe."

Dubric and Cadfan studied the device with curiosity. "How did you come by such a thing?" Dubric inquired.

Uthyr leaned back, a faraway look glinting in his eyes. "When I was a boy, hunting in the woods, I came upon a man unlike any I had ever met. He was cloaked in garments of green and brown, as if woven from the very forest, and he spoke in words both familiar and strange, a distortion of our tongue I could barely grasp. This metal box was a possession he showed me, then later left behind when, offended by something I said, he ran away and disappeared as swiftly and mysteriously as a spirit of the fae. I have never seen him since, though I searched many times."

Taking the magic box back from Dubric, Uthyr held it in his hand before them, driving home the reality of his story, adding, "He named himself Ma'erlyn, and this is the only proof I have of our fleeting encounter."

Dubric and Cadfan exchanged glances, then, bowing respectfully, left Uthyr's hall. As they walked, the weight of the king's tale pressed on Dubric. "Cadfan, could this Ma'erlyn be the same man we discussed yesterday? I should have thought to ask the king where he spent his youth."

Cadfan's eyes were thoughtful. "I had the same suspicion. And you know I do not put much stock in coincidences."

He halted, a sigh escaping him as he gazed out toward the vast expanse that lay before them. "An investigation is indeed in order. However, my pledge to Uthyr binds me. The upcoming parley requires my counsel, and I cannot shirk my duties if we hope to win over his affections."

Turning back to Dubric, his expression earnest, he continued, "And perhaps to do that, we must first find and win over this Merlin. He may hold the key to winning over the king. So, the task must fall to you. You would need to leave the congregation in the care of our kind host, with assurances of your return. It's a heavy burden, I know, but one I am convinced you're ready to bear."

Dubric met his gaze, feeling the weight of expectation and the urgency of the moment. "I understand, and you have my word. I'll seek out this Merlin and discern the truth of his intentions. The congregation will be in safe hands until I return."

A smile of gratitude crossed Cadfan's features as he clapped Dubric on the back. "Good. Then let us both prepare for the journeys to come and let faith be our hope and guide."

Chapter 9

Stories and Lessons

The sun was just cresting the horizon, casting long shadows on the dirt road as Marilyn, Ecder, and Kei made their way towards Afonffordd. The day's heat had not yet taken hold, and a cool morning breeze rustled the nearby trees, making the leaves whisper secrets to one another. The rhythmic clatter of hooves and the creaking of wooden wheels played a melodic counterpoint, occasionally punctuated by Kei's soft sniffles and the drag of his sleeve across his nose.

Marilyn had spent the morning, as they broke camp and began their ride anew, casting furtive glances at Kei. The boy was saddle sore from riding a horse too large for him. So Ecder had tied off the horse's reins to the back of the cart and sat Kei on the cart's bench seat next to him. As Kei sat there, he wore a distant expression, occasionally reaching out to touch the sturdy flank of the horse pulling the cart, perhaps drawing comfort from the beast's warm and steady presence.

As she rode along atop the piebald taken from the ill-fated brigands, Marilyn often reflected on the young boy's demeanor. She recognized the signs of mental and emotional trauma in him – a skill imparted by her military training, though she had never encountered someone exhibiting such symptoms before. He seemed like a soldier – scarred from battle – yet he was just a boy. His senses were heightened, and every rustle or sudden noise would jolt him back to the present, his body constantly on high alert.

"I need to walk around for a bit, Ecder. Travel by horse is uncommon in my land and the experience has taken a toll on my backside," Marilyn admitted, attempting to break the somber atmosphere.

Ecder chuckled, seizing the opportunity to engage Kei. "Ah, see here, Kei! The great and powerful Merlin has an all-too-human backside!"

Marilyn smirked but played along with the jibe as she climbed down from the saddle. "Mock me at your peril, mortal! Or face the wrath of my backside's mighty wind!" Then turning her back to them and looking over her shoulder, she made a faux flatulent noise and was rewarded with a giggle from the boy and hearty laughter from Ecder, who patted the boy gently on the back.

Pulling out some dried fruit from her saddlebag, she walked over to the cart. "You must be hungry, Kei," she said softly, offering it to the boy. He hesitated for a heartbeat before taking it, nodding in gratitude but not meeting her gaze.

Observing the sun, Ecder commented, "We should reach Afonffordd by late afternoon."

Marilyn, stretching her legs, retorted, "More like evening. I can't climb back up in that saddle right now. I can barely walk as it is! Riding again might finish me off."

"Why don't we switch for a while then, Merlin," Ecder offered, hopping down from the cart seat. "I'll ride the horse and you can keep Kei company up here in the cart seat."

Marilyn nodded to him gratefully and climbed up into the seat next to Kei. As Ecder settled into the piebald's saddle, Kei spoke up suddenly, surprising them both. Looking up at her, he inquired in a muffled voice around a bite of apple, "How do people travel in your land Merlin?"

Momentarily taken aback by the unexpected interjection, she soon recovered, her eyes twinkling with amusement. "In my homeland, we rarely use horses except for sport or show. We have carts of metal that move on their own, without horses," she replied with a playful smile.

Kei's eyes widened in awe, a mix of incredulity and wonder, but Ecder seemed skeptical. "Do not tease the boy, Merlin," he interjected with a tone that suggested he thought she was spinning tales. "The poor boy has been through enough!" Marilyn waved him off and winked at Kei, drawing a tentative grin from the boy. Ecder merely smirked and shook his head, urging the horse onward and setting the group back in motion.

As the landscape began to open up, allowing for a wider, more travelled road, Ecder pulled back from the lead to ride beside the cart, matching its pace. Looking at Kei, who sat between them, Ecder asked the boy, "Kei, do you have any family waiting for you back home?"

Kei dropped his eyes, fresh pain clouding his face with misery as he quietly shook his head. Seeing the boy's pain, Ecder gently urged his horse closer to the cart, until he could reach out and place a reassuring hand on Kei's shoulder. "I know you are hurting, scared, and feel all alone, lad," he began softly, his voice filled with empathy. "But your da' was well regarded by everyone in Solva. He was a good man, and his legacy lives on in you. I know the people of Solva. We take care of our own. We stand by each other and look after one another. And that includes you. Do you understand?"

As Marilyn watched the two of them quietly, Kei looked up, eyes shimmering with tears but also seeming to show a sign of hope and determination. He nodded quietly and sniffled, offering the older man a shaky smile. She could not help but feel a deep respect for Ecder – a man who, stoic as he had been at their initial exchanges, seemed a genuine, warm, and caring soul. The boy's presence only seemed to be drawing Ecder out, revealing a man of quiet strength behind the stoic mask – an observation that deepened her admiration and curiosity about him.

"Have you lived in Solva long?" she ventured, seeking to extend the conversation.

Ecder nodded, his expression nostalgic. “Born and raised there. My family has overseen the village for generations.”

Marilyn glanced at Kei, then back to Ecder. “And your own kin?”

A shadow passed over Ecder’s face. “Elain, my wife, and I… we have been unable to have children. But Solva is like family to us.”

Understanding dawned on Marilyn, then. The man had no children and the boy, having just lost his father through tragedy brought on by a cruel twist of fate, suddenly found himself blessed with a potential surrogate – someone willing and able to step into the role the boy so desperately needed – a fact Ecder only further reaffirmed by what he said to the boy next.

"Kei, listen. When we return to Solva, you and I could perform rites for your da’ – to ensure we give him a proper send-off and let the Jesus God know he is on his way. Would you like that?"

Ecder waited for the boy to look up at him and reply. Eventually, Kei looked up at him, sniffled and wiped his nose, then nodded gratefully, but wordlessly. In that moment, locking eyes with Kei, with a fierce intensity, Ecder continued. “I am not your father, and I would never pretend to replace him. But if you are willing, once we return to Solva, I want you to meet my wife, Elain. You can stay with us, be a part of our lives. As for me, I will honor your da’ the best way I can – by teaching his son what I know of being a man.”

Marilyn looked on as Kei just stared at Ecder with an unreadable expression. To her, it seemed a spark of hope in his eyes was at war with the sense of betrayal to his dead father. Her heart went out to him.

Ecder seemed to sense a similar degree of emotional turmoil in the boy. Placing a hand on the boy’s shoulder and smiling down at Kei jovially, he said, “Just think on it, lad. You need not decide anything now. But I have a feeling one bite of Elain’s apple pie will decide you!”

Kei's eyes rounded in amazement as they approached the town. A mix of awe, excitement, fear, and wonder swept over him in turns as they drew closer. Even from a distance, Afonffordd seemed to stretch on forever to Kei. In Solva, he could easily count all the cottages and buildings on his fingers and toes, with just one road running through the village.

Soon the trio passed the guard post at the town's entrance. A pang of fear gripped Kei as the guards glanced their way – a sudden memory of the armed men who had held him captive surfacing.

But as they moved beyond the post and deeper into Afonffordd, his apprehension was quickly replaced by wonder. To Kei, the town felt like many villages stitched together, roads branching out like threads binding a patchwork of cottages and grand buildings into a vast quilt of shapes and colors.

Ecder rode ahead, skillfully guiding the cart through Afonffordd's winding roads and pathways. Kei recalled his father often speaking of the alderman's annual trips to pay the tithes for the people of Solva and its nearby farms. His da' had let Ecder take their family's tithes last year in fact. The sudden memory stirred sharp feelings of regret as he stifled a sudden sob.

Hearing the small sound, Merlin turned his gaze down to Kei, concern evident. "Are you alright, Kei?"

Kei blinked rapidly, turning his face away, willing away the moisture in his eyes. His father's words echoed in his mind: 'Boys do not cry, and when they do, not where others can see.' His da' wasn't being cruel, just teaching Kei the ways of the world. "I was thinking of my da'," Kei admitted, voice shaky. "If he had let Alderman Ecder handle the tithes this year, he would still be here."

Merlin's voice was gentle, a balm on the raw wound. "Kei, cherishing his memory honors him. But regret for the past and dwelling on what cannot be changed is a trap. It blinds you – forcing you to always look backward instead of seeing the promise of tomorrow."

Kei pondered Merlin's words as the bustling market area came into view. The sheer number of people, the chatter, haggling, and laughter were unlike anything Kei had experienced. He could even hear the rhythmic sounds of oars slapping against water and the chatter of dockworkers somewhere nearby. Searching for the source, he glimpsed the occasional sparkle of water through the crowd along the busiest road leading away from the market square and toward the source of those sounds.

As the crowd grew thicker, Ecder chose to dismount, concerned for the safety of those around his horse. He led the way on foot, walking beside the piebald and calling out to clear a path. Once they reached the market's heart, he turned to address them. "I'll go find us a place to stay for the night. Merlin, while I'm gone, could you watch our goods?"

Merlin chuckled, "I might not know much about haggling here, but I can keep an eye on things." His peculiar accent reminded Kei that Merlin was an outsider, just as he felt in this big town.

Ecder turned to Kei after making some arrangements. "Would you like to come with me?" he asked. Kei, curious and eager to see more of the town, nodded enthusiastically. They soon found themselves at the open door of a sprawling building from which lively music and the hum of many voices spilled out into the road, washing over passersby.

To Kei, it felt like the building had grown over time, added on bit by bit with each section telling a different tale, some old and others brand new. It was like the patchwork quilt of the town itself, condensed into a single building. And the same nervous tension he felt when first entering Afonffordd struck him again now. Seeming to sense his apprehension, Ecder looked down, smiled reassuringly, and grabbed Kei's hand as they walked into the building together.

With the hustle and bustle outside, the tavern–styled great room in the lodge offered a brief respite for Kei and Ecder. Benches and tables were scattered around, each hosting a variety of guests. Sailors and farmers shared stories, their laughs echoing in the large room. Candle sconces punctuated the wooden posts, casting a gentle, flickering light across the space. Up above, square openings allowed the outside light to seep in, creating a serene ambiance. In one corner, a man plucked at a lyre, his voice rising and falling in a haunting melody.

Asking around a bit, Ecder soon found the innkeeper. But his subsequent haggling with the man to secure lodging for the night soon lost Kei's interest. Fortunately, the alderman finished quickly and began shuffling Kei toward the exit.

Once back in the bustling streets, the sights and sounds overwhelmed Kei, his eyes darting everywhere. Grateful for the reassuring grip Ecder maintained on his hand, he pondered the man's intentions. Kei didn't understand why Ecder was willing to take him in, but where else could he go? Though he had no other options, the alderman had presented the offer as a choice – one he was still waiting for Kei to accept. Finally, he decided to get to know the man better.

"There are so many people here – more than I ever saw my whole life!" Kei started, looking up at Ecder with uncertainty.

Ecder glanced down at him as they continued walking, a little surprised to hear Kei speak, and grinned. "Your life does not have many years on it, lad. Wait until you are my age!"

"How old are you?" Kei asked.

"Old enough to know that is a rude question when asked of the wrong person," Ecder chuckled. "I have celebrated thirty and five spring seasons."

Chagrined, Kei apologized and fell silent until Ecder gave a reassuring squeeze of his hand. Looking up and seeing Ecder's smile, Kei continued. "My mother died of the pox three summers ago…"

"I remember," Ecder interjected. "Dafydd was devastated. Good thing your da' had you to help him remember her. You favor her you know."

Kei nodded. "My da' tells…told me…that all the time," he replied, swallowing a sudden lump in his throat.

"Now they are both gone and…," Kei began. He didn't quite know how to say what he really wanted to know.

Seeming to sense Kei's struggle, Ecder picked up on Kei's thoughts as though they were his own. "You do not see any choice but to accept my offer. Is that about what you are thinking?" Ecder asked the air in front of him as they walked, without looking down.

Kei nodded and Ecder stopped, squatting down to look him in the eye. "Kei sometimes fate lays a finger on your life and bad things happen – things you wish did not happen. It can leave you feeling as though you have no choices – no control over the things that happen to you. I did not need to add to that. So, I gave you a choice rather than taking it from you. Do you understand now?"

Kei nodded again as Ecder smiled, patted his shoulder jovially and stood. "Besides…I think my wife and your mother were distant cousins. So, perhaps we are already family!" Ecder exclaimed and continued walking.

Kei smiled and continued watching the menagerie of characters they passed, when suddenly he heard a shouted warning as a large clay jar came crashing down in front of him. Instinctively he leapt away, stumbled into the street, and collided with a towering figure – a menacing looking man that might have fit in well with Kei's previous captors.

"Out of the way, mongrel!" the brutish man commanded as he lifted his hand to backhand Kei. An instant later, Ecder was there, having intercepted the impending blow, grasping the man's wrist firmly. "Forgive us," Ecder began, his voice steady and calm, "this is my son's first time in a big town. He is only a boy."

Kei stayed crouched, heart pounding, as the two men towered over him. Their eyes locked in a silent standoff, the strain evident in their tense arms. But, just as swiftly as it began, the confrontation ended. The brutish man's attention shifted up the street, and he yanked his hand away with a sneer. "Watch your welp, or it'll be his last visit," he snapped, before striding away briskly.

Kei watched as the man quickly caught up with a group of three others. One of them walked at the center of the group, looking proud, and wearing fancier clothes than the others. 'He must be someone rich and important, and the others are his guards,' Kei mused. The way other people in the street reacted to the group was also evident. Some averted their eyes to avoid notice, while others decided to walk a different way. The leader and his guards reminded Kei of a group of bullies from his village.

A tap on the shoulder and the sound of a clearing throat pulled Kei's attention back to the moment. Looking around, he saw Ecder extending a hand to help him up. "Come lad. Merlin awaits our return."

As they reentered the market square, Kei and Ecder discovered that Merlin had drawn a crowd. Adults and children watched as Merlin, perched atop Ecder's cart, narrated a story that had them all captivated.

Eager to see and hear more clearly, Kei tried to find a better vantage point, but the sea of taller figures blocked his view. Noticing this, Ecder chuckled, "Here lad, let me help." In one swift motion, he hoisted Kei onto his broad shoulders just as Merlin concluded his tale.

"Then the man removed the magic stone from the soup and everyone in the village shared a wonderful meal together!" Merlin said. "And the lesson of this story from my land is this: When people are clever and work as one, all benefit, from eldest to youngest," he continued, pointing at the adults and children in turn with a twinkle in his eye.

Taking a smooth pebble from his pocket, Merlin tossed it to one of the young boys at the front of the crowd. The boy stared at the rock in round–eyed wonder, then ran off through the crowd excitedly, trailed by chuckles and laughter from some of the adults who'd seen the exchange.

Loud applause followed, and Kei regretted missing the earlier parts. Suddenly, a girl about Kei's age called out, "Tell the story about the spirit again!" She excitedly gestured towards another girl, "My sister missed it earlier!"

Merlin, about to disembark from his impromptu stage upon noticing Kei's and Ecder's arrival, hesitated as Ecder called out, "Go on, Merlin! We have time yet!"

Kei listened intently from his elevated position as Merlin launched into his story again. "This is not a tale from my lands," Merlin began, "but a story I have heard while travelling your own!"

"A village that was once happy fell into hard times. The crops failed, and the rivers dried up. People grew thin and weak as their food ran out, and the people began to starve. But one man still had plenty to eat. He was the richest man in the village, and his storehouses were full of grain and meat – plenty for all. Yet he was greedy and would not share, locking them up to keep the food all for himself."

Merlin's voice dropped lower, drawing the crowd in. "One night, while the rich man was eating a fine meal, he heard a soft knock at the door. At first, he thought it was the wind. But then he heard a small voice - a child's voice - crying for help. When he opened the door, he saw a small, frail boy standing there. The child was shaking from the cold and looked ready to fall over from hunger. 'Please, sir,' the boy begged, 'just a piece of bread.'"

Merlin's eyes swept over the crowd, his voice filled with scorn. "The rich man sneered at the boy as if he were nothing more than a stray dog. 'Get away from here!' he said. 'I have nothing for you.' And he slammed the door shut."

Merlin paused for a moment, letting the silence linger. "The next morning, news spread that the child had died just outside the rich man's door. And that night, strange things began to happen in the rich man's house. The air turned cold, and the light of his fire seemed to fade. As he lay in bed, he heard it again – the voice of the boy crying for bread. But not from outside! It came from the dark corners of the room, growing louder and closer. He tried to shut it out, but the crying never stopped."

The crowd leaned in, some holding their breath. "The spirit would not leave him," Merlin went on. "Each night, the cries grew louder. The man locked his doors and called for guards, but they all ran away in fear. By the third night, the crying stopped, and the house went quiet. When the servants went to check on him the next morning, they found the rich man dead in his bed, his dead eyes wide with a frozen look of horror."

The crowd shuddered, and Merlin's voice softened. "Some say the spirit of the child still wanders the land, looking for others like the rich man, mean-spirited and filled with greed. It asks for bread, but if turned away, its touch will steal a man's soul. Others say it is a warning – that if you see the spirit, you have one day to change your ways, stop being greedy, and be kind to others. If not? The next night…"

Merlin made a ghastly sound as he reached out with his own hand, choking himself and feigning horror. Children squealed, clutching their parents, while a few adults chuckled nervously. Even Kei, who thought himself too old to be scared by stories, felt a shiver run down his spine.

Once the eerie story ended, Merlin bowed and excused himself to attend to other duties, and several folks tossed more coins around the small cache already near Merlin's feet. Ecder carefully lowered Kei from his shoulders, while Merlin busied himself gathering the coins left by the grateful listeners. The two joined Merlin, and Kei assisted in collecting the scattered coins.

"How did that all begin?" Ecder asked curiously, his gaze fixed on the coins.

Merlin, with a glint in his eye, recounted, "As most things do for a stranger. Some children saw my strange clothes," he gestured to his outfit, "and asked who I was…with that curious bravery all young people seem to possess," Merlin continued, winking at Kei and smiling.

Then he shrugged, "I told them I am Merlin – a storyteller from a far–away land. Before I knew it, stories flowed, and a crowd gathered."

"But you said the story about the spirit was something you heard from our land, Merlin," Kei piped up, a hint of concern in his voice. "Is it true?"

"Ah, that!" Merlin replied, grinning as he finally collected the last coin and stood. "No, Kei, that was also a tale from my own land, although usually told a bit differently. But earlier, there was a particularly greedy looking rich man in the market who was using his guards to bully free food and goods from sellers. When he stopped to listen to me, I told that story hoping he might think about being kinder."

"Yes, I believe we crossed paths with one of his men on our way here," Ecder interrupted.

Merlin nodded as Kei handed him the remaining coins he had collected. "Was the pebble you gave that boy magic?" Kei asked, intrigued. "I only just heard the ending of that story."

Merlin grinned. "Are you certain this is the same boy, Ecder?" he asked. "You left with a mouse and returned with a lion," causing Kei to blush as Ecder chuckled.

"In my experience, Kei, the magic a thing has is only the magic we give it," Merlin finally replied, winking again and ruffling Kei's hair. Kei wasn't sure that answered his question and found himself wondering if Merlin had indeed given the pebble some magic. Seeing the look on his face pondering Merlin's words, Ecder just laughed loudly for some reason.

The next few hours passed in a flurry of activity as Ecder got them moving again. As they approached the docks, Kei's gaze was immediately captivated by the vast expanse of water. He had never seen such an immense river, its sheer magnitude making him feel small and filled with wonder. Nearby, boats bobbed gently, their sails whispering stories of far–off places. The hive of activity around them was mesmerizing: men moved with purpose, scurrying industriously from ship to dock and back, like ants on an anthill.

While Ecder delved into haggling with a ship merchant, Kei remained lost in the scene, the wonders of the dock momentarily drawing his attention away from the weight of the day's events. As Kei watched a particular ship with no sails, instead driven against the gentle current of the river by several men paddling oars, he couldn't help but wonder where all the water in the river came from.

Ecder's discussions with the ship merchant wrapped up quietly and efficiently, his face as unreadable as ever, but Kei noticed a slight nod of satisfaction as coins exchanged hands. Men then came over, setting about the task of unloading their cart with practiced hands.

"Now that I have the coin to pay tithes for the village, let us stable the horses and cart at the inn and head over to the tax house," Ecder announced. "Perhaps when we are done, we can return to the inn for something to eat. The lamb I smelled roasting there earlier has left me hungry since!" With that, the trio set off from the riverside.

Kei felt a steady knot of unease as they stood in line at the counter. The big man who had almost hit him earlier was right outside the tax house, and it was unnerving. While Ecder and Merlin tried to reassure him, Kei couldn't shake off the feeling that they were walking into the "den of thieves" he'd heard in tales.

The rich man from before lounged in a chair in the corner, cleaning his fingernails with a knife, while a stern-faced man at the counter dealt with those paying tithes.

"Village?" the man asked as Ecder reached the counter.

"Solva," Ecder replied. The man eyed Ecder, appraising him like a pig being sold at market, then did the same to Merlin. After a moment, he signaled to the rich man, who gave Ecder another scrutinizing look, held up some fingers, and resumed his nail cleaning.

Kei did not fully understand counting or coins, but Ecder's shocked expression said enough. "That's outrageous!" Ecder burst out. "That is more than twice last year's tithes!" He pointedly looked at the man in the corner, demanding, "Where's Prefect Llewcius? And who are you to ask for so much?"

The man briefly looked up, saying lazily, "Prefect Llewcius is my father. As he has more important matters to attend than making sure tithes are paid, he has left the responsibility to me."

Standing up and approaching them, he continued, "You country oafs for too long have lived under my father's protection, while paying a mere pittance of what you should. Now you can pay the tithes you owe, or I will ensure men are sent to…" he paused, looking to the man at the counter, "Where did he say?"

"Solva," came the reply.

"Solva," he echoed with a smirk, "where they will collect the appropriate tithes – plus a little extra for the trouble, of course" he added, sneering.

Ecder's face turned red. "What protection?" he demanded. "We were attacked and forced to defend ourselves on our way here!"

"Where is this…Solva?" the rich man asked derisively.

"To the west and north a day's ride," Ecder answered, trying to remain calm. Kei felt a chill run down his spine as the two men at the door, having heard the heated exchange, began looming with menace.

The prefect's son turned to one of his guards, "Hywel, did we not send a patrol that direction recently?"

"Rhys, Cadoc, and Efan went that way three days ago," Hywel confirmed. Kei's heart began to race as he recognized the names of the men who had killed his father and taken him captive.

Ecder recognized the names too. His eyebrows shot up in outrage, and he looked ready to attack before Merlin's firm hand stopped him. "Our apologies." Merlin murmured. "We came ill-prepared to pay so much, but we will return tomorrow."

Ecder seemed shocked by Merlin's interjection, and while Kei didn't understand everything, he was just glad they were leaving as Merlin forcefully ushered Ecder out the door. As they departed, the rich man's voice rang out, "See you tomorrow!" prompting derisive laughter from the guards inside.

On their way back to the inn, Merlin's stormy face spoke of plans brewing. The fear and anxiety that had taken root when Kei was at the tax house now subsided, replaced instead by a growing concern.

"Merlin, I did not like those men," Kei finally managed, gathering the courage to speak. "And I think the men he talked about were the ones that killed my da'."

Merlin's face, tight with anger, softened when he looked down at Kei. "I know, Kei," he replied. Then, a hint of mischief crept into his eyes. "But perhaps we can do something about this little…" He paused, searching for the right word. "In my language, we have a crude word for the hole in your backside to describe such men. I do not know it in yours."

Ecder burst into laughter. "You mean 'arsehole'?" he offered, amusement clear in his eyes.

Kei's eyes widened. That was a word he had heard from grown–ups, and his da' had warned him not to say it. Merlin merely nodded, repeating it, "Arsehole."

"What do you have planned, Merlin?" Ecder inquired.

Glancing down at Kei, Merlin grinned, the twinkle of mischief still in his eyes. "I have an idea," he said, "and Kei here is just the right person to help!"

By dusk, the three sat in the room Ecder had procured for the night, bellies full from a shared meal in the common room. Kei, dressed in sackcloth rags, tried not to fidget as Merlin carefully painted his face with mixtures from two small crocks – one of flour and fat drippings and the other, ash and fat.

Ecder watched skeptically, eyebrow raised. "You scheme to convince the prefect's son that Kei here is the spirit child from your tale, Merlin. But even to my eyes, he is no more than a boy in costume."

"Patience, Ecder," Merlin replied, a look of concentration on his face. "I have a few tricks to help bring this spirit to life!" Finishing his work, Merlin wiped his hands on a spare bit of sack cloth and stepped back, nodding in satisfaction.

Reaching into his pack, Merlin produced a long black rod about the length of Kei's forearm, and something flat and shiny. Handing the latter to Kei, Merlin said, "Here Kei, take a look at yourself."

Kei was so shocked at the visage staring back at him that he dropped the object. "Careful Kei," Merlin gasped. "It is easily broken! It is only a looking glass. Like seeing yourself in still water."

Holding the glass again, Kei studied the fearsome figure mirrored back. As he raised a hand to his face to reassure himself that the reflection was indeed his own, Merlin slapped his hand away, grinning. "You will ruin all my hard work!"

"I look like the spirit child!" Kei exclaimed, his excitement palpable.

"Just wait! I am not done," Merlin replied grinning as Ecder took the looking glass from Kei and examined his own image.

"I am quite the handsome fellow," he announced, stroking the beard of his chin. "My wife is a lucky woman!" he added, winking at Kei.

Taking the looking glass and returning it to his pack, Merlin smirked at Ecder, "Your humble nature knows no end," he said, drawing a chuckle from both Ecder and Kei.

Turning his attention to the black rod, Merlin said, "This is…let us call it my moon scepter. It is harmless, so do not be alarmed by its magic." With a click, the room illuminated brilliantly, drawing gasps from both Kei and Ecder.

"By all the Gods," Ecder murmured in awe, staring around at the brightly illuminated room. "What sorcery is this?!"

"Be calm you two," Merlin replied. With another click, the room dimmed, and Merlin handed the rod to Kei. The rod was surprisingly heavy, and Kei wondered at its construction.

"Hold the scepter to your chest under your chin like this. The light will emerge from this end, so face it at the floor," Merlin instructed, taking Kei's hand, and helping him to position the rod. "Stand here," he continued, "and use your thumb to press here to show the light, and again to extinguish it."

Kei held the rod and did as instructed. Suddenly, his robe of sack cloth and the floor before him were bathed in an eerie light. Kei grinned, confident from the look on Ecder's round–eyed face that the light had the desired effect. Using the looking glass, Merlin allowed Kei to see himself anew. His painted face, now under the spectral glow, seemed even more haunting. Kei grinned widely, which only added to the effect, causing him to giggle giddily and start making faces, trying different looks out.

"If I had not seen the making of him Merlin," Ecder replied, still round–eyed in wonder, "I could believe he is the spirit boy from your tale myself."

"Wait. There is more," Merlin replied grinning. Rummaging through his pack again, he extracted two identical looking black boxes and set them down beside him. "These…" Merlin began then seemed to falter. "I do not have a name for them."

After a brief pause, Merlin asked with a contemplative frown, "Are you familiar with the practice of using birds to carry a message from one place to another?"

Ecder nodded, "The Roman soldiers I trained with in my youth had a dovecote for that very purpose – to send messages between Londinium and Camulodunum."

"Then let us call these 'bird boxes'," Merlin proposed. "Only, instead of a message, one's voice is carried from one box to the other across vast distances, as if by an invisible bird."

Seeing Ecder's skepticism, Merlin fiddled with each of the boxes, eliciting odd chirping and clicking sounds. To Kei, it seemed as if there truly was an invisible bird within, and he stared at the boxes in round–eyed wonder. Ecder looked taken aback, but Merlin appeared completely at ease, no doubt accustomed to the marvels of his magic.

"Take this," Merlin instructed, "and handle it with care, Ecder. I would be most displeased if it were to break. The two of you go and stand over in that corner with it. When I give the command, press here and speak into it."

Merlin took position in the opposite corner of the room. A moment later, Ecder nearly fumbled the box in astonishment as Merlin's voice suddenly came from it. "Ecder, can you hear me? Press where I told you." Pressing where he was told, Ecder spoke tentatively, "Y–yes, I can hear you."

"Well done! Now place the bird box in the pouch sewn inside Kei's garment and come join me in this corner to watch," Merlin instructed. To Kei, he said, "Kei, you stay there and hold your mouth open wide like so," demonstrating the facial expression.

Guided by Merlin's voice from the mysterious box, Kei soon found himself gliding smoothly about the room like a leaf floating in a stream, bathed in an ethereal glow. From within him emanated haunting moans, cries, and pleas for bread. Ecder looked on with a blend of awe and mirth, no doubt as tickled as Kei at Merlin's attempt to play act a haunting child's voice. All the while, Merlin's face was lit with a triumphant smile. Kei, sharing in the delight of the ruse, grinned and laughed in response, marveling at the wonders of Merlin's magic.

Kei and Merlin waited patiently until Ecder strode out of the tax house, a wide grin across his face. Kei, having been so discomfited the day before, had asked to wait outside with Merlin and the horses. Now he was wondering if he should have gone in with Ecder.

Merlin, his brow arched playfully, mused, "That look suggests things went favorably?"

Ecder's eyes twinkled. "Indeed, more than well. The prefect himself was inside. Would you believe his son has barricaded himself in his room and refuses to come out?" Laughter bubbled up as he ruffled Kei's hair. "Our young spirit here played his part exceptionally last night."

"So, what happened?" Kei and Merlin asked at the same time, both curious, then grinned at each other.

"Word has swept through town since dawn," Ecder began, relishing the recount. "The guards who fled his manor grounds first told the prefect of the spirit child come to steal his son's soul. He dismissed such talk, only to be assailed by the townsfolk echoing your tale in the market square and swearing they had seen the spirit child with their very eyes."

Kei's thoughts drifted back to last night, giggling to himself involuntarily. He had, without a doubt, sent chills down the spines of a few late–night wanderers. But he had especially enjoyed seeing those formidable guards scatter in panic as he approached the manor. And nothing could top the glee he felt when, upon responding to his pounding at the door, the prefect's son had shrieked in terror, slammed it closed, bolted it, his frantic steps echoing as he fled.

"It might have ended there," Ecder continued, "but then some of the older guards and a few outspoken townsfolk told the prefect about his son's arrogant and greedy behavior while in charge. The prefect looked fit to flay the young man's hide himself!"

"Flaying is a little harsh perhaps," Merlin snickered, "but the young man may be safer locked in his room until his father's temper cools."

Ecder nodded, grinning back, "In any event, tithes have been restored to normal, and even reduced for those that appear in need."

As the trio walked away from the tax office back toward the center of town, Kei could not help noticing the aftermath of last night's adventure. He overheard bits of conversation as they passed people talking in the street, claiming to have personally witnessed the spirit child wandering through town, or to have knowledge from a reliable source who witnessed it. Others were recounting parts of Merlin's tale, a few even pointing him out with awed whispers as the three of them passed.

Occasionally, Kei spotted a loaf of bread lying at the foot of a cottage door, sometimes accompanied by a lone coin. He was surprised to see that no one would go near to take it. He could not help grinning every time he saw it, but Merlin would become quiet, a distant look in his eye. "Are you okay, Merlin?" Kei asked finally, concerned. "The loaves or coin trouble you?"

"What? Oh! No Kei," Merlin responded, snapping back to the moment, and smiling down at him. "In my own land, people often celebrate a custom – a feast of fall, where children dress up and pretend to be spirits and fairies and goblins, much as you did last night. Then the children visit each house to receive a small treat from those inside. The bread and coin simply remind me of that custom."

Merlin's face became thoughtful again as he mumbled to himself, "I wonder now if my actions…" Shaking his head as if to clear it, he grinned at Kei again. "It is a fun tradition, even for the grown-ups."

As they came to a crossroads, Merlin stopped, causing Ecder and Kei to pause as well. "This is where I leave you," he said without preamble. "I must make for Moridunum still, and the ferry across the river is that way," he added, pointing down the road to the east.

Kei found himself shocked to suddenly be on the edge of tears. He had only known Merlin for two days but had grown to like him. Words escaped him as he ran up and embraced Merlin, who hugged him back, ruffled his hair, and said "Keep being magical, Kei," smiling down.

When Kei stepped back, Ecder stepped forward, and the two men clasped forearms. "We both owe you more than a life debt, Merlin. Remember that" Ecder said.

Merlin nodded solemnly, then turned and walked away down the road toward the river. As he and Ecder stood silently for a moment, watching him go, Kei wondered if he would ever see Merlin again. Then they turned the other way toward home.

CHAPTER 10

Parley

Ygraine sat on a small wooden bench beside the open double doors, basking in the sunlight. A warm salt breeze came in from the garden terrace overlooking the vast expanse of the sea, where her daughter sat, working her tiny fingers around a garland made from freshly picked flowers.

Surveying the room she shared with her husband, Ygraine felt a swell of pride for the effort she'd invested in creating such a welcoming space. Gorloys liked everything just so, and she endeavored to ensure it was. Stone walls and thick wooden beams were adorned with the bright glow of numerous sconces. Rustic furnishings complemented the large bed, its plush furs a testament to comfort. Vases filled with fresh wildflowers adorned corners, striking a delicate balance between ruggedness and grace.

"Will you be gone long, mama?" the young girl asked, her innocent eyes shining with curiosity.

"No, Morghais, my sweet. Your father and I will return from the parley in just three days," Ygraine responded with a gentle smile.

Morghais tilted her head slightly, "What is a parley?"

Ygraine pondered for a moment, searching for words a seven–year–old child could grasp. "It is like… when you and the other children make up a game and you talk, deciding the rules so that everyone can be happy and have fun."

Before the conversation could progress, Gorloys strode into the room with a gleam of anticipation in his eyes and something concealed behind his back. But upon seeing Morghais, his expression faltered, and he took on a commanding look. "Send the girl off to play," he said, his voice not harsh, but expecting obedience.

"We are almost done, husband. A moment more…" Ygraine began, trying to set Gorloys at ease and allow Morghais to finish.

"No, now! I wish to be alone with you," Gorloys interjected.

Not wanting Morghais to witness any tension between them, Ygraine gently instructed, "My sweet, why don't you take these flowers to your room and finish the garland? You can show mama later."

"Yes, mama," Morghais whispered, her voice timid as she hastened out of the room.

Gorloys, his gaze following the child as she left the room, relaxed visibly, the playful gleam in his eye returning. Pulling the object from behind his back, he announced, "Here. I have brought you something."

Ygraine's eyes lit up, "Oh, husband! For my twenty–fourth birth year?" The package, bound delicately in cloth and wool string, unraveled to reveal a stunning dress. Holding it against herself, she turned to Gorloys, a mixture of delight and apprehension in her eyes. "It is beautiful!"

Gorloys stepped closer, "I want you to wear it the day of the parley to show everyone how beautiful you are," smiling warmly. He gently brushed the back of his hand against her cheek. The tender touch was betrayed by her involuntary wince. "You should be more careful, my dear," he added.

She lowered her gaze, "I will try harder, husband."

The moment was interrupted as Magra entered the room. "You summoned me?" she asked tersely, seeing the two of them standing together.

Ygraine nodded, showing the healer her swollen cheek, the yellowing bruise prominent, "I must look my best for my husband when we go to the parley, and I need your help with this."

Seeing the bruise's location, Magra cast a suspicious glance at Gorloys. But, noticing the self–satisfied smirk spreading across his face, she held her tongue. Focusing instead on Ygraine, she examined the bruise. "I cannot heal it in two days, but I can help soothe and conceal it."

Gorloys, watching the exchange, commented indifferently, "It will be sufficient."

Magra's hands worked diligently, her voice edged with cynicism, "Child, have you been this clumsy all your life? Of everyone I have treated, you collect more bruises, welts, and cracked bones than the rest combined!"

"Oh, yes! I was always clumsy," Ygraine chuckled lightly, "Though this time the bruise was my horse's doing. Something spooked him and he threw me."

Magra raised an eyebrow, "I see."

Gorloys interjected, his tone ambiguous, "I suppose you would like to replace him with something easier to handle?"

Knowing her husband as she did, Ygraine sensed a double meaning in his words. "Oh, no, husband! He's perfect! He did nothing wrong! Had I minded myself better, Magra would not be here now," she quickly reassured him.

Gorloys' eyes held hers for a moment longer, searching her face, before he relaxed, a smug satisfaction in his smile. "Then let this be a lesson for you. You must learn to respect his power. Then you will find more pleasure when riding him," he said casually. "If not, next time he could hurt you much worse," he added, his voice low, the double meaning unmistakable.

Ygraine dropped her eyes and spoke meekly, "Yes, my husband. I will heed your advice…and your warning."

A brief nod from Gorloys confirmed her answer sufficed. "Good. I will see you tonight. Remember to pack the dress," he said, leaning in to seal his words with a kiss.

But Ygraine, in a quiet act of defiance, turned her head just so, offering the bruised side of her face to his lips instead of her mouth. It was a silent scream, a whisper of rebellion. 'See this? This is your doing. This pain belongs to you,' the evidence insisted.

The air hung heavy, charged with unspoken truths, and she wondered if he understood her message. Gorloys paused, his lips barely brushing her marred skin, the heat of his breath mixing with the sting of the bruise. His eyes searched hers, a flicker of something unreadable within their depths. Then, without a word, he straightened and left the room.

Once the door closed with a soft thud behind him, Magra cast a dubious glance at it, then shook her head in disgust. "Powerful or not, that is one stallion that needs a good whip," she muttered under her breath, just loud enough for Ygraine to hear.

Ygraine's lips twitched into a smirk, and with a conspiratorial gleam in her eyes, she whispered, "Can I tie him to the rack and watch?" The remark, unexpected and vivid, sent them both into quiet fits of laughter, the sound a mixture of true mirth and a desperate relief that they clung to in the moment.

As their laughter subsided, the women regained their composure. Magra's expression turned serious, the lines around her eyes deepening. "Ygraine, if you ever…"

"I know, Magra," Ygraine interrupted softly, her voice a mix of weariness and resolve. "But I have no more family, and… horrible as he can be – especially when he drinks – he provides a good life for me and my daughter. I stay because of Morghais… and he is her father, no matter how much he wishes she were a boy." She paused, the weight of unspoken words hanging in the air. "If I did not have her, though…"

The sentence hung unfinished, a world of possibilities contained in their absence. They shared a look of understanding, the silence speaking volumes more than the missing words ever could.

After their shared moment, the room fell into a comfortable silence, filled only with the quiet sounds of Magra's continued ministrations. The healer worked with a gentle efficiency, her skilled hands moving with care over Ygraine's bruise. The silence wasn't awkward but filled with a mutual understanding that no more words were needed for now.

Finally, with a confirming nod at her handiwork, Magra stepped back. "There, that should hold for the time being. But make sure you see me again before you depart for the parley," she instructed, her tone no longer terse but imbued with a soft concern.

After the door closed behind Magra, Ygraine approached the stone basin of her reflecting pool, the dark, still water reflecting her visage. The candles about its rim cast an ethereal glow upon her face, enhancing the illusion of unblemished skin and untouched beauty that Magra had meticulously crafted. As she assessed the healer's handiwork, a wave of exhaustion washed over her. She hadn't realized she had been as taut as a bowstring drawn back for release when Gorloys had entered. Now, as she forced herself to relax, tears threatened to surface, but she staunchly held them back. If she cried, it would mar all of Magra's efforts. If she cried, he would win. She refused to permit that victory.

Ygraine's horse picked its way carefully through the rugged terrain, the wild expanse of the upland moor stretching out in every direction. Gorloys, riding beside her, seemed wary and tense, his eyes constantly scanning their surroundings. Ygraine couldn't decide whether she should be wary too. Looking behind her, a group of twenty armed men followed, the sound of their mounts' hooves a constant, dull thunder in the background. 'Those men should be ample protection,' she thought. 'Why is my husband worried?'

She knew that, with his current demeanor, Gorloys could be emotionally volatile and quick to agitate. Choosing her words carefully, she finally asked, "Is anything amiss, husband? The way you survey the moor, one would think we ride into the jaws of Cerberus himself. Should I fear the men of the wild, or do they cower, knowing Gorloys, the fierce protector of Cornwall, patrols his lands?"

The flattery seemed to work; Gorloys' chest puffed out slightly and the lines of his face softened, but only for a moment. "It's not the men of the wild you should fear, woman," he said, his voice a low growl. "It's the ambition of men who call themselves kings. Men like Uthyr, who would see all kneel before him." His hand instinctively went to the hilt of his sword as he fiercely proclaimed that he would bow to no one.

"But why here, amidst these age–old stones and untamed land?" Ygraine queried, her gaze sweeping across the moor, trying to fathom her husband's strategic mind.

"The moor, my dear, is a land ruled by no man, a wild divide between the lands I rule and the lands to which that overreaching Uthyr lays claim," Gorloys explained, his voice tinged with disdain. "The Standing Stones of Scorhill are as ancient as their legends, known to all who roam these lands. Some fools believe the stones to be magic - standing as witness to dealings within, bringing fortune to agreements and a curse to those that break them. No doubt Uthyr is one such fool. Still, it is as good a place as any for this parley."

His logic was sound, yet Ygraine felt a twinge of apprehension. "But if this Uthyr is as you say, why meet him at all? Would that not expose you to danger, my husband?"

At this, Gorloys' expression darkened, his pride pricked by her insinuation of vulnerability. The air around them seemed to crackle with his indignation. "Do you doubt me, woman? Do you doubt my strength? My cunning?" he snapped, the threat in his tone unmistakable.

"Is a wife not allowed to be concerned for the things she loves?" she asked, her voice maintaining a calm and steady timbre. While Gorloys would interpret her words through his own lens of arrogance, her inner thoughts sang a different tune, 'I love myself and my daughter. I would be safe at home with her if not for your incessant need to parade me around like a trophy.'

He regarded her with a piercing look, the fury still evident in his eyes, but her composed concern seemed to give him pause, softening the edge of his anger, if only slightly. "Uthyr may be ambitious, may claim what is not his, but only because he is a shrewd and cunning leader. He knows the value of perceived strength and has dared to venture into this barren land himself, showing a facade of bravery. To refuse his invitation would be perceived as cowardice, a weakness he would exploit. I will not give him that satisfaction."

Ygraine, trying to soothe him, replied gently, "You are anything but weak, husband."

A curt, humorless chuckle escaped him. "Indeed, I am not."

Still, her worry gnawed at her. "But what if it is a ruse? What if he intends to overwhelm us, not with strategy, but with numbers? Could his forces be lying in wait in these valleys, hidden among the hills, waiting to strike?" she could not help but ask, her eyes scanning the deceptively serene hills around them.

Gorloys' smirk held more than a hint of scorn. "Sometimes, I wonder if you are truly naïve or merely feigning ignorance to vex me. Do you think me a fool, believing that what you see is all of I command? You insult me, wife," he spat, pride in his strategy burning bright in his eyes. "The men you see are but a fraction of my escort. Scouts, my vigilant eyes in the shadows, scour the land ahead, ensuring no surprise befalls us, providing forewarning against both wild men and treacherous kings alike."

Quick to recover from her inadvertent provocation, Ygraine sought to mollify his bruised ego, "It seems I am the greater fool, husband. I lack the mind for such intrigues. Naturally, you have thought ahead to ensure our safety." As if on cue to underscore his foresight, one of

Gorloys' scouts galloped up to them, breathless with exertion. "My liege, the circle is just beyond the ridge. We have secured all quarters, and the other company awaits amidst the stones."

A wave of relief seemed to wash over Gorloys, the tension in his shoulders easing. His lips twisted into a satisfied sneer. "Good. Lead the men forward," he ordered, and as the scout nodded and dashed away, he turned to Ygraine, the sneer still playing on his lips. "Uthyr is already at the meeting place," Gorloys said, a smirk spreading across his face. "The bastard found himself forced to wait for our arrival rather than the other way around. This pleases me. Come."

Ascending the final ridge, they found a sprawling valley below, where a circle of stones stood as a silent witness to ages long past. In its heart, a pavilion tent, vibrant and stately, buzzed with the activity of men making ready. White pennants snapped in the breeze as symbols of safe haven for parley between adversaries. Seeing the openness of the valley, Ygraine understood why the two men had chosen to meet here. Such visibility afforded no opportunity for ambush by a hidden force. With her husband leading, Ygraine and the rest of the men descended into the valley as the stones of Scorhill called.

As their party reached the stone circle's boundary, a charged silence fell over the area. At Gorloys' signal, Ygraine stayed close, feeling dwarfed by the commanding presence of Gorloys, his First Sworn-sword, and his Guard Leader. Together, the four proceeded toward the pavilion tent at the center. Ygraine felt entirely out of place amongst these formidable men, their dominating presence casting her as a sheep among wolves.

They halted at the pavilion's brink, and opposite them was another delegation, including a man whose beauty took Ygraine's breath away. Gorloys' sudden scowl made her fear he'd caught her staring, but his attention was entirely on the delegation. The handsome stranger gave a subtle nod to one of his men. Recognizing the gesture, Gorloys relaxed slightly as the man acknowledged silently and retreated to the circle's edge.

Ygraine grasped the silent exchange's significance. The stunning man, undoubtedly Uthyr, had brought an extra person into the pavilion. With the departure, both parties were even, though her opposite number wasn't a woman but a small, elderly man, clearly unarmed and not garbed for battle. 'Could that be Uthyr's father?' she pondered.

With the parties equally numbered, the men advanced to the pavilion's heart, where a hefty wooden table awaited. Ygraine held back, as did the elder in Uthyr's retinue, both awaiting an invitation to join. Across the table, the men faced off in silent appraisal, hands upon sword pommels.

Ygraine's gaze was inexorably drawn back to Uthyr. Close to her own age, she surmised, he radiated a youthful vibrancy. Yet, when she turned her thoughts to Gorloys, guilt tinged her comparisons. Her husband possessed his own mature, regal allure, the silver in his hair and beard lending him a distinguished air. However, Gorloys' actual age was a subject veiled in deliberate ambiguity, a tender nerve she had once unwittingly struck, prompting a violent reminder never to question it again.

Uthyr was a vision of masculine vigor, his lean, muscular grace showing like a lion strutting among his pride. He stood unyielding, his authority unquestionable even in silence. And within Ygraine, an unexpected sensation began to stir, a tender ache blossoming unbidden, a soft heat building in her womanhood.

Breaking the contest of stares, Uthyr began, "I believe introductions are hardly necessary –" but he got no further. Ygraine noted the familiar tone of impatience and disdain as Gorloys interrupted, "We know who each other are…boy." Then, looking down his nose at the younger man, he added derisively, "The question remains, why have you brought us here? If you think to bend my neck and bring Cornwall under your rule, then you have wasted both our time making a long journey for nothing."

"Kinsman, I bear you no ill will, nor do I plot against Cornwall. But we do have serious matters to discuss. Let us share a cup of wine and talk…as men," Uthyr emphasized, countering Gorloys' belittling term.

Servants materialized with wine carafes and cups, pouring for all six men. Ygraine observed Gorloys, his expression taut, as he waited for Uthyr to drink first. Upon sipping, Gorloys offered a begrudging compliment, "The wine is refreshing," then added sardonically, "You serve me well, Uthyr."

Not knowing his character, Ygraine tensed, worried that the subtle insult might spark contention, or worse, violence. She knew her husband's provocations all too well and the peril they often invited. But instead, Uthyr remained unruffled by the veiled jab. Returning Gorloys' sardonic grin with a composed smile, he simply replied, "I'm pleased you enjoy it. The wine comes from a vineyard in Gaul. I have had the carafes chilling in a nearby stream since dawn. Sadly, we may not taste it's like again."

Gorloys' brow furrowed. "And why should that be?"

"That brings me to the point of this meeting," Uthyr replied, signaling an older man at the edge of the circle. "If I may?"

Before the man could take another step, Gorloys' voice boomed, "Hold!" His eyes narrowed on Uthyr. "You will understand if I require him searched." It was not a request. Uthyr accepted the condition with a tight nod, prompting Gorloys' Guard Leader to proceed.

In the midst of this tension, Uthyr's gaze shifted to Ygraine, and her heart skipped momentarily. "Gorloys, please forgive my lack of courtesy. I see you have brought a nursemaid," he grinned mischievously, then added, "Shall we ask her to join us?"

Uthyr's mirth was infectious and Ygraine barely had time to hide her grin by covering a feigned cough. Following Uthyr's gaze, Gorloys prompted Ygraine to approach. But, as she neared, Uthyr's voice continued playfully, "Shall I extend the same precaution and have her searched?"

Gorloys' gaze whipped back toward Uthyr dangerously, displeasure flashing across his face. "Mind your jests and search your tongue for manners if you have any wish to further continue this meeting, Uthyr." Then, turning to Ygraine with a forced composure, he introduced her. "My wife, Ygraine, Lady of Tintagel."

Uthyr bowed slightly, his eyes alight with undisguised admiration, as his flattery dripped with charm and grace. "Tales of your beauty have reached even my ears, and yet they do my eyes little justice to the truth. You indeed have found fortune, Gorloys. May I offer you some wine, Lady Ygraine?"

Ygraine, caught off guard by the direct flattery and all too aware of Gorloys' piercing gaze, felt her cheeks warm, blushing furiously. She stammered a thank you, accepting the cup with a trembling hand, her heart fluttering inexplicably. Words failed her as she grappled with how to address Uthyr appropriately, all too aware of the potential repercussions any misstep could invoke. Unable to find a suitable compromise, she simply repeated, "Thank you," and stepped back, eyes demurely lowered.

With Ygraine's retreat, the older man stepped forward, prompting Uthyr's introduction. "This is Cadfan, one of the many wise men who wander these lands, sharing the teachings of the Jesus god from Judea."

Before Cadfan could speak, Gorloys scoffed, interrupting. "You call this parley, proclaiming its importance, and yet you bring me this?! A wise man from a foreign land, spreading his…wisdom… about a foreign god. You waste my time," he spat, turning to leave.

He halted at the sound of a wooden cup slamming down. Uthyr stood, hands flat on the table, eyes aflame. "I have shown you respect and shared verbal swordplay with you in friendly jest as I might a brother under the peace of this tent! I offered you my wine and my hospitality. And you repay me with scorn! I will have it no longer! It is not this man's wisdom I bring you, but his news! I am no fool to carry foolish tidings. Do not doubt me. Or you will be the fool!"

At Uthyr's insult, loyalty drew the swords of Gorloys' men. The sudden tension grew instantly palpable as Uthyr's contingent mirrored their actions – the previously calm atmosphere was suddenly a maelstrom of hostility. As men all around the circle of stones answered the silent call to arms, drawing swords and knocking arrows, Ygraine felt the blood drain from her face as terror gripped her heart. Caught in the eye of an unfolding tempest, Ygraine's breath hitched as she gasped for air.

Gorloys seemed taken aback, stunned. Ygraine thought surely the day would end in slaughter, when suddenly, Gorloys' features morphed into amusement, and a wide grin split his face. He bellowed a laugh that seemed to cut through the thick air of tension like a knife. "He has a spine after all!" he proclaimed. "Perhaps I have underestimated you Uthyr! But why bring the wise man? Why not simply bring his news?"

Ygraine suddenly found herself taken aback, not only by her husband's completely unexpected reaction, but also by Uthyr's equally unexpected response. Her senses spun as she watched Uthyr drop his façade of contained rage, instantly adopting a jovial grin as though he'd been the butt of a grand jest. "The wise men of this Jesus god – they all seek the company and influence of powerful men." Uthyr replied. "He wanted to meet you," he added with a shrug.

The veiled complement acknowledging Gorloys as powerful appeared to mollify him as well. As instantly as it had begun, the tension evaporated as signals from both leaders were given, and swords beneath the tent and around the circle were sheathed.

Ygraine fainted.

Consciousness crept back to Ygraine not with the soft tendrils of morning light, but with the jarring urgency of rough hands. Her eyes fluttered open to see her husband looming over her, his face a stormy mix of concern and irritation. Pain throbbed in her cheek where Gorloys had slapped her to wake her up, clearing the cobwebs as her surroundings swam into focus. They were inside a tent, the ground beneath her blanketed with rich, woven rugs, and her body cocooned in a surprising softness of luxurious furs.

"Careful now," Gorloys' voice held a serrated edge, belying the gentleness one might expect in such a situation. "We would not want you swooning again, especially not after this grand display of Uthyr's chivalry," he jeered, waving a wine cup he was holding around, indicating their opulent surroundings. Taking a sip and continuing, with acid in his tongue, he added, "He sleeps under the stars tonight, while you, my dear, get to enjoy the comforts of his tent."

Ygraine's heart sank. A spark of gratitude for Uthyr's unexpected kindness flickered within her, quickly smothered by Gorloys' palpable disdain for her weak constitution. The gesture, meant as a kindness, had opened her up to more of her husband's bitterness. The warmth of the furs did little to stave off the chill that settled in her bones, an icy foreboding that the night was far from over.

"It appears he is willing to go to great lengths to impress you, my love," Gorloys continued, his words slurred with wine and malice. "Or perhaps he aims to humiliate me with his… generosity. No matter. Let us not allow his theatrics to spoil our evening." His hand, cold and unsteady, traced the line of her jaw, a promise of pain veiled as affection.

The lavishness of the tent, the softness of the bed, all became a prison as Ygraine lay there, steeling herself for what was to come. Uthyr's act of kindness, far from offering solace, served as bellows to stoke the coals of Gorloys' wounded pride and ego, enflaming his anger and jealousy.

Gorloys set his wine cup down with a careless clatter, the rich red liquid sloshing dangerously close to the rim. His gaze, clouded with a concoction of resentment and something darker, something predatory, roamed over Ygraine's form, taking in her state of vulnerability. There was a cruel sort of calculation in his eyes, the kind that came before the storm, an ominous thunder she had learned to recognize and dread. She shrunk back, cowering against the coming lightning.

"You've always had a flair for the dramatic, my dear," he remarked, the words a serpent's hiss as he leaned closer. "A faint at just the right moment. Uthyr's concern. All eyes on you." His hand snaked to her neck, fingers pressing just enough for her pulse to beat against his touch like a caged bird. "But I think we both know the truth! You revel in his attention – in the power you wield with just a bat of your eyes."

Ygraine's protest caught in her throat, a choked whisper of denial. "Gorloys, I –" But he silenced her with a swift, sharp motion, his hand striking her cheek with enough force that stars exploded behind her closed eyelids. The sting of it was a stark reminder of her reality, of the dangerous game that she didn't even realize she had been playing.

"Do not bother to deny it," he growled, his breath hot against her ear as he loomed over her. "Do you think I am blind?! I saw the way you looked at him!" Pausing, his voice was thick with scorn, he added, "And the way you enticed him to look at you." The atmosphere in the tent grew stifling, the furs now smothering in their heat. "We shall show that pretentious warlord exactly where you belong, and to whom you belong!"

The icy fingers of panic gripped Ygraine's heart, even as her body instinctively recoiled. She understood the storm that was about to be unleashed upon her, knew all too well that resistance would only fan the flames of his fury. Trapped, with the opulent tent serving as nothing more than a gilded prison, she braced herself for the inevitable.

Gorloys' brutal claiming began with him tearing her dress from her body, fragmenting her world into sharp shards of pain. With his escalating force, a stark realization dawned on Ygraine: this was not merely a husband asserting dominance over his wife; this was a message, a cruel demonstration intended for another. His every thrust, each more savage than the last, wrenched from her throat cries of pain, each louder than before. Amidst the agony and humiliation, she understood Gorloys' true intention, and, powerless, she complied. Her cries were meant for another, echoing beyond the tent walls and into the darkness of the valley beyond for all to hear.

As the violence reached its crescendo and Gorloys climaxed with a guttural yell, he collapsed, his seed spent, then rolled away and retreated into a fitful slumber. Ygraine lay shivering amidst the furs, her aches a throbbing reminder of her husband's cruelty. Breathing in heavy, quivering gasps, she strove to stifle her sobs as tears seeped silently into her hair. She allowed them freedom, for there was no one to witness her despair, no one to offer solace. Not really.

And yet, amidst the ashes of her despair and self–pity, an ember of defiance flickered to life. As she wondered if her cries had reached Uthyr's ears, a daring thought took hold: 'I hope he heard. I hope he heard every cry, and I will wake tomorrow to find he killed that bastard…' With visions of retribution cradling her thoughts, she drifted into a restless sleep.

When she awoke in the morning, the tent was empty save for herself. Dressing slowly in her riding clothes, she winced with every small movement – the remnants of throbbing pain that served as a cruel reminder of the night's events. The beautiful dress Gorloys had given her lay in tatters, a casualty in a war she never asked to fight.

She had just finished composing herself, checking her reflection in the polished bronze left near the opening, when Gorloys entered, his demeanor now cool and dismissive. "Prepare for our departure. We return home at once." There was no room for argument, not that she could muster any if there were. Numbly, she complied, her movements robotic.

It was midday on their journey back before she dared to speak, her voice a mere whisper. "What was the parley for? What did he want?" she asked, not daring to say Uthyr's name.

Gorloys' response was detached, as if the events of the previous night were already an afterthought. "The wise man, Cadfan, brought news of the death of the king of the Franks in Gaul. Raiding bands could trouble the southern coast. Uthyr sought allegiance, alliance, or assurance. I gave him none. I told him a man who cannot protect his lands should not claim them. The Cornish coast is my concern. What do I care if the Franks trouble that bastard? As long as they learn to stay off my shores."

"So, it was not successful?" she dared to ask him.

"Oh, I would not say that, my love," Gorloys replied nonchalantly. "Your performance last night was exquisite, prompting that preening gamecock to ask after your welfare," he added, chuckling.

Ygraine knew better than to take the bait and remained silent. After a moment, he smirked and continued, "I let him know that you were well and resting in the comforts of his tent, exhausted from your ecstatic cries of last night's passions. Is that not so, my dear?"

"Yes, that is so, husband," she replied mechanically. She remained silent the rest of the journey, despair, anger, desperation, and hatred all churning under the surface.

Uthyr sat silently upon his steed, his gaze following the last of Gorloys' retinue as they disappeared from the valley. Around him, his men worked efficiently, the pavilion tent collapsing with practiced ease to be stowed in the horse–drawn cart.

Cadfan approached, his eyes following Uthyr's fixed stare before offering a dry observation. "Gorloys is an… interesting man."

Uthyr issued a humorless chuckle as he turned to face the wise man. "An… interesting way to describe that bastard. I could hope the fleas of his horse infest his cock!" Turning back to stare at the retinue, he added sympathetically, "Only, that poor girl has suffered enough that no curse should befall him that would bring more misery to her."

Cadfan replied, his voice calm but carrying a certain weight, "Our Jesus tells us to forgive and pray for our enemies," following Uthyr's gaze. "But I suspect all the forgiveness and prayer in the world will not save that one from eternal damnation."

Uthyr turned to Cadfan with a knowing grin. "Do not think to bait me with that scent, wise man," he said, his voice rich with amusement. "You'll need to be a slyer fox than that to interest this hound."

Their conversation was cut short as the camp steward approached, breathless. "Sire, we're ready to pack up your tent."

"I no longer need it standing. Stow everything," Uthyr commanded. Then, his expression hardened. "Burn the bedding! I will not sleep where…" He shook his head, leaving the sentence unfinished. "Just… burn the bedding." Recomposing himself, Uthyr added final instructions, "And inform me the moment we are ready to leave. We make for Execaer, and I wish to be there by sunset."

As Uthyr rode, thoughts of Ygraine came to him unbidden, stirring visions of her beauty, innocence, and vulnerability within his mind's eye. These thoughts swiftly became daydreams – ones he welcomed – bringing secret smiles, whispered secrets, and imagined kisses to accompany him on his long journey home.

CHAPTER 11

Convictions

As Cadfan and Uthyr approached the southern border of Glouvum, Cadfan drew his reins, slowing his horse to a stop. The town was protected by a palisade, its integrity interrupted only by a modest guard post marking the entrance. The structure of wood and stone seemed more a tool for observation than a means of defense – a chokepoint for monitoring those who came and went.

Cadfan felt a twinge of impatience; after seven days in the saddle, his body ached for reprieve. 'The journey has had its rewards, though,' he reflected, a smile playing on his lips.

Riding beside Uthyr, he had found an unexpected companion in thought. The king's strategic mind, coupled with a keen curiosity, had led to many deep conversations on politics and religion – a topic that initially held little interest for Uthyr. Cadfan had witnessed the king's dismissive nature, yet with each passing discussion, Uthyr became more engaged, more open to the wisdom of the Christian teachings Cadfan shared. His heart, however, remained guarded, encased within walls as formidable as

Glouvum's palisade. 'I just need to find the guard post to his heart,' Cadfan mused, a sense of irony washing over him.

As they neared the guard post, Uthyr raised his hand in greeting. The guards, recognizing their king, responded with respectful nods of their heads. The one on the left beamed, his voice warm as he welcomed them, "Your journey was long, sire! Welcome home!"

"You seem in good spirits, guardsman!" Uthyr observed, pulling his horse to a stop.

"I am, sire! I was stationed here when you left three weeks ago. At that time, my wife lay sick in bed, and I was sick with worry. It seemed as if an ominous cloud had descended upon my home and, indeed, the entire town. But today, as you return, that cloud has lifted. My wife – and many others – are well again!" the guard shared, relief lacing his voice.

"That is indeed good news," Uthyr responded, his tone thoughtful. "I wonder what brought about this change of fortune…"

The other guard quickly interjected, "You have not heard, sire? Surely, you know of the sage physic who came to our aid. The whole town believes you summoned him; it is the common rumor."

Though seated further back than Uthyr, Cadfan immediately recognized the potential source of the town's good fortune. Hastily interjecting before Uthyr could refute the guard's assumption, he asserted loudly, "Indeed, King Uthyr summoned him." The king, an unformed reply still on his lips, turned in his saddle and cast a sharp, questioning gaze at Cadfan.

Maintaining steady eye contact, Cadfan continued, "Though he did so… indirectly. Sire, as you recall, when meeting with Brother Dubric and me, you demanded a demonstration of our God's grace in exchange for your support. You asked us to aid and heal your people. It seems, in our absence, Brother Dubric has risen to the challenge."

The air seemed to crackle as Cadfan held Uthyr's gaze, neither man breaking eye contact. The king's eyes searched Cadfan's face for a moment, as if weighing the truth of his words. Finally, Uthyr nodded slowly, his expression shifting from skepticism to contemplation, as he turned back to face the guard, now armed with a new understanding of the situation at hand. "Well then.... It seems the rumors were true. May fortune continue to favor you and your wife," Uthyr responded, his tone softened.

"Thank you, sire!" the guardsman replied, his gratitude evident.

With that, Uthyr nudged his horse forward, leading the way into town. Cadfan followed suit, his senses awakening to the transformation around him. The air, once thick with despair and apprehension, now seemed to vibrate with a newfound energy and vitality. The town had been weighed down by the impending threat of plague when they had left, but now, three weeks later, it was as if a miraculous change had taken place.

"Sire, I wish to seek out Brother Dubric and learn more of this matter," Cadfan said after a moment.

"That is well," Uthyr responded. "But leave the horse; my men will have need of it. And when you find this sage physic, bring him to me. I wish to meet him myself."

With a nod, Cadfan dismounted, bidding farewell to Uthyr and his entourage. He patted the horse's nose and turned in the direction of Aurelius' house, where he hoped to find Dubric and some answers to the town's recent turn of fortune.

Cadfan made his way towards Aurelius' house, his spirits lifted by the newfound vivacity that seemed to pulse through the town. The once ominous atmosphere, heavy with the threat of plague, had dissipated, replaced by a wave of optimism and energy. As he strolled through the streets, his observant eyes caught sight of something unusual yet intriguing. The doors of the houses, which were previously marked by the dread–inspiring red X's, now bore a different symbol: a simple, yet elegantly painted blue raindrop.

Puzzled yet intrigued, Cadfan tried to discern the meaning behind this peculiar symbol, but it eluded his immediate understanding. However, he couldn't help but notice the palpable change in the air around these homes. They radiated warmth and liveliness, a stark contrast to the somberness that once shrouded them. The sound of children's laughter filled the air as they played freely in the streets, a sight that had been scarce in recent times. Goodwives gathered, exchanging stories and laughter, their faces lit up with joy and relief.

The town, it seemed, had been reborn. The cloud of despair that had hung heavily over it had lifted, and in its place, a sense of hope and vitality thrived. Cadfan, now even more eager to uncover the mystery behind this transformation, quickened his pace towards Aurelius' abode, his mind buzzing with questions.

At Aurelius' house, Cadfan found himself in the midst of a passionate sermon. The guest chamber was filled, hosting a congregation more than twice the size of any he had seen at Dubric's previous gatherings. From his vantage point at the back, Cadfan observed faces illuminated by faith and enthusiasm as his one–time student, speaking with unwavering conviction, captivated the audience.

Engrossed in his oration, Dubric eventually lifted his gaze from the scripture, and upon noticing Cadfan, he flashed a smile of recognition. But, choosing not to draw attention to the new arrival, he instead seamlessly transitioned the sermon. "And so, to continue our reflection on the scriptures, I would like to turn the service over to Brother Aurelius. Brother Aurelius, would you lead the congregation in the next passage?"

With a gracious nod, Aurelius stepped forward, his voice strong and sure as he picked up where Dubric had left off. The crowd, seamlessly accepting the change, turned their attention to the new speaker while Dubric made his way quietly to the back of the room toward Cadfan.

"It's good to see you, Father," Dubric greeted, his voice filled with warmth.

Cadfan returned the smile, "Aurelius speaks with such conviction; he has quite the gift for oration."

Dubric's face softened with pride, "Indeed, he does. He has embraced the faith wholeheartedly, accepting baptism not long after you left. His leadership and commitment have been invaluable, his home has become a sanctuary for our congregation, and his standing in the community has greatly aided in spreading our shared faith."

Listening to Aurelius for a moment, Cadfan nodded in agreement, "His words reflect a deep understanding of the scriptures and a genuine belief in their power."

After a brief pause, Cadfan's expression turned more serious, "Aurelius appears to have things well in hand. Come. Let us speak in private." He gestured subtly towards the outside, leading Dubric away from the attentive ears of the congregation and into a space where they could converse freely.

Stepping out into the cool air, the atmosphere shifted as the muffled sounds of the sermon faded behind them. They found themselves alone, standing beneath the shelter of a large oak, its branches swaying gently in the breeze.

Dubric, still bubbling with enthusiasm, wasted no time sharing his incredible story. "You will not believe it, Father! When I reached Moridunum, there at the docks, as if by divine providence, was Merlin himself! He was waiting for a ship bound for Glouvum. It is as if our paths were meant to cross, just as you said – let faith be our guide!" His laughter was rich and heartfelt, and for a moment, Cadfan was swept up in the joy of the reunion and the miraculous turn of events.

However, as the laughter died down, Cadfan's expression grew more serious, his brows furrowing in thought. "That is indeed a remarkable meeting, Dubric, and I am glad to hear that you had so little trouble finding Merlin."

Dubric's eyes sparkled as he continued, "To make matters of fate or serendipity more interesting, I did not tell you why Merlin sought passage to Glouvum!"

His emphasis on the word 'why' piqued Cadfan's interest, who couldn't help his bemusement. Dubric's demeanor reminded him of nothing less than a goodwife with a delicious morsel of gossip she couldn't wait to share. Smirking, he didn't bother asking the question. He simply raised an inquisitive eyebrow at Dubric and waited.

Finally, Dubric broke the suspense, "Merlin is seeking Uthyr! He would not share his reason beyond that he needs Uthyr's aid. Oh! And one other reason of consequence now that I think of it!" Dubric smiled mischievously, waiting for Cadfan to bite.

Finally, giving in and pursing his lips, Dubric asked, "And why is that Brother Cadfan?"

"Merlin seeks to reclaim his magic fire box!" Dubric exclaimed excitedly.

At his words, Cadfan's eyebrows shot up in shock and surprise. "So…this Merlin and the Ma'erlyn of Uthyr's tale are indeed the same man," he confirmed as Dubric nodded enthusiastically, then queried with a hint of caution in his tone. "Tell me, where is Merlin now? I would speak with him."

"When we arrived in Glouvum together to find that you and the king had not yet returned, Merlin took up residence not far from here to wait," Dubric responded. "In that time, he has been a blessing to the community, Father, truly! His knowledge and wisdom have been invaluable," he added with deep sincerity.

Despite the reassurances, Cadfan couldn't shake off his concern. "I see that you trust him deeply, Dubric, and I am glad he has been a help to the town and its people. But I have yet to meet the man, and my instincts are to tread carefully. Please understand." He paused, choosing his words with care. "Merlin's powers and knowledge are beyond the ordinary. Scripture has many stories of sorcerers demonstrating powers beyond that of mortal men, intending to mislead. I simply want to ensure that Merlin's abilities are indeed gifts from God and not…" He trailed off, not wanting to voice the darker possibilities.

Dubric's face showed a flicker of surprise, but he nodded solemnly, understanding the gravity of Cadfan's words. "I know his ways are mysterious, Father, but his heart seems true. I have seen nothing to make me doubt him. In fact, he is currently overseeing the construction of a cistern at a nearby well. He has explained that the illness afflicting the town had something to do with the difference between the river and the well. I did not quite understand the details, but the people are already seeing improvements in their health."

Cadfan sighed, the weight of responsibility settling on his shoulders. "I hope you are right, Dubric. I truly do. The line between divine gift and deception can be thin, but I will withhold judgment until I have met the man." His gaze was firm, reflecting the seriousness of his words.

The two clergymen stood in silence for a moment, the rustling leaves above them bearing witness to the gravity of their conversation. Finally, Cadfan broke the silence, "Since you know where to find him now, let us go to him," signaling Dubric to lead the way.

The square, hosting the neighborhood well, teemed with activity as Dubric led Cadfan from the avenue. Despite its actual size, the space appeared expansive due to roads converging from six different directions. Amidst the hustle and bustle, a solitary figure directed a group of men as they poured sand into one side of a newly constructed, low–lying cistern adjacent to the well.

Upon closer inspection, Cadfan observed a dividing wall within the cistern, creating two separate compartments, with holes at its base between the two sides. One side was already filled with a mixture of sand, gravel, and chunks of coal, while the other side – shorter with a gap cut into the lip for water to drain out – was only now beginning to receive pails of fine sand and small pebbles. awaited its turn.

The construction of the cistern, though peculiar and enigmatic, paled in comparison to the man overseeing the work. He wore clothing of a remarkable single–piece construction, yet appearing as a patchwork of greens, browns, and tans that blended seamlessly together. His short hair and the long black coat that flowed past his knees added to the strangeness of his appearance. In his hand, he held a long staff topped with a curious metallic fixture, which he used to guide the workers.

All of these elements were odd in their own right, but Cadfan's astonishment peaked when Dubric called out to the man, and Merlin turned around. Cadfan had expected a middle–aged man, bearing the marks of a life well–lived. Instead, he found himself face to face with someone who appeared not yet old enough to have grown a beard. So taken aback by this unexpected sight, Cadfan involuntarily stepped back when Merlin extended his hand in greeting.

"Forgive him, Merlin," Dubric interjected, noticing Cadfan's apprehension. "Meeting you for the first time can be… unsettling," he added, eyes twinkling with mirth as a knowing smirk played on his lips. "And I must say, your clothing today…. You look as if the forest itself has claimed you! Though I must say it suits you. The black you have worn since we first met seem rather dull by comparison."

Merlin's grin broadened as he retracted his hand and leaned casually on his staff. "Yes, well… my usual clothes needed a good wash. Had I worn them any longer, they might have taken a stroll on their own!"

Cadfan's eyebrows shot up, a surge of unease tightening his chest. "Sorcery!" he exclaimed, his voice edged with wariness as he eyed Merlin's garments with newfound suspicion.

Merlin chuckled, his expression balancing between mirth and mockery, leaving Cadfan unsure. "No, only a jest – clothes cannot walk!" he replied, shaking his head with a wry grin. As he turned back to Dubric, he added, "You troubled me enough convincing you I was not in league with the devil. Will he be the same?" Merlin's voice was unassuming, his accent subtly altering the words, making his tone elusive and hard to pin down.

Dubric's grin mirrored Merlin's. "Perhaps even more so. This is my teacher, Father Cadfan."

"I see," Merlin said, his expression turning serious. "Ask what you will then…teacher?" As Merlin uttered the word 'teacher,' his voice carried a nuance that was hard for Cadfan to decipher. It could have been the tone of someone hearing and repeating a word for the first time, or it might have carried a subtle undertone of mockery. Cadfan found it challenging to determine which. For the sake of Dubric's opinion, Cadfan opted to interpret Merlin's words in the least offensive way possible. He paused, scrutinizing Merlin intently for a moment. Knowing that guile was often a tool of evil, Cadfan remained vigilant, despite Dubric's evident admiration for the man.

With an effort to stay objective, he addressed the man with a blend of caution and mild curiosity, his tone reflecting his underlying apprehension. "Cadfan speaks very highly of you, Merlin. You have certainly made an impression on him. But as he mentioned, my trust is not so easily granted. I do not wish to offend you, but your reputation has come ahead of you, even here – rumors and tales of sorcery and magic, things my faith warns us against." Seeing Merlin about to reply, he held up a hand and added, "I am not one to hastily cast judgment based on hearsay, but neither can it be easily dismissed. So, I am here to judge for myself."

Merlin locked eyes with Cadfan, a hint of amusement flickering in his gaze. "You have more sense than most to judge matters for yourself," he remarked. As he spoke, his expression shifted subtly, morphing into what Cadfan perceived as a sly, almost arrogant grin. "…and less than some to give weight to every whisper of the wind."

Cadfan's eyes narrowed slightly, his uncertainty evident as he tried to gauge Merlin's true intent. Around them, the workers at the cistern had stopped their labor, their attention now fixed on the unfolding dialogue, heightening the sense of unease. Cadfan, typically used to receiving a certain level of respect and deference, found the lack of it disconcerting. The crowd in the square seemed to sense the shift in atmosphere too, as more onlookers joined the workers to observe the exchange. Dubric, noting the increasing audience and the mounting tension, leaned in, his voice low but insistent. "Merlin, please…"

Merlin glanced at Dubric, then his gaze swept over the onlookers, seemingly registering the crowd's presence for the first time. He exhaled softly, turning back to Cadfan with a more conciliatory expression. "Forgive me, Cadfan. My ways and humor might seem rude, being from a foreign land. But I mean no disrespect."

Glancing at his staff and gesturing vaguely to his attire, Merlin continued, "I tell you, nothing I do, nor any item I possess, is magic or sorcery in the way that you mean. I simply have a greater understanding of the natural world." Motioning to the cistern, he added, "And I use that understanding to benefit others where I can."

Remaining cautious, Cadfan responded, "Yet, I must consider the source of this… understanding. Does it come from a place of good intent, or from a darker place, meant to deceive? I have met many charlatans. They may not be in league with the devil, but their goals are often selfish and harmful to people."

Merlin shook his head, a mix of frustration and earnestness in his expression. "Cadfan, consider this: Is the knowledge of forging a sword good or evil?"

Cadfan pondered briefly before answering, "Neither – it is simply a sword. It can be used for protection or to cause harm."

"Then you see, yes?" Merlin affirmed with sincerity. "One does not judge the blacksmith as good or evil for how the sword is used. My knowledge has neither harmed nor deceived anyone. But see the fruits of my labors and consider your own teachings – 'A tree is known by its fruit,' and 'A house divided against itself cannot stand.'"

Cadfan couldn't help but be impressed. Merlin's charisma was undeniable, his intellect disarming. Yet, as a man of faith, he knew the allure of such charm could be a cunning veil for deception. He found himself struggling internally to remain objective. But glancing at Dubric, who was clearly taken with the man, Cadfan resolved to steel himself for further scrutiny. "But what of your ageless appearance?" he pressed further. "Knowledge alone cannot grant a man eternal youth."

Merlin seemed taken aback to Cadfan, and turned to Dubric, his expression one of apparent confusion, "What is he talking about?"

"King Uthyr once shared a story of meeting you – or a man very much like you – when he was a boy," Dubric explained. "But that was ten years ago."

A smile broke across Merlin's face that seemed out of place to Dubric considering the solemnity of the conversation, "Ah, now I understand. Dubric, your companion is quite perceptive, catching a detail that escaped even you."

Turning back to Cadfan, he continued, "Indeed, we met when he was a boy. But that is more difficult to explain and has to do with knowledge that even I fail to understand properly. Yet still, it is not magic. Let it be enough to say that I slept in a certain cave by the sea for a night and awoke to find that the boy I had met the previous day – and the world around him – had aged ten years while I slept."

The skepticism on Cadfan's face must've been apparent because Merlin shook his head, adding in a conciliatory tone, "Okay, yes, even I must admit it was like some tale of the fae that the locals tell their children by the fire. But it was not my doing. Still…it is the truth."

Seeing lingering doubt on Cadfan's face, Merlin added, "No doubt the king's tale included my 'magic fire box'?" A sardonic smile played on his lips as he continued, "Those were his words, not mine. I have heard the whispers in town as well. The young man has a vivid imagination and I do not doubt that I left a strong impression. Combine those with a touch of mystery and…" Merlin trailed off for dramatic effect, then swept into a low bow, extending one arm theatrically. As he straightened, he revealed an identical box cradled in his other hand, from which a small flame danced. "…'magic', or so the tale might grow in the telling."

As Cadfan recoiled in alarm, Merlin regarded the taller man with a trace of irritation. "Do not behave like a child, Cadfan. This flame can no more hurt you than any other." Snapping the lid of the box shut, he passed it to Dubric, who accepted it with eager hands, ready to demonstrate its workings to Cadfan as Merlin elucidated, "In my land, this…box…is called a Zippo. Blacksmiths from my land have great skill with crafting things from metal. The box is filled with something very much like lamp oil. Tiny amounts of flint and steel built into the box light the oil as Dubric turns the wheel with his thumb."

"Astonishing!" Cadfan exclaimed as he leaned in to examine the box more closely.

"My apologies, but I do not know that word. Even my knowledge has limits," Merlin replied, looking puzzled.

Dubric chimed in to assist, addressing Cadfan, "Merlin is still learning our tongue." Turning to Merlin, he clarified, "'Astonishing' means amazed and impressed." He pantomimed strong emotion on his face, prompting a nod of understanding from Merlin.

"You see knowledge at work for good here, Cadfan – the easiest of my powers to show. The rest? It is mine to share when and where I choose," Merlin said, reaching out to retrieve the device from Dubric.

Cadfan nodded thoughtfully, then remarked with a hint of sagacity, "As you say, Merlin. But surely you understand that with great power comes great responsibility."

At this, Merlin burst into uproarious laughter, the sound echoing through the square and causing bystanders to stop and turn in curiosity. Cadfan, looking bewildered, asked, "What amuses you so?"

Regaining his composure, Merlin shared with a hint of nostalgia, "In my own land, a famous storyteller told a tale of a boy who gained the powers of a spider. This very wisdom was imparted to him. It seems true wisdom knows no bounds of time or place."

Cadfan was indeed impressed and stepped back to appraise Merlin through a more discerning eye. The strange clothing, the staff, the shoes – all he had seen thus far could be explained away with exceptional craftsmanship. Without even realizing it, the apprehension and fear he had felt upon meeting this man was suddenly replaced by curiosity. Gesturing to the cistern, he asked Merlin, "So, what knowledge do you employ here?"

"Now that is a question worth answering!" Merlin exclaimed. He led the priests to the cistern, explaining how the cistern cleans the water. At Merlin's prompting, the workers poured brown, murky water from the well into the cistern. Soon, clean water trickled from the lower side, eliciting a cheer from onlookers. Merlin tasted it, approvingly nodded to the workers, and congratulated them, reinforcing the crowd's enthusiasm. Cadfan hadn't noticed before, but several of the denizens in the square carried buckets or clay jars, and were now lining up to retrieve water from the cistern as the men continued to pour water into it from the well.

"When I came here, I saw the town was afflicted with sickness. Even so, some households were affected while others were spared," Merlin explained. "As I began to question people in homes, both sick and healthy, I determined the source of the illness – bad water pulled from this well by those in homes struck by sickness, while those drinking from the river remained healthy."

"So, the well is poisoned?" Cadfan asked.

"Not exactly," Merlin replied, shaking his head. "The world has creatures both great and small, yes? Name the smallest creature you can think of."

"I suppose, a fly," Cadfan replied.

Merlin nodded, "Even smaller are the fleas that infest an animal. Smaller still are the tiny bugs that make one's head itch."

Cadfan nodded, a memory flickering across his face. "Lice, yes. I once had to shave my head and boil my clothes to rid myself of them." Merlin repeated the word for 'lice', nodding as if etching it into his memory.

"But there are creatures even smaller than that," Merlin continued, his hands gesturing as if to conjure these unseen beings. "So small, in fact, that you cannot see them with your eyes. For them, a grain of sand is as vast as a town. These tiny creatures swim around in the water, and if they get inside you, they make you sick like the people in town – much like a dog with too many fleas."

Cadfan's brows furrowed as he tried to envision such minuscule creatures. He watched Merlin point to the brown water, then to the clear water emerging from the cistern, illustrating his point.

"Boiling the water kills these creatures, just as it kills lice. But the unpleasant taste and smell remains." Pointing to the cistern, he added, "The sand, gravel, and charcoal act as a sieve, pulling the creatures and the bad taste and smell from the water." He gestured towards a blue raindrop painted over a nearby lintel. "You saw the blue raindrop painted over doors in town?"

Thinking back, Cadfan recalled the blue raindrops and nodded, to which Merlin replied, "As I visited each home of the sick, I gave the same advice: 'boil the water before you drink it.' When I determined the source of the bad water, I added to that advice: 'Avoid well water and get your water from the river.' As the sick recovered, I told them the king had ordered their lintels be painted with the raindrop to show the water in their home was clean."

Cadfan looked at the lintel, then back at Merlin. A new understanding dawned on him, mixing awe with a trace of disbelief. "Incredible," he murmured, his eyes reflecting a newfound respect for Merlin's wisdom. "The king is going to want to hear of this," he added.

Merlin smiled and responded, "I have my own reasons for seeking the king out. But Dubric and I arrived to find you and he were still gone, so I have had to wait."

"Yes, Dubric mentioned before that you were awaiting a ship to Glouvum," Cadfan replied. "Why do you seek the king?"

Merlin's shoulders lifted in a casual shrug, a gesture that seemed to carry the weight of his predicament. "I was…marooned…in this land when I met Uthyr," he began, his eyes briefly drifting away as if recalling the memory. His gaze returned to Cadfan, carrying a reflective quality. "Even as a boy, Uthyr was both kind and curious, brave, and unafraid of my strange appearance. Well…strange to him, in any case." As he spoke, a faint smile flickered across Merlin's face, hinting at a fond remembrance of the young Uthyr.

He paused for a moment, his expression turning more serious, almost pensive. "So, I sought him in hopes he could help me return home." As Merlin spoke of his desire to return home, his hand briefly touched his chest. To Cadfan, it seemed like an involuntary gesture, perhaps reflecting a deep–seated yearning or an act of cradling a cherished hidden keepsake. "He was a boy then," he continued, his voice tinged with a mix of wonder and wistfulness. Merlin's eyes seemed to gaze into the distance, as if visualizing the past. "I discovered later the strange effects of the sea cave and that the boy had become both man and king while I slept." There was a touch of disbelief in his tone, as though he still found the passage of time hard to grasp.

Cadfan, his brow furrowed in contemplation, finally spoke, his voice tinged with curiosity. "Something you said earlier. You spoke of the teachings I share. You know of the teachings of Jesus?"

"Indeed," Merlin replied, his voice carrying a note of respect. "Even in my distant land, his words echo with wisdom. 'Do unto others as you would have them do unto you,' is a principle that crosses many borders."

A spark of intrigue lit Cadfan's eyes, and he gestured towards the path that wound its way to the stronghold, his robes sweeping the ground with his movement. "Let us make our way to Uthyr's keep," he suggested, a hint of eagerness in his tone. "Along the way, we may discuss these teachings further."

As they walked, the path unfurled before them, bordered by the verdant hues of the Welsh countryside. Dubric and Cadfan shared with Merlin their struggles to have Uthyr become a follower. Merlin chortled, his laughter echoing softly in the air. "My reputation may have traveled before me on the whispers of the wind. But that does not give me the power to influence a man I only met once as a boy ten years ago. Why do you come to me with this?"

"Based on my brief encounter with the king," Cadfan explained, his gaze steady and thoughtful, "you may have a great deal more influence than you think." At this, Dubric nodded in agreement, adding, "He speaks the truth, Merlin."

Merlin appeared to contemplate the ground before him as they walked, the gravel crunching softly under their feet. After a moment of silence, he finally spoke, his voice laced with a hint of solemnity. "I will lend what measure I can, Cadfan. But convincing a man to follow your faith, though perhaps a wise decision, is not within my powers any more than your initial concern that I possessed the power to turn men to evil. Neither is the case."

The trio continued their journey, the gentle rustle of leaves and distant bird calls accompanying their thoughtful conversation. The dialogue between them weaved through the complexities of faith, belief, and influence as they continued on toward the king's stronghold.

Eventually, their path led them to the front of the stronghold, where large, heavy timber doors, bound in iron stood open to allow entry. To either side though, guards clad in mail eyed the trio with a mix of recognition and suspicion, their presence bearing witness that casual entrance would not be permitted. Cadfan and Dubric, in their priestly garb, earned nods of acknowledgment, but Merlin's peculiar attire and air drew their caution.

Cadfan looked on as Merlin stepped forward, an impish grin slicing through his otherwise inscrutable features. "I seek an audience with Uthyr. Announce that the great and powerful Ma'erlyn has come to reclaim his magic fire box," he declared, his voice dancing with mischief.

Recalling his own previous interactions with the dismissive guards when trying to seek an audience with Uthyr, Cadfan was shocked as Merlin quipped, "And tell him to make haste, else he may find himself giving birth to a cow!" That Merlin's reputation had even reached the guards beforehand was apparent. His claim sent a ripple of shock through them as they wasted no time in dispatching a runner. The young man's feet pounded the cobblestones as he disappeared into the depths of the fortress with orders to be swift.

Shocked themselves, Cadfan and Dubric exchanged a glance of disbelief, their previous discussions forgotten as they both protested, "But you claimed to have no knowledge of sorcery!"

Merlin turned to the priests, his mirth barely contained. "I do not," he murmured to them furtively. "Among my people, it is but a jest to say someone making much of a trivial matter is giving birth to a cow." Then, his expression straightening, he added, "Perhaps you are right though," he added in contemplation. "Caution should have guided my tongue more so than humor – Uthyr has not seen me for ten years."

Before the priests could reply, a commotion erupted from within the keep's walls. The sound of hurried steps and clanging armor preceded the sight of Uthyr, barreling through the inner sanctum and across the courtyard. His face, a canvas of surprise and incredulity, was a stark contrast to the composed guards. Stopping short at the open gates, his breath heavy with haste and his eyes wide, he managed only a single word, "Ma'erlyn!"

Merlin's response was warm, his tone carrying both fondness and a tinge of respect, "Uthyr. It warms my heart to see you. It appears that bravery and ambition have served you well since our paths last crossed."

CHAPTER 12

Alliances

Marilyn observed Uthyr closely, noting the transition from boy to man and king in his stance and gaze, the lines of youth shed for the broad shoulders and stern visage of a king. He had grown into his authority, yet his eyes still held a spark of the inquisitive boy she remembered. Still sharp, his eyes missed nothing as they appraised her in return. She decided he was handsome in a rugged way, if a bit too hairy of face to suit her tastes in men.

Standing before the large open doors, his guards changed their posture to defend him, misreading the disbelief on his face. Marilyn was not surprised at his reaction or theirs. He had not seen her in ten years after all. Perhaps, she considered, it was her nearly unchanged appearance. In the time she had last seen him, little more than a month had gone by for her. The guards' armor clanked as they exchanged wary glances, their postures tense. One guard, without taking his eyes off her, cast a warning over his shoulder to his king, "Sire, be careful! This sorcerer threatened to use his magicks on you!"

"Peace, men!" Uthyr proclaimed. "Ma'erlyn is a friend." Though still uncertain, the guards obediently relaxed their stances and resumed their posts. "Ma'erlyn," Uthyr repeated, his voice, though tinged with disbelief, carried a familiarity and warmth that mitigated any remaining tension. His eyes, a mix of youthful fire and kingly scrutiny, swept over her, as if questioning his sight. "I thought never to see you again," he confessed. "And you have not aged a day from my memory of you! How can that be after ten years?"

"That is a tale not to be told standing out here at your gate, Uthyr," Marilyn responded with a smile, her tone light yet pointed. "Or should I say 'King Uthyr' now?" Her eyebrow arched sardonically, her gaze drifting momentarily over the keep's sturdy walls.

"This…yes…well…," Uthyr stuttered, momentarily at a loss for words. He composed himself and then gestured toward the inner courtyard. "Come. Let us talk inside," he managed, his voice regaining its steadiness. As he turned to lead the way, Marilyn noted the lingering traces of the boy in the man before her, recalling their first meeting and the unspoken, almost arrogant assumption in his departure – a silent expectation that he would be followed without question.

As she stepped past the guards to either side of the gate, Father Cadfan and Brother Dubric followed, moving with a deference that spoke of their many journeys to courts less welcoming than this. Marilyn noticed the guards' reactions; their faces were a mix of duty–bound resolve and uneasy curiosity. They seemed caught between the instinct to protect their king and a wary hesitance, as if standing too close would scourge their soul as surely as flame scorches flesh.

Once within the courtyard, a chorus of everyday sounds greeted Marilyn, echoing faintly the robust life within Uthyr's realm. The air was ripe with the scent of earth and woodsmoke, a fragrance that teased the edges of Marilyn's senses with a stark reminder of the passage of time. In the corner of her eye, she caught the sight of the young runner who had dashed off earlier, now peeking from behind a stone column, his eyes wide with a mixture of awe and apprehension. Marilyn couldn't help but grin at his reaction, musing internally on how reputation indeed wielded its own form of power, shaping perceptions even before one uttered a word.

The courtyard itself was alive with the stronghold's pulse; the steady beat of the blacksmith's hammer spoke of enduring strength, while the soft murmur of servants and the occasional snort from stabled horses wove together into a tapestry of ordered industry. Marilyn's eyes briefly flitted over these vignettes of vitality, acknowledging the prosperity that Uthyr had fostered.

Off to one side, men practiced their martial skills with wooden swords, the clacking, grunting, and banter triggered a pang of nostalgia in Marilyn, a momentary homesickness as she recalled similar practice in her own military training. Pushing aside the sentiment, she followed Uthyr across the courtyard to the inner sanctum.

Entering the great hall, Uthyr led them towards a long, sturdy oak table at the end, their footsteps echoing off the smooth marble floor. The hall boasted a high, vaulted ceiling, reaching some twenty feet, adorned with a blend of Celtic and Romanesque motifs. The walls, stark yet imposing, were intermittently broken by narrow, high–set slit windows, positioned well above eye level. These windows, barred and slim, were designed more for letting in daylight than for providing views, ensuring the keep's security.

Marilyn's gaze lingered on the interplay of light and shadow cast by these slits, creating patterns on the stone floor. A few wall sconces flickered gently, their light dancing over the austere stone walls. In the center of the ceiling, a grand chandelier made of interwoven antlers added a touch of rustic grandeur to the otherwise unadorned hall.

'Typical of a man not to decorate,' she thought with a wry smile, observing the room's utilitarian character.

Chairs were the first to arrive and the group settled about the table, with Marilyn and the priests on one side and Uthyr on the other, as other servants brought food and drink. Noticing the drink wine and not water, Marilyn turned to Uthyr, concerned about consuming alcohol while pregnant. "Can you ask them to mull my wine please? I do not usually drink."

Uthyr gave her a questioning look, then nodded to one of the servants without saying a word. She watched him during the exchange. Though a young man, he exuded an aura of command that would have named him king even without the simple brass crown on his brow. Yet, beneath that kingly demeanor, the inquisitive boy she had once met still lingered.

Marilyn wasn't sure how to begin. She had gone to great lengths to find this man, and now, words eluded her. Shaking her head at her own bemusement, she parted her lips to speak, but Uthyr was quicker.

"Ma'erlyn, I looked for you, you know; after you ran off," Uthyr said, a note of speculative interrogation coloring his words. "Where did you go?"

Marilyn raised an eyebrow, a playful spark in her eyes. "Do not take that tone with me, young man!" she chided, feigning indignation. She watched with amusement as the priests accompanying her widened their eyes in shock, their expressions of disbelief matching the drop of their jaws. No one, she surmised, had spoken to him quite so candidly for some time.

She held Uthyr's gaze, noticing the unfamiliar blush of humility on his face – likely a rare sight for those accustomed to dealing with him. Then, in an abrupt shift, amusement took hold of Uthyr as he laughed heartily, a clear note of respect underlying the gesture. His laughter was rich and surprising, a remnant of his less regal days.

"And just call me Merlin, please," she continued, maintaining her stern façade only for a moment longer before allowing a hint of a smile to form.

As the name 'Merlin' left her lips, a moment of realization dawned in Uthyr's eyes. The laughter faded into a thoughtful silence as he pieced together the puzzle. His gaze lingered on her, a mix of wonder and comprehension. "Merlin..." he murmured to himself, the gears turning in his mind. "The healer, the sage, the mystic… all these tales, all these whispers milling about my kingdom… it was you, all along?"

Marilyn nodded slightly, an enigmatic smile playing on her lips, allowing Uthyr to absorb the magnitude of his discovery. The myths and rumors that had woven their way through his realm had found their source in her – a truth more extraordinary than any legend.

Caught off guard, Uthyr's laughter subsided into a warm grin. He slapped his hand on the table in a rare display of unguarded mirth. "Yes, of course, forgive me… Merlin," he said, the realization still fresh in his expression. The tension in the room dissolved, replaced by a newfound understanding as Marilyn found herself sitting not just across from a king, but across from someone who had been the boy before the crown, grown into the man he was today.

As if to excuse his previously stern and suspicious behavior, Uthyr swept his hand, encompassing the grandeur of his hall. "One may only become king in this land by making many friends and allies," he said, settling back into his chair. His demeanor shifted to a more solemn tone as he lifted his wine. "And perhaps just as many enemies. A man may guard against the knives at his throat. But it is the dagger in his back that is a king's undoing."

"Et tu, Bruté?" Marilyn shot back with a smirk.

Cadfan and Dubric, unable to hold back their surprise, burst out simultaneously, "You know Latin, Merlin?!"

A chuckle escaped her. "Not really, no – just a few well–known sayings. That one is from a tale told by a famous bard in my land, about a king betrayed by his closest friend."

"You have mastered our language though admirably it seems," Uthyr interjected, recalling their past. "There was much hand–waving and pointing when we first met, as I recall."

Marilyn leaned back, her gaze steady and inscrutable. "Do not pretend to know me, Uthyr, nor of what I am capable, considering how little you truly know of what powers I possess," she replied, her voice edged with a subtle challenge. She watched Uthyr closely, noting the subtle changes in his expression. A flicker of surprise crossed his face, quickly followed by a look that hinted at curiosity. To Marilyn, it seemed as if Uthyr was beginning to understand that there was much more to her – to Merlin – than he had initially thought.

She didn't like having to manipulate him as she was, no matter how subtle or benign her intentions. But as her words hung in the air, Marilyn's mind briefly revisited a pivotal conversation with Ayesha. It was Ayesha who had first counseled her on the necessity of adopting the Merlin persona, a mantle of mystery and wisdom, in a world where being a woman could mean vulnerability and disregard. This was not just about survival; it was about gaining respect and maintaining authority in a land where her true identity might undermine her mission.

Uthyr was a king, and, like it or not, she needed his aid. However, she could not rely solely on goodwill to secure it. So, if playing the role of someone aloof and powerful was what it took to obtain his help, then that was the role she would embrace.

Uthyr's curiosity was evident as he leaned forward, his arms upon the table. "You are right of course, Merlin. The Fae are a mystery to me and you are the only one of their kind I have met. Before that fateful day, I had thought them children's tales told to teach lessons or scare a lass to snuggle a little closer by the evening fire," he remarked, a hint of wonder in his eyes.

Marilyn cocked her head, the edges of her mouth curling into a knowing smirk. "I am no magical creature Uthyr. I am as human as you. Though, I would ask that you keep that knowledge to yourself. Such a reputation offers its advantages," she confessed, allowing a full smile to show.

Uthyr studied her with narrowed eyes, skepticism threading his tone. "Such claims from one who seems untouched by time," he countered, an eyebrow raised.

Shaking her head in bemusement, Marilyn replied, "I will need to tell you my tale to convince you otherwise, Uthyr."

Acknowledging her response with a nod, Uthyr straightened, his curiosity now clearly outweighing any prior suspicion. "Yes, that brings me back to my first question, Merlin. Where did you go? What happened to you?"

"For leaving you so abruptly, I owe you an apology, Uthyr. But it is also why I sought you out," Marilyn began, her voice measured. "Ten years ago, I found myself marooned here in your land. I did not know where I was until you began drawing a map in the dirt. Do you remember?"

As the meal progressed, Marilyn narrated the beginnings of her tale with calculated vagueness. She spoke of being marooned yet omitted how; she mentioned her initial panic upon discovering her whereabouts but offered no explanation why. The only detail she explicitly shared – already known to the priests – was the time lapse she experienced in the sea cave and her shock at finding a decade had passed overnight.

The conversation naturally drifted to the rumors about her travels. Marilyn played her part skillfully, oscillating between stoicism and enigma, letting the priests and Uthyr piece together what they had heard, only smiling and nodding in response to their queries.

When Cadfan brought up his observations of Merlin's efforts in town, the topic of her Zippo inevitably surfaced. Marilyn cut him off with a stern look, "Yes, that reminds me, Uthyr – I would like my fire box back, please." Her gaze was expectant as Uthyr produced the pouch containing the Zippo, revealing it as his 'luck charm.' She swiftly reclaimed it, offering no explanation to the group like she had with the priests, her expression stern and lips pressed together in silent warning not to brooch that topic further.

Resuming the tale, Cadfan recounted how Merlin's efforts seemed to have halted the impending plague. The conversation culminated with Cadfan's abrupt interjection, "And now the bargain is met, is it not, Uthyr?"

Uthyr's expression clouded with suspicion. "What bargain?"

"Dubric and I stood in this very room when you promised allegiance to our God and our faith if, by His grace, your people were healed!" Cadfan explained. "It may not have been by the snap of His finger as you demanded, but faith seldom works on command. Still, in bringing Merlin to this place while we were at the parley, Brother Dubric brought about the means by which it was accomplished. So, by my reckoning, the bargain is met."

A stormy expression crossed Uthyr's brow as he stared at the priests for a moment. "Cadfan, I have grown to like and respect you over these past days. Do not spoil that by bending the truth to serve your cause," he replied staunchly.

"But…" Dubric started, only to be silenced by Uthyr's commanding gesture, his expression stern.

"Do not twist the facts!" Uthyr chided. "To begin, I never promised fealty – only a willingness to believe your god even exists! Secondly, the recovery of my people was due to Merlin's efforts, not your god's intervention. And by his own account, Merlin would have arrived here eventually and helped whether or not you found him, Brother Dubric."

Though Marilyn was impressed by Uthyr's surprising pragmatism, she felt a pang of sympathy for the priests. "Do not be so hasty to dismiss faith, Uthyr," she interjected, her voice carrying a note of sincerity. She remembered her vow to aid them in his conversion if she could and saw this as a moment to subtly influence Uthyr's thinking. "It can give hope when all seems hopeless and drives men to accomplish incredible things for the sake of a belief."

Uthyr looked at her, startled. "Merlin? You share their belief?"

Marilyn paused, considering her response. "I do… I did even before I met Cadfan and Dubric," she confirmed thoughtfully. "The wisdom they share has echoes even in my homeland." It was a delicate dance of words, a blend of truth and the persona she had cultivated.

Uthyr sat back, pondering her words. "I will have to give this matter more thought then," he finally conceded. "Perhaps I have been hasty to dismiss such concerns after all."

A look of unspoken gratitude passed between them as Marilyn glanced at the priests, her eyes conveying a silent message of support and understanding.

Returning to the topic of her tale, Uthyr finally asked, "But why are you here now, Merlin? Surely, you could have found a ship to carry you home by now?"

"I said I was marooned here, Uthyr. I never claimed I arrived by ship," Marilyn replied, her voice low, letting her words linger in the air for dramatic effect.

Uthyr furrowed his brow in confusion. "I do not understand. If not by ship, then how?"

'The moment of truth,' she thought pensively. 'You've come this far, Marilyn - time to take your shot.' She stared into the flames of the large stone hearth against the wall behind the long table as she considered her next words. Despite the warmth that it fed into the room, she suddenly felt cold.

Marilyn rose from her seat, gripping her staff. The tap of its end against the stone floor echoed through the grand chamber, a stark contrast to the sudden silence that had fallen over her audience. She stood before the hearth, silently considering her next words as she stared into its crackling fire. Then, as though uttering a sacred oath, she spoke into its flickering light. "This secret must never leave this room," she said quietly, her voice barely more than the whisper of the flames licking the embers.

She turned to Uthyr, her eyes meeting his with a mix of determination and vulnerability. "Because I need your help, I must trust you are an honorable man, Uthyr. But you two…" Her gaze shifted to the priests, steely and unwavering. "Swear on your faith to hold my confidence or leave us."

Marilyn watched as Cadfan and Dubric exchanged guarded looks. Curiosity seemed to win out over whatever lingering fear and suspicion either might have as they nodded to each other and made oaths to keep her confidence.

Satisfied, Marilyn continued, committing to her course of action. "If it is not already clear, I am not from this place…"

Soft chuckles filled the room at her statement of the obvious, but ceased abruptly as Marilyn activated her shock staff. The glow and hum of its tip intensified the dramatic effect. "I am not from this world," she added.

"By all the gods!" Uthyr stammered, echoed by Dubric's exclamation, "By the one true God!" Cadfan sat pale-faced and stunned, staring at the staff before mumbling breathlessly, "Sorcery!"

Marilyn grinned at him, bemused. 'Avery was right,' she thought. 'To these people, science really is like magic.'

"The more you speak, the more stories from my grandmother come to life, Merlin!" Uthyr said in wonder. "Are you sure you are not of the Fae?"

Marilyn considered his question. 'Perhaps it's best not to disabuse him of the notion,' she thought. "If it helps you to believe so, Uthyr," she said, "then let it be so."

She waited as their expressions settled, seeing curiosity slowly replace the stunned shock on all their faces. But before the inevitable questions could rise to their lips, she continued, "I arrived here by…a door – in the same sea cave I spoke of earlier – entirely by chance."

The men's eyes widened, reflecting a mix of astonishment and disbelief, the shock of her second revelation perhaps nearly equal to the first. 'And the hits just keep on coming,' she thought, a wry smile playing on her lips.

"Yes, that is why I needed your oaths," Marilyn confirmed their unspoken thoughts.

Finally breaking the silence, Uthyr asked, "Can you not simply return to your realm through this door? Why seek my help? What aid could I possibly offer one of the Fae!?"

"The door on this side is set wrong, Uthyr. For lack of a better explanation, it is stuck by the rocks in the sea cave," she explained. "I require men with mining tools to free the door from the rock's embrace so that I may open it and go back to where I belong."

Uthyr's voice bore the weight of his kingship, each word laced with a weariness that seemed too heavy for one man. "I wish I could help you, Merlin. After all you have done… But my men are stretched thin as it is. I only returned to Glouvum to give over governorship of the town to my steward and move my house to Execaer. Troubles there demand my attention."

Marilyn's eyes, sharp and assessing, locked onto Uthyr's. "What troubles would draw a king from his stronghold, Uthyr? If I can find a way to ease your burdens, could you then spare the aid I require?"

Unexpectedly, it was Cadfan that interjected. "The southern shores are under threat from Frankish raiders turned pirates. The king must bolster defenses to protect the people and the land."

Uthyr nodded grimly, his gaze distant as if picturing the coast and its dangers. "And that is only part of it. I sought an alliance with Gorloys of Cornwall, hoping for a united front. But that meeting… it was a disaster. The man is as stubborn as he is treacherous. Rather than offer aid, he is as likely to take advantage of any weakness in my ranks for his own gain."

Marilyn tilted her head, a thoughtful glimmer in her eyes. "Men often resist the yoke when force is the method of persuasion, Uthyr."

Cadfan interjected with a rueful shake of his head. "Uthyr's description of Gorloys is generous. I witnessed the parley and its aftermath, which was indeed a disaster." Shifting his gaze to Uthyr, he added with a wry grin, "Though the king could learn a few lessons in not baiting a man who is overly prideful, he approached with respect and diplomacy, not force." Uthyr blushed at the apparently private jibe Marilyn did not understand, as Cadfan continued, "Gorloys responded only with scorn. He is a man who knows only the language of power and fear."

Uthyr's blush faded as he contemplated Cadfan's words, the earlier embarrassment subsumed by the gravity of the situation.

Marilyn began to pace back and forth in front of the hearth, her staff clicking on the stones as her mind began working through the complex weave of problems, politics, and pride. "Were this a battlefield, I could offer guidance in defeating your enemy, Uthyr. But that is not the case, so I cannot aid you against the Franks," she conceded. "But Gorloys… perhaps I can find a way to bend him to your will. I need time to think on it though – I will not help you to kill him though. War and bloodshed are the paths of other men, not mine. If I journey with you to this Execaer and find a solution, will you pledge your support in freeing my door?"

"I am a man of ymarferoldeb, Merlin," Uthyr began, his voice firm. "You seek my aid to return to your realm, and I seek the unity of mine. Gorloys is a thorn in my side – a thorn that must be removed or turned to point against my enemies. Either way, if you can accomplish it, then you have my word as king – you will have your men and tools."

Marilyn paused and turned to Dubric, her expression inquisitive. "Ymarferoldeb? What is this word?"

Dubric, seeing her confusion, explained in more straightforward terms, "It means making decisions based on what is possible and achievable, rather than on one's hopes and desires." Nodding in understanding, Marilyn internally translated, 'Ah…pragmatism…' she thought.

"So be it," Marilyn declared, accepting Uthyr's terms. But as she spoke, worry at finding a solution plagued her mind. "My knowledge for your strength. I will find a way to bring Gorloys to heel," she added with determined resolve, even as the challenge of the task loomed in her thoughts.

Cadfan then spoke up, "Sire, I am weary of travel and intend to remain here. But if you will allow it, I want the church to continue to be a part of these matters, offering aid where it can, and prayer for divine intercession when needed. I would ask that you allow Brother Dubric to accompany you for that support."

Dubric seemed surprised by the sudden request, or so it seemed to Marilyn. But she had gotten to know the man on their journey from Moridunum, as well as their time together in Glouvum since then. Glad to have a familiar friend along, she voiced her pleasure at the notion, and Uthyr, lacking any particular reason to deny the request, acceded.

As the first light of dawn painted the sky in hues of orange and pink, Marilyn set off with Uthyr and his entourage. The men were rugged, their faces weathered by wind and sun, a stark contrast to the polished knights of her anachronistic fantasies. Their armor, though functional, was far from the gleaming suits of steel she had imagined; instead, it was a patchwork of leather and metal, worn and dented from use. The horses, sturdy and unadorned, bore none of the regal trappings she had seen in storybooks.

Uthyr himself rode at the head, his presence commanding yet devoid of any ostentatious display. He wore a simple tunic and trousers, his sword hanging at his side the only hint of his status. The crown she had seen him wear in the great hall was nowhere in sight, replaced by a practical helmet.

As they rode through the gates of Glouvum, Marilyn couldn't help but compare this reality to the tales she had grown up with. In her world, kings and knights were figures of grandeur, shrouded in romance and mystique. Here, however, they were men of practicality and necessity, their lives and roles dictated by the harsh demands of their time.

Even the weapons carried by Uthyr's men were a testament to this reality. Swords and axes were well-used, their blades nicked from battles past. Bows slung over shoulders and quivers of arrows at their sides spoke of readiness for conflict, a constant companion in this age.

Marilyn mused on these observations, her mind contrasting the romanticized images of her time with the gritty reality of this one. It was a world stripped of glamour, where survival and duty reigned supreme. She felt a pang of respect for these men and their unadorned valor, a stark reminder of the differences between her world and the one she now found herself in.

By midday, their path had led them through a bustling settlement. Marilyn suspected that this little village, now known simply as Abona, would someday grow into the city she knew as Bristol, though she lacked the convenience of GPS to confirm her suspicions. The location just south and west of Glouvum seemed about right though. As they rode through Abona, Marilyn observed Uthyr's interactions with the villagers, noting a remarkable lack of the arrogance she might have expected from a king.

As they passed through the center of the village near the edge of a wide river, they were met by the village alderman. Uthyr greeted him with the warmth and familiarity of an old friend. "How fares your family, Eilif?" Uthyr inquired, his tone genuine and devoid of formality. The alderman, a man of middle years with a weathered face, responded with a bright smile, updating Uthyr on the village's well-being and the recent harvest.

Uthyr sent his men off to mingle among the stalls in the village market, their eyes drawn to the vibrant array of fruits and goods on display, as he continued to talk of things with Eilif and introduced Merlin and Dubric. Uthyr seemed to take mischievous delight in introducing her. Still wearing her camouflage field dress, she stuck out amongst the locals and he was taking advantage of the fact to her chagrin. Finally exasperated, she muttered "How would you like to puke toads for a night, Uthyr?" eliciting a mirthful guffaw from Dubric as her query was met with round-eyed silence. Afterward, he took a more respectful approach when introducing her if he mentioned her at all, which suited her fine.

Once done with the alderman, Uthyr joined his men at the village market. Despite being offered fruit for free as a gesture of respect, Uthyr insisted on paying. "No, let the coin flow as it should," he said firmly but kindly to the vendor who had tried to refuse payment. "Your labor is worth its reward." His men followed his example, exchanging fair coin for the produce they desired.

Marilyn watched this exchange with a growing respect for Uthyr. His sincerity and lack of pretension were refreshing, a stark contrast to the tales of kings and their courts she had grown up with. In this moment, Uthyr was more than a king; he was a man deeply connected to his land and his people, understanding the value of mutual respect and the importance of supporting the local community.

This small window into Uthyr's character deepened Marilyn's appreciation of the man leading them. It was clear that his strength as a ruler lay not just in his ability to lead in battle, but in his genuine care for his people, a trait that would surely be crucial in the challenges that lay ahead.

As they left Abona, the journey took them through a tapestry of verdant landscapes, untouched by the march of time. Rolling hills stretched out like emerald waves, interspersed with clusters of dense woodland and meandering streams. Marilyn found herself captivated by the unspoiled beauty, so different from the future she knew, where mankind's relentless mark of deforestation had scarred much of the land.

As they passed through other villages and sleepy hamlets, scenes of rustic life unfolded before her. Thatched cottages huddled together, their gardens abloom with a myriad of colors. Villagers paused in their daily chores, their gazes following the small entourage with a mix of curiosity and caution. Children playing in the fields would stop and stare, their games momentarily forgotten.

The simplicity of these scenes belied the complex nature of life in this time. Here, life moved at a slower pace, dictated by the rhythms of nature rather than the ticking of a clock. It was a world far removed from the hustle and bustle of her own time, where the constant noise of progress drowned out such tranquil serenity.

Marilyn reflected on this contrast, the tranquility of the journey offering a momentary respite from the weight of her task. She thought about the trips she had taken between Gloucester and Bristol in her own time, where the land bore the evident scars of human intervention. Here, however, the landscape was a living painting of nature's unbridled splendor, a reminder of what the world once was before humanity's heavy hand reshaped it.

Occasionally, their path would wind along a dry run through a marshy landscape, the reeds swaying gently in the breeze. It was during one of these moments, amidst the peaceful isolation of the marshlands, that Marilyn's pregnancy pressed upon her with an urgent need. Politely excusing herself, she rode a short distance from the party to find privacy amongst the reeds near the water's edge.

The marsh itself was a serene expanse, a symphony of nature's quiet whispers. The soft rustle of reeds swaying in the gentle breeze, the distant croaking of frogs, and the occasional splash of a startled fish created a backdrop of natural sounds. Marilyn dismounted, her movements careful as she navigated the spongy, uneven ground near the water's edge.

As she crouched down to relieve herself, the unstable footing beneath her shifted suddenly. Instinctively, she reached out, grasping at a clump of reeds to steady herself. In her haste, she pulled too hard, and several reeds snapped, their hollow interiors revealed as they came away in her hand.

For a brief moment, she stared at the broken reeds, her initial annoyance giving way to curiosity. She examined the hollow tubes, turning them over in her hands. The texture, the strength, and most importantly, the hollowness of the reeds sparked a sudden insight. Her eyes widened as the seeds of an idea formed, a plan that could turn the tide in their favor against Gorloys.

A smile slowly crept across Marilyn's face, her mind racing with the possibilities now unfurling before her. It was a simple, yet potentially ingenious solution, hidden in plain sight within these unassuming plants of the marsh.

Regaining her composure, she finished her business and stood, still clutching the snapped reeds. She looked back towards where Uthyr and his men waited, a new determination lighting her eyes. This unexpected discovery, born from a moment of vulnerability, could be the very key she needed in her quest to bend Gorloys to Uthyr's will.

Rejoining the group, Marilyn carried an air of newfound purpose. She strode towards Uthyr, the snapped reeds still clutched in her hand, her expression a blend of determination and mystery. Uthyr and his men, noticing her approach, turned their attention towards her, a collective sense of curiosity palpable in the air.

"Merlin, is everything all right?" Uthyr asked, his eyes flicking to the reeds in her hand.

"Better than all right," she replied, her lips curling into a secretive smile. "Uthyr, I need you and your men to gather reeds, but not just any." She held up the broken reeds as examples. "They must be large enough for a man's finger to fit inside and as tall as a man's chest," she instructed, her voice laced with an enigmatic undertone.

As Uthyr's brows knitted in confusion, Marilyn shook the reeds at him, her eyes gleaming with excitement. "I may have stumbled upon the key to bending Gorloys' neck!" she exclaimed, her tone implying a breakthrough in their challenging quest.

The men exchanged puzzled glances, intrigued by her unusual request. Uthyr, however, merely nodded, accustomed to her enigmatic ways. "How many do you need?" he inquired, his tone indicating his readiness to comply without understanding the reason.

"As large a bundle as each man can secure behind his saddle as possible. I may not actually need that many, but I have no desire to go hunting for reeds again. So, I would as soon get all I need now and then some," Marilyn responded, her voice firm yet enigmatic.

Uthyr prodded his men into compliance, and they set off to cut and bundle the reeds. They moved with efficiency, yet their faces mirrored their confusion over the purpose of such a task. Marilyn watched them work, her gaze intense and thoughtful. She turned to Dubric, who had been observing the proceedings with a mixture of curiosity and skepticism. "Trust me," she said to him, her eyes twinkling with a mischievous glint. "Sometimes the simplest things hold the greatest power."

Dubric nodded, albeit still puzzled, as Marilyn's gaze returned to the bundles of reeds. She smiled to herself, her mind already weaving the reeds into the fabric of her plan. Her mysterious grin hinted at a strategy forming, a plan that promised to be as unconventional as it was audacious.

As the entourage resumed their journey, Marilyn found herself riding at the rear, her gaze fixed on the bundles of reeds now secured behind each saddle. A mischievous grin played on her lips, the gears of her mind turning with possibilities and plans. Beside her, Dubric rode in quiet contemplation, casting sidelong glances at Marilyn and the reeds, his curiosity unmistakably piqued.

"What are you thinking, Merlin?" Dubric finally ventured, unable to contain his curiosity any longer. "Those reeds… they're not just for show, are they?"

Marilyn turned to him, her eyes twinkling with amusement and secrets untold. "Oh, Dubric," she said, her tone playful yet elusive. "If I told you everything now, where would the fun be in that?"

Dubric sighed, half in frustration and half in admiration, shaking his head at her reticence. "You are full of surprises, Merlin. I just hope this plan of yours works."

"Trust is a two-way street, my friend," Marilyn replied, her gaze returning to the reeds. "Just wait and see. We may yet turn the tide in Uthyr's favor."

CHAPTER 13

Dragon's Breath

The initial awe of Execaer's thrumming vitality had scarcely diminished for Marilyn, even as days turned since her arrival with Uthyr's entourage. The city stood as a testament to the flow of progress, a dynamic heart where the River Exe and the looming fortress, from which the town drew its name, provided both lifeblood and protection to nurture trade and culture.

Gone was the monotonous tranquility of the verdant landscapes and sleepy hamlets; here, the cobbled streets – relics of Roman influence – burst with activity, a stark contrast to the quiet journey that had brought them.

Stone structures, some graced with the patina of bygone Roman grandeur, shouldered against the newer wooden edifices, creating a mosaic of history and ambition. Along the docks, where Marilyn now found herself, the river's embrace harbored a fleet of diverse ships. Their sails and hulls were storied tapestries that spoke of far–off lands and the confluence of distant lives.

The language of commerce here was as varied as the wares on offer, with traders engaging in a cacophony of dialects, haggling over goods that spanned the spectrum of known riches. The air was rich with the scents of brine and fresh catch, mingling with the earthy fragrances of trade: wool, leather, and exotic spices that hinted at the breadth of Execaer's reach.

Within this vibrant sprawl, Marilyn sought the next component of her plan that would enable her to fulfill her promise to Uthyr. She knew her objective and hoped that the port's diverse economy would provide what she sought. With an expectant heart, she let her nose guide her through the bustling tableau laid before her.

After three days scouring Execaer's bustling markets and pungent docks, her perseverance had paid off. A whiff of rotten eggs rose from the river, guiding her toward a secluded vessel tethered away from the main flotilla. As she neared, the stench of sulfur grew overpowering, enveloping the air in its noxious embrace.

She observed the ship's cargo bay wide open, workers bustling within its bowels amidst glowing braziers. The ship was being cleansed, purged of all vermin and potential contagions accumulated during its sea–bound travels. Having gotten her degree in chemistry, as well as her doctorate, sulfur's role in this ritual of purification was well–known to her – a potent disinfectant, albeit one whose fumes relegated the task to the lowest ranks of dock labor.

Wrinkling her nose at the pungent odor, she understood why the ship was kept isolated during the fumigation – an outcast until deemed clean. But to Marilyn, the acrid scent was more than a mere byproduct of nautical hygiene; it was a key component to her plan. As she approached the ship, she saw another crew along the wharf – rat catchers with nets, intent upon collecting the vermin that leapt from the ship to escape the noxious smell and swim ashore.

Fortunately, in Execaer, sulfur was not just a tool for sailors but a traded commodity. Donning a perfumed cloth to try and assuage the smell, she sought out the man who led the ship fumigators. Negotiations ensued, and before long, Marilyn had brokered a deal to procure several pounds of the elemental crystal. With the transaction complete, she accompanied the laborers as they hoisted crates of the precious substance, making their way from the stench of the docks to the security of the fortress.

As Marilyn walked beside the laborers, she pondered the ramifications of what she planned to attempt. In her grasp, the sulfur was not merely a fragment of the earth's depths but a means to an end – part of a desperate plan to fulfill her promise to Uthyr and secure the aid she needed from him. But she was toying with knowledge that would not reach Europe for centuries and worried that her actions might be tantamount to opening Pandora's Box and changing history forever.

It was this worry that prompted her to demand from Uthyr a place to work in private when their entourage arrived at the fortress – a place where she could keep her secrets guarded and locked away from prying eyes, a room to which only she had the key. At the top of a stout lookout tower to the southeast of the main keep. Ostensibly, the tower was meant to keep an eye on the river inlet to provide ample warning in case of coastal raiding parties. But for now, it was her sanctuary.

So, once she arrived at the fortress with the bearers carrying the crates of sulfur, she soon had the crates secured away and whisked the men out of the room the moment each deposited his crate, then locked the door and stowed the key in her backpack. She was not about to give away the secrets of her alchemical knowledge to a sixth century world that wasn't ready for it by being careless.

The next morning was no less equal to the last in bearing the fruits of her endeavor. Amidst the lower quarters of Execaer, amongst the stock yards of animals kept penned for sale or slaughter, away from the bustle of the more populated areas of town, she found what she was looking for. Here, where the animals of the city were kept, their waste was piled high, left to sit and stew in its own natural processes. 'Why the hell does the job of getting the things I need have to smell so damn bad?' she mused.

The mounds were not a place where many would care to linger, but for her, they were a goldmine. Four stablemen, who had been busy with their work, stopped what they were doing and eyed Marilyn with suspicion and a hint of disdain as she approached the dung heaps, first probing them with a stick, then scooping up the white crystalline crust that formed on the surfaces with a spade she'd brought for the purpose.

Marilyn tossed the scoop aside and stood, surveying the work before her. If she attempted the job herself, she would be at the task all day. But worse, Marilyn worried that she might permanently stain her camouflage fatigues. The stains might blend in, but her fastidious nature simply couldn't accept the possibility. 'Besides,' she thought, 'I might never get the smell out!'

Choosing to let the experts handle the matter, she cast her gaze toward the stablemen – to one in particular. She mused at how such men tended to be so easy to spot amongst the work crews at the dregs of society. It was no different the day before with the men at the ship. The man in charge of the crew always cast an air of self-important arrogance – one who expected to be treated with respect regardless of his station in life. He would be the man who cast back a challenging stare that said, 'Who the hell are you to bother us in our work?' while others would simply drop their gaze, ignore your presence, and continue with their labors.

Marilyn walked over to the man she thought lead the crew and pulled eight leather sacks from her backpack where she'd had them neatly folded. Addressing the stableman, who still eyed her with suspicion and curiosity, she held up the bags and a small pouch of coins.

"A day's wages for each of your men and two day's wages for you, for your labor and your silence," she stated firmly, her voice leaving no room for negotiation. "No questions asked. I need this white powder atop the dung heaps collected into these bags." Her tone was authoritative, yet there was an undercurrent of enigma in her request.

The stablemen exchanged glances, the allure of easy coin overcoming their initial hesitance. She was offering a full day's wages for a matter of a few hours of work. They knew it, and she knew that they knew it. 'Money talks,' she mused, grinning inwardly. One by one, the other three looked to their leader waiting to hear the answer they wanted him to speak.

Finally, he nodded and accepted the bags, doling two each out to his crew. As they began the task of collecting the white powder, Marilyn watched them for a moment, ensuring they understood what she wanted, then stepped back, allowing them to work.

The murmurs and speculations among the stablemen continued, but now with a sense of purpose as they scooped the strange substance into the bags. Marilyn, standing a discreet distance away, kept a watchful eye on the proceedings. Occasionally, one of the crew would cast a speculative gaze in her direction. She would only smile and nod mysteriously. 'Let them think what they want,' she thought. 'So long as they get the work done.' They had no idea what she was about, and that was exactly as she wanted it.

She would have to refine the raw material, of course. The process of leaching the substance with water, collecting the runoff, and then evaporating it to leave behind the potent salt was not complicated, but it was tedious. Nevertheless, the result would be worth the toil. The purified saltpeter, when carefully combined with the sulfur she had secured earlier and the finely ground charcoal she planned to produce, would yield the potent mixture she sought – black gunpowder, crafted in precise proportions for maximum efficacy.

Late that afternoon, as she meticulously worked to separate the precious white crystals from the pungent mixture of dung and straw, the clanging echoes of the fortress watchtower's bell reverberated in her memory. The day she had arrived, that very bell had announced the arrival of the king and unwittingly provided the spark of even more inspiration for the endeavor she now pursued. The people of this century were certainly a superstitious lot – a factor she could exploit with the appropriate level of theatrics added to her plans.

The next morning dawned bright over Execaer, casting long shadows on the cobblestone streets. Marilyn, her presence still an anomaly in this bustling port town, navigated her way through the throngs of early risers. Her unusual attire and demeanor drew curious glances; some townspeople eyed her with a mix of intrigue and suspicion, while others, less brave, scurried away, whispering to each other. Occasionally, she heard the name 'Merlin' uttered. 'I guess the king's entourage has started the rumor mill,' she thought, amused.

Undeterred, she approached a group of locals congregating near a market stall. "Pardon me," she began, her voice firm yet non-threatening, "I seek the bell founder - the one who made the bell in the fortress tower. Could you tell me where to find him?"

A burly man, mid-bite into his morning bread, scrutinized her before replying. "The bell founder, eh? Anselm is his name. His workshop is down by the riverbank. Near impossible to miss it – always clanging and banging." He pointed southward, his finger directing her towards a soot-stained part of town. "Head that way," he added. "When you get close enough, just listen and follow your ears," he advised.

A woman, her arms laden with market goods, interjected, her voice tinged with a mix of wariness and intrigue. "Why do you seek Anselm? You have not the look of someone in need of a bell?"

Offering only a secretive smile in response, Marilyn said, "I require his expertise for a matter of personal interest. Thank you for the directions." With a gracious nod, she turned away, leaving the speculations behind as she followed the path to Anselm's workshop, her thoughts already weaving through the intricacies of her plan.

Upon reaching the riverbank, Marilyn found the bell founder's workshop, a soot-blackened stone building distinct against the bustling port's backdrop. From within echoed the constant clang of metal, a testament to the artisan's dedication. Attached to the main structure was a quaint wattle-and-daub shop, its roof thatched with wood tiles, presenting a stark contrast to the foundry's industrial aura.

Stepping inside the shop, Marilyn was greeted by a woman whose demeanor suggested she was the bell maker's wife. The woman's eyes swept over Marilyn's unusual attire, joining the chorus of curious glances she'd received since her arrival in Execaer.

The shop was a trove of smaller bells and chimes, their craftsmanship evident in every curve and edge. Some were wrought from iron, others from brass, and a few from metals Marilyn couldn't immediately recognize – perhaps tin or nickel. It was a reminder that in a port town like Execaer, even rare materials could find their way into skilled hands.

"Your husband makes fine things," Marilyn commented appreciatively.

The woman chuckled lightly. "Thank you. I'm sure he'd love to hear that, though his head is big enough as it is." She then asked, "Is there something particular you're looking for? We have many fine bells and clychau."

Marilyn repeated the unfamiliar word, "Clychau?"

The woman pointed to a set of chimes hanging above the door, which clanged melodiously as the door moved. "Clychau," she repeated.

'Ah… chimes,' Marilyn thought, mentally translating. "May I please speak to the smith responsible for their making? I have a special chime I need made."

After a speculative glance, the woman nodded and led Marilyn through a door into the foundry at the back.

Entering the foundry, Marilyn was immediately struck by the array of bell molds and half-finished creations. Sketches of bells and chimes adorned the walls, some of which she recognized from Execaer's watchtowers and churches. This was the domain of a master craftsman, his work woven into the very fabric of the town's life and safety.

Anselm, the bell founder, stood among his creations, his presence as sturdy as the materials he worked with. His hands, calloused from years of shaping metal, paused as he looked up at Marilyn. "Welcome to my foundry," he greeted warmly. Quickly appraising her appearance and clothing, so different from the usual townsfolk, he asked, "You're not from around here, I take it? What brings you to my workshop?"

Marilyn surveyed the workshop, recognizing the extent of Anselm's skill and reputation, likely renowned well beyond Execaer's borders. "I'm here on a unique errand," she began, preparing to unfold her unusual request to the curious craftsman.

Amidst the tang of hot metal and the din of hammers still being worked by apprentices, Marilyn broached her unusual request. "Anselm, I need a chime crafted, not for a steeple or a church, but for a purpose that must remain between the king and myself," she began, her voice steady over the clamor of the foundry.

Anselm, his curiosity piqued, leaned closer. "A secret chime for the king? Tell me more of what you seek."

Marilyn outlined her specifications. "I need it crafted of brass, uniform in size and thickness. Measure it as deep as your arm, with walls two fingers thick. The capped end should be three fingers thick and include a hole about the size of your smallest finger." She gestured with her hands to give him a better idea of the dimensions. "The hollow must be wide enough to fit a man's fist."

Anselm rubbed his chin thoughtfully, his experienced eyes visualizing her description. "A chime of such proportions would be quite weighty," he remarked.

"Yes, and for that purpose, just as it is with any large bell, I need thick pegs attached on either side, about a third of the way down from the capped end to provide the yoke," Marilyn instructed with clarity. "And above the hole in the capped end, add a squared hoop to allow attachment of a rope for ringing." She did not explain that the chime would not be used for its intended purpose but knew he would understand the concept and not question her instructions.

The bell founder nodded, a smile of craftsmanship spreading across his face. "A hefty task, but I relish the challenge. It is not every day one gets to create something so unique and for the king no less! My reputation will grow even greater!"

His wife, who had been listening from a corner of the workshop, couldn't help but chime in with a mix of affection and teasing in her voice,

"As if your head could swell any larger, Anselm." Her eyes twinkled with a blend of pride and amusement.

Anselm let out a hearty laugh, acknowledging her jibe with good humor. "Well, one can never have too grand a reputation, especially in the art of bell making," he replied, winking at Marilyn.

Marilyn paused, considering her next question carefully. "One more thing, Anselm," she began. "Do your skills extend to bronzing over a clay figure?"

Anselm stroked his beard thoughtfully. "Indeed, it does. Bronze is a fine material, and I have some experience in layering it over clay for decorative pieces. What did you have in mind?"

Marilyn's eyes lit up with satisfaction. "Excellent. I have a particular design in mind, something… symbolic. I can bring the clay figures to you when they are ready. But, as you said, I am new in town and do not know anyone. Do you know of a skilled sculptor capable of working in fine detail? Someone you have worked with before perhaps?"

Anselm scratched his already soot-marked brow, adding to the stains there. "Wynfor," he finally said. "He is a master with clay, able to breathe life into the mud. But if you think to have me bronze his work," he added, a knowing glint in his eye, "tell him to use the finer river clay. It holds up better to the heat and detail. You said 'figures' – I assume by that you mean to have more than one chime from me?"

Marilyn smiled, amused by his astute observation. "Yes," she replied. "Identical." Removing her backpack to retrieve a purse of coins, she said "Wynfor it is, then. Could you give me directions to find him?"

Anselm wiped his hands on his apron and walked over to a cluttered desk, drawing a quick map on a scrap of parchment. "He is not far. Down by the southern market, near where the cobblers ply their trade. You cannot miss his workshop; it is always surrounded by children, fascinated by his magic with clay."

Marilyn nodded, taking the map. "Thank you, Anselm. You have been most helpful." Her eyes danced with a mischievous twinkle. "But if I am to bring this together, I will need a measurement – a precise width for the chimes you intend to craft."

Anselm nodded expectantly. "Yes, of course," he said, taking two small slips of wood down from a shelf. He laid both beside each other and held them down with his fist, then cut notches into the wood on either side of his fist, scoring the wood. Then he placed two fingers on the outer edge of each cut and repeated the process. Handing one of the sticks to Marilyn, he said, "Fist-sized chamber with two fingers of thickness the walls of the chime per your instructions."

Marilyn took the stick, nodding. "That should do well enough for Wynfor – tell him I said hello when you see him. It will keep him more honest with his price," Anselm added, grinning. "Anything else?"

"Just your discretion," Marilyn replied, a hint of secrecy in her tone. She paid for the commission of the two chimes, adding a little extra for his priority. "Consider this extra to make them your priority," she said seriously.

Anselm appraised the coin in his hand a moment, a look of pleasant surprise on his face. "The king is most generous!" he exclaimed. "It is appreciated. I will get started on your chimes right away."

She put the coin purse and the measurement stick in her backpack. "Thank you, Anselm," she said, "I will bring you the figures when he has them completed – hopefully soon." With that, she turned and left the foundry, the sound of clanging metal fading behind her as she stepped back into the bustling streets of Execaer, her mind already weaving the next thread of her intricate plan.

Later that afternoon, as Marilyn turned the last of the dung mixture through the sieve, separating the grains of saltpeter, she couldn't help but feel a kinship with both Anselm and Wynfor. They both shaped the world with their hands, masters of their craft, just as she was with hers.

And as the late afternoon sun dipped lower, casting long shadows across the makeshift lab she had set up, Marilyn simply felt at peace. Her plans were coming together perfectly! Wynfor had proven to be as masterful as Anselm at his craft. Such artistry had always escaped Marilyn as a child. Her drawings, at best, looked like a badly mimicked Picasso. In Wynfor's hands however, the process looked like magic. Scratching marks of charcoal and chalk on a wooden panel meant for the purpose, he had taken her words and transformed them into a drawing like an expert police sketch artist.

The result had been something akin to a snake-scaled cat, crouched to pounce. Only this cat has a long neck ending in a roaring head of long teeth and large horns. To that, she had him add taloned bat wings spread as though about to take flight. Lastly, she had added instructions to make the head and neck a separate piece intended to hold a log that was long, straight, and slender, giving him the wooden measurement stick Anselm had provided.

Thinking back now, Marilyn felt a mix of impatience and trepidation. She was eager to see the result of Wynfor's bronze work – a fearsome, snake-scaled feline creature poised menacingly, a vision straight from mythical lore. Assuming the visual was anything like the image in her mind's eye, the anticipation of combining this visual spectacle with her planned fireworks display filled her with a sense of nervous excitement.

Yet, she could not help her trepidation as she contemplated the potential impact of her actions. She intended to use "shock and awe" – a phrase she had first heard when she was ten years old during the 2003 Iraq War at the height of her father's diplomatic career. She later learned in her military training that the term had been borrowed from a book on military strategy written almost a decade earlier. With any hope, she planned to use that strategy to cow Gorloys into submission, eliciting his cooperation and discouraging him from treachery without a drop of blood. She also had no intention of introducing gunpowder-based warfare into sixth century Europe, with potentially devastating butterfly effects to the timeline.

Three weeks had passed since Marilyn's dealings with Anselm and Wynfor, and now, tucked away beneath tarps in the stables of Execaer's fortress, lay the culmination of their combined artistry – two impressive bronze dragons, each perched on a small four-wheeled cart. These sculptures, crafted with exquisite detail, were more than just a testament to their creators' skills; they were integral to Marilyn's grand scheme.

To Anselm, who had the task of bronzing the pieces and questioned their odd design when he saw them, she had explained the dragons away as elaborate wall sconces, with the brass tubes functioning as pivoting candle holders – a cover story to mask their true, more enigmatic purpose. For now, they remained hidden, their formidable forms and the secrets they held concealed under the heavy canvas.

Now, as she stood amongst the horses in the stable with Uthyr, ready to pull back the tarp, Marilyn felt a blend of excitement and apprehension. She knew the unveiling of the dragons would be a pivotal moment, one that could shape Uthyr's perception of her plan.

Still very circumspect, she looked up at Uthyr and nodded toward the stable hands. Two were mucking out stalls and paying no apparent attention to their presence, but a third man was busily currying a horse, acting as though he held no curiosity. But she had already seen the man glance at her and Uthyr more than once. "Can you ask them to leave?" she asked.

Looking around, Uthyr caught the eye of the man currying the horse just as he chose the wrong moment to glance up rather than mind his own business. "We need a moment to talk privately," Uthyr said. "Please take them with you as well," he added nodding to the men mucking the stalls. "I will come get you when we are done." Recalling how he had treated those he met along their journey to Execaer, Marilyn could not help but be impressed with how polite Uthyr always seemed to others, no matter their position in life.

As the stable doors closed behind the departing workers, Marilyn surveyed the area, her eyes scanning for any lingering presence. Once satisfied they were alone, she turned her attention back to Uthyr. With a steady hand, she drew back the heavy canvas, revealing the bronzed forms of the dragons in all their intricate glory. Uthyr's eyes widened slightly as he took in the sight, a mix of surprise and curiosity etching his features."

Marilyn chose her words carefully, letting a mix of earnestness and caution color her voice. "Uthyr, as I have said, I will not help you to kill. So, the next best approach is to demonstrate overwhelming power. And when true power is beyond one's grasp, deception with a touch of theatrics becomes the tool of choice."

Uthyr's sneer was evident as he scrutinized the bronze dragons. "Children might be frightened by these statues, Merlin, no matter how grand," he chided. "But how do these help us?"

Marilyn met his gaze, her expression a blend of seriousness and mystery. "With the knowledge and powers I possess, I plan to summon the dragon's breath!" As if that shock were not enough, she explained with a mischievous smirk, "But such a thing must be carefully contained to prevent destruction. Since I cannot summon real dragons from my realm, these bronze dragons must work in their place."

She watched as Uthyr's expression transitioned from skepticism to shock, and then gradually gave way to a flicker of curiosity. "Yes, you see? Even these seemingly ordinary statues are central to my plan," she confirmed, responding to the unasked question in his eyes. "They must be kept under close watch."

"Until when?" Uthyr asked, his tone a mix of skepticism and intrigue. "Dragon's breath?" he echoed, as if trying to comprehend the scope of her revelation.

"Indeed, dragon's breath," Marilyn confirmed with a nod. "But the task of doing so requires a degree of… secrecy. The work I must do may draw unwanted attention with its noise and visibility. Given how close we now reside to Gorloys' domain, I fear spies may reveal or worse, steal the secret of my work.'"

Uthyr's expression shifted as he pondered her words. "So, what do you propose?" he inquired, a hint of newfound respect in his tone.

Uthyr considered her words, his expression thoughtful. After a moment, he nodded in understanding. "Where do you suggest we go for this... secretive work?"

"I suggest that, until my trials and attempts to summon and capture the dragon's breath are done, we move to a more secluded location, one where I can work without the fear of prying eyes," Marilyn offered. "Somewhere like the fortress at Moridunum; it is remote enough to offer the seclusion I need." She hoped he would see the wisdom in her suggestion, understanding the delicate balance between secrecy and the need to wield a show of force convincingly.

Uthyr considered her proposal, his expression a mixture of contemplation and nostalgia. "Moridunum..." he mused, his voice tinged with memories of a past long gone. "The place where I grew up. It would indeed be good to return, to oversee things in the north."

He paused, his gaze momentarily settling on the stable walls around them, reflective of his broader responsibilities. "We've only recently shifted my house from Glouvum to Execaer so that I could personally oversee the security of our southern coast," he said, more to himself than to Marilyn. "Perhaps things here are stable enough now, or at least well in hand, for me to leave for a while."

His focus returned to Marilyn, now filled with a determined resolve. "Yes, we will move to Moridunum. It will be an opportunity to check on my northern kingdom and ensure all is well." A chuckle escaped him as he then added, "Besides...I have cousins there I have not seen in more seasons than I care to admit!" He nodded decisively. "Prepare your dragons, Merlin. Once you have captured the dragon's breath, we shall return. I am eager to see if your theatrics can indeed sway the stubborn heart of Gorloys."

Marilyn breathed a sigh of relief, a subtle smile playing on her lips. The next phase of her plan was set into motion, a dance of deception and power poised to unfold.

CHAPTER 14

Legends Come to Life

As Marilyn and Dubric walked along a path uphill from the wharf, she gazed across the bustling wharf, her eyes taking in the diversity of the ships. "Quite a sight, is it not?" she remarked, her tone reflecting a mix of awe and curiosity.

Marilyn glanced over at Dubric who was quietly observing the busy seafarers, lost in contemplation. Breaking from his reverie, he replied, "Yes, Merlin. Seeing so many different ships and people makes me wonder at the size of the world and God's creation. So many people… How can the church ever bring Christ's salvation to all of them?"

Understanding the enormity of the task from her unique perspective of the future, she offered an encouraging response. "The message of the church will travel far and wide, much like these ships. Just as each vessel finds its way to distant shores, so too will the teachings of your church reach far beyond what we can see here. It is a journey, one step at a time."

Dubric shifted his gaze to Marilyn, his eyes reflecting a mixture of wonder and curiosity. "You speak with such certainty, as if you know this beyond doubt," he remarked.

With a mysterious grin and an arch of her brow, Marilyn replied, "Does it surprise you that among my gifts lies a limited knowledge of the future?"

Dubric, both shocked and amused, shook his head. "After all I have witnessed from you, no. It does not surprise me that you might be a teller of fortunes."

Marilyn chuckled softly. "You mistake my words, Dubric. I am no teller of fortunes. I cannot foretell your future any more than I can foretell the next rainfall. Tell me, in your teachings, do you not speak of a man named Elijah, who foretold Christ's coming? In my tongue, he is known as a 'prophet.'" She carefully pronounced the word 'prophet' in her native English, not knowing the appropriate translation.

Dubric's eyebrows rose in realization. "Yes, 'Propheta'! Are you one of these, a prophet?"

With a shake of her head and a knowing smile, Marilyn responded, "No, I am not a prophet." Her chuckle carried a hint of enigma. "But perhaps my gifts are closer to that than fortune-telling." Glancing over at him, she saw the look of doubt still on his face as he continued to contemplate the people milling about the wharf. "Even without such a gift Dubric, it is truly a matter of numbers in any case," she added.

Dubric looked puzzled. "A matter of numbers? What do you mean?"

"Suppose you tell five people and only two believe you. But then the next day each of the new believers tells five more each with the same result. This continues each day for each new believer," Marilyn said. "How many new believers will the church have after ten days?"

Dubric pondered for a moment. "I do not know," he admitted. "Perhaps a hundred?"

Marilyn smiled at the shock and disbelief that spread across his face as she corrected him. "No, my friend. More than ten times that many. And in twenty days, the number is so large I do not know it in your language. But imagine a hundred groups of a hundred men - then imagine a hundred of the hundred groups!"

Dubric shook his head, "That is not possible, Merlin. Do not jest."

"I do not," Marilyn assured him. "If you do not believe me, then see for yourself. Take a piece of parchment and put a mark on it. The next day, draw two marks below it, then four marks below that the next, and so on. Count up the marks after ten days," she instructed. "You will see I speak the truth."

As the two of them walked along Marilyn noted how the wharf and river were both alive with activity. Anglers skillfully cast nets from smaller boats, their movements practiced and precise. On larger vessels, workers busily loaded and unloaded a myriad of goods – barrels, sacks of grain, and even livestock. And slender vessels sped along, with men at the sweeps, carrying men and horses back and forth across the river – either travelers or residents that worked or lived in the smaller villages along the far shore. The air was filled with the sounds of commerce and the salty scent of the sea.

Marilyn's attention was drawn to a few ships adorned with modest decorations – painted symbols on their sails or simple carvings on their prows, perhaps emblems of their home ports or the symbols of their owners. The lack of elaborate mastheads or figureheads hinted at the utilitarian nature of these vessels, yet there was a certain beauty in their simplicity and functionality. They were certainly more rudimentary than the anachronistic visions in her mind, the product of too many fantasy novels and Hollywood movies.

Recalling that Takashi's barracks room was adorned with several ships in a bottle, Marilyn decided to capture this unique moment for him. She delved into her backpack, retrieving her Polaroid camera. As she aimed it at the bustling scene before her and pressed the button, the camera clicked, capturing a snapshot of a moment in mankind's history. A moment that, given the time period in which she found herself, Takashi would never find in a history book. The camera's whir as the film slid out drew a curious glance from Dubric.

"What sorcery is this?" Dubric asked, his eyes wide with wonder as he watched the film slide out of the camera.

Marilyn chuckled softly. "Not sorcery, my friend." She waved the developing photo in the air. "Call it… 'magic parchment' if you like. But do not tell Cadfan of this," she teased with a wink, "Or he might think the devil himself handed me the parchment!"

Dubric's laughter mingled with the sounds of the wharf. He watched in amazement as the image slowly came to life on the film.

As Marilyn was about to stash the photo in her backpack, her eyes caught a glimpse of a ship in the picture that seemed perfect for their journey. She looked up, spotting the actual vessel among the others. It was wide and flat, with a large square sail hanging from the yardarm on its central mast. Five sweeps were aligned on either side, and its deck had a wide, lowered central strip for cargo along the spine.

Pointing towards it, Marilyn exclaimed, "That ship is perfect!"

Dubric followed her gaze, his eyes settling on the robust vessel. "It seems sturdy and well-suited for our needs," he acknowledged.

As she and Dubric approached the ship moored along the wharf, Marilyn heard a man yelling commands to his fellow crewmen in what sounded eerily like Farsi – a language she had never taken the time to learn, but which she had heard many times growing up in the shadow of her father's diplomatic career. If not Farsi, it was certainly some similar Arabic tongue, or perhaps its ancient precursor.

It was evident the man was the captain; as he yelled and pointed, the other men crawling about the ship jumped to do his bidding. Approaching the wide gangplank, Marilyn stepped onto it, drawing the captain's attention. "Who are you and what do you want?" he demanded unexpectedly in Old Welsh. She had anticipated needing hand signals and coin to negotiate passage, so the fact he was able to speak a shared language came as a welcome surprise.

Looking up at him, Marilyn found herself momentarily taken aback. The man's striking features – black eyes, long, curly hair, olive skin, and a muscular, lean physique – were complemented by a boyish, pearlescent smile. He stood at the boat's edge in nothing but baggy white trousers held up by a colorful sash, into which was tucked a wicked-looking scimitar. 'No shirt, no shoes, no problem,' she mused admiringly. His ensemble, or lack thereof, along with his striking appearance, made him resemble a figure straight from the cover of a romance novel.

"You are far from home," Marilyn said, smiling.

The man grinned. "My home is the sea," he replied. "And that is found right here!" he added, motioning to the water arrayed beyond ship and wharf. "But I take your meaning. I come from Antioch as do my men. Ah! But I forget Najat the Unspeaking!" he added shaking his head. Pointing to one of his men he added, "We found Majat abandoned and left for dead on a beach at Cyprus. Since he cannot speak, I do not know where he is from. But Zarathustra surely chose to bless him that day in our finding him. We named him and gave him new life. He has been with me since. He can hear but not speak. Someone removed his tongue for him."

"I am Merlin," Marilyn started. "On behalf of the king in this land, I seek passage for the king, my companion here, and myself, along with the king's men and…some things we must bring with us." She realized suddenly that she didn't know the Old Welsh word for 'cargo' and reminded herself to ask Dubric later.

"May the winds carry the honor and fortune of our meeting, Merlin," he replied poetically. "And may that honor be buoyed on the tide of newfound friendship," he added. "I am Sinbad, greatest sailor on the seas!" he announced, bowing with a flourish of his hand.

'It can't be!' Marilyn thought with shock. 'There is just no way that is possible!' She stood there dumbfounded as he straightened and beamed a perfect smile, then reconsidered. 'I am pretending to be a man from myth written about centuries after he supposedly lived,' she thought ruefully.

'Why should I be surprised that Sinbad of all people should step out of fairy tales and into the world!'

Marilyn realized she had been standing there slacked-jawed and quickly closed her mouth blushing as Sinbad broke the momentary silence. "I see my reputation comes before me on the tides even to this place!" he exclaimed. "But perhaps not. Your friend seems…confused," he added, with a nod at Dubric.

Looking up, Dubric chimed in. "Forgive me captain. I do not travel often by sea. My stomach does not agree with it," he said ruefully. "So, though Merlin may have heard of you, I have not."

Sinbad nodded. "Where does your king wish to travel upon the seas?" he asked. "I have travelled far to bring spices from my homeland to this place. But I know little of the land beyond his port."

Nodding, Marilyn took off her backpack and pulled her laminated map from a side-pouch. "Come, let me show you," she said, motioning to come onto the wharf. As she unfolded the map and stooped down to lay it out, it was Sinbad's turn to be shocked, taking on a dumb-founded expression.

"By the endless depths of the hidden sea, how did you come by such a map?!" he asked in breathless wonder. "I would give all I have and passage besides to own such a map!" Marilyn smiled, contemplating what such knowledge might afford such an enigmatic sailor. His eyebrows climbed even higher if that were possible as he pointed to the top right corner where a location key to which she had paid almost no attention resided. "That…that is the whole of the world! I have seen maps very much like it!" he added.

Examining the corner more closely, she realized that it contained a basic outline encompassing an area covering all of Europe and included the entire Mediterranean Sea and coast along northern Africa. Within this was a small red square outlining the area detailed by the larger map that showed only the southern half of the island and coast of what would someday be called France along the English Channel.

"How I came by such a map is my own business," Marilyn replied, glancing up at Dubric, intent on having him remain silent. He stood there quietly stunned, likely in round-eyed contemplation of his earlier thoughts concerning the size of the world and the number of people in it. "I cannot sell you this map, Sinbad," she added. "But if you swear it to secrecy and never share its knowledge, I will have a copy drawn to parchment for you by morning in exchange for the passage I require to…here." She pointed to the river inlet south of Moridunum on the map.

Sinbad leaned over the map, his initial awe giving way to the focused gaze of an experienced sailor. His eyes traced the lines and contours with a practiced precision, the gears of his mind visibly turning as he navigated the charted waters in his imagination. It was the look of a man who had spent a lifetime reading the language of the sea, now confronted with a new dialect in the form of Marilyn's remarkable map. He noted a line on it in the bottom corner, recognizing it for what it was. "This is a distance line, yes?" he asked, already confident of the answer. "How far does it measure?"

Marilyn had no ready answer, offering only a vague suggestion based on the 20-mile scale. "I do not know exactly," she replied. "I have no head for sailing. But by land, that is about the distance a man can walk along a clear path from dawn to dusk."

Nodding, Sinbad studied the map a bit more and announced confidently, "If we leave at dawn, I will have you at this place in six days."

"There is a…." She didn't know how to say 'complication' she realized. "…a problem to think on," she continued. "Along here lives the king's enemies," she said, pointing to coastline east and west of Tintagel roughly forty miles in each direction. "What we bring with us is as precious to the king as this map will be to you. We cannot put ashore along here and risk its loss to the enemy."

"Have no fear," Sinbad replied with a confident grin. "My crew and I have sailed many treacherous waters and are as quick as the wind to avoid danger and as fierce as the storm when we cannot. We will deliver you and your king's treasure safely." Bowing with a flourish, he added, "On my honor," then trotted back across the gangplank to rejoin his crew., transforming seamlessly from grandiose sailor to focused captain. His orders rang out decisively, echoing across the deck as he began preparing his crew for the journey ahead.

Marilyn stood coughing, gagging, and waving a hand in front of her face to try and clear the lingering smoke. Amid the chaos, Dubric burst through the door of her tower room, his face etched with terror. "What in Almighty God's name was that thunderous noise?!" he asked excitedly, his voice tinged with alarm.

Catching her breath as the smoke drifted out the window of the tower chamber, Marilyn replied, "That…(cough)…was the sound…(cough, cough)…of success!" She beamed, despite the smoke.

"And the smell of it too, it seems," Dubric remarked, wrinkling his nose.

"It was not that loud," Marilyn countered, a wry smile on her lips. "Given the proper materials, I could make a dragon's breath capable of destroying this tower." She surveyed the chamber, where charred remains of reeds and parchment confetti littered the floor. Outdoors, the firecracker's noise would have been less dramatic, but within the stone walls, its echo amplified the impact, lending credibility to Dubric's description.

The structure, more an adjunct to the wall surrounding the small fort than a true tower, stood about 30 feet high. Its Roman engineering, a remnant withstanding the wear of time, provided an almost anachronistic contrast to the rustic palisades and wooden stronghold around it. Regardless, the noise likely carried into the town below.

She had already made something of a reputation for herself when she had come through Moridunum before in search of Uthyr. And in the eight days since she and the king had arrived from Execaer with Sinbad's help, her ongoing experiments, marked by smoke and unexpected flashes of light from the lookout window, only further fueled rumors, speculation, and the mystery surrounding her activities. To maintain secrecy, Marilyn had even resorted to nocturnal testing of her firework rockets, launching them into the river under cover of darkness. But their sparkling trails only heightened the intrigue. As a result, the residents began referring to the place as “Merlin’s Fort” regardless of any official titles. And now that her experiments had met with success, it was time to return.

“Dubric, please inform the king of our success and let him know we should prepare to return to Execaer and set up a meeting with Gorloys. Sinbad promised to return on the first day of the full moon, which, if my reading of the waxing moon is correct, is in three days,” Marilyn instructed as she began sweeping the remnants of her experiment into a pile.

As she worked, her thoughts drifted back to the voyage from Execaer and its aftermath. Sinbad had been true to his boasts; the speed and skill of his ship and crew had more than lived up to his claims. After rounding the corner of the Cornish peninsula, he had boldly chosen to sail overnight straight to the river inlet south of Moridunum, skillfully avoiding landfall in enemy territory. This daring maneuver had cut a day from their journey, a feat that did not go unnoticed by Uthyr.

Impressed by Sinbad’s nautical prowess, Uthyr had invited the sailor and his men for a well-deserved respite within the keep. But before Sinbad prepared to take his leave, Uthyr presented the sailor with a new challenge. “The map used on our journey here – do you have it with you?” Uthyr inquired.

She recalled Sinbad’s furtive expression as he glanced over questioningly, mindful of the secrecy she had imposed. “Show him,” she nodded, sensing his hesitation. Sinbad pulled the parchment map from an inner pocket and carefully unfolded it across the table.

Even more, she remembered Uthyr’s amazed expression and keen interest as he examined the map, his fingers tracing the coastal outlines. "I know these waters!" he exclaimed. Shaking his head in wonder, he pointed at one of several locations Marilyn had marked. "We are here, yes?" he inquired, pointing to Moridunum on the map, though Marilyn had written '(Carmarthen)' instead - the name of the city in modern times.

"Do you have the tools to add more markings?" he asked, directing the question to Marilyn. "I must add more points along the coast here," he said, tracing his finger along what would someday become the Bristol Channel.

At the time, Marilyn had produced a pen from her satchel and handed it to Uthyr, thinking little of it. "Use this," she offered. The memory of his marvel over such a mundane instrument for the modern world brought a smile to her face.

Uthyr added marks to the map with precise strokes, writing the names of towns next to each point. "I have another task for you, Sinbad," he said, his voice carrying a tone of solemnity. "I have messages that must reach the governors and aldermen of each town I have marked here. Can you complete this task and return by the full moon?"

Sinbad studied the map for a moment, then replied seriously, "It can be done, but such a journey will exhaust my men. I cannot fairly ask this of them without reward."

Uthyr nodded in understanding. "I am in dire need of conscripts if I am to succeed in the south," he explained. He motioned to a clay jar within which stood a set of tightly rolled scrolls, each sealed with wax. "These are the messages for each town. Each has symbols matching those I scribed on your map," he added, indicating the importance of each destination.

Smiling then at Sinbad's concern for his crew, Uthyr asked curiously, "What were you paid for bringing us to Moridunum? Merlin never spoke of it."

"My payment was this wondrous map before you!" Sinbad beamed in satisfaction. "It is a treasure all its own in the hands of a sailor such as I!" he boasted with bravado, then added trivially, "I paid my men from my own purse."

Uthyr's gaze shifted to Marilyn, frowning in disapproval, but saying nothing. "Complete this task, and you shall receive fair payment for both journeys," he assured. "Upon your return, we will make a final journey to Bearda Market," he added, marking another location on the map. "Tell your men a feast awaits them – with wine, women, and song!"

Sinbad's face broke into a wide grin. "It will be done!" he proclaimed, gathering the sealed messages. With renewed purpose, he left to prepare his crew for the challenging voyage ahead.

Lost in her reverie, Marilyn pondered whether Sinbad would meet the tight schedule. She certainly hoped so. She had been in this land for three months now, and her pregnancy was just beginning to show. The last thing she needed was for the secret of her true gender to be discovered. So, to conceal the growing evidence of her condition, she had resorted to wearing her trench coat constantly, using it to mask her slowly changing silhouette.

Finally, looking up, she realized Dubric was still standing there. "Is everything okay, Dubric? Do you need something else?" she inquired.

"Yes…no. You look…tired, Merlin," he said, his concern evident. "You should eat and rest."

Smiling at his concern, she nodded. "I will," she replied. The last eight days she had been working from sunup to well past sundown. It was no surprise that she might look haggard.

"And take a bath!" he added with a smile, glancing around the room one last time. "You stink of brimstone," he quipped, closing the door behind him before she could respond.

Marilyn sat in a corner of the great hall in the bustling riverside town of Bearda Market, enjoying the gaiety of the feast in spite of being unable to imbibe for fear of harming her unborn child. Regardless, it was a scene that seemed lifted from the pages of an ancient tale like Beowulf.

The venue, a grand feast hall more than an inn, was a sprawling structure of hefty hewn timbers, its interior resonating with the warmth and vibrancy of the gathering.

Cots and beds made of straw and fur were arranged along the walls of the hall, offering rest to those who would later seek respite from the night's revelries. The heart of the space was dominated by an enormous fire pit, where the scent of roasting boar filled the air. Two massive specimens turned slowly on a giant iron spit, tended by boys at each end, their faces glowing in the firelight.

Occasionally, the proprietor – a portly man with a balding crown capping snow-white hair – would walk over and scold one of the boys for turning too fast or too slow, then return to his own duties. The fire pit provided the hall's only light source, lending a mystical quality to the space with its warmth flickering across the hall, casting dancing shadows that glowed in the smoke drifting out through a hole in the center of the roof.

Along the wall beside her, large barrels of mead stood like sentinels, where the proprietor busily drew the sweet, potent drink for the guests or wenches that approached. 'World's first bartender,' Marilyn thought, amused.

The hall was a hive of exuberant activity, alive with the raucous spirit of celebration. Sinbad's sailors and Uthyr's soldiers mingled freely, engaging in boisterous contests of strength and agility, their laughter echoing through the space. Amidst the rough and tumble of arm-wrestling and mock wrestling matches, uproarious cheers and shouts of encouragement filled the air.

The women, more than mere onlookers, actively participated in the gaiety, moved among the men with ease, their laughter mingling with the din. They teased and were teased in return, some engaged in playful tickling matches that ended in giggles and mock protests. In the dimmer corners of the hall and along the bedding-lined walls, couples, not all of them traditional pairings, were lost in intimate moments, sharing kisses and whispers. Marilyn noticed the unexpected yet tender interaction between one of Uthyr's soldiers and Najat the Unspeaking, their affection for each other as open and genuine as any other.

Dice clattered on makeshift tables as gambling games unfolded, the shouts and jeers that erupted with each roll drawing a crowd of eager onlookers. Coins exchanged hands amidst good-natured banter, the stakes seemingly less important than the camaraderie it fostered.

In one corner, the gentle strumming of a harp filled the air, its melodies weaving through the din of celebration. Some of the men, emboldened by the music and mead, took to dancing and making merry, their movements a blur in the firelit hall.

Marilyn observed it all, a sense of wonder at the uninhibited joy and freedom of the moment. The diversity and acceptance evident in the hall were surprising yet heartening, a stark contrast to the more restrained and formal gatherings she was accustomed to. This night at Bearda Market was a celebration of life in its most unvarnished and authentic form, a quintessential gathering that brought to life the tales of old. In this moment, Marilyn, amidst the echoes of history and legend, felt the pulse of a world both ancient and alive.

"Will you not join the king and I for a drink?" she suddenly heard from above. Looking up, she saw Sinbad standing over her.

Smiling up at him, she replied, "I need not drink to be merry, Sinbad." Patting the empty fur beside her, she invited, "But come! Sit! I have been wanting to speak with you. I have a tale to share."

"To have the friendship of one such as you is my honor," Sinbad replied sincerely, bowing before sitting beside her.

"One such as I?" Marilyn inquired, arching an eyebrow.

"Forgive me. I do not mean to offend. But I have heard much about you I did not know," he offered cautiously. "To hear the tales, you are like one of the Peri!" Scrutinizing her shoulders with a teasing smile, he added, "Though I see no wings to prove it!"

Now she understood. The rumors of her powers and reputation had apparently reached even his ears. A 'peri' must be the Persian equivalent of a fairy – or so she assumed. "Enough drink will make any fish the size of a whale," she chided, causing Sinbad to laugh uproariously in agreement.

"I may not be one of your… 'Peri.' But that does not mean I am not without certain gifts," Marilyn said with a mysterious smile. "I have another for you," she continued.

"You have already given me a treasure beyond asking," Sinbad responded, patting his breast where he kept his new map. "What more need have I than to call you friend?"

"I have little doubt you could charm a snake, Sinbad," Marilyn said, shaking her head in amusement as he blushed. "I said I have a tale to tell. But first, I have something to show you," she continued, becoming serious as she removed a folded parchment from her trench coat pocket and handed it to him.

"What is this?" Sinbad asked, curiosity in his eyes.

"Open it," Marilyn encouraged, watching as he unfolded the parchment. In the face of his confusion, she added, "It is another map, Sinbad. Take out the one you already have."

When he had retrieved it, she laid one atop the other, matching the coast of the Mediterranean Sea along the east, extending the scope of his known world. She looked down with a hint of pride; her drawing included the Middle East and coastal areas surrounding the Arabian Sea, though not to scale – the Red Sea, the Horn of Africa, the Persian Gulf, and the western coast of India were all represented.

"The waters you sail now are not your destiny, Sinbad," she confided, her voice low and knowing as she pointed at his map. "Your fortune, your true destiny, lies at the heart of this sea," she said, her tone prophetic, as she pointed at the new one.

Sinbad gazed at the new map with a mixture of awe and incredulity. "But how? How do you know these lands so well? Your knowledge… it is beyond any sailor's."

Marilyn smiled, her eyes twinkling with a mixture of mischief and wisdom. "If you could become a bird and fly high above the world, could you not then draw what you see?" she asked cryptically.

His eyes widened in shock, and Marilyn chuckled. "I cannot become a bird, Sinbad," she teased. "But I will keep my own counsel on my journey to greater knowledge. The map is drawn from my memory of others I have seen."

"And I must travel to these lands to seek my fortune?" he asked, his voice filled with a mix of wonder and disbelief.

"Yes," Marilyn responded with confidence. "Return to Egypt and sell your current boat. Then buy another that embarks from this land." She pointed to Egypt, then to Ethiopia on his new map.

Sinbad pondered her words, his gaze intently studying the parchment. "Sell my ship and buy another…" he mused, considering the possibilities. Then, with a glint of playfulness in his eyes, he added jokingly, "Or perhaps I should add wheels to it and sail across the lands here!" He pointed to the land bridge dividing the Mediterranean and Red Sea on the map. "A ship that is both of land and sea – a chimera of a vessel!" At Marilyn's obvious confusion and query, he explained, "Chimera – a boat of …fancy…of dreams…"

Marilyn's laughter joined his, her eyes sparkling with amusement at his inventive idea. "You have the heart of a true adventurer, Sinbad. Follow it, and it will lead you to fortunes untold."

He nodded solemnly, then with a spark of determination in his eyes, promised, "As you say, Merlin. I shall seek my fortune in these new waters. Who knows what mysteries and treasures await?"

Marilyn fixed Sinbad with a serious gaze. "Sinbad, I give you this knowledge. But it comes with a price."

Sinbad's eyes narrowed with suspicion "What price?"

"You and your crew must leave here at dawn to carry a message for me," Marilyn said.

Relaxing, Sinbad replied, "A message? That is no price! It would be my honor."

Marilyn's voice held a gravity that caught Sinbad's attention. "That is not the price. The price will be of time. Where I need you to take this message," she indicated a spot on his old map, "here…is a magic cave where time itself is a mystery. Within its walls, moments stretch into days in the world outside. You must not linger there."

Sinbad's eyes widened in disbelief. "A magic cave where time… What will we find within? And to whom am I delivering this message?"

"Within, you will find a wall of jagged rocks. It is difficult to explain, but through these rocks, you will see another world, as if looking through stormy waters to the sea floor. The message is for those you see through the jagged rocks - my friends. Show it to them," she instructed. Handing him another parchment. On it were the carefully written words in large letters:

COMPLICATIONS BUT OK.

BARGAINED FOR HELP SOON.

3 MOS. TELL DOC SHOWING.

XOXO 2 FLIP

Sinbad looked at the cryptic symbols, unable to decipher them, but Marilyn assured him, "My friends will understand. I am trusting you beyond measure, Sinbad. This must be done. Tell your crew nothing until you find the cave. And remember! Do not linger; leave the cave immediately once you show them the message."

Sinbad's face took on a look of solemn resolve. "On my honor, it will be done," he replied as he had once before. He carefully tucked the message and his new map into his coat, his expression contemplative, hinting at the depth of thought provoked by Marilyn's mysterious task.

CHAPTER 15

Confrontation

The morning was crisp, a tangible chill hinting at autumn's approach. Gorloys sat at a table beneath a sprawling tent atop a small rise overlooking the open field. The vast field was mostly barren, speckled by small boulders laden with bits of grouse and scrub - a natural battleground kissed by the first rays of dawn.

He leisurely enjoyed his breakfast – eggs and ham cooked to perfection over the campfire – savoring each bite with the ease of a man accustomed to power. His eyes, however, were fixed not on his meal but on a peculiar sight in the distance. A lone torch, its flame unwavering, stood planted at the center of the open field, a solitary beacon in the otherwise undisturbed landscape. Small boulders littered the landscape, with most concentrated near the torch. He briefly wondered if the torch was placed among them with purpose.

As he pondered the torch's purpose, his aide, a sturdy young man with keen eyes, quietly stepped into the tent. He knelt at the entrance, head bowed in deference, awaiting Gorloys' permission to speak. The tension in his posture spoke of urgency, yet he maintained the disciplined patience required in Gorloys' presence.

Gorloys took his time, enjoying another mouthful of his meal, letting the silence stretch. He prided himself on his ability to command respect, to instill a sense of awe and fear in those who served him. Finally, with a casual wave of his hand, he granted the aide permission to break the silence.

"Report, Jory" Gorloys commanded, his voice firm yet devoid of haste. His demeanor was calm, but his mind was as sharp as the blade he carried - always ready, always calculating.

The aide rose, his voice steady as he relayed the latest observations. "Pen Gorloys, scouts report that Uthyr's men await at the far end of the field – about two score in number. One in four have horses, but all are unmounted." Then a perplexed look crossed the aide's face as he added, "The scouts also report something strange in the camp – two large carts, pulled by oxen, each carrying what appears to be a large crate. What is beneath each is concealed by cloth though. So, the scouts were unable to discover more."

Gorloys nodded thoughtfully, his gaze still fixed on the distant torch. The presence of Uthyr's men was expected, but the crates piqued his curiosity. His mind, always seeking the strategic advantage, pondered their contents. "And what of Uthyr?" he inquired, a hint of intrigue lacing his words.

"Uthyr is not mounted either, though he has a horse present. According to our scouts, he seems to be preparing more for defense than to attack," the aide continued, his report concise and detailed.

Gorloys absorbed this information, weighing each piece in his mind. The mention of unmounted horses and the number of men sparked a tactical analysis within him. "The ground is far too uneven and treacherous to trust the footing of horses," he confided. "So, they are of no consequence."

He then turned his attention to the peculiar formations on the field. "And what of the encampments to left and right?" Gorloys asked, his curiosity evident. "They just sit there. I have not seen a man move since dawn." The groups of men were too distant to make out any detail other than a rough count – about the same distance as Uthyr's encampment, only to left and right rather than directly across. Within each cluster were about a score of men, but that was all Gorloys could see from this distance.

"Perhaps Uthyr plans a three-pronged attack," Gorloys mused, stroking his beard. "No matter. My father taught me how to read a battlefield and defend against such moves." Pondering one of the many lessons his father had bestowed in a cruel fashion involving bullies he had hired for the purpose, he added quietly, "How I hated that man."

Jory hesitated, uncertainty flickering in his eyes. "The groups to left and right…they carry the strangest tidings of all, Pen Gorloys. The scouts claim that the two groups…they are not real! Only men of straw and brush dressed for battle and made to look real from a distance. They do not even bear weapons."

"Huh, ho!" Gorloys guffawed. "Do you not see, Jory?! The fool thinks me a fool!" It seemed a naive effort at deception, a poor attempt to inflate the numbers of his army in the eyes of the unwary. He let out a soft chuckle, amused at the thought. "A child's ploy, Jory" he mused, his confidence unshaken. "He hoped to trick me into believing he had greater numbers when he was unable to gather even half the men I bring to the field. The crates you describe likely held the spare armor he brought to dress his straw men."

Jory nodded in contemplation, "Yes, that fits well with the information we have, my liege. You are a wise commander of the field. Surely, you will destroy him."

Gorloys gave his aide a stern look. "Do not simper platitudes," he stated. "Now…Assemble the men for battle," he commanded. "Let us be done with this upstart king!"

As Jory turned to go, another scout burst into the tent, his face flushed with urgency. "Pen Gorloys! You must see this for yourself!"

Gorloys stood, placing his utensils down with deliberate care. He strode out of the tent, his eyes scanning the field with a commander's acumen. What he saw brought a frown to his face. Uthyr and another man, unarmed save for a long pole with a white cloth tied to it, were walking towards the lit torch. Uthyr himself only bore a sword, currently sheathed at his side.

"A final parley?" Gorloys muttered under his breath. The very notion seemed ludicrous, yet there it was, unfolding before his eyes. He could almost taste the opportunity to demean Uthyr one final time before the inevitable clash of arms.

With a decisive nod, he amended Jory's instructions. "Send Branok to me," he commanded. "I could likely kill the boy easily, but as my father often said, 'Over-confidence will get you killed.'" Branok was the largest and fiercest of his commanders and Gorloys felt confident he could offer sufficient protection should the need arise. "I will go to meet this upstart king and his standard-bearer. I am curious to hear his final words. I would have Branok with me."

Accompanied by Branok, Gorloys approached the lit torch where Uthyr stood waiting. His mind was a whirlwind of thoughts - memories of his demanding father, the scorn he had endured and the harsh man's upbringing, and the power he now wielded all swirled together. This was his moment to assert dominance over a rival who dared challenge his authority. His eyes were drawn to the white cloth tied at the top of the long pole, fluttering gently in the breeze. A sneer curled his lip as he glanced up at it, and with a mocking tone, he asked, "Why the white standard?"

Uthyr, standing tall with the dignity of a king but the earnestness of a young ruler, glanced up at the cloth and then back at Gorloys, a gleam of amusement in his eyes. "I had… an advisor… confide to me that such a thing is a symbol on the field of battle. He told me its meaning - 'I come in peace', he said." Then chuckling, Uthyr added, "Then again, he also told me it can mean, 'I surrender'." He shrugged noncommittally.

Gorloys' eyebrow arched in response. "So, you have come here to surrender?"

Uthyr's chuckle this time was tinged with nervousness. "No, nothing like that, cousin. I came hoping to appeal to you one last time as a fellow kinsman. I would have you as an ally, not an enemy." His gaze swept across the open field and the encampments of men on either side. "Our land suffers enough from outside threats without fighting amongst ourselves. I need strong men such as you to help defend our lands."

"I told you last time, boy. Defend your own lands if you wish to call yourself a king." The word 'boy' dripped with derision from Gorloys' lips, a deliberate echo of the contempt he once endured. He looked dismissively at the surrounding field. "And this is the largest force you can pull together? And half of them made of straw no less…"

He scoffed, interpreting Uthyr's silence as a failed attempt at cunning. "Yes, I see it in your eyes. Your attempt at deception has failed! My scouts informed me of their true nature. Did you think I was a fool to fall for such tricks? You disappoint me… boy…"

As Gorloys uttered the insult, old resentments stirred within him, remembering how his father called him 'boy,' even after he had grown into a man. How it had stung each time, igniting a fire within him to prove himself. Now, he wielded the same word as a weapon, using it to belittle and diminish Uthyr, just as he had been diminished.

Uthyr stood silently for a moment longer, his gaze hardening as he faced Gorloys. Then, with a voice that carried the weight of authority and resolve, he declared, "I came once again under truce seeking friendship and alliance. Yet still, you mock me, Gorloys. Enough of this! Surrender now - swearing oath to enforce the king's will - and live. If not, you will meet your end on this very field today."

Gorloys' response came as a sneer, his contempt for Uthyr as palpable as the morning mist. "And how will you achieve that? With that flock of lame ducks at your back and your straw warriors?" he scoffed. "Do you truly believe you can challenge me with such a pitiful force?" His words dripped with scornful skepticism, belittling Uthyr's authority and the strength of his band of men. "You bore me with your pretensions of kingship… boy."

He turned his back on Uthyr, a clear dismissal, his confidence unshaken. Beside him, Branok, despite his burly stature, was surprisingly agile. He remained facing Uthyr, his stance alert and ready to retreat defensively if needed, eyes locked on the potential threat. Before walking away, Gorloys glanced over his shoulder, his eyes full of disdain. His voice, laden with scornful assurance, echoed his contempt as he spoke. "You may yet live long enough to see the true meaning of strength before you die this day…King Uthyr!" He bestowed the title with the same undeserving derision his father had often used when bestowing undeserved qualities on people, referring to cowards as brave, the weak-armed as mighty, and the weak-minded as cunning. "Prepare yourself and your pitiful band of men. You wish for battle? You shall have it – and it will be your undoing!" he added derisively.

As he turned away again to leave, before he could take more than a step, the very terrain seemed to shift before his eyes. What he had perceived as a mere rock, adorned with scrub, abruptly stood, revealing itself to be not a part of the landscape, but a man. This figure, clothed in a manner that made him nearly indistinguishable from the surrounding ground and vegetation, stood holding a long, black staff with an odd metallic head.

"He said nothing of battle," the figure announced, his voice cutting through the tense air. Gorloys' mind raced to comprehend this apparition, this man who had been a rock only a moment before. It was a trickery of battle he had never seen nor imagined – a man hidden in plain sight, an ambush made flesh.

Gorloys stood frozen for a mere moment, his initial shock swiftly giving way to anger. "Treachery!" he bellowed, his voice echoing across the field. Branok reacted instinctively to the outcry, spinning around to discover the reason for the alarm. Caught unaware, his eyes fell upon the figure standing defiantly before them. The same shock that had gripped Gorloys a moment before now spread across Branok's face and hand, almost of its own accord, flew to his sword, readying to confront this unexpected and wild adversary.

From Gorloys' encampment, a low, bass rumble of outcries echoed across the field at the sudden turn of fortune. His men, seeing the sudden danger to their leader, prepared to charge, their reactions mirroring his shout of alarm.

As Gorloys went to draw his sword, the figure, far from adopting a defensive stance, stepped forward with surprising swiftness. In a fluid motion, he swept the base of the staff at Gorloys, catching him off-guard and knocking his feet from under him. The abrupt incapacitation must have distracted Branok who stood there stunned and looking down at Gorloys, his sword still in mid-draw. Before Gorloys could react, the figure carried through the momentum of his initial swing. In a heartbeat, the staff's head crackled with energy, arcing above him like lightning. With precision, the metallic head struck Branok's, emitting menacing pops and crackles as tiny sparks of lightning shot into his temple. The burly warrior's eyes rolled back as he crumpled to the ground, motionless.

Lying on the ground, Gorloys could only watch as the figure refocused the head of the staff on him, the sparking staff head now mere inches from his own face. The reality of his vulnerability, combined with the sudden and bizarre turn of events, left him momentarily disoriented. Was this the end? His mind raced, grappling with the shock of this unexpected foe and his strange weapon. Was Branok dead? Was he next? He had often heard that a man facing his demise would see his life flash before his eyes. But staring into the sparkling head of the lightning staff, all he could see was the abyss of his end.

"I am Merlin of the Fae," the figure announced. "And if I wanted it so, you would be dead already. Your men are preparing to charge the field. If you wish to continue living, stand and tell your men to hold. Then…listen to the king."

Merlin stepped back, allowing Gorloys to sit up and observe his men forming into deadly groups as he had trained them, preparing to charge the field. As Gorloys struggled to his feet, he drew his sword suddenly in a swift motion. Facing Merlin, who stood casually leaning on the still sparkling magic staff, Gorloys adopted a defensive stance, crouching low with his sword out before him. "Why should I do that?" he retorted, his voice a mix of challenge and disdain. "Now that I have seen your tricks Fae, I am more than able to defend myself until my men reach us and overwhelm you!" he boasted.

Glancing over, Gorloys noticed that Uthyr had remained unmoving and patient the whole time, a casual observer to the conflict – a fact that infuriated him even more. He recalled the casual indifference his father had shown when goading him into conflict, drawing first swords, and then blood as the older man easily bested him time and again – until one day, he did not. Scars scattered across Gorloys' body were enduring reminders of those brutal encounters. Caught in the sudden reverie, Gorloys momentarily felt the same rush of excitement as he imagined running his sword through the heart of this arrogant young king, just as he had done to his own father on that fateful day so long ago.

As Gorloys began to move backward toward his encampment, he had only managed two shuffling steps when Merlin called out loudly in an unfamiliar tongue. The sound resonated across the open field, briefly stilling the growing tumult from Gorloys' camp. As if Merlin's words were some sort of incantation calling out to nature, three score more men emerged from hidden positions in the terrain. They materialized from the nooks and crannies of the uneven ground where they had blended into the natural landscape or transformed from the shapes Gorloys had mistakenly taken for nearby rocks or small boulders, much like Merlin had earlier.

Each disguised apparition, covered in nature's elements, held a bow with arrow nocked and trained on Gorloys, but not yet drawn. From Gorloys' encampment, an even louder rumble arose as his men initiated their charge. Merlin stared at Gorloys, his gaze steady and unreadable. "Call off the attack, Gorloys, or die here and now. The choice is yours," he said flatly. Kicking Branok, who groaned, but remained unconscious, Merlin added, "Perhaps when this one wakes, he will have the wisdom to rule your people on behalf of the king in your place."

Gorloys surveyed the field, his gaze darting across the men now encircling him, as the rumble from his charging forces grew louder. He noticed some of Merlin's archers shifting their focus towards the approaching men. His own troops, still out of bow range, were rapidly closing the distance – but not quickly enough. A sinking feeling overcame Gorloys as understanding set in. His men, caught off guard and ill-prepared for such an ambush, were at a grave disadvantage. If he didn't act swiftly, he risked losing the majority of his forces to the archers' onslaught before they could even reach his position.

Uthyr raised a hand, catching Gorloys' eye. It was clear he too saw the imminent outcome. "If blood is spilt this day…something I do not desire…I swear to you Gorloys, yours will be the first!" Uthyr interjected firmly. "I suggest you do as Merlin says before your time is up," he offered, nodding to the closest archers as they began to draw their bows and train them on Gorloys.

Quickly coming to a calculated decision, Gorloys took his sword and held it high over his head horizontally in both hands – grip in one hand, blade in the other – and began yelling as loud as he could, "CORNWALL HOLD!", repeating the phrase over and over until the roar and charge of his men ceased.

"You show wisdom, Gorloys of Cornwall," Merlin stated flatly, as Gorloys turned to face Uthyr once again, stunned and defeated, the haunting words of his father ringing in his memory. 'Over-confidence will get you killed,' it mocked and chided, over and over.

Marilyn stepped back as the two men faced each other. Gorloys, his posture deflated, stood in disbelief. The sword that had once been a symbol of his defiance now hung limply at his side in resignation. In stark contrast, Uthyr's expression shifted fluidly from stern resolve to a hint of joy, and then settled into a look of purposeful concern.

"All this time, Uthyr, I thought you were the fool," Gorloys sighed. "Perhaps you deserve the crown you wear after all," he admitted. "It is I who has been the greater fool!" he added. Marilyn barely knew the man, but even she could tell he seemed disgusted with himself, perhaps disappointed at falling into this trap, though he didn't know it was she who had engineered it.

"Nonsense, cousin!" Uthyr proclaimed. "You are a proud, strong, cunning warrior who commands the loyalty and love of his men. And, by all accounts, you show no mercy to your enemies!" As Gorloys looked up at the king, his expression revealed surprise, mirroring Marilyn's own reaction to Uthyr's string of compliments. Uthyr then added, with a rhetorical edge, "Why do you think I wanted you as an ally and not an enemy?"

Uthyr's apparent concern for Gorloys' pride struck Marilyn incongruous, yet noble. The compliments and acknowledgment of Gorloys' prowess seemed to have the mollifying effect Uthyr was aiming for. Gorloys, perhaps without full awareness, sheathed his sword and stood a little taller, akin to a man whose bravery came from a bottle, forced to pretend he was only acting in jest when the bouncer suddenly appeared - attempting to salvage his pride after a self-inflicted blunder.

Following Uthyr's lead, Marilyn decided to adopt a non-threatening stance. She deactivated her shock staff, silencing its distinctive hum and crackle. This abrupt change caught the attention of both men, but almost immediately, the groan of the unconscious man on the ground redirected their focus. With a reassuring smile, Marilyn addressed Gorloys, "The power in my staff only stuns; it does not kill unless I make it so." She retrieved her canteen, removing the cap, and held it out to Gorloys. "It is only water," she stated. "Rouse your man. His head may ache for a few days, but he will be fine."

Gorloys accepted the canteen, eyeing it with curiosity. She was aware of how different it must seem compared to the waterskins of this century and would not have revealed it but for the immediate necessity. After taking a cautious sip and seeming satisfied, he crouched beside Branok. "Branok! Branok, wake up!" Gorloys urged, beginning his efforts to rouse his companion. A series of actions ensued – splashing water, mild slapping, urging Branok to drink, followed by sputtering and coughing – as Gorloys diligently worked to revive Branok.

Eventually, Branok regained his senses and stood, surveying his surroundings with a growing awareness. His eyes widened in shock and alarm at Marilyn's presence and the sight of the scores of other men arrayed around them. Instinctively, he reached for his sword, but Gorloys acted swiftly, firmly grasping Branok's wrist to halt him. "Peace, Branok!" Gorloys commanded, locking eyes with Branok in a stern, meaningful gaze. Marilyn observed this silent exchange, sensing an unspoken message being passed between the two men.

"Your companion bade me listen in exchange for my life, Uthyr," Gorloys finally spoke up, nodding toward Marilyn without shifting his gaze from Uthyr. "What words are so vital that you would go to such lengths to say them?"

Uthyr, adopting a pragmatic yet cordial tone, responded, "Our fathers hated each other. By my father's account, your own was a hard and spiteful man. I do not know the truth of his words, but I know the hatred was shared by their fathers and their fathers before them." He shook his head in a gesture of regret. "And all likely over some quarrel between two farmers over a bit of grazing land generations ago. I have no wish to continue with such senseless ire. We should not hate each other simply because our fathers did so, cousin."

"Why do you do that? Name me 'cousin'?" Gorloys inquired, his voice tinged with consternation. "You have done so before, yet we share no blood." Marilyn observed Gorloys' struggle to restrain his arrogance, his demeanor revealing the effort it took.

"I meant no offense, Gorloys - truly," Uthyr replied placatingly. "We are all Britons – men whose ancestors were born of this land whether Welsh or Cornish, or even the Umbric to the north. In that sense, compared to foreign invaders, you are my cousin – a fellow Briton. We should work together to drive out the Angles, Saxons, Jutes, and others who have come to our shores since the Romans departed, seeking to carve out a piece of our land - our land! - for themselves."

Gorloys began to speak, his tone hinting at impatience, "I have already told you…" but Uthyr quickly interrupted, his voice tinged with urgency.

"I know…I know! Please, cousin! Just hear what I have to say, and then decide," Uthyr implored. "Afterward, you may return to your men unharmed, and I to mine," he added, his eyes earnest. "If you still wish my death, then we shall have your battle."

Gorloys paused, his eyes narrowing as he weighed Uthyr's words. After a moment of contemplation, he nodded slightly, "Very well…speak your peace."

Uthyr spoke earnestly, his hands gesturing slightly for emphasis, "Despite my earlier demands, I do not seek to rule over you or Cornwall. Nor do I seek levies from you or your people. An alliance is not even my demand, though it remains my hope."

Gorloys' brow furrowed, a mix of surprise and suspicion coloring his expression. "Then what is it you want, Uthyr?"

Uthyr leaned forward slightly, his voice steady, "Cooperation! My focus must be eastward to repel the Saxons and Angles. I aim to reclaim Lundenwic. The Jutes already raid my southern borders, demanding vigilance. And now, the Frankish threaten our lands! I cannot commit my forces to the east if I must constantly guard my flank," he explained, emphasizing the strategic dilemma.

Gorloys stroked his beard pensively, absorbing Uthyr's words, yet remaining silent.

Uthyr continued, a hint of urgency in his voice, "If you require more reasons, cousin, consider this. The longer I do nothing, the stronger the Saxons grow. Eventually, they will gain enough strength to overwhelm me."

A sly smile crept onto Gorloys' face, revealing a fleeting satisfaction at the thought of Uthyr's defeat. Marilyn observed the play of emotions, the subtle shifts in Gorloys' demeanor. But Uthyr, perceptive to Gorloys' reaction, smoothly countered, "And when the invaders are done with me, who do you think they will target next? With an even stronger foundation no less!"

The smile vanished from Gorloys' face as the implication of Uthyr's words sunk in, reshaping his earlier stance of hostility into one of reluctant acknowledgment. "You make a good point," he finally conceded. "Like it or not, your lands are a shield to the east. But if I am to yield, I need something in return, or I risk appearing weak."

Beside them, Branok nodded in silent agreement, acknowledging his leader's strategic acumen.

Uthyr, sensing an opportunity, spoke with a tone of resolution. "You make a good point. Very well. My men and I came from Bearda Market to this camp, a land I claim for levies. But the river at Bearda Market forks to the east and south. Let us split the difference. I will relinquish my claim on the lands along the south river to you, claiming only levies along the east river, expanding your claim, and reducing mine. By this agreement, we will end our father's feud. And to add honey, by this agreement where we stand puts me in your lands. You can return home and tell your people you faced me, ready for battle, and sent me away defeated, claiming more lands for the Cornish!"

As Uthyr laid out his proposal, Marilyn observed Gorloys closely. His expression was a mix of calculation and conflicting emotions, hinting at the internal struggle between his personal desires and the pragmatism of Uthyr's offer. She could see the decision in his eyes as he cast an uncertain glance at Branok, as if worried whether the man would remain silent.

Before Gorloys could voice any second thoughts, Marilyn abruptly reactivated her shock staff. The sudden hum and crackle of the staff startled all three men. With a sardonic smile, she warned, "If your man cannot hold his tongue, I can ensure his silence permanently by sending his soul to wander the mists of Annwn, never to find peace and ensure his eternal silence."

Branok recoiled from Marilyn, his eyes wide with fear, as he turned to Gorloys. "You have my silence, Pen Gorloys, on my oath! Take my tongue if you must, but please, do not let this sorcerer take my soul!" he pleaded desperately.

Gorloys, in response, remained silent for a moment, his gaze lingering on Branok. There was a certain satisfaction in his eyes, a sense of power over his terrified subordinate. Marilyn, witnessing this, felt a surge of anger at herself for inadvertently contributing to Branok's fear. 'This man probably drowned kittens and pulled the wings off flies growing up,' she thought disgustedly. After a moment, Gorloys turned to Marilyn and stated firmly, "That will not be necessary." Then, addressing Uthyr, he declared, "We have an agreement."

Uthyr extended his forearm in a gesture of accord, which Gorloys grasped firmly. Marilyn watched the exchange, a mix of relief and anticipation in her heart. This agreement was a pivotal moment, potentially bringing her efforts to a successful conclusion. If things went well from here forward, she would be returning home soon.

Releasing arms, Gorloys unexpectedly adopted a magnanimous tone. "I must say, the clever deception disguising your men was well done, Uthyr" he admitted. "And though I thought them a pitiful attempt to deceive, I now see the groups of straw warriors were only a distraction to draw attention from your men in hiding."

"You misunderstand, Gorloys," Marilyn interjected. "The straw men are not meant as a distraction but are placed there for demonstration."

"Demonstration?" Gorloys inquired. "How so?"

"There is a saying that comes from my realm – one in fact concerning agreements resolving conflict. The best translation I can say in your tongue is, 'Trust, but seek assurances'," Marilyn replied.

Two days earlier, Marilyn had stood alongside Uthyr in this very field, brimming with anticipation to showcase the culmination of all her efforts since their arrival in Execaer.

"Will it work?" Uthyr had inquired, his eyes reflecting curiosity as he observed the makeshift missile that Marilyn had prepared. During their wait for Sinbad's return in Moridunum, Marilyn had utilized the time to test an array of fireworks. Each one was meticulously engineered, varying in length to achieve different intensities of lift charges. She had devotedly charted the correlation between each lift charge's length and the angle at which the dragon's head was positioned. Considering all these variables, her preparation had led to a significant level of precision. If she accurately estimated the distance to the target, her chances of hitting the mark were high.

Marilyn's creation went beyond the basic pyrotechnics of the lift charge, which itself left a trail like a shooting star. She had crafted an effective payload for her firework using reeds wrapped in parchment, tightly packed with gunpowder, and sealed with wax at the ends. This combination resulted in a modest yet impactful explosive. When encased in a sheep's intestine filled with tarry pitch, further wrapped in another layer of parchment and oiled, the resultant impact was visually striking. Upon detonation, the firework exploded outward, igniting the pitch, and creating a spectacular burst of flame that spread widely upon impact.

With Gorloys' scouts still days away, Marilyn had chosen that moment to demonstrate the launch to Uthyr – both to prove the functionality of her invention and to acquaint him and his men with what to expect. Despite being a mere demonstration, the sight of the firework arcing gracefully across the open field and then erupting into flames about five hundred yards away had instilled a sense of awe and fear in Uthyr's men.

After the initial demonstration, Uthyr showed no signs of fear; instead, he gazed thoughtfully at the remaining fireworks. He suggested an enhancement: coating the "dragon's breath" in pine resin and igniting it with a torch as it launched from the statue's mouth. He quickly dispatched men to gather resin from a nearby copse for her.

Observing the results of the improved launch, Marilyn was impressed. "Nicely done," she murmured to herself. The addition of the pine resin had transformed the spectacle. As each firework left the dragon's mouth, the torch at its mouth ignited the resin, creating the illusion of a massive comet-like projectile soaring through the air.

She had then selected four of Uthyr's bravest men and meticulously trained them in the art of launching the fireworks, operating the dragon statues to make the wings flap, and other necessary tasks. The others were assigned to extinguish the flames at the impact sites and to set up groups of straw man soldiers.

That night, sleep had eluded Marilyn. Her mind was a tumultuous blend of doubt and certainty, hope, and despair. Now, standing before Gorloys, poised for the final display, she hesitated momentarily. Then, rallying her resolve with the mantra 'Success never comes to those who don't try', she lifted her still-lit shock staff high and twirled it, signaling the commencement of the demonstration.

Within Uthyr's camp, all but four men separated themselves from the crates, giving them a great deal of room per her instructions to Uthyr's men the night before. Pulling back the tarps on each crate, the men revealed the dragon statues.

With their bronze scales glinting in the morning sun and the men working concealed levers to bring the hinged wings and pivoting neck to life, the marionette act was highly effective from this distance. The dragons indeed looked like the glorious living creatures she had hoped to display before these superstitious people. Uthyr's men knew their true nature, but even they reacted with some sense of the shock and awe she had hoped to achieve. Gorloys and Branok stood wary and speechless, their eyes rounded by the spectacle before them. But at such a great distance, the dragons were too small to really see from Gorloys' encampment. Even so, from her position mid-field, she could see men pointing and hear a soft murmur coming from his camp.

Looking over at Gorloys, she continued, "I lent Uthyr the smallest of my dragons. The agreement has been made and it will be trusted." Uthyr interjected, his face suddenly stern and commanding. "And this is my assurance," he said, drawing his sword and pointing it in the direction of one of the straw warrior groups, signaling the men working at the dragons.

As she had hoped, the first dragon unleashed a spectacular flaming missile, soaring across the field and erupting upon impact with the straw soldiers. The explosion, a mixture of pitch, flames, and shrapnel, decimated the mock soldiers, eliciting alarmed cries from Gorloys' encampment, the men there pointing and shouting.

To drive the point home, Uthyr repeated the performance, pointing to the second group of straw warriors. The resulting explosion was even more spectacular, its reverberations echoing across the open field, intensifying the unrest among Gorloys' men.

Branok, overwhelmed by fear, had already bolted towards his camp. Marilyn noticed, with a mixture of revulsion and sympathy, a dark stain running down one leg of his trousers – a silent testament to his terror. His hasty departure left Gorloys isolated in the face of Uthyr's overwhelming show of force.

Gorloys, now alone and visibly shaken, seemed lost, his mind grappling with the scale of Uthyr's new power. Marilyn watched as Uthyr allowed Gorloys a moment to absorb the scene, the smoke and smoldering remains of the straw soldiers a testament to his dragons' might. Then Uthyr spoke again, his voice as steady as his resolve. "I am a merciful king to my allies, Gorloys. But to my enemies, I show no mercy." He sheathed his sword with a deliberate gesture, his eyes fixed on Gorloys, and delivered a final warning, "Break our agreement, and I will have my dragons raze Tintagel to the ground."

His usual air of arrogance and defiance had vanished, replaced by a stunned realization of his own vulnerability. He sank to his knees, a gesture of submission as profound as it was unexpected. He raised his eyes to Uthyr, his face stripped of its former pride and prejudice. "You have my fealty and my oath," Gorloys acknowledged, his voice a blend of resignation and deference. He lowered his gaze and, swallowing hard, uttered the words that cemented his capitulation, the finality of his submission evident in his voice, "…King Uthyr…Pen Dragon."

Gorloys, standing alone in the aftermath of Uthyr's dramatic demonstration, watched as Uthyr and the enigmatic figure who introduced himself as Merlin retreated towards their encampment. In the distance, he observed the once fearsome dragons now covered and seemingly disregarded by the men in the camp. To him, these magnificent creatures, now hidden beneath tarps, resembled hooded birds of prey, their potential for ferocity momentarily restrained. The idea – that such powerful beasts could be tamed and used at will – intrigued Gorloys, stirring a mix of awe and curiosity within him.

His gaze lingered a moment longer on the destruction wrought by the dragons, the scorched earth and obliterated straw warriors testifying to their might. As he turned to march back to his own camp, his mind churned with thoughts of the newly tilted balance of power between himself and Uthyr. He couldn't help but distrust Uthyr's intentions, suspecting that once the Angles and Saxons were driven out, Uthyr's gaze would inevitably turn back towards Cornwall. It was, after all, what he would do if their positions were reversed.

As Gorloys strode into his encampment, a hush fell over his men, their eyes following his every step. With a gesture of command, he gathered them around, his gaze piercing and authoritative. Amidst the assembled warriors, Branok stood, visibly shaken, his eyes avoiding Gorloys' stern gaze.

"Do not be deceived by what you believe you have witnessed this day!" he began. "Uthyr has chosen to yield in the face of our show of force and your steadfast courage in the face of his tricks and fiery display! He has agreed to retreat and has given up lands to the east to Cornwall in exchange for my promise not to attack!" His declaration sparked a wave of cheers among the men, their spirits lifted by his words. Gorloys' smile broadened as he basked in their adulation, praising their firmness and resolve.

Then, shifting his focus, he called out, his voice deceptively calm, "Branok!" The man slunk forward, head bowed in shame, muttering apologies under his breath. Gorloys placed a hand on his shoulder, offering soothing words of comfort that belied the cold fury in his eyes. The surrounding men fell into an uneasy quiet, instinctively sensing the undercurrent of tension.

Then, with a suddenness that took everyone by surprise, Gorloys' demeanor outwardly shifted. His hand, which had rested reassuringly on Branok's shoulder, suddenly gripped the man's hair, yanking his head back with ferocity. With a swift, brutal motion, he drew a concealed dagger and slit Branok's throat. Blood spurted between Branok's fingers as his hands flew to his neck, his eyes wide with disbelief and pain. Still gripping Branok's head, Gorloys stared mercilessly into his eyes as the man tried to speak, his mouth opening and closing like a fish out of water, his pleas for mercy unvoiced as blood bubbled on his lips and dribbled down his chin.

Gorloys released him, letting Branok collapse to the ground, a growing pool of blood marking his final moments. The entire camp grew silent, remaining motionless, their expressions a mix of shock and fear. Gorloys turned to face his warriors, his voice resonating with cold authority. "Is there any among you who would willingly follow a man like him into battle, knowing he might abandon you out of fear?"

A heavy silence answered him, the men exchanging uneasy glances, none daring to speak. Gorloys' gaze swept over them, his message clear. "Cowardice will not be tolerated," he proclaimed firmly. "Someone clean this mess."

Without another word, Gorloys walked away, leaving his men to deal with the aftermath. He motioned for Jory to follow him to his tent. Once inside, he inquired, "You saw the man with Uthyr, the one who wielded the strange black staff? He calls himself Merlin."

"Yes, Pen Gorloys," Jory responded, his voice betraying a hint of apprehension.

As the two men sat in his tent, Gorloys shared his observations and suspicions, detailing the fiery display he had witnessed, its source in these dragons that Gorloys' camp had been too distant to clearly witness, and his concerns about the future balance of power between himself and

Uthyr. "If Cornwall is to remain free from the tyranny of a king, we must restore the balance of power, Jory," he concluded. "If I can acquire even one of these dragons…"

"Given what you have told me Pen Gorlois, I doubt very much he will be persuaded," Jory complained.

"Persuasion comes in many forms," Gorloys replied matter-of-factly, but with a hint of menace in his tone. "Send our best scouts to keep a watch over Merlin without attracting notice. I want to know his every move. And if the chance to capture him or seize these dragons arises, they must take it and return immediately."

Jory nodded, understanding the gravity of the task at hand, and turned to leave. "Have the men break camp as well. We return to Tintagel," Gorloys added as the man stepped out of the tent. "Yes, Pen Gorloys," came the curt reply as Jory set off to carry out his orders.

As they reached the edge of the camp, Uthyr glanced over at Merlin. Though he could not have been more pleased with the outcome, especially the surprise of having Gorloys acknowledge him as king, he said, "That went better than I expected" in an understated tone, hoping to tease a reaction from Merlin.

"Better than you expected?!" Looking up to see Uthyr's mirthful grin, Merlin realized he was trying to provoke a reaction and grinned back. "I admit, it was unexpected to see that man give you his fealty," came the reply, echoing his own thoughts.

As they walked through the camp, each of them began issuing orders, with Merlin sending men to tend to the dragon statues while he directed men to begin breaking down the camp. As he glanced over at Merlin, who took to ordering the men with an authority that belied her true nature, he found himself continuously impressed by her leadership and resilience. In this world where men dominated the spheres of war and strategy, she navigated with an ease that often made him forget her disguise.

He never revealed that he knew her secret though. She worked very hard to conceal the fact, pretending otherwise to the world. 'She must have her reasons,' he mused. Looking out over the camp full of men, he began to contemplate her possible reasons more deeply though.

The two of them never discussed the lands from which she came. But in his world, a woman's authority seldom went beyond the confines of her household and family. Here among all these men, he began to respect her choice to hide her identity, understanding the complexities and dangers she would face as a woman in this world.

Some men treated women as little more than a means to sate their lusts – especially among warriors who thrived on camaraderie, often boasting, and competing in virility and prowess. Desire to prove themselves or satisfy such carnal needs sometimes even drove men to forget a woman's honor in a despicable act of taking what they desire by force.

Even so, she had proven herself intelligent, resourceful, cunning, and more than able to defend herself in combat. Against any man – or perhaps against even two or three given what he had just witnessed with Gorloys and Branok – she surely would be capable of stopping a man's unwanted attention. Observing her now, he found himself adding to her admirable qualities – she was a natural leader, giving orders and delegating tasks authoritatively with the greatest of ease.

'So, I suppose she does have her reasons,' Uthyr thought, a sense of admiration lacing his contemplation. The more he observed her, the more he understood the precarious balance she maintained in this world dominated by men. Confronting her about her true identity, even if he meant well, could unsettle that balance, something he was loath to do. He realized that his silent acknowledgment of her secret was not just about preserving her disguise, but also about respecting her choices and the strength it took to make them.

Uthyr's interactions with Merlin had subtly shifted his understanding of strength and leadership, extending beyond the traditional norms to which he was accustomed. Silently acknowledging this, he vowed to maintain the status quo. 'As long as I treat her as one of the men, others will follow suit,' he mused. And he was keenly aware that a secret, once share, often led to a loose tongue, a careless word said at the wrong moment exposing her secret to others. In his mind, this was not just a strategy to protect her secret, but a gesture of respect for her courage and resilience, qualities he had come to admire deeply.

He began thinking back to when he knew with certainty and why he chose to remain silent. He had to admit that she had done a fair job of keeping her identity concealed. But Uthyr had always prided himself on being observant. At first, her enigmatic nature and almost otherworldly behavior had him convinced that she was not human, that perhaps the fae his father's mother had told him tales of as a child truly did exist and Merlin was one of their number. The soft hairless face, the pale unblemished skin, the short hair, her softer more lyrical voice, the strange clothing, her magic staff – all these things fed his beliefs that she was from another realm and not of this world.

But now, having spent the last two moons with her since their fateful reunion at Glouvum – travelling, camping, and living amongst each other – he had observed enough signs to see the truth. His first clue, thinking back, was her resolute insistence on solitude when bathing or relieving herself. At first, he accounted it as an act of modesty or perhaps a belief among her people. But other small clues eventually led him to the truth – the way she walked with a casual sway rather than a trudging gait, the furtive glances she cast at handsome men like Sinbad, the occasional softness in her voice when she thought no one was paying attention.

Then one morning, as she stood near, the light struck her just so, highlighting a detail of her features – or rather a lack of that detail – that made him realize the truth of her identity. She lacked any semblance of the characteristic knot in her throat that most men he knew shared. With that realization, all the other subtle clues came rushing back, clicking into place so well he was momentarily stunned that he had not realized it sooner.

"I see we are breaking camp," Dubric's voice pulled Uthyr from his thoughts as the man approached. His eyes surveyed the bustling activity with curiosity. "Does this mean your efforts met with success? Or with ill fortune?" he asked.

"Great success!" Merlin said just as Uthyr replied, "Triumphant success!" both of them speaking in tandem. Dubric chuckled, his amusement clear. "One at a time, please!" he laughed, shaking his head at their eagerness. Uthyr and Merlin grinned at each other, then competed to share the news with Dubric, eventually falling into a rhythm, sharing the tale in an energetic back-and-forth, their camaraderie evident in every word.

As their shared narrative wound down, a thoughtful shadow crossed Uthyr's face, dimming the mirth in his eyes. His gaze drifted away, settling on the distant hills as he pondered the implications of their victory. The weight of his promise to Merlin, to aid her in her quest to return home, pressed heavily on his mind. It was a promise born of gratitude and respect, and he intended to honor it.

Dubric, observant of the shift in Uthyr's mood, tilted his head slightly, concern evident in his tone. "You seem distant suddenly, Uthyr. What burdens your thoughts?"

Uthyr exhaled deeply, his voice carrying a somber tone. "Dubric, our victory today is not without its obligations. I made a vow to Merlin, a promise to help him return to his world. It is a matter of honor, and I must see it through."

Dubric nodded, his expression reflective. "You and Merlin seem to have formed a strong bond of friendship. I am sure his departure will be a loss. But a man's worth is often measured by his ability to keep his word. It is a trait that earns respect and marks true leadership."

Merlin, having listened silently, spoke up. "You have become a good friend, Uthyr. When we first made an agreement, I did not really know you. I had to trust that you would honor your promise, and I admit, I worried you would not." Waving her hand to their surroundings, indicating the whole of their accomplishment, she added, "Or that your success would overshadow your promise perhaps. But you have proven yourself to be a man of integrity who will keep his word. And for that, you have my gratitude. Your help means more to me than you can know."

Uthyr met her gaze, blushing a little at the praise from both. With a bashful smile, he replied, "I had no doubts of our success, Merlin. And it was a success even greater than I had hoped!" With a glint of mischief in his eyes, he added "Indeed, I was so confident we would achieve our goal that, before we left to meet Gorloys here, I had arranged for a mining crew from the Cuantuc Hills to be ready at Bearda Market to sail upon our return. Your path home will be cleared."

Later that day, as they rode quietly at the head of a large group of men, Uthyr noticed Merlin frequently glancing back at the carts holding the concealed dragons and then casting furtive looks in his direction. "It seems you have something to say but are unsure how to begin, Merlin," Uthyr finally remarked. "Speak your mind, my friend."

Merlin took a deep breath, her expression grave. "Uthyr, I have given much thought to the dragons and the dragon's breath. I have come to a decision… they cannot remain here with you."

Uthyr, surprised by her declaration, responded, "But Merlin, consider the advantage such power would grant us in repelling our foes. It could be the key to securing our lands."

Shaking her head, Merlin's tone was resolute. "The risk is too great, Uthyr. I have exposed your world to a power it is not prepared for. Should your enemies capture some of the dragon's breath, they may be able to study my secrets and learn to make more. I cannot allow that. I will not be responsible for risking such destruction."

Uthyr frowned, pondering her words. "I understand your apprehension, yet such power could shift the balance of our conflicts."

Merlin met Uthyr's gaze with an earnest intensity. "I am aware, but this world is not ready to wield such knowledge or power responsibly. The risk of harm is too great. The fate of your world must unfold as if our paths had never crossed, free from the influence of my knowledge. I must take it back."

Uthyr nodded slowly, absorbing the significance of her decision. "I understand your point, Merlin. Though I may wish to keep this power, I respect your judgment. I will have the statues and dragon's breath loaded onto your ship when we return to Bearda Market."

Offering a small, appreciative smile, Merlin replied, "Thank you, Uthyr. I will miss you, my friend."

"And I, you," Uthyr said warmly.

A moment later, Uthyr chuckled and said, "So much for that," talking to himself.

"So much for what?" Merlin asked.

"Gorloys called me Uthyr Pen-dragon. But without dragons, I suppose the title is meaningless!" Uthyr replied.

"Pen? What is this word?" Dubric, who had been listening stoically, suddenly chimed in.

"It is an old title – a formal title intended to convey respect – used since before the Romans came, before the people of this land had any idea the world beyond their village or their tribe was so vast," Uthyr informed him. "It means 'chief' or 'leader'. He named me 'Chief of Dragons' in essence."

"I like it!" Merlin piped in. "The name – the title - it has a certain…nobility. You may not keep the dragons, Uthyr. But you can keep the name," she added, smiling.

"Uthyr Pendragon! First Christian King of Britannia?" Dubric proclaimed but arching his eyebrow with a questioning grin of hope.

'The man is certainly persistent,' Uthyr thought, smiling inwardly. Outwardly, he chuckled. "Perhaps one day, Brother Dubric," he responded. "Perhaps one day…"

CHAPTER 16

Reunion, Heartbreak, and Hope

Standing at the self-serve station in the mess hall, Philip had just finished pouring himself a cup of coffee when his phone dinged, barely audible above the cacophony of sound emanating from the crowd of base personnel eating breakfast. 'Thirty minutes,' he thought worriedly. "Mare's been there three months," he said to himself quietly after a quick calculation in his head. "God, please let her be okay," he added in silent prayer.

As he turned around to head back to the lab, Ayesha came bursting through the double doors into the mess hall drawing attention from several nearby diners. Alarmed, Philip signaled her as she scanned the room, then locked eyes with him and stooped to catch her breath. Pointing back in the vicinity of the lab, she panted, "Flip…control room…now!" between breaths. Carelessly dropping his coffee on a nearby table, he rushed by her and out the double doors as she turned to follow.

He rushed down the hallway, yelling for people to move as he fumbled for his security badge. Finally arriving at the control room door, he frantically scanned open the door and demanded, "What's the emergency?!" to anyone and everyone in the room, hoping someone would answer quickly.

Naomi Higgins turned around from her workstation calmly as Ayesha skidded to a halt in the doorway behind Philip. "Look," Naomi said plainly, pointing at the artifact through the control room window.

Philip's heart pounded in his chest as he stared through the control room window, through the clear surface of the artifact, as though watching a scene unfold through a window. The cavern beyond, illuminated by the eerie glow of the artifact, presented a scene straight from a movie screen. More than a dozen olive-skinned men, barefoot and barely clothed, moved about the cave with a mixture of curiosity and awe. By their looks, attire, and swaggering walk, Philip concluded they must be sailors – they certainly shared the quintessential image of Arabian seafarers of the time as portrayed in his imagination: robust, with muscles honed by years at sea, clad in loose trousers and half-open vests that revealed rugged, sunbaked chests.

One sailor, his dark hair tied back, held a pair of women's dress shoes with a puzzled expression, turning them over in his calloused hands as if trying to decipher their purpose. Another, younger and with a curious glint in his eyes, was fixated on a cardboard box. He carefully picked through its contents, examining a wad of foil and some plastic utensils with the fascination of a child discovering a new toy.

And nearby, a burly man with a thick beard had found a length of metal cable. He twisted and turned it, his brow furrowed in concentration, occasionally glancing at his companions as if seeking their approval or understanding. His fascination was palpable, his gestures conveying a mix of awe and confusion at this strange, flexible metal snake.

All these items – things Marilyn left behind when she left the cave which was, for her, over three months ago – were a treasure trove of mystery to these ancient sailors. Some things, such as the thermos, were simple to understand though mysterious in their construction. Others, like the discarded GPS locator held greater mystery, but oddly enough, less interest.

But it was one figure who drew Philip's attention the most. Standing apart from the others, a man of medium build and an authoritative air examined the artifact itself. Unlike his companions, he wasn't distracted by the objects scattered around the cave. His focus was solely on the artifact. From the sailor's side, Philip imagined he was looking at a dense forest of crystalline protrusions, all displaying a fractured piece of the laboratory beyond. The sailor's eyes were scanning the crystal structure intently, as if he were trying to mentally fit all the pieces together to form a coherent image of the world beyond his perception.

As the sailor stood there looking into the artifact though, Ayesha said, "He's got a message, Flip!" Philip hadn't noticed until she pointed it out, but the sailor was indeed holding up a parchment. It was upside down, but even Philip could see it was English, though he couldn't make out the message from where he stood in the control room.

"How long have they been in the cave?" Philip inquired.

"One minute and 47…48…49…," Naomi counted, when suddenly, the unexpected unfolded before their eyes. Marilyn herself burst into the cave, her stride purposeful, followed by a scruffy-looking group of men. They were dressed for heavy labor, each carrying bags, packs, or water skins, but more importantly, they wielded mining tools.

From the control room, Philip and his team watched the scene unfold like a silent film. Marilyn approached the sailor holding the message with a familiarity that suggested she knew him, yet her demeanor was tinged with annoyance. She launched into a fervent argument, her hands gesturing emphatically first at the message, then the artifact, and finally back toward the cave entrance. The sailor, in response, vigorously shook the parchment, pointed at the artifact, and shrugged, countering her points with equal fervor.

Philip leaned closer to the window, trying to decipher the silent exchange. Marilyn's body language was unmistakable – she wanted the sailors to leave the cave. However, as the sailor began rallying his men, Marilyn's expression shifted to one of resigned authority. She pointed firmly to the ground, her stance unyielding. It was a clear command for them to stay.

The team in the control room exchanged puzzled looks. "Seems like she can't make up her mind whether she wants him around," murmured Philip, more to himself than anyone else.

"I'll have him around!" Naomi piped up, drawing Philip's attention. Ayesha followed closely behind. "Mmm Hmm," she muttered appreciatively in non-verbal affirmation. To Philip the two looked like a pair of desert castaways about to fight over a found canteen full of ice water. Looking back through the portal himself, he cast a more appraising eye on the unknown sailor and silently resolved to spend a little more time at the gym. The fellow certainly was easy on the eyes.

A moment later, Marilyn began walking over to the charge station to retrieve her earpiece, prompting Philip to tell the team he was headed to the platform as he ran out the control room door. The scene before them had raised more questions than answers, but one thing was clear: Marilyn was orchestrating something crucial.

By the time he had descended the stairwell, got through the security door to the lab, and made his way across the catwalk to the platform, Marilyn had managed to retrieve her earpiece and fit it to her ear. The sailors all around her watched in wonder as she did so, her apparent comfort with the artifact as enigmatic to them as she likely was. She was still facing the cave wall when, a moment later, he heard her voice over the comms. "Lieutenant Colonel Marilyn Morgan reporting. Can anyone hear me? Over."

The leader of the sailors had turned his attention back to the crystalline forest of the artifact and registered Philip's sudden presence with shock and surprise as Philip replied, "You're comin' in loud and clear, Mare! Turn around," he responded, his voice a mix of excitement and anticipation.

Marilyn turned slowly, her face a canvas of emotions. Though he could see her clearly, he knew her image of him was being filtered through the broken edges and planes of the crystalline protrusions extending from the artifact in the cave. He imagined that to her he must look like some geometric Cubist representation of himself – a stained-glass Picasso rendering. Even so, the moment she laid eyes on him, standing on the platform, a mixture of joy, relief, and unspoken longing filled her expression. For her, it had been over a hundred days in a world far removed from this lab, far removed from him. For Philip, it was as if she had left only half an hour ago, yet the intensity in her eyes told a different story.

The two shared a quiet moment – a moment that said more in silence than a novel of words could have conveyed. "Sorry, Flip," Marilyn finally said. "But you've no idea how good it is to see you. To hear your voice! To speak English!"

Philip found himself struggling to grasp what it must be like to be in her position. Having last seen her less than an hour ago, he hadn't really had time to develop the fondness of absence and the longing associated with it. So, for her sake more than his own, Philip's heart ached to bridge the gap, to hold her, to assure her that she wasn't alone in this vast and unpredictable journey. Marilyn's eyes glistened, a tear tracing a path down her cheek, a silent testament to the hardships she'd faced and the resilience she'd shown.

"This is so strange Mare," he finally said with a boyish grin. "I saw you less than an hour ago and now here you are. Your hair's longer and you've gone and got yourself tanned!" At his appraisal, Marilyn almost without thought reached up and tugged at a lock of hair and glanced at the back of her hand.

Marilyn's lips quivered into a smile, a mix of sadness and happiness. "Well from this end, my time here has seemed endless, Flip," she whispered, her voice laced with a longing that transcended time. "But seeing you now, I feel like a soldier returning home from a harrowing tour of duty. Only I can't hug you in the airport lobby!" Sighing, she added, "I'm happy but frustrated all at the same time!"

"I know Mare. But from the looks of these men, we're almost there. We'll have the artifact freed and you home in no time!" he said encouragingly. Turning his attention to the sailor standing next to her, Philip jabbed a thumb in his direction. "So, what was the tussle with this fella about?" he inquired. "I saw you arguing with him before we got on the comms."

Marilyn turned her head and leveled smoldering eyes at the sailor. The annoyed look, coupled with a sardonic smile, disturbingly reminded Philip of his mother when he was a boy and had done something ill-advised; her annoyance at war with amusement over whatever stupid thing he'd done. Marilyn held that same look now.

"I asked him to deliver a message I wrote almost a week ago. I warned him of the time dilation effect in terms he could understand and told him to get in, deliver the message, and get out," she informed the team. "He didn't listen. In any case, he's here now and I could use the extra labor. So, I told him to stay."

She paused for a moment as if considering, then inquired, "Is the whole team on comms?" Following a series of confirmations, she turned and introduced Philip to the man saying something to him in a language Philip didn't understand but ending with Philip's name.

"Team, meet Sinbad the sailor," she finally said, extending a hand toward the sailor as if presenting him like a game show contestant. He bowed, extending a leg forward with a curly cue flourish of his hand as a cacophony of disbelief and incredulous exclamations broke out over the channel. "What?!...No way!...For real?!...The Sinbad?" were all followed by the same appreciative mutter of "Mm hmm" coming from Ayesha.

Turning to Philip with a mischievous twinkle, she added glancing furtively in Sinbad's direction, "He is rather dishy isn't he?" she smirked. "I bet Naomi and Ayesha are panting right now..."

"Am not!" came an immediate, but obviously insincere protest from Naomi in tandem with another appreciative, "Mm Hmm" from Ayesha. The rest of the team laughed at their responses as Marilyn quietly snickered.

"That can't be the Sinbad, Mare," Philip exclaimed, emphasizing the article. "Wasn't he just some fairy tale like Ali Baba or Aladdin from that Arabian Nights book? I don't know when exactly, but that's got to be another four or five hundred years in the future from your perspective!"

"You all have me running around pretending to be some legendary wizard that won't be written about for another four or five hundred years," Marilyn interjected. "And here I am making that legend a reality. Is it so hard to believe that a legend from another culture could've had similar origins in a real person?"

"Lieutenant Colonel, please tell me you got a picture of his boat – The Chimera," Takashi suddenly interjected over the comms.

Smiling, Marilyn said, "Sinbad used that word to describe a make-believe ship with wheels that would allow him to sail on both land and sea, Tak. But perhaps one day it will be a reality."

"Oh," Takashi replied, disappointed. But repeated "Oh!" again more excitedly when she told him she had a picture of ships in a harbor from the era so that he could add to his bottled ship collection.

Returning her focus to Philip, Marilyn because serious. "We have a problem, Flip. The time dilation factor troubles me," she admitted. "In the four or five minutes I've been back in the cave, half a month has passed outside. Even working around the clock, it's going to take these men days to break the artifact free on this end. Some of these men have families and lives. I can't expect them to give that up. But a day in here means more than a decade will go by outside!"

"What are you proposing then?" he asked, suddenly afraid of the answer he knew was coming,

"Our only option is to turn it off while we mine it free," Marilyn replied, her voice steady but filled with the weight of her decision.

Apprehension filled Philip's veins. "That is one hell of a risk that could leave you stranded there forever, Mare…"

"I know!" Marilyn replied, then taking a deep breath, continued more calmly, "I know. But I don't see any other choice."

Philip swallowed hard, nodding in silent agreement. The courage in Marilyn's eyes spoke volumes, reinforcing his respect for her leadership and resolve; that same courage was only one of the many qualities that earned her the rank she held.

"Let's at least test it then," Philip suggested. "We'll cut the power to the proton emitter, then repeat the original experiment and reestablish contact." Strapping himself into a new harness installed at the workstation, he added, "I may not be dangling over the artifact like you were, but the first time there was some sort of energy bubble that seemed to reach out and grab you. We don't need two of us over there!"

"I remember that bubble," Marilyn said, a shadow crossing her face at the memory. "Let's just get this test over with before I lose my nerve. How long do you need to setup?"

"A half hour should do it," Philip responded after a brief consultation with the team.

Marilyn nodded, her expression resolute. "I'll clear out the cave for the next four hours. That should give you enough time."

Philip nodded, replying "I love you, Mare! See you soon!" with all the confidence he could muster, his voice steady despite the knot in his stomach.

"I love you too, Flip," she replied with a smile, then turned to usher the sailors and workers out of the cave. Once the last person disappeared down the passage, Philip turned to the team. "Cut the power, Tak," he ordered, his voice betraying a mix of fear and hope.

The gentle lap of waves frolicked in the background as Marilyn stood on the beach facing Sinbad. His boat, along with the one she had arrived on, bobbed in the shallow water nearby.

"How is it you are here, Merlin?" Sinbad asked, his tone a mix of curiosity and concern.

Marilyn sighed, her eyes reflecting the weight of her journey. "I tried to tell you that moments in the cave became days in the world out here. I last saw you five days ago. If you had stayed within overnight, years would have passed, changing everything you know."

Sinbad's brow furrowed in thought. "Then how can we be expected to help? I cannot ask this of my men."

"You saw the …door… to my world, yes?" Marilyn inquired, receiving a nod from Sinbad. "The magic that makes moments become days only happens when the door is open. I told my friend we must release the magic - close the door - so you could help me without sacrificing your lives out here. When we are done, he will reopen it." As she continued, explaining the need and the risk of possibly being abandoned in this world, Sinbad listened intently.

"The great and wise Zarathrustra says, 'Do not be sorry and dejected or have fear and anxiety for that which has not come to you.' It will be well," Sinbad finally said. "And if it is not, then you have worried over what cannot be changed. Let us focus on the moment and the task at hand then."

Marilyn nodded, surprised and appreciative of the wisdom shared from such an unexpected source. A small smile of realization touched her lips as she accepted the truth in his words. Resolving to think positively, she shared her plan. "When we go back into the cave, my friend is going to open the door again for a short time just to be certain it can be done," she explained to Sinbad. "Then he will turn it off again for three days. Do you think that is enough time to free the door within the cave?"

"You are my friend Merlin!" he responded with a boyish grin. "We will free your door in two days!" he added boastfully.

Marilyn grinned. "The rock is hard my friend. Three days will be enough."

Four hours later, she and the men were once again standing before the artifact. She'd had them set up torch poles along the back wall to provide light while she watched and waited with growing anxiety. Holding back panic while counting the minutes, a sudden rush of relief came flooding through her when she heard Naomi's voice over the comms as light reemerged from the artifact.

A cheer went up from the entire team as she acknowledged her presence. The sense of relief for the entire team was palpable in their voices, but Philip was standing before her on the platform. His voice, his body language, all spoke of the stress he had endured for the incredible, but necessary risk they had taken, one from which he may not have recovered easily had the outcome been unfavorable. "Everything is okay, Philip," she said encouragingly. "Now do me a favor before we close this thing and get me some toothpaste!" eliciting a smile from Philip and a chuckle from the team. Soon, the team had a plan in place to power down again and back up again in three days to check the miner's progress.

The workers and sailors murmured in awe when a tube of toothpaste shot out of the artifact's rough surface, seeming to materialize from nowhere. "See you in three days my love," Philip said, this time with confidence as Marilyn and the rest of the men in the cave watched the light from the portal dim and fade out.

Marilyn stood beside Sinbad, watching his men work to free the artifact, her anticipation growing. 'Many hands make light work,' she mused, grateful for the unexpected assistance Sinbad and his sailors provided, making the task a greater deal easier. Her own crew of miners, originally tasked with this job, rested at the back of the cave, conserving energy for the next shift. She did not think another shift would be needed though, and moments later her suspicions were confirmed.

The sounds of chipping and scraping that filled the air ceased as, with a soft grinding noise, the last stalactite gave way, and the crystalline device was released from its rocky prison. But when the sailors moved to steady it, a moment of confusion seemed to wash over them. As they began to babble with each other and with Sinbad in their own ancient tongue, Marilyn turned to Sinbad with worry. "What's wrong? What are they saying?" she asked quickly.

"Nothing is wrong my friend. Your…door - by the large size, it should be heavy, yes?" he inquired. She watched as Sinbad issued more commands in his own language and most of his crew backed away, leaving two men on either side of the artifact who lifted it with ease while a third held it steady. "It is not," he said with a sardonic grin.

"Have them turn it around," she requested with even more anticipation. Sinbad spoke again, interpreting her request to his crew, but as they pulled the artifact away from the wall, a cloud of ancient dust billowed out, emanating from a hidden chamber revealed behind it, scattering the nearby sailors as they coughed and sputtered, trying to recover.

As the artifact teetered, Najat the Unspeaking – one of Sinbad's crew whose name Marilyn had previously learned – rushed forward to steady it and keep it from falling. He turned, smiling at Marilyn quietly as she returned the smile, nodding in gratitude. "Thank you," she said, not knowing if he would understand. But the message seemed clear as he mimicked his captain's flourish of hand, accompanied by a nod rather than an attempt to bow.

Once they recovered their breath, the men guiding the artifact resumed their positions and turned it, revealing what Marilyn had hoped and prayed to see – a glassy, smooth surface identical to the one she had left behind in the present. The sight brought an immediate smile of satisfaction. Hope, joy, and excitement bubbled within her as she continued to direct the men.

"Lean it against the wall there," she said, pointing to an area of the cave wall to the left of the newly revealed opening into the unexplored chamber beyond. The sailors complied, needing no interpretation of her signals, setting it down with caution where she indicated. Their attention, along with Sinbad's and Marilyn's, then shifted to the dark opening of the chamber, the mysterious void beckoning with unspoken secrets to be explored and revealed.

Sinbad grabbed a torch pole from the collection along the back wall and murmured something to his crew, drawing a questioning look from Marilyn. "I told them to stay behind while you and I go within," he said. "If there is treasure to be found, I want first pick!" he added with a mischievous grin. Marilyn wasn't sure if he was joking though. Grabbing another torch pole herself, she allowed him to lead the way.

Sinbad led the way into the unexplored chamber, torch in hand, with Marilyn close behind. As they stepped across the threshold, the light of Marilyn's torch revealed that the rough-hewn edge where the artifact had been trapped ended abruptly, giving way to the glass-smooth walls of a short perfectly cylindrical passage. She held her torch up to the surface and felt it, expecting some sort of manufactured material. But instead, she found natural rock that appeared the have been smoothly cut somehow, marred only by the cracks and fissures of time.

Suddenly, she bumped into Sinbad as he stumbled and stopped, muttering, "There is something on the floor." He lowered his torch to see what had obstructed him, revealing the bleached bones of an obviously humanoid creature about the size of an adolescent. At first, he seemed only startled, exclaiming, "This is a tomb!"

But as Marilyn brought her own torch closer to shed more light on the remains, Sinbad yelled out in abject terror and fell back on his behind. Shocked at his sudden reaction, she watched him scramble backward in a crab walk yelling, "Ghūl! This is a cursed tomb! Ghūl! We must leave at once, Merlin!" The fear in his eyes was palpable, yet she felt it was more for her sake than his own. Still, his fear was infectious and, not knowing what a ghūl might be, she allowed the same instinct to flee to take over. As he gained his feet with her help, they both ran for the exit back into the main cave only a few yards away, leaving his torch where it lay next to the remains.

As they reached the exit together, she glanced over her shoulder and let out an anxious breath. "Nothing followed us, Sinbad." Hands on his knees, catching his breath, he looked up and nodded. "Good!" he replied, continuing to steel his nerves.

Fascination and curiosity winning out, she sat aside her concern for him for the moment and peered back around the corner into the darkness of the chamber, listening for any noise. 'Perhaps it was a snake or spider of some sort?' she mused. She finally turned to him and asked, "Sinbad, what is a ghūl?"

"A ghūl is a creature that was once a man whose greed drove him to rob the graves of the dead. He becomes cursed with an insatiable hunger, but the curse also keeps him imprisoned in the tomb he robbed," he informed her. "His hunger drives him to eat the flesh of the dead," he added. "…and the living – other graverobbers," he gulped, glancing into the darkness of the chamber.

"But, moments ago, you were willing to go in and take any treasure you found," she said with confusion.

"True," he responded. "But only hidden treasure. We would not steal from the dead!"

"I understand," she said. Though she did not believe such tales, he obviously did. Who was she not to treat his beliefs with respect, no matter how superstitious she thought them? She believed in God herself, and by extension, angels and demons. Even so, her scientific need to know more drove her desire to explore the chamber further. Pondering the situation for a moment, she turned to Sinbad and said, "I think I have just the magic that will protect us. A powerful light to fend off evil!" she informed him.

Fishing her flashlight from her backpack, she added "This is my scepter of moonlight," remembering what she had called it when creating the costume for Kei. As he looked down in wonder at the shiny aluminum casing, she asked, "Will you come with me to explore the chamber so we may guard each other?"

She could see the fear in his eyes slowly being subsumed by a strong desire to see her magic in action. Finally, drawing his sword from its scabbard, he nodded. As she turned on the flashlight and flooded the interior of the chamber with light, startled gasps of awe emanated from the cluster of men behind them. Glancing over at Sinbad, she saw that his eyes too were large and awestruck. He looked at the chamber, then back at the flashlight several times before simply accepting its power and leading her back into the chamber once again.

She smiled with amusement, shaking her head. 'Fear and belief,' she thought quietly, then muttered, "Powerful motivators..." to herself, finishing the thought aloud. Looking back toward the chamber entrance, she saw the soft, flickering light of the torches against the back wall of the main cave silhouetting several curious, but fear-stricken onlookers as they crouched around the edges of the chamber entrance, too afraid to enter.

Ignoring them, she approached the closest remains where Sinbad had dropped his torch and shined her light down, revealing a scene straight from a sci-fi horror novel. The creature was humanoid, though obviously inhuman, given the elongated shape of its skull, larger than normal eye sockets, and diminutive upper jaw and lower mandible, both of which contained the sharp teeth of a predator race rather than the omnivorous variety found in humans.

As if offering proof of its extraterrestrial origin, the alien wore a tattered uniform reminiscent of something an astronaut might wear, similarly marked by the faded symbols of its race. Marilyn's fascination mixed with a somber respect as she squatted down to examine the alien's remains more closely. But as she traced a finger along one of the uniform symbols, the fabric crumbled under the lightest touch, collapsing the arm into a mote of dust that kicked up, making her cough.

Standing once again, she shined her flashlight around the remainder of the chamber. Perhaps five yards of its walls, nearest where the artifact had been excavated, were perfectly round smooth-hewn stone. But this soon gave way to the coarse walls of a natural cave roughly another 10 yards deep. It was as if the artifact had been used as the drill bit of a tunnel boring machine, used to carve a cylindrical tunnel through the solid rock and left abandoned before the project was complete.

Lying about the chamber - some by themselves, others in clumps of two or three – were the desiccated remains of more than a dozen humanoid creatures like the one in front of her. She looked at Sinbad and said quietly, "These are not ghūl, Sinbad. They were… explorers – perhaps much like you – only their ship sailed the sea of stars. The door you helped free was made by them. I only stumbled through it by accident."

"Then what are they doing here? Trapped within this cave?" he inquired. "Could they not use their door to leave?"

"I do not know," she admitted. "Perhaps we will find an answer if we look around." Nodding, he picked up the second torch and held both over his head to alleviate light blindness as the two of them set off to peruse some of the other clusters of remains and explore deeper into the cave.

"These poor creatures!" Sinbad eventually murmured quietly from over in a corner. Walking over to him to observe what he'd found, she saw he was examining a pile of bones and bits of cloth smeared with dried and blackened stains of blood. Though gruesome, the scene reminded Marilyn that even this alien race likely shared all too familiar physiological characteristics with humans, such as iron-rich red blood.

"We once came upon a small island where we found a broken ship, smashed against its rocky shore," Sinbad recounted. "When we went ashore and searched for survivors, we found a scene much like this. Like the men we found, these creatures must have been marooned here, trapped within the cave, where starvation led to…desperation," he suggested, his voice echoing eerily in the chamber. She felt a wave of revulsion but understood the harsh reality of survival, mentally recalling a movie she had seen about plane crash survivors in the remote Andes Mountains who resorted to cannibalistic practices in a desperate attempt to survive.

Even so, the realization that these beings met such a tragic end stirred a deep empathy within her. Mentally, she said a silent prayer of thanks that she had not shared their fate as a hint of worry began to worm its way into her thoughts. When the accident happened, why had she not come out of the artifact into this chamber instead of the sea cave? Based on the evidence before her, when she went through the artifact surface, she should have come out trapped in the chamber like these poor creatures. Shuddering, she dismissed the frightening thought before pondering the implications any further.

Piecing together what she knew of the crash site in the present, and reviewing the scene within the chamber, she could only imagine the outcome. It was all guesswork of course, but she surmised that the two artifacts formed some sort of propulsion system – an Alcubierre drive perhaps. A catastrophic event aboard the alien's ship must have somehow torn the thing apart, flinging one half across time and space to carve out a smooth-walled cavity in the rock where they stood. These poor creatures must have somehow been dragged along to be trapped behind the sealed space that then became their unwitting tomb. How they could have survived such an event in the first place though, separated from the main ship half a planet away, was beyond her ability to speculate.

With Sinbad off exploring deeper within the chamber's recesses, she decided she should document her findings and fished her Polaroid camera from her backpack to take pictures of the alien corpses. This quickly led to the discovery of what appeared to be a small notebook journal mostly concealed by one of the corpses, but which had reflected the camera's flash.

Moving the body to the side, she discovered a small cache of seemingly ordinary paper sheets, although a bit waxier looking. They appeared to be what remained of a notebook since one edge contained rust stains as evidence of a metal binding that had long since disintegrated. While trying to preserve their order, she began thumbing through the pages, trying to make some sense of the handwritten symbols and diagrams recorded in some indecipherable language. Glancing at the corpse, she could see the bones of a six-fingered hand still grasping a hollow plastic-looking tube – likely a writing instrument whose guts had long since rotted.

Pondering the rather well-preserved state of the pages, she was amazed at their level of preservation until she considered how the cave must have been sealed from the elements like a tomb, untouched by untold centuries. Then too, calling it "paper" was a bit of a stretch. While it served the same function, this paper neither looked, nor felt like any variety with which she was familiar. Otherwise, the paper and pen struck her as extraordinarily mundane – an unlikely correlation with humanity despite their advanced technology and ability to travel the stars.

Marilyn collected the pages and stuffed the stack neatly into her backpack with her camera. In the meantime, Sinbad had returned from the rear of the cave carrying something. "There were two more creatures at the back of the cave," he informed her. "From the gouges in the wall, they were trying to dig their way out with this."

He handed her something shaped like a small cup or bowl that mirrored itself on both ends, except that one end was slightly narrower than the other. Made from the same crystalline material as the artifact, she decided it was not likely meant for drinking and added it to the contents of her backpack. She knew her team, like her, would be eager to study it as well as the pages when she returned.

As if thoughts of her team were a summoning invocation, chatter erupted from the men in the main cave, causing Marilyn and Sinbad both to glance toward the chamber's entrance. The far wall of the main cave began to glow with the reflection of an all too familiar light emanating from the artifact. Excitement and anticipation replaced curiosity and a desire to explore as Marilyn stood and rushed toward the chamber exit with Sinbad trailing her heels.

Marilyn was surprised and overwhelmed with a moment of tearful happiness as the two of them exited the chamber into the sea cave. Standing on the platform in the lab, clearly and beautifully visible through the flat surface of the artifact, was the entire team, including Doctor Bennett.

But something was different, she realized. The team wasn't looking down at her over the edge of a platform railing. Instead, a piece of that railing had been cut away and it appeared as though Philip had had a work crew turn the artifact on its side and position it so that she would be able to step through directly onto the platform. She smiled warmly at his thoughtfulness as she moved to grab her earpiece. But as she turned it on and looked back at her team, she noticed something else subtly different. She was now seeing a ghost image of dimly lit cave walls superimposed over the image of her team.

"Flip, I see something strange from my end. I can see the team clearly. Thank you for moving the artifact by the way. But now I am seeing another image on top of it, like a reflection in a window, of the cave behind the artifact."

It was Avery that responded though to her curious observation. "We're seeing the same thing…well, something similar anyway…from this side boss," he interjected. "Only in our case, it's a shadow of the wall you leaned the artifact against. Makes sense though."

"Why is that?" Marilyn asked, curious.

"We're basically seeing an effect not unlike privacy glass," he replied. "When it's light outside, you can't see into the house. But at night, when someone has a light on, you can. The same is essentially true for them. During the day, they see outside, but at night, they mostly see the reflection of their living room over a dark image."

"I see," she said, pondering his explanation. "Whichever side of the artifact has the strongest light will show the clearest image."

"Exactly," Avery confirmed.

Shrugging it off as interesting, but ultimately unimportant, she turned back to Sinbad, and all the men who had helped, to thank them for everything. But the look of shock and surprise on Sinbad's face drew her attention. "Are you okay, Sinbad?" she asked, concerned.

Shifting his gaze between her and her team, he swallowed and muttered, "It must be…"

"What must be?" she inquired, now a little alarmed. "Sinbad, look at me!" As he focused on her, grinning, she asked again, "What must be?"

"I have seen many lands, met many people," he began. "But none as strange and mysterious as you, Merlin. King Uthyr claimed you were from another world – one of magic and dragons; that you are not human…as with the creature we found," he mused thoughtfully.

Marilyn couldn't help but smirk at Uthyr's description of her as Sinbad turned his gaze to her team. "But seeing your crew…" he continued, "you are as human as I! Though seeing that world beyond your door, I could believe it is a magical place." Shaking his head and nodding at Philip, he added, "And though I cannot hear them, the language of your body and face says a great deal that made little sense to me before now. But I see now that you are a woman! That man there is your life mate, is he not?"

"You are too clever for a man, Sinbad," she chided shaking her head, drawing a grin from him that she returned. "And yes. He…", she pointed at Philip, "is Philip – and I love him." She turned and shifted her gaze to Philip, smiling warmly, then back to Sinbad as she continued. "But you must understand, history must remember Merlin as a man and tell his tale so."

She watched as more pieces of the enigma of Merlin clicked into place for him. She could practically see the proverbial lightbulb of enlightenment flicker on. Watching his face, his eyes rounded in realization as he spoke, nodding toward the portal, "That place – that is the land of tomorrows. It is how you know my destiny!"

Marilyn smiled without confirming anything. But for Sinbad, lack of denial seemed equal proof of his words. "And this…door – it is more like a ship that sails on the winds of time! I understand now. You are like a sailor in a leaky boat, trying to get home with no sail and a broken oar!"

He laughed at his own cleverness as she smiled and walked over to grab her earpiece. "Just remember Sinbad. What you believe must never leave this cave. Do you understand?" she asked him seriously.

"You are my friend, Merlin," Sinbad replied with heartfelt sincerity. "I will keep your secrets."

Nodding, Marilyn put in her earpiece, facing him with a grave expression. "This also means that when I leave, this door will close forever. Can you promise to cast it into the deepest sea depths you can safely reach?"

Sinbad's smile was warm and unwavering. "It will be done," he assured her.

With a mix of determination and sadness, Marilyn gathered the discarded GPS locator, thermos, and charging station. She gave Sinbad and his crew a final wave of farewell, then turned to step through the artifact, back to her team.

But as she stepped forward, she collided hard against the artifact's smooth surface. Shock registered on her face, a mirror of her team's stunned expressions on the other side. Panic surged within her as she pushed against the unyielding surface, her hands pressing futilely against its smooth surface – the glass screen over a television show she could not enter. Dropping her backpack and belongings, her screams of "No!" filled the cave, growing in desperation, volume, and tempo. She beat against the surface relentlessly, her cries echoing her team's distress.

Finally, Marilyn slid hopelessly down the smooth surface of the artifact, her eyes closed as she wept and clutched at the world she could not reach. As she collapsed into a pile in front of it, she heard Philip, his frantic voice coming through the comms, "Let me go, goddammit!" She looked up through her tears to see her team holding him back, preventing his desperate attempt to jump through the magic door and reach her.

As she sat there sobbing, in the muddy wetness of the cave floor with one hand pressed against the artifact's surface, she felt strong arms lifting her up, enveloping her in a consoling embrace. Sinbad's presence was a steadying force as she wept into his chest, the reality of her situation sinking in as keening wails escaped her throat unabated.

Sinbad held Merlin close, her tears soaking into the fabric of his vest as he gently stroked her hair. Though each moment in the cave's embrace meant days, maybe weeks outside, he deemed it worth the cost to let her grieve. He understood the depth of her despair, feeling her sobs ebb and flow like the tides he'd navigated all his life. This was a storm of the soul, and he, for the moment, was the only anchor she had.

He looked up, his gaze piercing through the now clear artifact, to see her people on the other side. Among them stood the man she had introduced as her life mate, the man she called Feelip, clearly distraught yet stoic. Outwardly calmed, his people no longer restrained him. Yet there was a storm in the man's eyes. As their eyes met, a nod of silent understanding passed between them. Sinbad could see the love and pain etched into Feelip's features and knew that the man wished he were the one holding and comforting Merlin instead, his eyes holding a silent plea for Sinbad to care for Marilyn in his stead.

Unable to hear each other, and likely unable to understand even if they could, Feelip began to gesture. He pointed to himself, clasped his hands over his heart, then pointed to Marilyn. Sinbad didn't need words to understand the message: "I love her." Feelip's next gesture – a fist to his chest followed by a breaking motion – conveyed his heartbreak. Sinbad nodded once more in understanding. He was struck by this silent communication, pondering how the simplest and most profound messages require no words.

He leaned down to Merlin, his voice soft but firm. "Merlin, we cannot remain much longer in the cave. The days pass in the world beyond." As he spoke, Feelip frantically pointed to something on the ground in front of Merlin's door. He gently released her and picked up the magical adornment Merlin had worn on her ear earlier. 'It must have fallen out when she fell,' he mused. As he stood, he looked up to see Feelip speaking and pointing to Merlin. The sounds coming from the magical adornment matched Feelip's mouth movements, though he could not understand the words, and he realized the thing must be how the two of them spoke to each other across the strange barrier.

He handed the adornment to Merlin and waited as she wiped her nose and placed it around her ear once again. She and Feelip matched each other's movements as both began to pace back and forth, gesturing to one another. Though he could not understand her words, her tone, facial expressions, and body language said much. At first awash with hopelessness, the two of them transitioned to frustration and thoughtfulness. Finally, one of her other crew said something, and Merlin's face lit up. Sinbad could not understand her words, but the change in her demeanor was sudden and unmistakable. There was desperation there, yes, but also a flicker of hope – a sailor fallen overboard, suddenly tossed the end of a rope, grasping desperately for it.

With renewed urgency, she turned to Sinbad and said, "I need your men to lay the... door... on the ground with the smooth, flat side up." He nodded and began directing his men as she retrieved the goblet they had found earlier in the star sailors' tomb. Once the door's position was shifted to the floor, he watched as she began awkwardly trying to show the goblet to the people in her world. Then, she also pulled a stack of parchments covered in strange symbols and pictures from her pack.

"You found this in the tomb as well?" he inquired.

"Yes," she replied. "These are writings from the star travelers," she explained, her voice a mix of awe and urgency. "The parchments lay concealed under one's remains. Within these parchments may live that answers I seek – a way to fix the door so that I may return home. But my people need to study them; the language is unknown to us."

With renewed purpose, Merlin began laying the pages out one at a time on the door's smooth surface. Satisfied, she spoke to the magic ear adornment and several flashes of light bled from the door and around the edges of the pages. A moment later, she turned the parchments over and spoke again into the magic adornment with the same result. More flashes of light followed.

After another excited conversation with her people, she turned to Sinbad and asked, "Is your ship large enough to carry that?" as she began to collect the pages and stow them away in her pack again.

Sinbad stared at Merlin in admiration. Though he couldn't understand her language, it was clear from her tone, her crew's reactions, and the way they deferred to her that she was their leader, much like his men followed him. Moments ago, she was lost at sea and floundering, weeping into his chest in hopelessness. But now? The change was as remarkable as it was surprising. For all he knew, the hope to which she now clung so desperately might only be a bit of flotsam stumbled upon in the storm. Yet she treated it with such lifesaving certainty that her hope was infectious. He could see it in the eyes of her crew. All was not lost. The storm could be weathered, and the ship could be saved from the rocky shoal. He saw why her people had made her a leader. More than charisma, she exemplified a courage he had seen in few others in his life.

"Sinbad?" she queried again, pulling him from his musing. "Is your boat large enough to carry the door?"

Pondering its size for a moment, he answered, "No. But if we tie both your boat and mine together to make a wider boat, we can carry it." Considering the potential problems this might present, he added, "The trip will be slow because we cannot use sails. The men will have to row the whole way." None of his men understood the language he spoke to Merlin, but her men did. A collective sigh and groan emanated from them as she nodded and looked down at her crew in the door lying on the ground. Moments later, after sharing what appeared to be words of encouragement from her crew and an affectionate exchange with Feelip, the image and light faded. The door was closed.

CHAPTER 17

Capture

Gorloys sat quietly in his favorite chair, staring into the fire of the enormous stone hearth, its light dancing across his hardened features. Outside, the oncoming winter's first chill wind clawed its way through the coastal air, seeping into the very stones of his home at Tintagel. Built on a peninsula jutting into the sea, the place served as a comfortable abode in the spring, summer, and early autumn, with salt air breezes helping to keep the inside of his home cool and comfortable, even in the hottest months of summer.

But in winter, those breezes turned bitterly cold, with buffeting winds that churned the sea and brought a damp mist. In the coldest months, it frosted the exterior paths, making them icy and treacherous. Tintagel, a robust construction of timber and stone, stood stubbornly against those howling winds, a testament to raw, unadorned strength that held the worst of winters at bay.

The fire danced in fits, battling the chill of winter winds gusting over the sea, across the peninsula, and down the flue. Its dancing light helped to give life to the memories now playing in Gorloys' head of the power of the dragon's breath Uthyr had demonstrated, a gift from this mysterious Merlin. Though the yoke was light, Cornwall was now subject to the will of a king – something that its people had not had to suffer since the Romans abandoned the land – due to the demonstration of that power. The fact rankled Gorloys' thoughts, seeking some means to restore the balance of power, searching the flames for some hidden answer that he knew would never come.

A sudden commotion and the stamping of feet in the outer chamber drew his attention as a messenger named Taran opened the door. Still stamping his feet against the cold as he entered the room, he closed the door quickly to keep out the cooler air of the outer chamber. "Pen Gorloys," the man shivered, "I bring tidings from my brother Jowan - your man at Bearda Market."

Usually stern and commanding with his men, ironically the winter seemed to soften Gorloys' demeanor. Though he usually demanded a certain amount of respect and obedience, the bitter cold made him more forgiving of the man's lack of formalities. He neither knelt, nor waited for permission to speak. Besides, Gorloys was eager to hear his report.

Still, there were some things Gorloys would not do, such as look up at a subordinate from a seated position. Standing and turning to Taran, he welcomed the messenger. "Come Taran! You must be cold! Warm yourself by the fire. Then perhaps I can hear your report without all the teeth chattering?"

Nodding gratefully, Taran took up position in front of the hearth. After warming his hands and rubbing the chill from his arms, he finally turned, put his back to the fire, and nodded again gratefully. Then suddenly, seeming to remember the formalities, his eyes rounded in fear as he dropped to one knee and cast his eyes downward in deference.

Gorloys had already forgotten the minor infraction and moved on. But the subtle reminder both amused and pleased him. Taran's obedience and loyalty reminded Gorloys of the power he wielded and the respect he commanded. "Rise and report, Taran," he finally commanded.

"Jowan kept vigil at Bearda Market, loosening tongues with drink and coin. Merlin hired a ship and, strangely, a crew of miners to accompany him to a place on the far shore to the north across the channel." A bemused expression then crossed Taran's face. "But my brother reported that Uthyr does not possess the dragons," With a pensive look, he added "Merlin took the statues with him."

Confused, Gorloys stared at the man, unable to make sense of what Taran was saying. "What has any of this to do with statues?" he finally asked in frustration, pulling Taran from his moment of reverie.

"Forgive me, Pen Gorloys!" Taran exclaimed. "Jowan reported that the dragons were not real! They were merely artifice of stone and metal! Their power comes from Merlin, whose magic includes the crafting of something Uthyr's men called dragon's breath!"

"So…" Gorloys began pacing, deep in thought. "This dragon's breath holds the real power, and Merlin knows the secret of its making."

Taran nodded in confirmation, then continued his report. "The night before Merlin was to set sail, Jowan secretly chopped a small hole in the boat, then paid a shipwright the next morning to mark the vessel with pitch while fixing the damage so that the boat could be easily recognized from others."

"Smart thinking," Gorloys conceded. "Was the shipwright of Cornwall?"

"No, Pen Gorloys," Taran gulped, shaking his head. "When the deed was done, the shipwright…suffered a drunken accident, having fallen and broken his neck."

Gorloys pondered the information with a smirk. Of the two brothers, Jowan was the larger and more willing to resort to aggression when needed. Taran was both younger and smaller. But as often happened with such sibling rivalries, he had also become the more cunning of the two. "Did Jowan follow the ship then?" Gorloys inquired.

"Yes, Pen Gorloys," Taran responded. "He hired on as a mercenary guard aboard a trade ship headed to the same port at

Moridunum where Merlin's boat first docked. But Merlin continued on from there, sailing along the coast to the west. So, Jowan followed his ship, trailing by land, until it outpaced him."

"So, Merlin is gone? That is all you can tell me?" Gorloys demanded, sudden ire rising in his voice.

"No, Pen Gorloys! There is more!" Taran replied quickly, no doubt hoping to stem the tide of Gorloys' anger. 'What more he has to say had better be worth saying,' Gorloys thought ruefully, 'or I will send his ears back to his brother as trophies for failure!'

Before he could say more, the frightened messenger hurried on. "The ship appeared again in Moridunum five days ago! With Merlin aboard! But…Pen Gorloys, there was a strange thing." Receiving only a stern look when he paused, Taran went on. "The vessel had been gone for over two moons," he said. "When it returned, it was bound together with another ship, both sharing the burden of a thing too large for either ship to carry alone."

"So, Merlin is in Moridunum then," Gorloys responded.

"No, Pen Gorloys! Jowan secured employment with their crew as a merchant guard and sailed with them back across the channel to the river port near Abona. When he arrived there, he sent word to me of these things by sealed message while I awaited his return in Bearda Market." Shaking his head and smirking, he confided, "I think my brother feared to return home these last two moons bearing news that he had lost track of Merlin."

"As well for him that he stayed and picked up the scent again," Gorloys responded sardonically. "What table?" he then demanded.

"Oh! I have gotten ahead of myself again! That seems to be the reason for the mining crew Merlin hired," Taran answered. "Though it is covered in cloth, it is no more than an enormous stone table – a gift from Merlin to the king apparently."

"Uthyr is no king," Gorloys said, his voice low and menacing. "He is a pretender sitting atop a throne of lies he created. Do not forget that."

Taran, realizing his mistake, hastily bowed his head, his voice trembling slightly as he spoke, "Forgive me, Pen Gorloys. It was a slip of the tongue in the cold."

Gorloys, after a moment's intense gaze, let out a slow, controlled breath. "Continue," he said tersely, motioning for Taran to carry on with his report.

"As I report, Jowan is among the small group of merchant guards taking it by land from Abona to Execaer," Taran continued, more cautiously now, perhaps hoping the additional news would mitigate Gorloys' annoyance. "He sent a second message from Abona to have me come tell you: the guard group is small, and Merlin is with them, but he dare not try to capture Merlin alone."

Gorloys' veins suddenly flooded with nervous excitement and energy. After months of waiting, now was the time to strike and capture Merlin so that he could attain the secret of dragon's breath and restore the balance of power. Barely containing his elation, he clapped Taran on the shoulder. "Excellent!" he exclaimed, with a cold grin. "Tell Jory to gather those men I usually take hunting with me. We ride at once!"

As Taran acknowledged the command, Gorloys made his way to the room he and Ygraine shared to change into clothes and boots that would keep him warm in the harsh winter conditions. Looking up from her sewing, Ygraine saw that he was dressing to leave and inquired, "My husband, where are you going?"

"Out," he replied sternly. "I have matters that require my personal attention."

"But husband…" she began as he interrupted her. "I will brook no argument Ygraine. I am leaving. I will be back in perhaps ten days. I will discuss it no more."

With that, Ygraine quieted, pouting as he pecked her cheek and marched out, calling for his guards.

A chilling gust from the first winds of winter tugged at Marilyn's long coat as she plodded along the cart path beside her precious cargo – an ox-drawn four-wheeled cart, laden with a burden too large for its confines. The artifact, her link to the future, lay hidden under a tarp, its edges hanging over the sides of the cart. The enormity of the object made the cart seem almost comically undersized, a testament to the desperate ingenuity that had led them to this moment.

Tightening her long coat around her and adjusting the collar, she cursed the cold and her forgetfulness in not asking Philip for a warm pair of gloves. Living in Texas for these last few years, she had forgotten just how bitterly cold and wet the winter months in England could be. Fortunately, with the deepest part of winter not having arrived yet, the cart path skirting the northern edge of the abutting marshland was mostly dry.

Yet, evidence of overnight snow flurries could be found in the shelter of sparse evergreens, refusing to melt under a weak, waning sun. Barren branches of leafless trees were delicately encrusted with icicles, glistening as if adorned with nature's own fragile jewelry. Along the edges of the nearby fen, a thin crust of ice formed, a clear sign of the deepening chill.

To the south, through the mists of the marsh, the village of Glestinga rose on an enormous, rocky hill, appearing like an island amid the swirling vapors – a 6th-century vision of what would one day be known as Glastonbury Tor. The map her team had provided contained only a few pre-marked locations, relying on the fact that such Neolithic sites would be easily identifiable even in this century. The tor and the ruins of Stonehenge forty miles to the east were two such markers.

Recalling her previous journey with Uthyr from Glouvum to Execaer along this same route, she remembered her awe that the site – a historical landmark in her time – supported an entire village along its terraced levels in this era. In modern times, the land around it had been drained away by land management efforts. But, in this century, its mystical presence within the fog-laden bog seemed both a beacon and a refuge to those who traversed these ancient lands.

As she pulled her beanie cap down further to protect her ears, some of the hired guards that accompanied her cast furtive glances or openly smirked at her appearance. Clad in fur-lined hides beneath rudimentary bits of leather or chainmail armor, she found herself once again contrasting their rustic, functional attire to the anachronistic vision of medieval men-at-arms that cinema often portrayed. Their armored caps had fur-lined flaps that covered their cheeks, protecting them from the elements, a feature Marilyn found herself envying despite the advantages of her more modern clothing.

The procession moved with a deliberate, plodding pace, the oxen's breath visible in the cold air, forming clouds that dissipated quickly but rhythmically. The guards wrapped themselves tighter in their cloaks, their breath forming similar clouds as they spoke in low tones or kept silent vigil. The winter landscape was a silent witness to their journey, an indifferent witness to their otherwise silent passing. Occasionally though, a loud crack echoing through the mists broke the silence, startling Jowan, the mercenary guard nearest to her. Each time, he would stare into the fog, trying to pierce the veil with his gaze, mumbling something she took to be a prayer or ward of some kind. Eventually, she turned to Jowan and asked, "What is a bucca, Jowan?"

His expression shifted to one of shock. "You are of the Fae! You do not know?" he exclaimed.

"Do you know every creature in this world? Or the name of every human?" she replied, arching her eyebrow with a wry smile. "No, I do not know."

Nodding, apparently satisfied with her logic, Jowan explained, "A bucca is a spirit of the swamp. They live within the mist. In summer, their lights draw unwary travelers away from safe paths to their doom. In winter, they roam the mists, felling trees, and breaking limbs with their passage. Can you not hear it?"

Marilyn shook her head, amused by his superstitious belief. "Be at ease, Jowan," she finally said. "The cracking you hear is not from a bucca. It is nothing more than branches, whose sap has frozen and become hard and brittle, overcome by the weight of the ice they bear. When the wind blows just right…" She clapped her hands together loudly to mimic the sound echoing across the marsh, "…they break," she finished matter-of-factly.

Jowan turned and stared into the mist for a moment, then nodded uncertainly and resumed his watch in silence. As more cracking sounds echoed, his unease abated, and the sound barely earned a glance in their direction.

As the cart creaked and the oxen plodded forward, a fresh gust of wind tore another silent curse from Marilyn's lips. She found herself quietly lamenting the prolonged time spent in the cave, which had forced them to emerge at the onset of winter. If only they had been quicker, if only the artifact had been freed sooner, they might have traveled under more forgiving skies. But most of all, she regretted the time lost while she wallowed in self-pity, crying hopelessly. Though probably not long, she felt sure it stole weeks of the autumn months that would not have so complicated each step of her return to Execaer.

Had those weeks been available, Sinbad could have taken them by sea straight to Execaer, despite the necessity to row without sails, as the artifact's immense size and shape precluded any traditional maritime speed. But with winter coming on, the decision to disembark at the river-side port near Abona and continue the journey by land became a reluctant concession to expedience. She had considered landing at Bearda Market, which was technically closer to Execaer by land. Yet, that option had been dismissed early on. The land between Bearda Market and Execaer was known for its wild and rough terrain, unsuitable for pulling a heavily laden cart. There were no proper cart paths, only narrow runs and trails snaking through dense woods and over rocky outcrops, an impossible route for their cumbersome convoy.

As for Sinbad and his crew, they were accustomed to the warmer climates and life aboard their ship, neither liking the cold nor willing to accompany her on an overland journey. After ensuring her safe passage to the port, Sinbad had made the decision to seek warmer waters, following the map she had given him that pointed towards the Arabian Sea and his destiny. She understood his decision, though she keenly felt the absence of a familiar friend.

The distant thunder of hoofbeats suddenly pulled Marilyn from her reverie, drawing not only her attention but also that of the entourage of guards. Suddenly alert, they turned with one accord to face the growing sound. The rhythmic pounding grew louder, more urgent, as armored figures on horseback began to resolve out of the mist. As they drew closer, the details of their armament and banners became clearer, sending a jolt of recognition through Marilyn. Leading them was a figure she knew all too well: Gorloys. She muttered his name incredulously and gripped her shock staff, activating its charge with a flick of her wrist.

But before she could react further, a heavy blow to the head sent her world spinning into darkness. When she finally came to, the world was a blur of pain and motion. She found herself bound and slung over the back of a horse, the rough gait jostling her with every step. Her wrists and ankles were tightly tied with a thong stretching under the horse's belly, making every movement a study in agony.

Through her throbbing headache, Marilyn forced her eyes open, catching sight of Jowan speaking to Gorloys. "The bodies have been disposed of in the marsh, Pen Gorloys," Jowan reported with a casual indifference that chilled her to the bone. "What of the table, cart, and oxen?"

Gorloys, toying with her staff with a mix of curiosity and disdain, barely glanced at Jowan as he responded. "The table is of no consequence and will only slow us down. Let the marsh have it as well. Burn the cart and set the oxen free." His words were final, dismissive of the artifact that had been her hope and burden.

Marilyn watched helplessly as the men uncovered the artifact and eased it off the cart, sending it rolling into the marsh shallows with a heavy splash, its flat side facing up. As the artifact sank into the murky water, so did her heart, despair surfacing like the slow rise of bubbles as the marsh took it – a despair she felt more deeply than the cold that seeped into her bones.

In a growing panic, she frantically scanned the surroundings for any familiar landmark, anything that could give her a sense of location. Glestinga, the village adorning the tor, was still visible through the mists to the south, a ghostly silhouette against the gray sky, but nothing else offered a clue to her whereabouts. Then the realization hit her: her backpack, with all its contents, was gone. She started to struggle against her bonds, her movements growing more frantic, drawing the attention of Gorloys.

He approached her with a cold, calculating gaze, assessing her struggle as one might observe an animal caught in a trap. "Calm yourself, Merlin," he said, his voice a blend of mockery and command. "Your journey with us has only just begun."

As Marilyn's eyes met his, she knew that whatever lay ahead, it would take all her cunning, all her strength, and perhaps even some luck she didn't know she had, to survive and find her way back home. But for the moment, her primary concern was her pregnancy. Steeling herself against the ache in her head, she focused instead on the immediate problem: the painful pressure against her belly as she lay bound across the horse's back. She knew she had to reposition herself not only for her comfort but for the safety of her unborn child, a secret that must remain hidden at all costs.

"Might I speak, Pen Gorloys?" Marilyn asked, her voice steady despite the situation. Her use of his title was deliberate, a small concession aimed at appealing to his sense of importance and authority.

Gorloys paused, seemingly surprised by her composed request. "Speak, Merlin," he replied, his curiosity piqued.

"It seems to me you wish to talk, perhaps even negotiate," she replied. "Else you would simply have had me killed. Being trussed to a horse like this causes me a great deal of discomfort and – let us be honest – does not lend itself well to discussion." Grunting and trying to shift her weight, she added, "And if you desire cooperation from me in negotiation, you would be better served to allow me to sit properly."

Gorloys considered her words, his gaze sharp and assessing. Marilyn could almost see the thoughts swirling behind his eyes, weighing the potential risks and benefits of her proposition. Seeing him ponder, she hurried on, "I understand my position here, Pen Gorloys. I am at your mercy. Agree to my request and you have my word that I will not attempt escape and will keep an open mind if negotiation is your aim."

After a moment, he nodded slightly to one of his men, who promptly removed the thong binding her hands and feet beneath the horse's belly, and then pulled her down from the horse. While she stood there having her feet unbound, another man stepped forward and threw a riding blanket across the horse's back and began re-saddling the horse properly. Marilyn quietly breathed a sigh of relief as she noticed her backpack stuffed into a saddle bag attached to the back of its high cantle. With her feet untied, she was allowed to mount herself upright, though her wrists were still tightly bound and the rope end secured to Jowan's saddle. Should she attempt to run, she would only unseat herself.

"Let it not be said that I am without mercy," he stated, a hint of self-satisfaction in his voice. "But make no mistake, Merlin; any attempt at escape or trickery will result in consequences far more uncomfortable than your current position."

Marilyn nodded, understanding the thinly veiled threat, but said nothing. Her primary concern was alleviated, but now she needed to find out why he had captured her and hopefully negotiate her way out of her present circumstances. The road ahead loomed ominous and uncertain though. She feared she knew what he wanted - his own pair of dragons - and she could not afford to give him that.

Marilyn sat quietly while some of Gorloys' men unyoked the oxen and pushed them off to the side as others began chopping splinters of wood from the cart to provide kindling for a fire. Preoccupied with directing his men, Gorloys had left Jowan to guard her. But Jowan sat his horse as far from her as the rope between them would allow, casting occasional furtive glances her way, but never quite meeting her eyes. 'Perhaps he feels a hint of shame for his part in this,' she mused, 'or perhaps only fear of retribution.'

Suddenly, Jowan spoke, his gaze fixed on a man striking flint and steel against wool to start a fire. "Not all of them we killed," he said, nodding toward the man as the wool began to smolder. "Fynn there, and three others live, all loyal to Gorloys."

Marilyn's anger flared. "Does that somehow justify the deaths of the five that were killed, Jowan?" she said, seething. "Does it relieve the grief and sorrow of their wives? Their children?" Disgusted, she spat finally, "Or does sparing the lives of the other men cleanse the stain of treachery from your black heart?"

With each question, she noticed Jowan shrinking slightly, like a boy being scolded by his mother for wrongdoing. Still never looking at her, he chose instead to sit in sullen silence.

Eventually, Fynn had a fire stoked, and men pushed the cart over the growing flames. As the flames began to lick away at the dry wood, one of the men approached Gorloys and pointed at the oxen. With Gorloys' quiet assent, the man pulled one of the docile creatures off into the spongy turf a short distance away.

Marilyn watched as the man snicked and cajoled the ox with a carrot, then suddenly slit the creature's throat. As it collapsed with a gurgling mewl and bled out, the sight momentarily turned her stomach, igniting a brief internal debate about her dietary choices in life. She enjoyed steak but had never given much thought to how it arrived on her plate. Recognizing the harsh realities of survival in this time though, she pushed aside her revulsion and looked away as he continued to slaughter the beast.

"We camp here for the night, men!" Gorloys' voice boomed out, breaking her contemplation. His declaration was met with enthusiastic cheers as the promise of fresh meat and warmth rallied his men. Marilyn silently gave thanks for the morbid markers they left behind: the ox carcass, the discarded yoke, and the remnants of a robust fire. These otherwise mundane remnants provided relatively lasting landmarks, a mental catalogue she could use to find the artifact again if she hoped to survive this encounter and return home one day.

As Gorloys' announcement echoed through the camp, Jowan dismounted and assisted Marilyn down from the horse. With a firm but kind grip, he guided her to the side, retying her hands and feet securely. She sat quietly, observing as the camp came to life around her. Her cart, once a symbol of hope and transport for the artifact, now lay collapsed in the fire, its destruction marking the end of one journey and the uncertain beginning of another. One of the men, seizing the opportunity provided by the blaze, set up a spit over the flames, skewering chunks of ox meat to roast.

Jowan occasionally glanced Marilyn's direction, ensuring her continued presence and lack of escape attempts. She considered the possibility of furtively untying her bonds and fleeing into the night but quickly dismissed it. The sky overhead darkened to a deep grey, and the scant light that filtered through the barren branches offered no promise of guidance. Without a light source, she knew she risked stumbling into the treacherous bog, a fate of freezing or drowning she wasn't willing to chance. Besides, though she could see it from where she sat, there was no way to retrieve her backpack without notice, and she would need its contents if she had any hope of survival in the wilderness alone.

As dusk settled into twilight, the misty fog from the nearby swamp seemed to come alive, tendrils creeping over the cart path, curling and twisting as if imbued with a life of their own. Yet, they were held at bay from the campsite itself by the roaring fire and torches that the men had placed strategically around the perimeter. The wilderness around them was alive with the sounds of nature: wolves howled in the distance, owls screeched from hidden perches, and even the cautious eyes of a curious fox could be seen at the edge of the firelight, darting in and out of the shadows, hoping to snatch a bit of carrion from the ox carcass.

In this setting, with the encroaching darkness of the outer world pressing in, Gorloys approached Marilyn, his footsteps deliberate and measured. In his hand, he carried her shock staff, a symbol of her ingenuity and power. His expression was unreadable, a mix of curiosity, calculation, and perhaps a hint of respect. As he neared, the firelight flickered over his features, casting shadows that seemed to dance with the questions undoubtedly swirling in his mind.

Marilyn watched him approach, her mind racing with the possibilities of what he might say or do next. Despite her bound state, she readied herself for whatever conversation or confrontation lay ahead, aware that, in the end though she was at his mercy, she could not allow herself or her knowledge to be used to change the course of history. Not for the first time, she regretted not asking Ayesha how Merlin's story ends in all the tales and folklore about him.

"I have worked out how to make the magic within your staff come and go," Gorloys confided, his gaze fixed intently on the staff's head. He demonstrated his newfound knowledge by flicking it off and on again. "But what does this magic do?"

"Touch it to your forehead and find out," she said acidly, knowing that a blow to the head with it was highly dangerous, even lethal.

"Come now, Merlin," Gorloys smirked, seemingly amused by her defiance. "There is no cause for a lack of manners," he added, flicking the staff off again. In response, Marilyn held up her rope-bound wrists, her eyebrows arching in a silent, accusatory manner. "Yes, well," he added with a slight nod, "lack of trust breeds precaution."

"You have me at an advantage for the moment, Gorloys," she responded, attempting a brave façade she did not feel. "But I promise you that if harm should befall me at your hands, the fae will hound you to your dying breath. You will find no peace in Annwn."

Shaking his head dismissively, Gorloys admitted, "It is not my desire to harm you, Merlin." Then squatting down, he locked eyes with her intently, adding with a tone of accusation, "But you came into this land, unbidden and unwelcome, and with your magicks, upset the balance of power."

As Marilyn contemplated his words, she realized she had judged Gorloys primarily through others' eyes but had never really taken the time to learn of the man herself. And she had only ever met Gorloys once – in the field where she had demonstrated her fireworks to cow him into submission under Uthyr's rule. Considering his point, she was forced to concede the truth of it. In her effort to strike a bargain with Uthyr and obtain his help, she had indeed lent her knowledge and skills to Uthyr's cause and upset the balance of power between these two leaders without ever really considering Gorloys' perspective.

Gorloys stood, pulling Marilyn from her thoughts. He looked off into the darkness before continuing, "For four generations since the Romans left, Cornwall has been free, unburdened by the yoke of a king." Casting his gaze back to her, he said sneering, "Then you showed up with your…dragons…and changed that."

Accepting his viewpoint, Marilyn conceded, "I see truth in your words, Gorloys." Then, with the simple hope of appealing to present circumstances, she added, "I realized my error in judgment already, took back my dragons, and set them free. Uthyr no longer possesses them; your balance can be restored."

Gorloys' expression hardened with irritation. "Do not insult me with lies and half-truths, Merlin," he warned sternly. "I now understand that your dragons were mere statues, their power lying in what you call dragon's breath."

Shock flitted across Marilyn's face, confirming Gorloys' assertion. Witnessing it, he casually mentioned, "My father once remarked that truth lives in a flagon of mead." Seeing her confusion, he elaborated, "He only meant that enough drink often loosens the most loyal of tongues." He smirked, adding, "And when that fails, idle boasts in the arms of a whore reveal secrets not even a mother would hear."

Marilyn shook her head, preemptively answering with denial the question she knew was coming. "I cannot give you the secret of dragon's breath for the same reasons I could not leave it with Uthyr, Gorloys. Such secrets are not meant for your world yet."

"Then you leave me in a difficult position, Merlin. So long as you withhold the secret of dragon's breath, I cannot risk you returning to Uthyr to give it to him once again," Gorloys replied. As she started to forestall him with guarantees, he cut her off, "Spare me any assurances, Merlin. I would be a fool to trust them," he sneered. "So…Until you change your answer, you will become my…guest…at Tintagel. Think on it."

With that, he stood and walked away with her staff in hand, leaving Marilyn to confront the grim reality of her predicament, wondering if her first borrowed impression of the man was likely the more correct one. She doubted very much that she would enjoy being his guest. If she was going to survive, she needed to find a way out of this trap.

CHAPTER 18

Imprisoned

"Stop making excuses for him!" Magra chided as she tended the darkening bruise on Ygraine's cheek. The salve she used did not smell pleasant, but it alleviated the worst of the pain and reduced the swelling, though it did nothing to conceal the brown and yellow discoloration.

Ygraine turned to the reflection pool, appraising her cheek. "He is only angry and frustrated because Merlin will not cooperate!" Shaking her head, she said, "But Merlin has been locked away in that cold cellar for what? Ten days now? And still, he will not say a word!"

"And how is that your fault?" Magra demanded. "One man's stubbornness makes another decide you are to blame?!" Shaking her head vexedly, she added, muttering, "Even if you were to blame for the first acting ox-brained, that gives no right for the other to play the ox's backside."

Ygraine turned on her stool and stood, looking about the room. Deep down, she knew Magra was right. But she could not meet the older woman's eyes while denying it openly. "It is my fault because I have failed him," Ygraine sighed.

She stared at the floor in front of the pallet of furs where she and Gorloys had made love three nights ago. 'That is when this whole business started,' she mused internally. 'I should have kept silent.'

Reminiscing about that night, she recalled how his lovemaking had been particularly aggressive, but not cruel or painful. He simply seemed filled with frustration, releasing his frustration and his seed in a hoarse, guttural yell. Typically, after having used such energy, he would collapse into her bosom for a time, then roll away to sleep.

That night was different though. Afterward, he had instead gotten up and begun pacing the floor in front of their bed, prompting her to ask the fateful question that led to this moment. 'What troubles you, my husband?' When he told her of the man locked away under guard in the cellar and the secret the man held, Ygraine had suggested that perhaps this Merlin believes once his secret is shared, Gorloys will simply kill him anyway.

Returning from her thoughts, she turned to Magra and shared what more she knew. "Merlin knows some secret my husband calls dragon's breath," she said. Responding to Magra's silent, but questioning look, she added, "I asked Gorloys what it was as well. He told me it is an elixir that grants immortality."

"Pfaw!" Magra exclaimed, "Gods help us if that man should live forever!"

Ygraine smirked in answer, "I did not believe him." Peering off into the distance, as though she could see Uthyr across the miles, she added thoughtfully, "But whatever this dragon's breath is, King Uthyr has it." Then, glancing back at Magra, she finished, "And that is why my husband wants it."

"Why should this Merlin share this secret of dragon's breath with him?" Magra asked. "No doubt he believes Gorloys will only kill him afterward."

Nodding, Ygraine replied exasperated, "I said much the same the night he demanded my aid!" She struck a pose, lowered her voice in a mocking tone, and mimicked Gorloys' demands that night: "Then you must convince Merlin I will not! Convince him of my benevolence! Show him that I am a loving husband, father, and leader who only seeks an earnest accord for the people of Cornwall!"

Magra chortled in that tone reserved only for wise old mothers, then scoffed. "Loving husband, eh?" gesturing to Ygraine's face.

Ygraine sighed, gently caressing her tender cheek with her fingers. "What can I do Magra?" she pleaded. "Every day I go and speak to Merlin. But he just sits there like a lump, a wretched man nesting in the squalor of that horrid cellar, refusing to speak a single word to me!"

Magra stared at her for a long while, a look of consternation on her own face, then finally spoke. "What can you do? You could leave this place – leave him. That is what…"

She paused as Ygraine, shocked at the notion, shot her a dangerous look. She stared until Magra looked away, albeit with an expression of disgruntlement. Calmed, Ygraine replied, "However you may disapprove of his treatment of me, we have a daughter. He provides us with home and comfort. And even if he ignores her, she loves him."

"Then you make this house as much a prison for you as the cellar to this Merlin," Magra mumbled with a sour look.

"Enough, Magra!" Ygraine demanded loudly, cowing the old woman into sullen silence. "Now," Ygraine continued more calmly. "Do you have any advice to help me secure Merlin's cooperation or not?"

Magra sighed as she ambled over to the hearth and began poking the coals. "Put another log in there, will you dear?" she asked.

Ygraine complied as Magra returned to her chair and settled in. "Do you recall when we first met?" she asked. "You would hardly say two words to me."

Ygraine nodded but said nothing as Magra continued. "Now look at us. Over the years, you have gone from aloofness and silence to confiding in me your deepest secrets. Merlin needs a friend Ygraine. Not someone seeking to dig information from him."

Ygraine lit up with delight. "Of course!" Turning to Magra, she spontaneously grabbed the old woman in a strong embrace, whispering, "Thank you for being my friend, Magra."

"I have come to speak with Merlin again as my husband commands me," Ygraine spoke as she approached the man guarding the heavy door to the cellar. Though she knew Jowan by name, Gorloys had told her that when she addresses a man informally, he perceives her as an equal – something Gorloys would not tolerate. But since then, Ygraine had come to believe her husband's reasons were pettier, stemming from his own insecurity rather than a need for formality.

"As you wish, Penêsek," Jowan replied, unbarring the door, and glancing within to ensure there was no danger. She hated that title and wished Gorloys would simply allow people to call her by her name. But he insisted on the honorific, likely for the same reasons she was not allowed to call others by name. The only person he had ever allowed such familiarity was Magra; and that only because the old woman had stood up to him and blessed him out for trying to prevent it. 'I was there when you came bawling into this world, young man! I will not put up with that nonsense from you!' He had covered shock with amused allowance and walked away; a fond memory that still tickled Ygraine when she thought of it.

Grabbing a torch from a nearby sconce, she stepped into the cellar. Except for the faint light and weak warmth of a torch sputtering its last breaths on the cellar's stone floor, the room was dark and cold. Merlin lay huddled next to it for warmth, shivering and in the same dark clothing he had been wearing since she first met him. As she stepped closer, he opened his eyes and sat up, leaning back against the wall.

"Hello, Merlin," she began. As before, he only stared at her, his piercing eyes glinting in the light of her torch, watching her warily. Ygraine sighed, realizing she should have asked Magra how to begin. He never spoke. She wasn't even sure he understood her words. Finally, she simply said, "You have not uttered a word to me so far. I suppose I should not expect any different today." Shrugging, she bent down to pick up the guttering torch and relight it, then left her own fresh torch in its place, something to offer more light and warmth than the meager stump she held in her hand now. "The least I can do..." she said. "I will see you tomorrow," then turned to go.

"He hit you," came a hoarse croak from behind. So surprised by the unexpected interjection, Ygraine whipped around, covering the bruise on her face with her free hand. "How...? What? No! I... I tripped and fell! I am rather clumsy you see and..."

Suddenly she realized that, as she had done so many times before, she had naturally stepped into the role of covering her shame with pretense and lies, and to a complete stranger no less. What Merlin said was not a question. It was a statement; an assertion of truth that he somehow simply knew. Stopping, she hung her head and nodded. "He is...unhappy with me...with my progress," she admitted. "This is the first I have ever heard you speak. Do all fae sound like a frog that can talk?" she asked curiously.

Merlin arched an eyebrow at her and snorted. Nodding toward a pail in a corner, he croaked, "No. The water they give me is unclean. It has made me ill." Seeing its contents, what looked like brackish water, Ygraine was incensed. She had mistaken it for a wash pail or chamber pot.

Wrinkling her nose in disgust, she grabbed the pail by its handle, turned, and began banging on the door. From the other side, Jowan unbarred and opened it, stepping back with sword drawn. Annoyed, she tossed the pail on the floor in front of him where it spilled out, splashing on his boots, forcing him to jump back further in surprise. "This man needs clean water," she demanded. "Clean! Do you understand me? Whatever purpose my husband has for him cannot be served by his death. And water like that..." she said, nodding at the brackish puddle on the floor, "will cause it."

Shocked, he only stared at her a moment before finally responding, "But Penêsek! If I leave my post, Pen Gorloys will have my head!" A worried look crossed his face as he added, "And I would like my head very much to stay where it is," as he sheathed his sword, sensing no immediate danger.

"You will lose it even more quickly if this man dies," she replied. "I will keep watch while you are gone. Bar the door if you must but do as I say."

"Yes, Penêsek," he said finally, nodding. "But are you not worried for your safety?" he inquired.

"I am in no danger," she replied confidently. "Now go!"

As she turned away from the door, hearing Jowan shut and bar it behind her, Merlin, still sitting in the same spot arched his eyebrow and croaked, "Are you so certain of your safety?"

"I doubt a man so concerned with harm to my face would then harm the rest of me," Ygraine replied simply.

Merlin smiled wryly, responding, "Fair…" but broke into a fit of coughing before he could finish whatever he was about to say.

Worried, Ygraine bent down and checked his head for fever. Worry became alarm as Ygraine stood. "You are burning up!" she announced. "I will call Magra; she is a wise woman. She will know what to do!"

Merlin's response was sudden and vehement. "No!" he croaked, holding up a weak hand as if to stop her, though Ygraine could go nowhere until Jowan returned. "I had a bag with me when I was captured," he rasped. "Find it if you can…. In the bag…is a metal box. In the box…is a bottle. And in the bottle…healing herbs like seeds…" Each phrase, each pause, was accentuated by a labored breath. Then Merlin's eyes rolled up as he fainted.

Panic-stricken, Ygraine turned and began pounding on the door, calling for help. Moments later, an eternity later, Jowan unbarred and opened the door. He stood holding a clean pail of water, and she grabbed it from him. "If you wish to keep your head this day, Jowan," she said with as much authority she could find within, "pick him up and follow me. He is at death's door. We must take him to Magra."

Round-eyed with shock, likely as much by the sudden change of circumstances as by the fact that she had used his name, Jowan simply stood there a moment, looking between her and Merlin. "Now!" she commanded loudly, breaking his stupor.

"Yes, Penêsek," he muttered breathlessly as he trotted into the room and swooped up Merlin to follow.

Ygraine gave a warning knock, then, not waiting for a response, barged into Magra's apartment with Jowan in tow carrying Merlin. Magra, who had been quietly sitting by the fire in her favorite chair, weaving something with a handloom by its light, looked up in surprise.

"Merlin is deathly ill, Magra! Please help him," Ygraine said, her voice urgent.

Magra's expression shifted from surprise to deep concern as she set her handloom aside and stood, motioning to Jowan. "Put him on the bedding there by the fire," she instructed, pointing to a pallet of furs lying nearby. As Jowan laid Merlin down, Magra turned to Ygraine and asked, "Is that drinking water?" Ygraine looked down at the pail she still carried, her concern having momentarily eclipsed her awareness of it. "Yes," she replied as she went to set it down, a hint of embarrassment in her tone.

"Do not just set it down, girl," Magra said with a tinge of annoyance. "Fill the kettle there and set it on the fire," she commanded, her tone leaving no room for hesitation. As she stooped down to assess Merlin's condition, feeling his forehead and checking his eyes, she continued, "If he is going to live through the night, we must break his fever with willow bark tea."

"Before he fainted, Merlin mentioned he had healing herbs in a bag taken from him when he was captured," Ygraine informed her, the bemusement in her voice betraying her wonder at Merlin's insistence. "He seemed quite firm about it."

"I know the one!" Jowan interrupted, his voice carrying a sense of realization. "I left it in my saddle bag, forgotten when I brought Merlin to the cellar." His expression became pensive as he added, "It is likely still in the stable with Cloud. I'll go and fetch it." With those words, he promptly turned and left the room, his sense of purpose evident.

Magra looked to Ygraine with a questioning glance, prompting an explanation. "If Merlin dies, my husband will not be pleased with him," Ygraine stated flatly, her voice a mix of fear and determination.

Ygraine sat quietly while Magra methodically flaked bits of willow bark from a small stem taken from a bundle on the mantle above the hearth. The mantle held several other crocks besides, some with contents all too familiar to Ygraine. Magra soon had a tea brewing when Jowan returned, the promised bag dangling from one hand.

Magra took it from him with a quick nod. "Now, out," she said briskly, shooing him toward the door. As he hesitated, beginning to protest, she firmly proclaimed, "The rest is women's work, young man; you will only get in the way. Guard my door on the other side if you must; but go!" With a gentle but firm push, she managed to usher him beyond the threshold and closed the door in his face, hiding his look of bewildered resignation as it shut.

Turning to Ygraine, she announced, "That is that. Now let us see what we can do for your new friend, eh?"

CHAPTER 19

Unexpected Allies

Marilyn awoke slowly, her sense of hearing being the first to achieve consciousness, bringing the soft crackle and hiss of a fire. Then came her sense of touch, registering the warmth and softness of wool and furs against her skin. Her nose joined in, picking up the savory scent in the air, like a roast in the oven. Her eyes slowly crept open to a ceiling with wooden crossbeams supporting a wood-shingled roof, where firelight softly danced. Achy muscles demanded attention as she stretched, and she sucked in a jaw cracking yawn that provided enough oxygen to her brain to clear the fog. Having achieved consciousness, her mind immediately raced back to the sensation of soft wool and furs against her skin. 'I'm naked!' she thought in sudden alarm, realizing she lay unclothed beneath the wool blanket covering her. Trying furtively to take stock of her surroundings, she noticed an old woman feeding strips of dyed wool through a handloom by the firelight.

"No need to fret, girl," the woman said quietly without looking up. "Your clothes are in the wash kettle there over the fire, stewing with some lye soap to rid them of the stink of squalor and sickness. I like to throw in a couple of holly sprigs too, to make it smell nice." The woman glanced over and winked knowingly and added, "Trade secret."

Marilyn's eyes followed to where the woman pointed, noting a bubbling kettle hanging over the flames. Beside it, a smaller pot emitted the savory aroma she smelled earlier. Sitting up slowly, testing the aches running through her body, she wrapped herself in the wool blanket; a makeshift toga that provided a semblance of modesty as she got up and ladled some of its content – a broth containing bits of carrot, potatoes, peas, and slivers of beef – into a bowl sitting by the fire.

As she sat down to slurp the broth quietly, Marilyn looked around the room, scrutinizing her surroundings, while the woman continued to work, her bony fingers working the wooden shuttle through the weft and methodically combing the weave. At the opposite end of the hearth, she saw Ygraine lying on a makeshift pallet. The rhythmic rise and fall of her chest indicated a deep, exhausted sleep. Marilyn's gaze then shifted back to the old woman, who had paused her work to look at her.

"She has been here all night," the old woman said, nodding toward Ygraine. "These old bones of mine need little rest these days, but what rest they took was thanks to her keeping watch over you while I slept. The cocks in the hen yard will crow soon enough though."

"I am Magra," the woman introduced herself with a gentle nod. "And you," she pointed at Marilyn, "are Merlin. Now the question I want to know is this." Magra paused for a moment and leveled a piercing gaze at her with an inquisitive eyebrow arched. "Who, or what, is a Flip?"

Registering Marilyn's surprise, Magra chuckled softly, then murmured conspiratorially, "You, girl, are quite a restless sleeper. You were talking in your sleep, quite the chatter. None of it made sense to me, words from a tongue I have not heard. But that word? You kept saying it over and over…moaning and groaning and carrying on." Marilyn blushed and buried her face in her bowl but said nothing.

Magra chuckled softly again and winked knowingly, a glint of amusement in her eye as she continued, "A lover then. I thought as much. Is he the one whose child you carry?" she inquired motioning vaguely toward Marilyn's midsection, then returned her attention to the handloom, waiting for an answer.

Suddenly alarmed, Marilyn dropped the almost empty bowl and snatched more covering around her, trying to hide the small bulge of her belly in more wool.

Consternation flashed across Magra's face as she glanced at the small mess on the floor in front of the hearth. "Pfaw! No cause to be making a mess, girl! I had three of my own and played midwife to so many more I lost count years ago. You look to be four or five moons along now, I would say."

Marilyn instinctively caressed her belly protectively. Magra softened, "Peace! Only the three of us in this room know." She nodded toward Ygraine, curled up on her pallet, snoring softly. Smiling fondly at Ygraine, she added, "When we began undressing you and Ygraine saw your girls there pop out of your shirt though," she turned back to Marilyn, a gleam of mischief in her eyes, "her eyes about popped out of her head!" As she said the last, the old woman pantomimed a round-eyed expression of surprise that sent Marilyn into an uncontrolled fit of giggling she quickly stifled against the back of her hand.

Magra sat back, a grin of mirth still on her face and in her eyes. "So, the girl can laugh," she proclaimed. Then her expression turned serious as she sat forward again. "I imagine laughter has not passed your lips in quite a while…hiding who and what you are," she added. Then, nodding toward Ygraine, she continued. "Her husband cannot find out, though. Whatever secret he wants from you, that git of a whore would use that baby of yours to get it."

"I know," Marilyn finally spoke, surprised to find that her voice was no longer nearly as hoarse as it had been. It still felt a little raw, but she sounded more like herself than a frog. "Thank you," she added.

Magra waved her off and stood, setting her handloom aside and knuckling the small of her back. She walked over to the wash kettle and began fishing bits of laundry out with a pole and draping them over pegs poking out of the mantle. As the clothing dripped, water drops began to fall and sizzle on the hearth stone nearest the fire. When Marilyn tried to rise and help, Magra waved her off. "Get you some more broth. You must eat to restore your strength. Come to that, take a third bowl to feed that little one in your belly if you can hold it down."

Nodding gratefully, Marilyn did as she was told and sat down to enjoy another bowl. Over the next hour, Magra tended to her laundry, turning and rotating it on the pegs while Marilyn tried to rest. But sleep never came and eventually, she could hear the crowing of a cock somewhere in the distance. As if trained to the sound, Ygraine startled awake, then relaxed, and knuckled the sleep from her eyes. When she glanced over and saw Marilyn staring at her, she exclaimed, "Oh, thank the spirits!"

Smiling, Marilyn said, "Thank your friend Magra. It was her doing," earning an embarrassed "Pfaw!" from the old woman.

Marilyn stood and checked her undergarments for dryness, then began getting dressed as Ygraine rushed over to a dark corner of the room. She returned carrying Marilyn's backpack and said excitedly, "Jowan remembered it and brought it straight away. Until yesterday, it had lain forgotten in the stables." Handing it to Marilyn, she added, "Magra and I found your healing herb seeds. We did not know how many to put in the willow bark tea she worked into you though."

Interrupting, Magra added "Some healing herbs do more harm than good. If too much is given, it could even kill. So, we used four seeds."

"Four is perfect," Marilyn said, earning a smile from both. She retrieved two more antibiotic pills from Doctor Bennett's first aid kit and asked for more of the willow bark tea if it was available. Magra grabbed a cup from the mantle, then poured the tea from a clay crock that had been resting on a warming stone at the edge of the hearth. The bitter taste of the tea made Marilyn cough, but she knew she needed the salicylates it contained to keep her fever at bay.

Checking the rest of her clothes, Marilyn decided they were dry enough and began to dress. Seeing her once again attempting to conceal her womanhood and pregnancy beneath layers of clothing, Ygraine parroted Magra's earlier comments. "If my husband learns your true nature, he will use it against you, Merlin. Is your secret worth the life of your child?" she pleaded. "He may be my husband," she began, brushing her fingers against the lingering bruise on her cheek as she stared into the fire with a look of regret, then glanced back at Marilyn and continued, "and I do not relish the thought of that man living forever. But, in your place, I would not trade the life of my daughter to keep the secret of the elixir from him."

Confused, Marilyn inquired, "Living forever? What elixir? You are not making sense Ygraine."

"The secret of dragon's breath," Ygraine replied, quizzically. "Gorloys claimed it to be an elixir that grants immortality."

Marilyn snorted, then shook her head. "Is that what he told you?" she inquired rhetorically, scoffing. "Dragon's breath is no such thing, Ygraine. It is a weapon of war to rain fire and destruction down on one's enemies."

"Pfaw! And you showed this to a man?" Magra interjected. "And Gorloys, no less! You fool girl!"

Unused to criticism, Marilyn turned to Magra, ready with an acid retort, but withered under the piercing gaze of the old woman, a mother who had just scolded her daughter. "I have been in this world coming on seventy winters if I make it to the next," she began as she threw some fresh logs into the hearth and adjusted them with a poker. Then, sitting back down in her chair, she continued with a sigh, "Sent two husbands and the second husband's son Branok to Annwn ahead of me."

Magra closed her eyes for a moment, her expression pensive, then continued, settling her piercing gaze on Marilyn once again. 'How do they do that?' Marilyn found herself thinking suddenly, feeling like the woman stood over her still, scolding her like a little girl, despite looking up at Marilyn from her chair. "In all those years, if there is one thing I have learned about every man, everywhere, it is this: Every last one of them is concerned with which of them has the bigger cock!"

An embarrassed giggle erupted from Ygraine, which she quickly stifled behind hands clasped over her mouth. But her hands did nothing to hide the burgeoning blush of her face. Magra glanced over at the young woman and nodded, continuing with a grin, "A boy has a stick and the next wants a bigger one. A man has a horse and the next wants a faster one. I once saw two farmers arguing over which of them had the fatter, longer carrots!" With the last comparison, Magra's face took on the same surprised expression that had sent Marilyn into fits of giggling earlier. Unable to help it, Marilyn giggled again. The old woman had a knack for spinning tales or sharing wisdom in a comical fashion.

Turning to Marilyn, she nodded, her expression once again serious. "And if a man has a sword, the next wants a shinier, bigger one," she finished.

Marilyn pondered her words as she stared into the hearth's fire. The old woman was right of course. The old woman was right, of course. But when Marilyn had cracked open this Pandora's Box, she hadn't expected to be placed in this position. Finally, turning to Magra, she admitted, "I do not know what to do, Magra; nor who to trust. Uthyr never demanded my secrets of me, only a demonstration of their power to goad Gorloys into submission."

"You know King Uthyr!?" Ygraine suddenly interjected with surprise. Glancing over at the woman, Marilyn recognized the same moon-eyed look she'd had herself, staring at a poster of the Jonas Brothers hanging in her junior high school locker as a teenager. For a younger man, she supposed Uthyr was indeed handsome. But being more like a younger brother to Marilyn, she had never looked at him with the starry eyes Ygraine suddenly possessed.

Marilyn looked over at Ygraine and grinned. "Yes, I know King Uthyr. I have given him counsel many times. We are friends," she confided. "Though he does not know I am here," she then added with consternation. "He thinks I returned to my own lands. But circumstances prevented me from completing my journey. I was captured by your husband while returning to him at Execaer. I had not thought to send word ahead of my return."

"If Gorloys knew how and where to find you," Magra replied acidly, "he likely had spies watching for you. Word would never have reached the king." With an assertive nod, she continued, "In any event, you speak the truth. You cannot share this secret with the man. The last thing this world needs is to give men better ways to kill each other. And you cannot be put back in that cellar; not with that baby in your belly."

"But then what do I do?" Marilyn pleaded. "I have no wish to return to the cellar either, but I cannot share the secret of dragon's breath either!"

"We need time to think and plan," the old woman replied with a perturbed look. "But, Gorloys has never been a patient…" As if saying his name too many times was a summoning invocation, pounding on Magra's door interrupted her and startled all three women. "Open up old woman!" came Gorloys' muffled voice from the other side.

"Hold on! I need to dress! Unless you want to see my wrinkly old hide sagging off these bones!" she called out, standing up again slowly.

Leaning toward Marilyn as she drew near, she demanded quietly, "Quickly; tell me of an ingredient in this dragon's breath." Seeing protest forming in Marilyn's eyes, Magra interrupted with exasperation, "Every good lie has a grain of truth, girl! I will ask for no more details but tell me now!"

Thinking quickly, Marilyn finally nodded in consent, replying, "You know of the yellow cakes that sailors burn to clear vermin from ships?"

Magra nodded confirmation and pointed to the pallet. "Go lay on the bedding over there, cover up, and pretend sleep," she whispered quietly as more pounding came. "Patience you goat!" she called out, then turned to Ygraine. "Go open the door for your husband while I settle back into my chair dear." Marilyn smirked but did as she was bid, admiring the old woman's quick thinking and composure despite the sudden panic she herself felt.

Gorloys shoved the door open the moment Ygraine had the inner latch undone and rushed past the threshold, forcing her to step aside or be knocked over. 'He is in a mood again,' Magra thought. Deciding to be pragmatic in an effort to calm him, she addressed him formally rather than talk to him like she would bend him over her knee. "Pen Gorloys," she said cordially, bowing her head slightly. "Forgive an old woman for taking so long to dress. What may I do for you?"

At first taken aback by her demeanor, Gorloys quickly glanced from Magra to the pallet where Merlin lay and stated angrily, "So, it is true! Merlin is here and not under guard in the cellar."

"Quiet down!" Magra demanded, quietly, but gently, attempting to breathe life into their deception. As Gorloys whipped his head around and settled his smoldering gaze of her, Magra added a belated "Please" then continued, "Merlin sleeps. He is very ill." She nodded toward Ygraine, warily standing by the still open door, adding "Your wife went to your cellar prison and found Merlin at death's door." Then she nodded toward the door. "She had Jowan there bring the man here straight away when she discovered it."

Gorloys' head whipped around once again toward the doorway, at the edge of which Jowan had been attempting to cast furtive glances into the room beyond. Attention suddenly drawn to him, he ducked back around the edge. "Jowan!" Gorloys growled loudly.

"Jowan is not to blame husband!" Ygraine interjected, drawing Gorloys stern gaze to her, as Jowan slunk into view. "Merlin's illness was his own doing. Before he fainted, Merlin admitted having taken a mouthful of water from the wrong pail."

'Clever girl,' Magra thought.

Gorloys, seeing the man wring his hands and cast a grateful glance at Ygraine, demanded, "Is this true Jowan? I will know if you lie!"

Jowan's focus jumped back to Gorloys. "Yes, Pen Gorloys!" he claimed vehemently. "Penêsek Ygraine speaks truly!"

Seeing doubt linger on the stubborn man's face, Magra offered some news she knew would please him, drawing his attention. "Merlin was mad with fever all night. But Ygraine had the presence of mind to question him about your dragon's breath while witless. She now knows the ingredients needed."

"Then we no longer need him," Gorloys said, glancing down at Merlin. "Kill him," he announced and turned to Ygraine to question her further.

"Pfaw! Even as a boy, you were rash and impatient!" Magra chided. "You may find out the ingredients, but knowing what goes in the pot does mean you can cook a stew properly. You need the recipe."

"Besides husband, you must wait until Spring in any event to make the dragon's breath," Ygraine quickly interjected. Magra wasn't sure where she was headed with their ruse, but hoped with all she had that the girl kept her wits about her.

Gorloys stepped out from between them, shut the door in Jowan's face, and pointed to a spot by Magra, turning a stern gaze on Ygraine. She moved to stand next to Magra and face him as he leaned against the door and crossed his arms over his chest. "Explain," he commanded, his expression still stern.

"The dragon's breath is made from the sap of pine trees," Ygraine began. 'Something that burns,' Magra thought. 'Good thinking.'

"And that is easy enough to collect in winter. But you must also have the fuzzy, brown flower tops of marsh rushes, which do not bloom until late Spring. And lastly, the yellow brimstone sailors burn to clear vermin from their ships is needed; something else that cannot be had until the ports open again in the Spring," she added. "Though I cannot think how these things combine to make a life-giving elixir," she said, taking on a quizzical expression.

With each ingredient listed, Magra watched Gorloys' expression shift from disbelief to pensiveness. Her last statement made him scoff in annoyance, however. "Do not be a fool, Ygraine. I only said that to avoid you blathering questions at me," he said reproachfully. "Dragon's breath is a weapon, one that will remove the yoke of Uthyr's rule from Cornwall's back."

He took on a thoughtful expression as he stared at Merlin lying still on the pallet. "My men reported the familiar smells of brimstone and pitch where the ground was scorched upon the field," he mused. "Perhaps you have discovered a portion of the secret." Then, looking up at Magra, his stern expression that laced with annoyance at having to admit the truth of her words, he stated, "But as I said…I need the recipe, not just the ingredients." He paused for a moment, glancing back toward Merlin. "Very well," he said. "When you have made him well again, lock him back in the cellar until he tells us the recipe."

"Pfaw!" Magra shot back, drawing his stern gaze back to her. "Ygraine has gotten more in one night of kindness than you have in ten days of cruelty! How many times have you heard me say that honey will accomplish more than bee stings?" Waving her hand at him dismissively in disgust, she continued, "I have said that since you were a boy and still you never listen. Ygraine told me what you were about. If you wish to gain Merlin's trust and get the whole secret, then try some comfort and kindness. Cruelty and cold have gotten you nowhere."

Gorloys stared at her skeptically, inquiring, "What are you suggesting old woman?"

"Leave the man here!" she replied, exasperated. "Jowan can guard my door just as easily as he could the cellar door. And besides, you charged your wife to win over the man's trust. She is a great deal more likely to do that here in comfort than in the dark cold of that cellar."

Gorloys stared at her, his expression thoughtful as he considered her arguments. "Very well," he finally said. "But I want that secret, you two. Your… honey… had best work or more than Merlin will feel my sting," he added acidly, then turned, yanked the door open, and stalked out, slamming it behind him.

"Ox's ass," Magra said staring at her door in consternation. "Ygraine, go latch the door. Merlin, you may as well get up," she commanded each of them.

Merlin let out a soft snore, mumbled something incoherent, and rolled over. "Poor woman. That soup in her belly is likely the first decent meal she has been able to keep down though." she murmured quietly, then turned to Ygraine. "Leave the latch, child. Merlin will improve now, but not without rest; she is exhausted. You can do nothing more for now. You may as well go for now."

Ygraine cast a doubtful eye at her, prompting Magra to snick in exasperation and shoo her out the door in protest. "He will be fine, Ygraine! I will call upon you if you are needed. You look like you could use a little rest yourself, come to it. Now go!"

With the door finally shut and latch secured, Magra turned around to go back to her chair. Merlin was sitting quietly on the bedding, with her arms wrapped around her knees, staring up at Magra with intensity.

CHAPTER 20

New Plans

Marilyn sat quietly on the bedding, her arms wrapped around her knees, her gaze intense and unwavering as Magra settled back into her chair. The room was still, save for the occasional pop and crackle from the hearth.

"So… you were playing the possum until we were alone," Magra began, breaking the silence. "You caught me off guard with your ruse. Not many can do that," she observed, her voice laced with both amusement and respect.

Marilyn shifted uncomfortably, her gaze settling on the fire's dancing flames. "I am a prisoner here, Magra. If I hope to survive and escape, I must find someone I can trust to help me." She paused, glancing at Magra's face to gauge her reaction. Her voice steady yet tinged with regret, she looked away, back toward the fire, admitting after a moment, "Ygraine is a sweet girl, but I do not trust her."

Magra leaned forward and arched a questioning eyebrow, drawing Marilyn's attention. "And why is that?" she inquired, her voice thick with curiosity, her gaze intense.

Marilyn sighed, remembering the struggles of a good friend from which she ultimately had to walk away; a painful memory that made her eyes glass over with unshed tears. With all her heart, she had wished for her friend to find the strength and courage to leave the bastard, hoping her support and encouragement would be enough. But it wasn't enough; so far as Marilyn knew, her former friend was still in that situation.

To Magra, she said, "I have seen the behavior before," her voice softening. "Women who endure cruel treatment, at the hands of someone claiming to love them, often betray trust, either to avoid further ill treatment or to win favor from the one who treats them poorly. It is not always the case, but it is a pattern I have observed – as though they have become trained to it, trapped by their minds as much as by their circumstances."

Magra nodded slowly, her expression solemn as she also stared into the fire. "Indeed. I love that girl like a mother loves a daughter, but I have seen it too. Ygraine grovels to Gorloys the way a beaten dog still licks its master's hand," she sighed, her gaze drifting back to Merlin. "So, you have chosen to trust me in her stead then. Why?" she asked Marilyn pointedly.

"Because you called Gorloys an ox's ass," Marilyn replied, grinning, eliciting a chuckle from Magra. Shaking her head with a weary expression, Marilyn added, "I may not like the man for the way he has treated me, nor for the way I see him treat others, but I have no wish to seek retribution for myself or justice for others. I only wish to go home. But I can think of no other way to win my freedom than to get a message to Uthyr that I am being held captive."

Magra pondered her words before voicing the same concern, the same conclusion at which Marilyn had already arrived. "If you involve Uthyr, it could lead to more bloodshed, more violence." Easing herself from her chair, she shuffled over to the hearth and tossed another log onto the fire, then began stoking it with an iron poker. As she did so, she continued. "You have the right of it that I do not like the man either. Yet, I must admit, though Gorloys mistreats his wife and shows no affection toward his daughter Morghais, he provides a comfortable life for them at Tintagel."

Magra prodded the flames to life as she worked in contemplative silence for a moment, then placed the iron poker back in its cradle and eased herself back into her chair. "I might wish to see that old goat's pride knocked off its horse a few times," she said. "But Uthyr is as likely guilty of that crime as any man. If those two go at it, innocent blood will pay the price for their pride." Magra sighed wistfully and fell silent.

Merlin wrapped the blanket tighter around herself, the weight of her predicament pressing upon her. "I know…But the only person who would be willing to stage a rescue is Uthyr!"

"And what do you propose he do?" Magra demanded, hotly. "Show up at Tintagel with an army at his back, demanding your release when he is not even supposed to know you are here?" Her expression turned sour. "Uthyr would have to sneak in alone while Gorloys' back is turned," she said acidly. "Even then, he keeps a handful of men housed at Tintagel or on the island, ready to ride at his word. Uthyr has no chance to sneak past the lot of them and take you out."

"Magra, you are brilliant!" Marilyn announced suddenly, her face lighting up. Like puzzle pieces that lay in a jumble, a plan began to form in her mind, the full picture of which was not complete. But the plan that began forming in her mind could work. It had to work!

"Oh, am I?" Magra said rhetorically, arching an eyebrow at Marilyn. Marilyn chuckled. "You all but said it yourself, Magra. If Uthyr is to rescue me, then Gorloys and his men cannot be here!"

"And how do you plan to see that happen," the old woman asked, her interest piqued.

"What is the one thing that would likely draw Gorloys and his men out of Tintagel?" Marilyn asked. She already knew the answer, but Magra's response only confirmed it.

Magra scoffed. "Pfaw! The chance to put Uthyr's head on a pike I imagine," she replied sardonically.

"Exactly!" Marilyn exclaimed, a mischievous grin spreading on her face. "But I will still need to send a message to Uthyr." Seeing a stubborn look in Magra's eyes, she held up a placating hand, adding quickly, "Be at ease, Magra. You and I are alike in that I want no bloodshed either. But I need your trust as much as I am trusting you."

Marilyn could still see doubt lingering in Magra's eyes. Nonetheless, the old woman said, "My son Lynok may be willing to carry a message. He has little love for Gorloys since the man shamed and executed his brother Branok."

"I am sorry for your loss," Marilyn said consolingly, but Magra waved her off. "The boy's shared a father – my husband, dead more than ten summers now. But Branok was almost a grown man by the time I knew him." Magra's expression became pensive and distant. "Lynok looked up to him though; and Branok doted on his brother from a young age." Then she focused again on Marilyn, saying, "His loss pains me a little, but not like it does Lynok."

"Can he carry a message to Uthyr without suspicion? Do you think he will?" Marilyn inquired, seeking confirmation. When Magra nodded with certainty, Marilyn said, "Then we may as well set things in motion. Call Jowan in here. I wish to tell him I have decided to cooperate with Gorloys and need his help."

Magra shook her head, a weary expression etching her face as she yawned into the back of her hand. "Whatever your plan, it can wait for tomorrow," she said assertively, her voice heavy with fatigue. "You are still ill and need rest. As for me, I need a bit of that stew and some sleep myself."

As she yawned again, Marilyn found herself involuntarily mimicking the gesture, a subliminal call to rest that spread between them. She nodded in agreement and laid back down on her pallet. As she lay there though, plans and contingencies began to race through her mind, and sleep did not come for a while.

"What do you want old woman?" Jowan asked gruffly, his gaze narrowing as he followed Magra back into the room.

Magra settled into her chair with a huff, her eyes flicking disapprovingly at Jowan. "Young people these days…no manners," she murmured grumpily under her breath. He displayed a snide grin at the elderly woman as Marylin drew his attention. "Magra did not call on you, Jowan; I did."

Surprise registered briefly on Jowan's ruddy face as he shifted his gaze to her. "After much thought, I have decided to aid Gorloys," Marilyn announced, her voice devoid of any obvious emotion.

His skepticism was palpable, his brows knitting together as he regarded her with a wary eye. "I do not believe you," he declared, his voice laced with distrust. "Why should I, after all these days?"

Marilyn's response was calm, almost detached. "This is not my country…nor even my world," she said, shrugging. Unused to being deceptive, Marilyn allowed her gaze to drift to the flickering flames of the hearth, masking her discomfort under his scrutinizing stare. It was all a ruse, of course; she had no intention of giving Gorloys the secret of making gunpower. But if she were going to make her plans work, she would need Jowan's unwitting cooperation.

"Why should I care who rules or who does not? I only became involved for the promise of aid to return home," she provided, hoping her casual demeanor would mask the lie, her heart beating a touch faster under the weight of her deceit.

Turning back to face Jowan, Marilyn tried to project confidence. "Gorloys has promised my freedom in exchange for my aid. And with that freedom, I will leave these lands and return home," she continued.

"Pen Gorloys is an honest man, Merlin," Jowan assured her. "If he promised your freedom, then he will keep his bargain so long as you keep yours."

Marilyn scowled at him. "You will forgive me if I do not take the word of the man who had a hand in my capture." Seeing him about to protest, Marilyn waved a placating hand. "Ygraine has assured me of Gorloys' sincerity," she said, then nodding toward Magra, sitting quietly in her chair, adding, "…and Magra has assured me of her honesty. So, I wish to secure that freedom."

Jowan's expression shifted to one of curiosity, a hint of interest creeping into his stern facade. "So, the dragon's breath… You will share the secret of its making with Pen Gorloys?" he pressed.

Marilyn met his gaze, her own expression unyielding. "No," she countered firmly. "I am no fool, Jowan. I will not share that secret. But I will make dragon's breath for him." She saw Jowan's scowl deepen, a flicker of confusion passing through his eyes. "So long as Gorloys has need of me, he has reason to keep me alive. Do you not see that, Jowan? If I share my knowledge, he has no more need of me, and I am as good as dead, no matter Ygraine's assurances."

The room settled into a tense silence, Jowan's eyes lingering on Marilyn, weighing her words. Marilyn held his gaze, her resolve clear even as she felt the precariousness of her position. She knew she was walking a thin line, one that could lead to freedom or further entrapment, and it all hinged on convincing Jowan.

Finally, he nodded, seeming satisfied that she was being forthright. "I will inform Pen Gorloys at once," he announced, and turned to go.

"Ygraine is already informing him," she interjected quickly, stopping him in his tracks. Turning around with a scowl, he inquired sourly, "Then why tell me?"

'Now for the hard part,' Marilyn thought as she paused a moment to take a deep breath, trying to calm her nerves. "Because I need your help if I am to help Gorloys," she replied, casting the line.

Jowan folded his arms, his suspicion apparent. "What kind of help?" he asked, his tone guarded.

Marilyn met his gaze steadily. "As you can see, I do not want my recipe for dragon's breath to become common knowledge. I must be very careful that no part of it falls into the wrong hands – even knowledge of the ingredients needed."

Jowan nodded slowly, but his eyes remained narrow. "So?"

Before Marilyn could respond, Magra interjected sharply, "Stop being so elusive, Merlin." Marilyn turned to her with a flat stare, but the old woman ignored her, saying to Jowan, "Merlin is trying to ask if you will get a message to your brother."

Jowan's scowl softened slightly. "Taran? What message?"

"I need him to keep an eye out for any ship that berths upon the river port at Bearda Market to cleanse itself of vermin. I have need of the yellow stone the sailors burn to do so," Marilyn explained, her voice steady, betraying none of her inner turmoil.

"That can be done," Jowan replied after a moment, the skepticism in his voice lessening. Marilyn noticed a slight shift in his stance, a lessening of his guarded demeanor – the hook was set.

"But how? You cannot leave your post, can you? And how do you ensure the message remains a secret? How do you know when a message comes from him and not from someone attempting to fool you?" Marilyn pressed on, her words pointed. "I will not seek your aid if you are so easily made a fool, Jowan."

A secretive smile flickered across Jowan's face as he reached up, untied a leather thong from around his neck, and pulled a small metal emblem from beneath his tunic. The emblem was a perfect five-pointed Celtic knot. "See the loophole in the knot at each point?" he explained, holding it out for her to see. "My brother has a twin to this emblem. If the messenger is true, he will have a bit of parchment bearing marks that trace the outline and where each knot hole in the emblem shows. If the messenger does not possess such a parchment, then I know the message is false. And the same is true for messages to him from me."

Marilyn extended her hand, her fingers poised with feigned casual interest. "May I see it?" she asked, her voice laced with careful curiosity. As Jowan handed it over, the small metal emblem felt cool and weighty in her palm. She turned it slowly, her fingers tracing the smooth, raised edges of the five-pointed Celtic knot. The emblem's surface was etched with fine lines, converging into a series of loops and whorls that spoke of a craftsman's skilled hand.

She noted the small, deliberate holes punctuating each point of the knot, like tiny eyes gazing back at her. They were evenly spaced, their purpose clear yet mysterious. Marilyn's thumb lingered over one of the holes, feeling its rounded edge, as she imagined the precision required to replicate such detail.

Her examination was meticulous, yet outwardly, she maintained an air of simple admiration. She tilted the emblem, watching the firelight dance and flicker across its surface, casting tiny shadows in the intricate crevices of the design. The metal was polished, reflecting the room's warm hues, yet it held a certain age, a testament to its history and significance.

"It is beautifully crafted. Such precision," she remarked, her gaze lifting to meet Jowan's. "How did you and your brother come by such detailed work?" she inquired, masking her true intent with a tone of admiration.

Jowan took back the necklace and emblem, beaming with pride. "Our father had them made when we were boys," he informed her. "He claimed that the crafting of a perfect five-point shape was itself a secret few knew," he added, tucking the emblem back into his tunic and retying the thong about his neck.

"So, the emblem cannot be easily copied," Marilyn confirmed to him. "Your father shows wisdom." She could see the praise and complements had the effect she desired. With the hook set, she had reeled Jowan in, netting him into her schemes, with him none the wiser. "Very well," she continued, a glimmer of resolve in her eye. "That will do nicely. Please have the message sent to your brother as soon as you can."

Jowan nodded, grinning happily, looking pleased with himself as he turned to leave. Marilyn watched him go, a sense of accomplishment mixed with apprehension swirling within her. 'One fish caught,' she thought to herself. But the real challenge lay ahead. As he reached the door, Magra's voice stopped him. "Jowan…" He turned back toward the two of them, his smile faltering as he took in stern looks from the both of them.

Her words were firm, laden with a gravity that held Jowan's attention. "Merlin has put trust in you, sharing knowledge I am sure he would rather keep to himself, and let you into a very small group," she said seriously. "Do not even share with your brother or for that matter, nor with your messenger, the reason for the yellow stone. Do you understand?" she demanded.

Jowan's gaze shifted from Magra to Marilyn, his earlier grin replaced by a more somber expression. Marilyn returned his gaze, her look one of quiet insistence. After a moment of silent contemplation, Jowan nodded solemnly. "I understand," he replied.

With Jowan's acknowledgment, Marilyn allowed herself a moment of relief as he turned again and exited the room, closing the door behind him. Once alone with Magra, Marilyn exhaled slowly, the tension of the moment giving way to the weariness of her still recovering body. She glanced at Magra, who gave her a subtle nod of support, then settled back onto her pallet to get some more rest. Her health was improving, but the intensity of her subterfuge had drained her of what energy she had.

As she lay back and stared into the rafters, she thought about the exchange with Jowan. She hadn't expected anything so complex as the emblem he had presented. She had expected something more along the lines of a secret pass phrase or secret knock, or some other simple, yet cliché exchange out of a 20th century spy movie. Replicating the emblem would not be easy, but she knew the trick of drawing a perfect pentagram Jowan had mentioned. The hard part would be carving it.

As if fate intervened though, a sudden realization broke through her fatigue, a potential solution to part of her dilemma. Turning to Magra, she asked, "Can you get me a spare wooden plank like those in the roof?"

The material from which she could easily carve a counterfeit emblem was literally above her, waiting to be utilized.

Magra's affirmative response was comforting, and with that, Marilyn felt a weight lift ever so slightly. A yawn overtook her, the exhaustion pulling her towards sleep. She curled up, the whispering keen of the wind down the chimney flue and the fire's warmth and dissonant, yet soft crackle conspiring to draw her into the rest she so desperately needed. As sleep embraced her, her last thoughts lingered on the carved emblem, the next step in her intricate dance of deception and survival.

"What the hell am I seeing here, Naomi?" Philip demanded. Having given Marilyn the two weeks she said she needed to transport the artifact to a new location, they finally decided to turn it back on and check in. What they saw instead was a chaotic blur – a strobing light show through a murky haze.

At first, Philip's heart raced, thinking there was something wrong with the artifact. 'What if it got damaged in transit?' he thought worriedly. Or perhaps their luck had run out and somehow their connection to Marilyn in the past was no longer attainable. These thoughts, each possibility worse than the last, finally sent him into a panicked race from the control room to the lab platform to see the artifact up close. He could not lose her. Not now! Especially now that there were two lives at stake – hers and the life of their unborn child – at stake.

"I don't know, Flip," Naomi responded, worriedly from the control room. "The monitors here aren't making things any clearer." Her worry only served to strengthen his own.

"I think I know," Avery interjected, levelly. "Naomi, what's the frame set to on the DARTS' video recorder?"

Philip forced himself to hold his own emotions in check. Avery's voice was so calm, so rational – the opposite of everything Philip was feeling at the moment, which only added to his frustration. He suppressed the urge to lash out at the man. 'How can you be so calm? My world is coming apart!' He said none of these things aloud though.

"It's running at thirty frames per second," Naomi replied, yanking Philip from his inner turmoil. "Normal frame rate."

"How high can you crank it up?" Avery asked over the comms.

Philip could hear the excitement in her voice as she caught on to Avery's line of questioning, just as he had. "Eighteen hundred!" she exclaimed. "Avery you're a genius!"

Knowing what the two of them were up to, Philip turned to head back to the control room. He listened to the two of them banter over the comms, sounding for all the world like Mac and Tosh, the overly polite gophers from Looney Tunes cartoons Philip remembered from his childhood. 'Good,' he thought. 'This place could use a little lightheartedness for a change.'

It had been a stressful couple of weeks for everyone to say the least. So, even the most mundane of good news or positivity was treated as though someone had won the lottery. He recalled fondly how, three days ago, Ayesha had burst into the control room excitedly bearing a cup of brown goo. "The mess hall has chocolate pudding today!" she had announced, presenting the cup like Montezuma's lost treasure. The team had cheered and, one by one, went off to get their own cup while Ayesha sat at her station spooning the delicious treat into her mouth, savoring every bite. 'It's the small things that keep us sane,' Philip thought contemplatively, remembering the look of child-like joy on her face.

Philip's strides back to the control room were hurried, his mind racing with worry for Marilyn. As the leader of this operation in her absence, he had always maintained a calm and collected exterior. However, as hours had stretched into days, worry and fear began to worm their way into his mind. More and more, he struggled to mask his concern and maintain professional detachment as the fear of losing the woman he loved chipped away at his façade.

He knew Marilyn could take care of herself – she was strong and capable. But it didn't stop him from feeling helpless, unable to do anything of consequence from this end of the time and space between them. The inexplicable light show coming through only served to heighten his anxiety. 'What if we've lost her? What if she's in danger and we can't reach her?' These thoughts hammered at him as he made his way down the catwalk and back to the control room.

"What are you two talking about?" Ayesha had finally asked after listening to Naomi and Avery banter back and forth for a moment.

Philip interjected, as much to let them know he understood the plan as to inform Ayesha. "Ayesha, have you ever watched one of those videos where they show a hummingbird in real time, and then the same hummingbird flapping its wings in slow motion?" he asked, forcing his voice to remain steady despite his anxiety.

"Ya?" she replied, quizzically.

"They do that with a high-speed video camera, then play back the video in slow motion," he responded.

"Ohhh," Ayesha replied as she caught up to their plan and what was about to happen.

By the time he had reached the control room, Naomi had increased the frame rate on the DARTS video recorder to 1,800 frames per second and recorded a minute of the light show coming from the artifact. By the time he had reached the control room again, they were done. "Cut the power until we figure out what we're dealing with here Tak," he commanded.

"Yessir," Takashi replied. As the familiar sounds of machinery wound down and the strobing from the artifact faded away, Philip and Avery gathered around Naomi's workstation.

"Flip, I think what we're seeing is… well… the world," Avery said.

Philip gathered with the team around Naomi's workstation and began playing back the video in slow motion. Even in slow motion though, the world beyond seemed oddly sped up. The strobing lights slowly revealed themselves to be the sun and moon reflecting off the surface of a thin layer of water that covered the artifact on the other end.

Right above the artifact, they witnessed a small school of bait fish fritter its way slowly across the surface of the artifact through a thin layer of murky water, while in the distance, the heavens sped by at incredible speed. All evidence suggested that the artifact currently resided in the shallows of a pond or some other naturally occurring fresh water source. As the realization dawned on everyone, a heavy silence fell over the room.

Philip felt a knot tighten in his stomach as his own fears gnawed at him. So, he turned away, appearing to ponder the circumstances, but more to conceal his face and mask his concern. 'Marilyn, what have you done? Why there, of all places?' he thought. Submerging the artifact in water, not knowing whether doing so would damage it, had been an incredible risk, and still might be. Just because the commercial claimed a wristwatch could survive immersion in fifty-foot depths didn't mean one should leave it in a glass of water on the bedside table overnight. Whatever he was feeling internally though, the team depended on him to lead. He needed to offer reassurance, show confidence he did not feel.

Straightening his features, and turning back to them, he cleared his throat, aware that all eyes were on him, waiting for him to make sense of the situation. He could see the same aura of concern had washed over them that he was feeling, unspoken fears just under the surface written across every face. They were looking to him for leadership and hope, even though all he felt at the moment was despair.

"Um, it makes sense actually," Philip started, his voice less certain than he would have liked. "She couldn't bring the artifact to a populated area and use it effectively. Maybe she hid it under the surface of a nearby pond or something, out of the way where it couldn't be casually observed from a distance."

As he spoke, part of him balked at his own words, knowing the explanation sounded a little far-fetched. Even so, perhaps his own heart was seeking a positive reason. Oddly enough, the explanation he gave the team kind of made sense.

Starting with the assumption that Marilyn had hidden the artifact with intent, the explanation did seem plausible – even practical – despite his earlier thoughts about the risk of immersing it in water. He found he was actually convincing himself as much as them, a desperate hope to which he could cling under the circumstances. It did make sense! Even if he had made up the excuse on the spot.

Naomi raised an eyebrow. "Underwater, really, Flip? Like dropping a cell phone in a lake to hide it?"

He met her gaze, his expression serious. "I know it sounds implausible. But remember, this artifact isn't like any technology we know. It doesn't have circuits or batteries that would short-circuit. It's survived in a salty sea cave, exposed to the elements and perhaps even tides, for who knows how long without damage. Whatever its purpose or design, water doesn't seem to affect it like it would normal electronics."

The room was quiet, each team member processing the information. Philip could see the concern in their eyes, mirroring his own worries. Yet, they nodded, accepting the explanation for now. It was the best they had, and in the face of the unknown, sometimes a tenuous hope was the best you could offer. Still, he didn't need them mulling over his explanation and worrying, so he turned to each and gave them something to do to keep busy.

"Tak, now that we know what's going on, make sure we can reestablish the connection," he ordered. "Now that it's out in the open, you have a window on the time dilation effect. We need to get a better handle on that if possible and learn to control the difference in the time flow."

With Takashi's acknowledgement, Philip turned to Naomi and inquired, "Higgins, what is our status on the linguist?"

"We brought in Doctor Lyle Okun - one of the top linguists in the field," Naomi responded. "Maybe even the best. He studied under Noam Chomsky at MIT back in the day!" she added excitedly. "We would've brought Chomsky in, but he retired over two decades ago." Then she shrugged, her expression almost apologetic, "And to be honest, we would've had a hard time getting Chomsky through security clearance given his history of political activism."

"So where is Doctor Okun?" Philip inquired.

"We gave him the empty office down the hall from the Lieutenant Colonel's, sir," she replied. "When I told him what he would be working on and showed him the pages, he got really excited." She snickered and shook her head, amused. "He's a committed one for sure. He cloistered himself off in there three days ago and has hardly come out since."

"Tell me about it," Avery interjected. "I went in there to talk to him about those technical-looking diagrams on the pages and the smell about knocked me over. I had to remind him that even geniuses need to shower and change clothes now and then!"

Philip chuckled at the jab. He had met that sort of fellow before – so preoccupied and passionate about their work that social conventions often took a backseat, all but forgotten in the fervor of their current focus. "Regardless, check on his progress," he ordered. "Find out if he has learned anything. And Avery, plug your nose if needed, but work with the man on interpreting those diagrams. If they are technical in nature, they will likely provide the best clues to help us get Mare home. I'd like a status report right away."

As he gave each order, he looked each of them in the eye, gauging their reaction. In each case, he could see their fears, worries, and concerns melt away, replaced instead by the confidence and sense of duty he had hoped to see, a mirror for the example he himself was trying to portray.

"What about me, sir?" Ayesha asked, wanting to be included. Just looking at her, he could see the difference in demeanor. In giving the others something to do, their focus and confidence had been greatly restored by a new sense of purpose and potential accomplishment. Ayesha on the other hand, still looked fretful. But her position as cryogenics specialist didn't lend itself to any special need at the moment. He glanced through the control room window at the platform and artifact below and thought for a moment.

"Actually, I do have a task for you, Ayesha," he said. "Something important."

"Ya?" she asked, hopeful.

"You said it yourself when all this started. Folks back then were a superstitious lot. We need something to ward off the casual wanderer from getting too close to the artifact," he said. "Otherwise, some curious farmer is liable to get too close, take a nap nearby, and pull a Rip Van Winkle!"

His suggestion not only pulled a chuckle at the thought from the entire team, but it also wiped the worry from Ayesha's face, replacing it instead with a wide smile. She nodded with an acknowledging, "I'll get on it, boss!" and headed off to brainstorm ideas.

Having delegated tasks, he watched his team spring into action, their earlier concern replaced by a renewed focus. It gave him a momentary sense of relief, a brief respite from the gnawing worry for Marilyn. Yet, as a flicker of light caught Philip's attention, drawing his gaze back to the control room window, his thoughts returned to her. Takashi had reestablished the connection and the strobing light show was back. Staring at the portal, he said a silent prayer, hoping his version of Marilyn's circumstances was close to the truth, hoping that she was safe and that they would soon find a way to bring her back.

CHAPTER 21

Deception and Loyalty

Marilyn heard the muffled sounds of a heated exchange outside Magra's door, the words not quite loud enough to be called a shout but tinged with frustration. "I need no excuse to see my own mother, Jowan. Now step aside," came a demanding voice.

A moment later, the door opened, and Lynok – Magra's son, whom Marilyn had met earlier – stepped through, latching it shut behind him.

"Is it done?" Marilyn asked without preamble.

Lynok, pausing to warm his hands by the hearth, eventually answered, "Yes, though not hidden in the cave you requested. A smaller, more secluded cave lies higher up and to the right that may only be reached by boat and then by climbing. None but sea birds ever venture there. Your box is safely hidden in a crevice within."

The news made Marilyn think back to what began this endeavor. Waking up nude when she had first been brought to Magra unconscious had been unsettling, to say the least. Magra and Ygraine had removed everything, including her necklace chain, which held her military dog tags and the engagement ring Philip had given her what seemed ages ago. Marilyn recalled promising him that she would find a place to stow it for safekeeping. As her health improved over these last two days and her mental faculties were restored, she realized one morning with horror that her chain was not around her neck.

"Magra, where is my chain?!" she had demanded in a panic.

"The one holding the bits of metal and the ring with stones that sparkle in the light? I put it in a pocket of your pouch," Magra had replied simply, pointing to Marilyn's backpack, propped neatly in a corner of the apartment.

Relief had washed over Marilyn when she found it and placed it around her neck once again. But that relief brought with it the reminder of her promise to Philip and a new resolve to see it through.

Later, to aid in keeping that promise, Magra supplied the very container Lynok had just finished hiding – a wooden box of herb crocks she had had sitting on the mantle. Now those crocks lined the mantle, adding an ambiance akin to some ancient apothecary.

As Marilyn had prepared the box for its purpose, she remembered pausing, contemplating if there was anything else of value she didn't want to risk being stolen. She rummaged through her backpack then, her hands searching among her few belongings. It was during this search that her fingers brushed against the cool, smooth surface of the crystalline cup Sinbad had found in the alien tomb, crafted from the same enigmatic material as the artifact.

Realizing its potential importance, Marilyn carefully placed the cup alongside the chain that held her engagement ring and dog tags, arranging them thoughtfully inside the box. She then sealed the lid with beeswax, ensuring the contents were securely enclosed. Now, with Lynok's help, that box lay safely hidden in a cave below the fortress. In that secluded spot, Marilyn hoped it would remain undetected, preserved for centuries, if necessary, until she could return with a metal detector to recover it.

"What of the boat?" Magra inquired, drawing Marilyn back from her thoughts.

"That is why it took me so long, mother," Lynok replied. "I waited for the tide to go out, then hid it within Merlin's cave, lashed to a rock deep within. No one should venture there in mid-winter, but if they do, it should remain concealed beneath the tide."

Magra nodded in approval, sparing no extra words. Marilyn couldn't help but smirk at the old woman's brevity. 'Not one to waste words,' she thought.

"And what of Gorloys?" Ygraine inquired meekly. Marilyn glanced at her worriedly. As loathe as she was to trust the girl, Marilyn found herself forced to have Ygraine become complicit in her deceptions. Of course, the powder and suet Magra had applied to Ygraine's face to make her look pale, weak, and sickly did not help. But Marilyn supposed that was the point of it. She knew Ygraine wasn't sick at all, but playing a part, even for Lynok's sake. If Gorloys ever discovered his or Magra's involvement in affecting her escape, their lives would be forfeit. Even so, ruse would be the limit of Ygraine's involvement, Marilyn had decided, as much brought about by her lack of trust for the woman as by a desire to not implicate her and put her in danger. Ygraine knew she was hatching plans to escape but knew none of the details. Such conversations had been limited to Magra and Lynok when Ygraine was not in the room.

'She will do well,' Marilyn hoped as she continued to appraise Ygraine's appearance. As an additional part of the deception, Ygraine had a small padding of wool wrapped tightly against her lower midriff, concealed beneath her dress. If all went according to Marilyn's plans, that padding, which held within it a magnet Marilyn had cannibalized from the speaker of one of the two-way radios in her backpack, would play a part in an even greater deception to come. Magra was sitting in her chair knitting with an iron needle that Marilyn had annealed in the hearth fire and magnetized earlier that morning with that same magnet. All was in place and ready.

Lynok turned to Ygraine while Marilyn pondered her plan with equal parts hope and worry. "Pen Gorloys has been told you are with child, but ill," Lynok replied.

For the second time in as many days, a pounding came to Magra's door at the mention of Gorloys' name. 'Speak of the devil and he shall appear,' she mused. She wrapped her dark long coat more tightly around her and moved to a shadowed wall of the room to sit as inconspicuously as possible, while Magra directed Lynok to open the door.

Unlike the time before when Gorloys had burst into the room with anger and outrage that Marilyn had been moved to Magra's apartment, Gorloys instead burst into the room with a sense of nervous excitement. "Your son brought news that my wife is with child, old woman!" he exclaimed failing to notice Ygraine, lying on a pallet just at the edge of the hearth's fire light.

Magra looked up from her knitting and arched an eyebrow, seeming to take a moment's pleasure in waiting to respond to him. Finally, she nodded toward Ygraine, then focused once again on her knitting. "It is as you were told. She is with child," she stated flatly. "But she is also ill and will need to stay here with me for the time being, perhaps until she has the child."

Despite the troubling news, Gorloys wore a satisfied expression as he turned to Ygraine, inquiring, "How far along?"

'Wow,' Marilyn thought. 'He really could care less about her health, so long as she brings him an heir. She is nothing but a vessel to him. What an ass!' Ygraine had warned her of Gorloys' disposition. But Marilyn was nonetheless surprised to witness it firsthand.

"It must have been the night of Uthyr's parley in the summer, husband," she replied meekly. "You have been preoccupied since then and have had no time for me. If all goes well, Magra says I will give birth in the spring."

Marilyn was taken aback by the sudden revelation, not so much because she found it easy to believe, but rather because Ygraine had voiced it in front of others. Ygraine had not shared that information earlier; only that he lacked in his duties as husband of late, assuring Marilyn that the ruse of her being pregnant was plausible. 'For a man so keen on having an heir,' Marilyn thought, 'he certainly isn't going about it with much effort.'

A smug smile spread across his face as he gazed down at Ygraine. It might have been a smile of anticipation upon hearing the news of her pregnancy, but Marilyn couldn't help but sense it carried a lecherous undertone, as if he were recalling the night of conception Ygraine had mentioned. "Perhaps this time you will bring me an heir," he said.

'There!' Marilyn thought suddenly, 'The opportunity I needed!' Though filled with the adrenaline of anticipation, she remained calm, sitting cross-legged in the shadows. "Have your people not learned how to tell whether a boy or girl lies nestled within the womb?" she inquired, derisively. She tutted a few times and fell silent, waiting for Gorloys to take the bait.

"Is this some trickery of yours, Merlin?" he finally asked, annoyed.

"No, only something of the natural world my people learned long ago," Marilyn replied enigmatically. "I see no reason not to share this knowledge though." She had previously rehearsed what she was about to have Magra do, and of the four people in the room, only the old woman knew what was coming. Not even Ygraine was aware of the speaker magnet concealed within the wool padding under her dress. Marilyn remained sitting in the shadows mysteriously as she led her charade. The less she was physically involved, the more she hoped Gorloys would believe in what he was about to witness.

"Magra, your darning needle is made of iron, yes? I thought so. Thread the eye with a length of wool about as long as your arm, then hand it to Pen Gorloys," she instructed.

When Magra had done so and handed the needle to Gorloys, Marilyn directed her next instructions at him. "Spit on it," she demanded.

"What?" Gorloys asked, taken aback in surprise.

"You are the father, so this magic requires a part of you to work," Marilyn replied, trying to sound impatient though she knew it was all a ruse. "Blood works best, but I would not ask you to harm yourself. Some men become squeamish at the sight of blood. So, spit on it."

She smiled inwardly, knowing the best parlor tricks involved distraction. As she expected, the subtle jab at his pride provided that distraction, committing him to the parlor trick without his even realizing it. Sneering at her, he yanked a dagger from his belt and squeezed his fist around it. A moment later, the darning needle was covered in blood from his palm.

"Magra, have Ygraine lie flat and, with a steady hand, dangle the needle over her navel," Marilyn continued, "If the iron does not move or sways back and forth, she will give birth to a son. And if it wobbles or goes round in a circle, she will give birth to a daughter."

Magra reached out to take the needle from Gorloys, but he yanked it back with a glare. "I will do it," he announced, his tone laced with distrust. He turned his gaze to Ygraine, his tone commanding, "You heard the man, Ygraine. Lie on your back."

Ygraine did as she was told and Gorloys soon had the needle dangling over her, about where her navel would be. As Marilyn had hoped, the pole at the tip of the needle was repelled by the speaker magnet hidden in the padding and began to wobble around in a circular pattern, avoiding the spot directly over the magnet. Both Lynok's and Ygraine's eyes rounded in wonder, while Gorloys watched with a stunned expression.

"This is some sort of trickery," Gorloys finally muttered incredulously.

"Come now, Pen Gorloys," Marilyn replied quietly from the shadows, trying to sound as mysterious and wise as possible. It helped that she was still recovering from illness and her throat was still a little hoarse, lending a throaty, otherworldly tone. Or at least she thought so.

"We both know the truths to be found in blood and iron," she continued. Her words were an artful fabrication but sounded sagely to her.

Regardless, this was the moment. He would either buy into the ruse or he would not. If not, they may all be in trouble.

Gorloys glared at her shadow, then yanked the needle up by the thread, snatching it from the air. His face spoke of anger and outrage as he tossed the needle across the small apartment to clatter against the wall beside Marilyn's head. Shifting his glare to Ygraine, his ire was obvious. He managed a single kick of rage that caused Ygraine to double up as she cried out, while at the same time, Lynok reacted, grabbing Gorloys' arm to pull him away. "Pen Gorloys!" he exclaimed loudly, then yanked Gorloys arm again, drawing his attention.

Gorloys' glare shifted from Ygraine to Lynok, who stepped back, but held his gaze, an earnestly shocked look on his face. The distraction seemed to clear Gorloys moment of rage as the haze of anger cleared from his eyes and he stopped grimacing, perhaps remembering that he was not alone in this room with Ygraine, Marilyn thought.

Ygraine's quiet weeping pulled Gorloys' attention as he turned from Lynok to stare back at her. She still lay on the floor weeping, with Magra stooped over her. Magra turned and met his gaze accusingly but said nothing.

"Stay here and whelp the brat then," he finally said with disgust. "But stay out of my sight until the deed is done." His parting words, laden with disdain, hung in the air as he turned abruptly and stormed out, the door slamming shut behind him with a resonant thud.

Marilyn exhaled slowly, a silent prayer of gratitude escaping her lips. The deception had held. While her pregnancy could no longer be concealed, they had gained precious time – time that could mean the difference between peril and safety for her and her unborn child. Yet, uncertainty lingered in the shadows of her hope. The success of her future plans, her very rescue, hinged on factors beyond this room, beyond her control.

The room was steeped in a heavy silence, broken only by the faint crackling of the hearth fire. Marilyn finally turned to Lynok, her eyes reflecting the gravity of what lay ahead. "Well… that is done," she stated, her voice steady yet tinged with the weight of the moment. "Lynok, you know what to do."

Lynok gave a curt nod and kissed Magra on the cheek. Then, with a final, determined look, he departed, the weight of his responsibility evident in his purposeful stride. Marilyn watched him go, aware that the seeds of her plans, for better or worse, were now sown. In the stillness that followed, her gaze lingered on the closed door long after he had disappeared, her mind racing. In the end, she could do no more than wait and hope. Whatever happened from here, the next moves in this intricate game of survival and subterfuge were no longer hers to make. She had set the pieces in motion; now, fate would have its say in her destiny.

Uthyr raised a fist, signaling his men to halt. A faint scent of decay wafted on the breeze, drawing his attention. He surveyed the sparse patches of yellowed marsh grass among the winter-barren woods lining the road to Glouvum, but the source remained elusive.

The overcast sky loomed above them, heavy with the promise of snow as Uthyr glanced upward appraisingly with a twinge of impatience. He was not eager to spend yet another night in the open but refused to seek refuge with his goal unmet.

Nevertheless, to the south across the fens in the distance, he could see the village of Glestinga, looming like a ghostly specter atop a terraced hill, its rooftops peeking through the ever-present winter mist that clung to the swampland below, mocking him with the offer of refuge that he could not yet seek.

Their party had passed the road to that village that morning, a meandering route through the bog, treacherous to follow in winter with the ever-present fog offering the unwary a watery grave. Yet, Uthyr mused, he'd rather find what they were looking for soon, even if it meant navigating that misty path to Glestinga for a night's refuge.

He returned his attention to the matter at hand, turning in his saddle and calling out to his men, "“I caught the scent of a dead animal on the breeze. Be alert for…"

He paused and turned to Lynok, riding beside him. 'The remains of an ox – those were Merlin's words?

"Yes, sire," Lynok responded. "He said it would be about ten paces from the path, across from the fen to the south."

Satisfied, Uthyr turned back to his men, and continued. "Keep your eyes open for the remains of an ox, in the woodlands to the north."

As he gently urged his horse forward, Uthyr cast a thoughtful glance at Lynok, then continued surveying the woods. "You call me sire and show me respect. But you also betray Gorloys in coming to me," he mused aloud. Then, turning a piercing gaze to Lynok, he demanded, "I would know why, Lynok."

Lynok matched his stare, seeming to ponder his words as Uthyr bobbed his head back toward the men following them. "The hundred men you see behind us bear witness to my caution," he added. "Your tale stretches belief, but I must follow the trail of it for Merlin's sake, treating it as truth. Yet I would not walk blindly into a trap."

Lynok sat stolid, resilient to Uthyr's withering gaze, then, seeming to come to a decision, nodded, replying, "I speak the truth. Merlin sent me to seek your aid on his behalf." He looked away, his expression pensive. "The day you and Merlin faced Gorloys on the field outside Bearda Market, my older brother Branok stood with Gorloys on the field."

"Ah!" Uthyr replied, jumping to a conclusion. "So, my dragons convinced your brother to switch loyalties, and in turn, he convinced you?"

"Do not mock me with continued deception," Lynok replied hotly, surprising Uthyr. "Gorloys knows the dragons were a ruse; mere statues in a play, concealing the real power within. That is the secret Gorloys is after," he continued. "That is why he captured Merlin."

Uthyr was shocked at Lynok's confession, and looked away, pondering the implications. "There must be spies in my camp," he muttered.

Lynok offered solace, replying, "Think nothing of it sire. Enough coin and mead will loosen even the most loyal tongue."

"But what has this to do with you and your brother?" Uthyr demanded, seeking clarity.

"My brother is dead," Lynok replied, acidly. "That day on the field, he witnessed the power of this dragon's breath, and it frightened him beyond reason."

Lynok's eyes became haunted as he stared ahead, continuing his story in a somber tone. "Our father was a cruel man when he drank. He would threaten to burn Branok, amusing himself with a nasty grin and wicked light in his eyes. As I grew old enough to gain our father's notice, I never received such… attention. My brother always stood in my stead, protecting me from that drunken, old wart. I loved my brother for that. But because of it, he feared fire above all else."

He looked over finally, anger and regret filling his words, "Tormented by those old fears, Branok was frightened by the dragon's breath. He fled, leaving Gorloys to face you and Merlin alone on the field. Gorloys executed my brother for cowardice that very day."

"So, you changed loyalties to seek vengeance," Uthyr concluded solemnly, believing he understood Lynok's motivation.

"No, not vengeance. Though if given the opportunity, I could not say what I would do in the moment," Lynok admitted, the quiet intensity in his voice revealing his inner turmoil. "I was loyal to Pen Gor… to Gorloys. But my loyalty to Branok, to my family, is stronger. I could not stay loyal to a man whose cruelty robbed me of my brother." Lynok's expression was one of pain as he contemplated his next words. "I do not deny that the desire for vengeance has gnawed at me. And though I may want it, I have neither the opportunity nor power to seek it. So, changing my allegiance to you, serving you instead of Gorloys, is perhaps the only justice I will find." His gaze drifted away, echoing the pain and conflict he felt inside.

Uthyr nodded slowly, his understanding deepening. Lynok's words struck him as more about balancing the scales than seeking blind revenge. It was a quest for closure, driven by a sense of honor that was rare and profound. Uthyr found himself not only understanding Lynok's plight but also feeling a newfound respect for the man. There was a sincerity in Lynok's struggle, a commitment to a personal code of ethics that Uthyr admired. He decided, in that moment, that he liked Lynok and could trust him.

A strong scent of decay brought their attention back to the task at hand. Uthyr paused and scanned the area. Spotting the carcass ahead, he pointed it out. "The ox is there," he said with a hint of eagerness. "What did Merlin say we should look for next?"

Lynok looked where Uthyr pointed, his eyes searching ahead, his voice steady, "We must look for the burn marks of a fire and the charred remains of the cart used to feed it. Merlin said they would be nearby." Then he looked up at the sky, scowling, then back down, shaking his head as if to clear it.

Uthyr glanced up, looking for what troubled the man, then back to Lynok. "Is something wrong?" he inquired.

Lynok glanced at him, replying with chagrin, "Nothing…I…For a moment, it seemed I could see the sun move."

"The sun moves across the sky every day," Uthyr replied quizzically.

"No…not like that. For a moment, when I glanced up, the sun was moving quickly through the tops of the trees; like watching a pill bug make its way across a log. I could see it!" he exclaimed. "It is high overhead now and I should be hungry, but I am not," he added. "The tree's shadows appeared to be shrinking much too quickly. That was what made me look up."

Uthyr nodded, urging his horse forward. "Perhaps such things are to be expected as we approach the threshold to Merlin's world?" he pondered.

"He said it might be so, but I did not believe him," Lynok responded, then shook his head. "That is not true," he added, denying his own words. "Merlin said time may stretch for us and shorten for the world around us. I could not understand what he meant at the time, so I said nothing. I am sorry sire."

Uthyr waved him off. "Let us be wary then for other signs as well." As if giving voice to his words, when they moved forward a few paces, Uthyr noticed the sun and clouds indeed beginning to move at a noticeable pace, and a sense of unease began to build within him.

With another step, a wave of disorientation washed over him, akin to seasickness – an entirely foreign sensation on solid ground. Both his and Lynok's horses grew restless, nickering and rolling their eyes in confusion.

Another pace, and the world seemed to spin. The sky whirled above him, increasing his sense of disorientation. Suddenly, his horse neighed loudly, its unease reaching a peak. Without warning, Uthyr found himself thrown to the ground as the horse bolted away towards the rear of their column.

Shaking his head to clear it, Uthyr looked up to see Lynok struggling to control his own horse. Dusting himself off, Uthyr's gaze turned back to his men. Those at the back of the column appeared to be moving faster than those nearby, their voices reaching him in high-pitched, accelerated tones.

Regaining his composure, Uthyr walked back towards his men, leading Lynok's horse by the nose. The closer he got, the more normal their movements appeared. One of his men approached him with concern. "Are you well, sire?" he asked.

Uthyr replied with a hint of sarcasm, "I am fine, Rhys. A horse has thrown me before."

Rhys shook his head. "That is not what I meant, sire. From a distance, you and this man," he gestured at Lynok, "appeared to move as if wading through honey. Your movements were slow as a slug. But as you approached, your movements returned to normal."

A realization dawned on Uthyr as he pieced together these bizarre events with the information Rhys had shared. The passage of time must change the nearer they come to the threshold of Merlin's world. The epiphany made Uthyr look back to confirm – the men at the back of the column and the world around them appeared to move with a speed beyond description. And from their view, he realized, the opposite must be true - his group must appear to move as the man had described – slow as a slug.

"Men, listen well," he announced, gathering their attention. "The threshold to Merlin's world is nearby. Do not fear, though you may witness strange and wondrous things. It is simply that time passes differently the nearer a man draws to it. This was to be expected!"

Walking over to his horse, he pulled his bow from its saddle holster and grabbed an arrow. "Watch," he commanded, then shot an arrow down the cart path. Exclamations of surprise and wonder erupted all around him as the arrow slowed to a crawl perhaps ten paces away, and appeared to hang in the air, its forward motion almost imperceptible.

Uthyr turned to his men and began issuing orders with a commanding presence. "Rhys, take a dozen men back up the road to the cutoff headed for Glestinga. Make camp there and tell any travelers that the road through here is closed by order of the king and that they must detour through Glestinga."

His gaze then shifted in the direction of the floating arrow. Pointing up the road, he addressed Owain, another trusted member of his troupe. "Owain, take a dozen men and provisions to make another camp. Horses will spook too easily to bring with you, so run along the road as fast as you can toward Glouvum until you reach the fork to Glestinga coming from the other way. Make camp there and do the same for travelers coming from that direction."

As Rhys and Owain began to gather their respective groups, Uthyr continued to lay out his plan, ensuring that every detail was covered. "I must go to the threshold of Merlin's world," he stated solemnly. "But I do not know how long I will be," he added, glancing once more toward the arrow suspended in its surreal state. "The rest of you will come with me. I will send a man from my group to each camp every so often to provide updates until we are done here. If it takes long, resupply in Glestinga if needed, but wait for our return!"

After giving his orders, Uthyr reached into his saddle bag and retrieved the leather tube of parchments Lynok had given him from Merlin. He looked at Lynok, seeing in him a shared sense of purpose. "Come with me," he commanded, his voice resonant with the gravity of their mission. With that, he led the way back to the head of the column, his thoughts now firmly fixed on reaching the threshold and the charge Merlin had entrusted him with once he was there.

As Uthyr and his group followed the path, evidence of his earlier warning manifested in startling ways. One of the men pointed at a distant cluster of evergreens, shaking as though trembling in the cold. Uthyr contemplated the trees, realizing that in this odd mashing of moments, even a limb swaying gently in a breeze would appear to dance frantically. This thought was confirmed as he glanced back at the group he had left behind, observing them moving with unnatural speed.

Conversely, when his gaze shifted towards Glouvum, where he had sent the other group ahead, their movements seemed to slow, taking on a languid quality that contrasted sharply with the frenetic activity behind him. Ahead of them, the arrow he had shot had nearly completed its flight.

In mere paces, the daylight suddenly dimmed as night fell all too quickly, only to be replaced by daylight once again with a few paces more. Uthyr was suddenly glad that he had thought to leave instructions with his men. Based on what he was witnessing, they were likely in for a long stay.

As his group aligned with the ox carcass off the path, day and night began to alternate rapidly, each transition marked by a count of ten. Lynok pointed towards the bog, where a flickering light caught his attention. "Sire! Look there!"

Approaching cautiously, they beheld the remnants of a fire and a charred cartwheel. Despite the disconcerting strobe of light from the shifting day and night, a mesmerizing light show played out from a spot near the water's edge, casting dancing rainbows into the fog.

They had found it – the threshold to Merlin's world. Uthyr felt a mixture of awe and determination as he unsheathed his sword and motioned for the rest of his men to hold back while he stepped toward the waters, prepared to confront the unknown.

Naomi couldn't suppress the yawn of boredom as she languished at her station, eyeing the clock and longing to join the Halloween party already in full swing in the mess hall. 'At least I have company,' she mused, glancing at Ayesha, her best friend on the base. Ayesha had embraced the festive spirit, garbed as Storm from the X-Men movies, her costume accentuated with a striking long white wig and a cleverly sewn plasma disk in place of the iconic X emblem. Naomi felt rather plain in comparison, donned in her fairy princess attire, albeit with wings that added a touch of whimsy.

Regardless, she appreciated the costumes and the excuse to wear them. It was a stark departure from their regulation uniforms – a nod to the day's levity and a rare chance to relax the base's strict decorum. It was a tacit acknowledgment by the higher-ups of the importance of maintaining a semblance of normalcy, especially given the underground, clandestine nature of their work. For a day, the base transformed, offering a fleeting taste of the world beyond its concealed walls.

"What's playing on that big screen in front of the portal?" Naomi asked Ayesha as she turned once again to watch the monitor. Captain Lawton had tasked Ayesha with finding a way to scare off any curious farmers near the portal. Her solution involved wheeling a big screen television in front of it, ensuring that anyone peering in from the other side would see whatever she chose to display. But from this vantage point, Naomi could only see the back side of the television.

Ayesha grinned and flipped a switch. "My lady jam!" she declared. Suddenly, all the monitors in the control room switched to an audio visualizer from some MP3 playing software. She flicked another switch and the control room filled with the sounds of Bruno Mars' "That's What I Like", with which the pulsing and beating of the audio visualizer kept time. Naomi grinned with amusement, as much because she liked the song as at the thought that anyone on the other end of the portal would probably think they were looking at a bizarre tunnel leading to the underworld, pulsing with what seemed like an electrical storm.

Seeing Naomi grin, Ayesha jumped up and drug her out of her chair. "Show me you can dance, girl!" she demanded with mirth as she leaned over and turned a dial, increasing the volume and filling the control room with music. The two started dancing, caught up in the rhythm, laughing and enjoying the moment. By the time the song ended, they were both breathless and giggling.

Switching back to the portal's observation feed, Ayesha froze. "Holy shit!" she exclaimed.

Naomi followed her gaze to the screen. There, standing on the artifact on the other side, was a man, stooped over and peering down into the portal. "He's holding a sign in English," Naomi said, a mix of surprise and curiosity in her voice. "I'm going down there. Go find Flip!" she instructed as Ayesha dashed out of the control room.

Naomi hurried to the platform, quickly pushing the big screen television aside to establish a clearer view. The sign held by the man on the other side was stark and simple: "I AM UTHYR," it declared in bold, unadorned letters.

She studied the man holding it, noting his strikingly handsome features framed by a rugged black beard. His attire was suited for winter, yet distinctly from another time. He wore a sturdy leather tunic, reinforced with metal rings sewn into the fabric, a design that spoke of practicality and durability. This was overlaid with a thick woolen vestment with wooden toggles, draping down to his high leather boots, providing protection against the cold. He was the very image of a hardy warrior, far removed from the polished knights of storybook tales. His sword, attached prominently at his side, appeared well-used and weathered, its glory days, if ever they existed, hidden beneath the patina of time. The raw authenticity of his look was a sharp contrast to the romanticized anachronisms Naomi had expected, with her imagined visions of chivalry and nobility. His presence, raw and unpolished, lent a startling authenticity to the surreal encounter unfolding before her.

Naomi could see the shock and surprise etched on Uthyr's face as he gazed upon her. Dressed in her fairy princess costume, complete with wings, she couldn't help but feel a bit self-conscious, realizing how magical and outlandish she must appear to him. With a bashful giggle, she covered her embarrassed smirk with her hand, then twirled around gracefully and looked back over her shoulder at him. As she playfully tugged at her wings, demonstrating they were not real, Uthyr's initial surprise softened into a warm grin.

Turning back towards him, Naomi pointed at his sign, then attempted a curtsy – a clumsy yet charming gesture, given her 'sexy fairy' rather than 'ball gown princess' costume. Uthyr, in response, grinned even more broadly. Despite his crude attire and the awkwardness of his position, he managed a surprisingly graceful bow, complete with a flourish of his hand.

Their whimsical exchange was suddenly interrupted by Philip's voice, echoing through the cavern from a loudspeaker near the control room platform. "If you are done flirting with our new guest Officer Higgins, perhaps you could take a moment to reach over to the workstation and put on your comms?" His tone, more expectant than requesting, brought a flush to Naomi's cheeks.

Holding up a finger to signal Uthyr to wait, Naomi hurried over to the platform workstation. She grabbed the comms unit from its charging station and slipped it into her ear. "Sorry, Captain," she muttered apologetically, then returned to her spot in front of the portal, facing Uthyr once again with a more composed demeanor, ready to proceed with the unexpected encounter.

Naomi watched with anticipation as Uthyr, standing atop the artifact, shuffled through the stack of signs he held. Philip's voice echoed through the comms, tinged with concern. "What is he holding?"

Naomi relayed what she saw, pointing at Uthyr's signs for emphasis. "A sign that says 'I am Uthyr,' but it looks like he has three or four more signs tucked under his arm." Uthyr seemed to understand her gesture, nodding as he examined the stack and selected another sign.

Gasping at the new message, Naomi couldn't mask her shock. "Flip, you're not going to like this. His next one is in all caps and says, 'Mare in peril' and then 'Captured'."

A heavy silence followed, broken by Philip's anxious voice. "He couldn't have written these signs himself. Mare must have sent him. What does the next one say?"

Naomi, maintaining her composure, gestured again to Uthyr, who swiftly presented another sign. "I think you're right, Flip. The next sign says, 'Help him Flip' and then 'Need decoy' on the next line."

Philip's muttered response over the comms sounded both ponderous and anxious. "Need decoy? What the hell are you talking about, Mare?" After a pause, his voice returned, louder and more urgent. "Does he have any more signs?"

"Yes, one more," Naomi confirmed, motioning to Uthyr once more. He showed her the final parchment. "It says, 'A symbol' then 'The Prestige' then 'Trojan Horse' on three separate lines. That's the last one, Flip. But I don't understand. What does it mean?"

Philip's tone shifted from confusion to a sudden understanding. "I think I actually get it! Clever girl, Mare!"

Naomi heard Ayesha's curious voice. "Get what, sir? What does it mean?"

Philip's voice crackled with a mixture of realization and urgency through the comms. "Trojan Horse," he began, his tone reflective yet instructive, "is a reference to a mythical story where the Greeks used a decoy wooden horse. They hid inside of it to gain entry into the fortified city of Troy, effectively ending a ten-year siege." There was a brief pause, as if he was contemplating the depth of the analogy. "There's even a type of computer virus named after the story. The principle is essentially the same. Mare must be asking us to help Uthyr to get into to wherever she's being held."

His words hung in the air, a blend of ancient myth and modern technology, drawing a vivid parallel between the legendary subterfuge of the past and their current predicament.

Naomi interjected, practical and slightly skeptical. "But how are we supposed to pull that off? We can't exactly make a big wooden horse. Much less get it through the portal!"

"That's where the other clues come in," Philip continued. "'Need decoy', 'A symbol', and 'The Prestige' are all a part of it."

"So, what are you saying?" Ayesha chimed in with a mix of sarcasm and genuine curiosity. "He needs a symbol? Like a big red 'S' and a cape?"

"Hey! Don't mock the costume, lady!" Avery suddenly interjected, eliciting a round of chuckles across the comms channel, momentarily lightening the atmosphere. He and Takashi had dressed as Superman and Batman this Halloween, which explained his protest, Naomi figured.

Philip steered the conversation back. "We can't turn him into Superman, but he needs something distinctive. A flag or standard might be a good starting point."

Naomi assessed Uthyr's appearance. "The cape idea is stupid but look at this guy. Anything you give him clothing-wise is going to be an upgrade! A fur cloak maybe? Or a replacement for that shabby-ass sword of his?"

In the midst of their brainstorming, Ayesha's voice suddenly brimmed with excitement. "Oh my God! Of course!"

Philip's voice came through the comms, alarmed. "What?"

Ayesha's revelation was swift and enthusiastic. "If this really is history in the making, and the lieutenant colonel is supposed to be Merlin, then that dude there has gotta be the king!"

Confusion was evident as Philip and Avery responded in unison. "What king?"

Ayesha elaborated with a sense of discovery. "King Uther Pendragon, father to the legendary King Arthur! If that man there is him, then he needs his sword! Excalibur!"

Realization dawned on Naomi as she grasped Ayesha's line of thought. "Go and get it Ayesha!" A clatter sounded as Ayesha dropped her comms and hurried out of the control room. Naomi turned to Uthyr in the portal, nodding to convey her understanding and signaling for him to wait.

Philip's voice echoed with confusion. "Naomi, what is she after? Where is she going? What the hell is going on?"

Naomi responded, her voice tinged with regret. "Sorry, Flip! You know the lieutenant colonel is into Harry Potter, right? Well, Ayesha and I decided to have a functioning replica of the Sword of Gryffindor from the movies made for her. We were going to give it to her on her birthday, but…well…" Her voice trailed off, the unsaid words hanging in the air.

Philip's tone shifted to one of realization. "Hey that's a great idea! Speaking of which, doesn't she have a scarf, with a cartoon dragon or a lion or something like that on it, hanging on the coat rack in her office? We were just talking about a flag or standard. Maybe that would work."

"It's a scarf, and it's the standard of Gryffindor House," Ayesha smirked.

"Now is not the time, Ayesha," Philip chided. "Just grab it."

Avery chimed in, practical as ever. "There's just one problem, Philip. If you expect to get anything over to him, you'll need to get him to flip the artifact over on his end. Whatever we try to send through comes out of the rough side. He looks surefooted standing on that thing though."

Philip acknowledged the obstacle. "Ah, jeeze! You're right Avery!" he exclaimed. From this side of the portal, they couldn't tell how the other side was actually oriented. Given that Uthyr stood steadily atop it, Philip mused that Avery's observation was indeed the case. "Avery, grab that whiteboard out of conference room B and wheel it down to Naomi at the lab platform," he ordered. "Looks like we're in for a game of Pictionary with this fella."

Lynok observed with a mixture of curiosity and awe as Uthyr waded into the shimmering water, then stepped up onto something just beneath the surface. The object bathed the area in flickering light, as bright as a bonfire, casting an ethereal glow that painted everything in rainbow-like hues – yet far more mesmerizing.

To Lynok, Uthyr appeared like a figure from legend – something more than just a man, haloed by the light as he stood seemingly atop the water. The men onshore whispered and muttered, sharing perhaps the same mixture of fear and wonder that Lynok felt. In spite of it though, he remained stoic, remembering Merlin's forewarning that he might see extraordinary things, but need not fear.

Lynok watched intently as Uthyr selected one of the parchments Merlin had provided and began displaying it toward the water. The sight struck Lynok as both peculiar and whimsical. A memory surfaced, a tale his mother, Magra, had recounted to him during his youth – a story about a fisherman who ensnared a magic fish capable of granting wishes. The parallel seemed almost comical under the circumstances.

'Perhaps this fish can read,' Lynok mused quietly to himself, allowing a brief smirk to cross his face. The thought was absurd, of course, but the levity of it offered a momentary distraction from the weight of their situation. The flickering light from beneath the surface seemed to listen, casting a dancing glow over Uthyr's earnest figure.

Lynok watched intently as the chaotic dance of lights beneath Uthyr steadied into a gentle, consistent glow, and a smile spread across his face. His facial expressions and actions became more deliberate, an indication that he had established contact with something – or someone – beneath the water. He watched Uthyr, his movements deliberate, holding up parchment after parchment in response to unseen cues.

Although the exchange was a silent dialog, an unheard conversation whose words were a mixture of hand gestures and body language, the eerie spectacle reminded Lynok very much of another occasion where he had witnessed the ravings of a madman given to conversing with shadows. The sight of Uthyr, so intently focused on the watery surface below him, pacing, then pausing to nod or shake his head, seemed a similar exhibition. Indeed, whispers of disbelief and concern began to ripple through the men behind Lynok. They began to mutter among themselves, their words tinged with unease at the sight of their leader communing with the unseen.

The murmurs of confusion and concern began to grow and Lynok was about to turn and silence their doubts with a stern rebuke when Uthyr's voice, clear and commanding, cut through the cacophony. "Lynok, bring three men with you and come here!" he called out, pulling Lynok's focus sharply back to him. The urgency in Uthyr's voice was unmistakable, a call to action that allowed no room for hesitation, momentarily silencing the men.

He seized the chance to summon the three men who had been the loudest in their talk of madness, ordering them to follow him as Uthyr had commanded. With their voices suddenly silenced, unable to instigate further doubt in their companions, the remaining men fell quiet to observe the unfolding of events.

With further directions from Uthyr, Lynok and the three other men trudged into the water and took up positions around what Lynok could now see was a circular platform upon which Uthyr had stood. Exclamations of shock and wonder were ripped from all of them as, looking within, they saw a beautiful woman in a pale green dress lying within the depths of the hard surface.

'This must surely be one of the fae!' Lynok thought, observing sparkles of light glittering from her cheeks and large, diaphanous wings like those of a dragonfly. As she turned her gaze to him, smiled, and arched an eyebrow, he looked away embarrassed, realizing that he must have been staring, his mouth agape. He had never seen such a beautiful creature.

"We must turn over this…stone," Uthyr commanded, his gaze fixed on the circular platform beneath the water's surface. The term 'stone' came hesitantly, as if the word was a placeholder for something he couldn't quite define. Lynok understood the hesitation; the material beneath them was unlike any stone he, or likely any man, had ever encountered.

Together, they pushed against the structure, which, to Lynok's astonishment, was surprisingly light. The underside revealed itself – a wild, uncharted terrain of spines and jagged edges, a stark contrast to the smooth surface they had just disturbed. The material, foreign yet familiar in its solidity, carried within its depths the same beautiful fae woman as before, only now his view of her was broken up into a thousand small pieces. 'Stone,' he mused, 'as good a word as any….'

Once flipped, the stone submerged once more, leaving Uthyr standing in the shallow water, his attention captured by the glow that now softly illuminated from below. Lynok, along with the three men, returned to the bank. By the looks on their faces and the quiet murmurs of questioning that grew as they rejoined their companions, Lynok supposed their minds, much like his own, were racing with thoughts of what they had just witnessed.

A collective gasp suddenly escaped the group, drawing Lynok's gaze sharply back toward the luminous waters. Lynok watched in stunned silence as a sword, unparalleled in its splendor, surpassing in beauty any blade he had ever seen, slowly emerged hilt-first from the water's surface.

The sword's quillons and grip boasted an exquisite symmetry, their craftsmanship surpassing the finest work of any smith Lynok knew. Adorned with a delicate filigree, the patterns and emblems presented an exquisite testament to a master's hand.

Bright gems, as red as fresh blood, crowned the hilt and the tips of the cross-guard, their clarity and brilliance startling against the soft glow of the artifact's light. Even from a distance, their sparkle was undeniable, each facet catching and reflecting the light, adding to the sword's mystique.

As the sword continued to emerge from the water, the blade's edge gleamed with a sharpness that seemed to split the very light around it, reflecting it back with an intensity that rivaled the sun glinting off polished bronze. Yet, unlike the warm hues of bronze, this material shimmered in shades of white and gray, a luster that Lynok had never seen in a metal before, hinting at a substance both known yet wholly beyond his experience.

A breeze, oddly warm for this time of year, caught the tail of a cloth that had been tied loosely to the hilt and dangled behind the sword. The cloth of deep red and gold colors, bore an emblem of a creature that seemed both fierce and noble, echoing the majesty of a lion, but with the forked tongue of a serpent, suggesting something more mythical – perhaps a creature of that other world from whence the sword came, Lynok supposed. He glanced up to see the new growth of an early spring slowly begin to emerge from the foliage surrounding them, reminding him that time near the threshold to Merlin's world passed as rapidly as a galloping horse.

Uthyr seized the sword, lifting it with a grace that belied the strength such an act must have required. Even Uthyr seemed shocked at the ease with which he handled it, twirling and swiping to test its balance. As he did so, the light played off the blade, casting a spectrum of colors that danced across the faces of all who watched.

Finally, he emerged from the water's edge and held the sword aloft, pointing it at the sky. "I am Uthyr Pendragon!" he proclaimed, his voice carrying with it the weight of history in the making that Lynok felt surely swept through the hearts of every man present. "By the gift of this sword and symbol, you bear witness at the threshold to Merlin's world, by this quest where Merlin himself sent me, that the queen of the fae, the lady of the lake, proclaims me king of all Britannia!"

As cheers erupted from all the men, including Lynok, Uthyr raised a hand to quell them, then continued. "From this day, let us all share what we have seen, what we have learned! Let us go forth and, under this symbol, proclaim the union of this kingdom under one king! Remember well this day!"

As cheering erupted once again, the weight of his words hung in the air, a declaration not just of kingship but of destiny unfolding. Absorbed in the solemnity of the moment, Lynok understood this was not merely the anointing of a king. He was witnessing the birth of legend in the flesh, an event that would inspire stories and tales told long after the men here were gone from this world.

CHAPTER 22

Perspective and Forgiveness

Gorloys paced back and forth impatiently along the wide corridor before Magra's apartment door, his boots echoing against the stone floor with each heavy step. Worry allied with his impatience in an ongoing battle for dominance over the annoyance he felt at Jowan.

The man stood casually beside Magra's door, one foot propped against the wall as he chewed his nails, acting as though this were just another day. Each nail spat, each furtive glance, would strike a blow of annoyance in his mental battle, only to have impatience and worry push back when a fresh wail and the old woman's urges to push emerged from within.

He hated that Jowan was witness to his rare display of agitation, but at least the man had the good sense to remain silent. For that reason, Gorloys could not decide whether he wanted to send Jowan away and endure these moments alone, or whether company in these moments was preferable. Concern for Ygraine gnawed at him, sharply contrasting with his indifference toward the expected child – yet another daughter – who meant little in his quest for a male heir. Then annoyance pushed to the battlefront again as Jowan finally spoke.

Jowan cleared his throat, attempting to breach the heavy silence. "Magra knows her craft well, Pen Gorloys. You have no need to worry." His voice, meant to offer solace, felt misplaced against the gravity of Gorloys' turmoil.

"So. That is your excuse for standing there so calmly?" Gorloys barked, glaring at him.

Looking abashed, Jowan replied uncertainly, his tone apologetic, "N-no, Pen Gorloys! I have stood at this door four moons now. In that time, two other women have come to Magra's door laboring with child. Both times, the mother and child went away healthy. And neither woman was as young and healthy as Penêsek Ygraine! Surely, she and the baby will be well."

Oddly, Jowan's words suited, calming his worries somewhat as he scowled, harumphed, and continued to pace. Moments later, an eternity later, a resounding wail – the loudest yet – was replaced by soft murmurs. Gorloys and Jowan shared a tense look, the air thick with anticipation, until a sharp slap followed by the crisp sound of a baby's cry could be heard from the other side.

The baby's cry was a siren song signaling a change in his anxiety, exchanging worry for his wife for more practical concerns. Though the sound offered a sort of relief, it also encouraged new worries for the future as his thoughts momentarily veered towards the child, another daughter for which he would eventually need to find a suitor.

Setting aside thoughts on what to do with the child for the time being, he allowed his concern for Ygraine's wellbeing to take hold once again. The sudden realization that, despite his prior frustration at her for giving him another daughter, he missed his wife. He had never spent so long separated from her, he realized, separated for so many moons while she remained cloistered away in Magra's apartment under the old woman's care. The baby's cry signaled an end to it, a break in his fast. But the door remained a barrier, a final threshold that kept him from seeing, from knowing, that she was well.

As the infant's crying subsided, Gorloys' hand balled into a fist, ready to pound at the door and demand entry. But at the last moment, he realized the disturbance it would cause within, and paused. He glanced over at Jowan, who was smirking, intentionally looking straight ahead. "What?" he demanded.

The smirk broke into a smile as Jowan responded, "You have been parted for a long time." Then turning his head to face Gorloys, he grinned widely, adding, "Any man would be anxious to see his wife after so long."

Mildly abashed, Gorloys returned the smile, then loosened his hand and rapped gently on the door. His knock was met with an annoyed, yet somewhat hushed response from the other side. "The mother and child are fine, Jowan!" he heard the old woman exclaim. "Go report the news to Gorloys!"

"It is I, old woman!" Gorloys announced. "Let me enter. I wish to see my wife."

An interminable silence followed before Magra responded again. "A moment please, Pen Gorloys, while I help Ygraine to compose herself for you."

His voice rose slightly as he allowed annoyance to once again creep in. "I have seen my wife at her best and at her worst. Let me enter!" he demanded impatiently.

"Pfaw! Patience you…! These old bones do not move so quickly at my age," Magra replied. Finally, he heard the wooden latch loosed and her door swung open.

The apartment was more dimly lit than the hallway, forcing Gorloys to pause and let his eyes adjust. As his gaze swept across the space, they landed on Ygraine, who lay reclining on a pallet of wool and furs, cradling a quietly sleeping bundle, a vision of serenity laced with exhaustion. Her haggard eyes and a wan complexion spoke of a night marked by weary toil. She had a right, he supposed, given what she had been through.

Magra grimaced at Gorloys' silently, no doubt annoyed at his unexpected presence, he mused. After dropping a bucket beside the doorframe with a deliberate thud that seemed to echo her disapproval, she turned and ambled with tired resignation to a blanket laden chair near the hearth.

He smirked at her back as he followed her inside, where the smell of sweat mixed with the metallic tang of blood and the musty scent of afterbirth drifting from the pail. The combination assaulted his senses with a distinctive and unmistakable odor, lingering in the air as a visceral testament to the strength and vulnerability of both mother and child in the moments following birth.

As Magra reached the chair, a moan from the shadows beyond the edge of the firelight pierced the quiet, drawing their attention. Gorloys narrowed his eyes, fixating on the unexpected presence of Merlin, lying on a pallet, wrapped in a wool blanket. He appeared to be sleeping fitfully, though a rictus of pain furled his brow. "That man was in the room while my wife lay exposed?" he demanded, his voice a controlled mix of shock and anger, yet careful to keep the volume low.

Magra scowled at him with a withering glance as she turned and wandered over to Merlin, then bent down to wipe his brow with a cloth she had produced from somewhere. "Merlin is ill again and lay with fever dreams all night," she said brusquely.

The shock he felt at the impropriety of the situation, regardless of the circumstances, must have been evident in his eyes. Glancing at him as she stood once again, she waved a perfunctory hand and turned back toward her chair. "He saw nothing," she proclaimed dismissively.

Gorloys glanced down, scrutinizing Merlin's prone figure, when Ygraine interjected unexpectedly, pulling his attention. "It is true, husband," she said quietly, but with forceful earnestness. "Merlin has hardly stirred this whole night!" Shifting his gaze back to Merlin, Gorloys relaxed. 'He looks worse than my wife,' he thought, dismissing any further concerns. 'Perhaps I thought in haste.'

He shifted his gaze back to Magra as she pushed a hand against the small of her back and winced. She too looked rather haggard, more worn than could be accounted for by her age alone. As she began to slowly make her way back to her chair, she spoke almost dismissively, talking to the space in front of her as she walked, rather than looking at him. "You have come, you have seen. Ygraine and the child are well," she began, then turned to face him when she reached her chair. Her gaze held an unyielding intensity. "The night has been long for us all," she proclaimed expectantly, adding, "Rest is what Ygraine now requires, and soon the babe will stir, hungry for her milk."

"Magra, do not be rude!" Ygraine chided, quietly. "If he wants to see his daughter, then he should be allowed," she proclaimed around a wide yawn, adding, "She is right though, husband. I have been through much this night and would like to rest."

Magra glanced over at Ygraine in annoyance, her voice carrying a mix of authority and irritation. "I have helped a great many more mothers to bring their babes into the world in my years, child. If I say you need rest, then you need rest!" Her admonishment given, she turned back to Gorloys, an expectant look in her eye.

Caught in the midst of this exchange, Gorloys was taken aback by the old woman's boldness despite Ygraine's attempted intervention. 'She wants me to leave?' he thought incredulously, his mind racing. He could feel his simmering annoyance at her beginning to boil over into anger. Of late, she had gotten bolder in showing a lack of respect. Not for the first time, he entertained thoughts of slapping her to the ground with the back of his hand, giving the bitter old crone a reminder of her place in the world, a reminder of the man to whom she spoke with such insolence.

Yet, the respect for elders ingrained in him stayed his hand. Striking Magra would only diminish his standing among his men. Such an act only showed weakness of mind, allowing the words of an old fool to rule your emotions, only to be checked by a show of brutality. 'No,' he decided, 'This old hag needs a reminder of who leads here, but not through brute force.'

"Leave us," he commanded, his voice stern. He glanced over at Ygraine, noting the quiet concern in her eyes – a concern for which he knew he was at least partly responsible. While he still held no interest in the child beyond the burdens it placed on him in the future, he felt a compelling need to apologize to Ygraine for his words when last they spoke. His anger had been misplaced; she had no control over the child's birth, and it was unjust of him to have blamed her. He wanted to tell her these things. Indeed, he knew they needed to be said. But he was not going to do so in front of this old woman who had taken to acting above her place.

"Did you not hear me?" Magra replied, aghast.

"I heard you, Magra," he responded, his tone edged with smugness. "But it appears your hearing fails you in your old age." Gorloys cast an appraising eye around the modestly sized apartment, speaking in a deliberately casual manner, "I was thinking… now that the baby is here, my new daughter will indeed need her own room."

He stepped just past the old woman, casually inspecting the mantle, wiping it with a finger and dusting his hands, before moving on, subtly asserting his presence in the cramped space. Turning to Ygraine, he commented, "This room feels quite cozy. Would you not agree, my love?" Clearly astonished, Ygraine lay there round-eyed and speechless. Seeing her face, Gorloys lips pursed into a smirk as he rounded once again on the old woman, a mischievous glint playing in his eyes.

"What do you think Magra?" he inquired. "Surely the needs of a child are greater than those of an old woman. Of course, we would need to move you elsewhere – a place more suited to your meager requirements." He stroked his chin as if giving the matter serious thought. "The cellar, perhaps?" he added, arching an eyebrow.

His amusement was palpable as Magra's indignation flared and her eyebrows climbed in comprehension of the veiled threat. "Pfaw!" she spat out, her pride wounded but recognizing the futility of further protest. As she moved to leave, Gorloys couldn't resist one final jab. "And do take the pail with you," he pointed out, nodding towards the bucket by the door.

Casting a final look of mixed frustration and resignation over her shoulder, Magra picked up the bucket. "Pfaw," she muttered again, this time more softly, as she exited. Gorloys' grin widened, watching her departure, satisfied with the assertion of his authority.

Gorloys stood silent for a moment, his gaze fixed on the door Magra had exited through, as if it held answers to unasked questions. "It seems clear that woman does not like me," he muttered, more to himself than to anyone else in the room.

Ygraine's voice, stronger than he expected, cut through his musings. "I suspect the feeling is mutual," she said, her words pulling him from his reverie.

He turned towards her, a dismissive wave of his hand accompanying his response. "That is not fair, Ygraine. She aggravates me, but she is just an old woman. When someone lives beyond their years, they have little left but their dignity. And as even that leaves them, they turn to bitterness. But Magra? She has never shown even a token of affection to me."

"You have shown me…many times…husband, never to question you," Ygraine whispered, looking down at the child, cuddling it gently when it cooed. Then she looked up and locked eyes with him, adding, "Magra has never asked questions directly, and I have never spoken out against you. But I think she knows my bruises and hurts are not due to clumsiness or being thrown by a horse."

Her whispered rebuke in the quiet of the room struck him as forcefully as any blow. Firelight from the hearth danced in her eyes, now wary, where once there was trust. The room felt colder as her words hung in the air. Gorloys, lost for a moment, found himself unable to meet her gaze. He turned away, unable to respond, unable to find words in his defense.

Breaking the silence, Ygraine's voice held a tremor of boldness he hadn't heard before. "You can be a hard man to love at times, my husband." She paused a moment, then continued, "But you are my husband. So, I must find it in me to do so."

Her words hit him unexpectedly, shaking his resolve. He sank down, trying to hide his shaken state, sitting cross-legged before her. "You no longer love me?" he asked, the unexpected vulnerability he suddenly felt unnerving him.

Ygraine's reply was a search for understanding rather than accusation. "I am not sure you know what love is, husband," she sighed. She smiled down at the infant she held and tickled her chin with a finger, smiling gently. "What it means to love someone," she concluded.

Gorloys sighed, a sound heavy with resignation. "Perhaps. But in the time we have been separated, I have come to miss you greatly. Does that not account for love?" He stared at her, awaiting a response, feeling very exposed and raw, emotions utterly foreign to him.

Unable to take the silent reproach in Ygraine's eyes any longer, Gorloys' gaze drifted to the infant in her arms. He felt a pang of jealousy for the affection she showed the child but withheld from him. A new curiosity, or perhaps something deeper, sparked within him. "May I…?" he began tentatively, extending his arms towards the child with a hesitance that betrayed his usual confidence.

Ygraine hesitated, her arms protectively tightening around the baby. At the same moment, a loud moan emanated from Merlin's cot, startling them both. It was a sound full of protest and anguish that only heightened Ygraine's protective instinct as she coddled the child even more. As he looked into her fear-filled eyes, she whispered, "Gorloys, you would not…?" She searched his face, unable to finish, perhaps seeking a hint of anger or deceit.

"I will not hurt her," Gorloys said softly, his voice laced with a gentleness that seemed at odds with the strong, commanding, and stoic man he had always portrayed toward her. This…tenderness…he was attempting to show was no doubt as foreign to him as to her he mused. "I just…wish to hold her, Ygraine. To…meet…my daughter."

Another low moan escaped Merlin's pallet in the dim light, causing Ygraine to glance over. But this time her expression seemed to be one of annoyance at the sleeping shadow. With a slow, almost reluctant motion, Ygraine transferred the infant into Gorloys' arms. His hands, so often clenched in anger or command, now cradled the child with a surprising delicacy.

Holding his daughter, Gorloys felt a wave of something indefinable wash over him – a mix of awe, fear, and an unexpected tenderness. He realized in that moment that he was so focused on his desire for a son, that perhaps he had overly neglected his other daughter, Morghais, whom he had never bothered to hold with such tenderness. This baby in his arms was so fragile, so in need of his protection, more so than anyone else in the domain of his rule. Holding her, he was forced to admit that he was failing in his duty as a father, trading it for a duty he understood – that of a leader.

He smiled and tickled the child under the chin, watching her as she slept and instinctively suckled the air a moment, looking for a teet that wasn't there. When he looked up at Ygraine, who had remained silent, her eyes were filled with wonder, watching him. Gorloys took a deep breath, the infant's warmth against his chest grounding him. "Ygraine, before you, the only relationship I have ever known was with my father. My mother died before I ever knew her," he said softly, his voice steadier, the presence of the child offering an unexpected anchor in the tumult of his emotions.

"You have spoken seldom of your parents, but I remember as much," Ygraine replied.

Gorloys nodded, then continued. "My father was a hard man. His were lessons in respect and obedience, with harsh retribution for any shortfall, and no accommodation for forgiveness or kindness."

Ygraine's soft interjection, "Oh, Gorloys…" was met with a flash of his ingrained defensiveness. "I do not want your pity," he snapped, immediately regretting the harshness in his voice, softening at the sight of her wounded expression. "Forgive me. It is perhaps the worst of my father's lessons, that to show any part of the softer, gentler emotions – warmth, kindness, compassion – is a weakness to be exploited by others."

In the quiet that followed, the flickering shadows cast by the fire reflected his own inner turmoil. For a moment, he allowed himself to just observe Ygraine, taking in the details he had often overlooked – the softness in her eyes, the gentle rise and fall of her chest as she breathed, the serene expression and curve of her lips as she gazed upon and smiled at their daughter. It was as though he was seeing her for the first time, not as his wife, not as the mother of his children, but as Ygraine, the woman he had vowed to cherish but had failed so profoundly.

As he held the child, he noticed the slight furrow of her brow, the peacefulness of her sleep, and the innocence that seemed to emanate from her. The serenity of both mother and child was a stark contrast to the storm raging within him, a tempest of emotions he neither fully understood nor could scarcely navigate. The realization hit him with the force of a physical blow, a clarity emerging from the fog of his pride and anger. 'I have been a fool,' he admitted to himself.

In the momentary silence, the baby suddenly tooted, drawing a small giggle from Ygraine, who hid her unexpected outburst behind her hand. As Gorloys looked down in surprise, sharing a smile, the little one's face took on a sour expression, followed by a faint gurgle of distress. Taken aback, Gorloys instinctively began to rock her gently, murmuring, "Shush…shush…shush…little one. It happens to little ladies too!" His attempt to soothe her was clumsy yet earnest, a moment of levity and tenderness that surprised even him and drew a smile from Ygraine, her wary eyes softening.

Gorloys, feeling slightly more at ease but still holding onto the child, continued, "I know I have not been the husband you deserved, Ygraine. I will try to… soften… toward you. With your patience and help…" His voice trailed off, the words unfamiliar and difficult, but the presence of the child in his arms making them feel less daunting, less foreign. Looking down at his new daughter, he finally asked plainly, "Will you show me how to love you, Ygraine? To love our daughters?"

His gaze shifted from the child to Ygraine. She seemed perplexed, searching his eyes and face, looking for something, but he did not know what it could be. He had never allowed himself to be so vulnerable with her, and the experience was proving to be a strange and foreign land, an unexplored territory he broached with uncertainty. "You say you have missed me all this time husband, but you never sought me out," she finally replied. "Why?" she inquired in puzzlement.

"At first, I suppose, shame," Gorloys began, the weight of holding his daughter making his confession feel more profound. "I grew angry when Merlin said you were having another girl. You know I long for a son." He paused, his gaze shifting from Ygraine to the baby and back again. "But I took my frustration out on you, though you have no more control over fate than I do. For that, let me apologize."

Ygraine's face brightened, a soft smile playing on her lips. "I accept!" she exclaimed, her eyes momentarily glancing down at the infant cradled in Gorloys' arms.

"Have you named her?" Gorloys inquired, a hint of curiosity and newfound warmth breaking through his earlier solemnity.

"Morgan or Morgana; I have not yet decided," Ygraine mused, her gaze affectionate as she looked upon their daughter.

Gorloys frowned, confusion evident. "But we already have a daughter named Morghais?"

"A family tradition," Ygraine explained, her voice carrying a hint of amusement. "Mothers name their first daughters in homage to their mother's mother and second daughters in homage to their mother."

"But your name is Ygraine?!" Gorloys' confusion only deepened.

Ygraine smirked, the amusement now clear in her eyes. "I am a third daughter – named for my father's mother's mother. Now let it be. When I give you a son, you can name him."

The thought seemed to lighten the mood, a smile spreading across Gorloys' face as he asked, "When?" His smirk mirrored hers, eyebrow arching in playful inquiry.

"Not today, you lecher," Ygraine teased, her laughter soft yet clear. "But soon enough," she added, bringing a smirk to his lips. After a moment, she gently reached out. "May I have her back now?" she asked, her voice a tender whisper. Gorloys, with a slight nod, carefully passed the baby back to her, his movements deliberate and careful. The baby safely nestled in her arms once again, she seemed to relax even more, releasing an almost imperceptible tension he had not realized was there.

Her expression then shifted, becoming slightly more serious as she ventured into the space of unanswered questions. "You said 'At first'. Is there another reason that has kept you away?" she inquired, the softness in her voice belying the weight of the question.

Gorloys' demeanor changed almost imperceptibly at her inquiry, the brief interlude of lightness giving way to a familiar shade of annoyance. "Uthyr's latest mischief is causing me no end of trouble," he admitted, the frustration evident in his tone.

He stood once more, somewhat bemoaning the loss of the intimate moment they had shared, as the harder emotions brought about by his external struggles resurfaced. It was time to tell Ygraine his other reason for coming to see her.

In the dimly lit confines of Magra's stone-floored apartment, Marilyn lay quietly, fighting exhaustion as she listened to Gorloys unfold his plans to Ygraine. The birth of her new daughter had taken its toll. As the adrenaline rush of the final push – a climactic moment of intense pain and exquisite release – began to wear off, the ability to remain alert and focused became more elusive.

And yet, as Marilyn overheard their conversation, she could not help but be intrigued. She came to realize, with a perspective only afforded a spy – a fly on the wall whose presence is unaccounted for in the privacy of the bedroom – that Gorloys was a great deal more complex than she had given him credit. Still, her visceral emotion at the thought of him holding her child, and her helplessness to do anything more than moan in protest, shocked even her. It was an unexpected emotion in the aftermath of what she'd just been through and the lack of connection with her child that she had initially felt.

The ordeal of childbirth had been a tempest of sensation, a raw and visceral experience marking Marilyn with a pain and power uniquely hers, a profound journey no man could ever walk. At the end of it, Marilyn lay exhausted beside the hearth, enveloped in a tapestry of emotions that seemed at odds with the monumental act she had just performed. The process had been a convergence of power and vulnerability, an intimate battle waged in the silence of the night, punctuated only by the crackle of fire and the whispers of ancient stone walls.

And now that exhilaration of bringing life into the world was tempered by a profound exhaustion, a physical depletion that seemed to seep into her very bones. Beyond the threshold, she had expected an immediate flood of maternal love, a bond forged instantaneously in the crucible of labor. Yet, what she found was a weary detachment, a desire to retreat into the depths of sleep and escape the intensity of her recent experience.

Magra's presence had been both a comfort and a reminder of Marilyn's vulnerability. The old woman's experienced hands had guided her through the ordeal, but in the aftermath, Marilyn had felt adrift, uncertain of her own feelings. The anticipation of motherhood, with its promises of joy and fulfillment, felt distant, obscured by the fog of fatigue and the messiness of birth.

It was a quiet acknowledgment from Magra, seasoned by countless births she had attended, that offered Marilyn a semblance of reassurance. As Magra had swaddled the girl and tried to hand the baby to her, Marilyn had shaken her head and retracted, her eyes no doubt filled with the sudden shame she felt inside. Magra, seeing the look on her face, smirked. "Pfaaaw," she had said gently, drawn out in a sympathetic tone. "That love thing they say you are supposed to feel? It will come," Magra murmured, her voice carrying the weight of wisdom and understanding. It was a simple affirmation, but to Marilyn, it was a beacon in the darkness, a reminder that her feelings were not a failing, but a part of the complex tapestry of motherhood.

Seeing Marilyn's face transform into gratitude, Magra had instead turned to Ygraine and instructed, "Hold her for a moment, Ygraine, while I cut the cord. We still have work to do. I know you are tired Merlin, but you have one final push before this business is done."

Marilyn's reverie of those final moments continued as she heard Gorloys ask Ygraine what she would name the baby. She smirked as she lay under the covers, recalling the earlier conversation when Ygraine took the baby into her arms. Her face had lit up with a mixture of awe and joy. "She is beautiful, Merlin! Have you thought of a name?" she had asked, looking down at the newborn with tender eyes.

"Morgan – it is a family name," Marilyn had responded, her voice soft but filled with pride.

Ygraine had chuckled softly, the sound a gentle ripple in the quiet room. "That sounds like a man's name! You need something more fitting for this pretty child! How about Morgana?" she had suggested, her gaze still fixed on the baby's peaceful face.

Magra, her patience wearing thin with the diversion from the task at hand, had interjected with a note of annoyance in her voice. "There will be time enough for that talk. Let us be done with this!" Her focus had remained unwavering, the practicality of her experience guiding her actions amidst the emotional swirl surrounding them.

Marilyn pushed one final time, then Magra dropped the resulting afterbirth into a nearby bucket as they heard a gentle knock at the door. Her memory of the moment was now blurred – a mad dash of rushed anxiety as Gorloys announced his presence on the other side of the door that put the three women into a chaotic scramble to conceal Marilyn's ordeal and stage Ygraine as the would-be mother.

In the rush of the moment, Marilyn's exhaustion had been momentarily forgotten, replaced by a sharp focus on the need for deception. The reality of her situation, stranded in a time far from her own, giving birth in secrecy, and now participating in a charade to protect her child, was starkly illuminated by that singular knock. It was a reminder of the precariousness of her position, of the lengths she would go to for the safety of her newborn, and of the complex web of lies and truths that now enveloped her life. Now that it was over, the initial adrenaline rush of the frenzy was waning, chipping away at her consciousness.

As Magra hurriedly cleaned up, whispering instructions to Ygraine on how to cradle the baby to make the deception more convincing, Marilyn couldn't help but marvel at the old midwife's efficiency and calm in the face of potential discovery. There was a resilience and resourcefulness in Magra that Marilyn found both reassuring and daunting, a testament to the strength required to navigate this ancient, unforgiving world.

This realization struck Marilyn with the weight of her new responsibility: to teach her daughter the skills to learn, adapt, and survive - just as Marilyn had done, just as Magra was still doing in her old age. But now, it was no longer just about survival; it was about laying a foundation of strength, wisdom, and resilience for her daughter, preparing her for the complexities of their shared reality, and hopefully providing her the tools needed to thrive amidst the uncertainties of their new life.

"What? Why? Surely, she is too young?" she heard Ygraine cry out in fear, pulling Marilyn from her reverie and moment of contemplation and startling her baby to wakefulness.

"Because there is no guarantee you will ever give me a son, Ygraine," she heard Gorloys explain as the baby began to cry. "I have spent little enough time with the girl, but I know that playing with dolls and weaving garlands of flowers will not teach her about the real world. I thought you would be happy!"

"I am!" Ygraine replied as she attempted to soothe the infant. "There, there little one…shush, shush, shush…. Morgana is hungry, Gorloys. Can we speak of this later?"

"I will go, but no. I leave at first light tomorrow and I am taking Morghais with me," Gorloys responded firmly.

"Then…keep her safe, husband," Ygraine pleaded. "Promise me."

Marilyn listened to the tread of Gorloys' boots as they moved toward the door. "I am her father, Ygraine," was his only response before the apartment door creaked open and his heavy footsteps faded down the outer passage. A moment later, she heard sounds of the door being shut and latched, followed by Magra's voice. "It is safe now Merlin."

The momentary silence that followed Gorloys' departure was palpable. Marilyn, suddenly alert and protective, sat up with a sense of urgency driven by her daughter's cries. Her gaze, intense and focused, locked onto her daughter in Ygraine's arms. Without a word, she reached out, her arms instinctively extending towards her child. "Give her to me," she stated, her voice carrying an edge that brooked no argument.

Ygraine, taken aback by the sudden demand, hesitated for a moment before gently transferring the baby into Marilyn's waiting arms. The shift was smooth but charged with unspoken tension that only increased when Marilyn demanded acidly, "Why did you let him hold her?" A veil of shocked hurt fell over Ygraine's face as she opened her mouth to respond, but Magra interrupted whatever she was about to say. "What right have you to speak to her that way, Merlin?" she scolded. "Is the child not safe in your arms? Does Gorloys remain none the wiser?"

Shocked at Magra's biting interjection, Marilyn tried to defend herself around the siren calls of her hungry child. But once started, Magra's berating only continued, making Marilyn feel smaller by the moment. "Ygraine has done all she can to protect you and your child! And at great personal risk! Can you imagine the cost to her had you been found out?"

Magra shook her head in disgust and looked away. "Pfaw!" she said loudly to an empty corner of the room, then turned her piercing gaze back to Marilyn. "Apologize," she commanded in a tone only a scolding mother possessed.

Marilyn sulkily looked over at Ygraine, whose eyes were watering; whether because Marilyn had hurt or feelings, or because of deeper feelings surfaced by Magra's defense of her, Marilyn could not tell. "I am sorry,

Ygraine," she said sincerely. "New mother…overly protective. Please understand," she pleaded.

Ygraine smiled and nodded, wiping the excess moisture from her eyes with her palms. "You are holding her wrong if you want to feed her," she offered as Marilyn struggled to hold her new baby and nurse her while wrestling with a wool blanket in an effort to maintain a sense of modesty.

"After all the bare parts of you we have witnessed, now you feel shy?" Magra chided gently as she smirked, her eyebrow raised. With that, Ygraine came over next to Marilyn and coached her into a position that felt more natural as her baby latched on.

Marilyn cradled her daughter closely, her movements tender but firm. As she looked down at the infant, a mix of awe and protectiveness washed over her, grounding her in the moment. It was only then, with her baby safely in her arms, that she allowed her attention to drift back to the larger concerns at hand.

"My mind drifted at the end. What happened? Why did Gorloys leave in such a hurry?" Marilyn inquired, her tone now softer, tempered by the warmth of her daughter against her. "I would like to know myself," Magra added with eagerness. "Send me out of my own room," she grumbled. "Pfaw!"

Ygraine grinned at the old woman, but then her eyes took on a distance expression, her tone a mix of puzzlement and concern. "Uthyr is causing trouble across Cornish lands, flaunting a sword and a sigil he claims were gifts from your queen. Gorloys has taken it upon himself to confront Uthyr's provocations," she explained, her voice laced with worry. "Though I thought Uthyr and my husband had reached an accord after their meeting on the field near Bearda Market?" she added quizzically.

Marilyn, cradling her daughter and listening intently, felt a twinge of curiosity mixed with bewilderment. "My queen?" she echoed softly, her mind racing. The mention of a queen and gifts of a sword and a sigil sparked a multitude of questions. 'What is Uthyr's game, and why invoke my name in his machinations?' she pondered, her thoughts a whirlwind of speculation and concern. “I was there, remember? It was more of an uneasy truce than an accord, Ygraine,” she finally offered.

“What is the sigil?” she asked curiously, smirking as Ygraine described the golden beast on a field of red. ‘One of my team must have grabbed the scarf from my office,’ she mused. ‘My queen must be Ayesha or Naomi,’ she snickered inwardly. ‘Wait until they hear this story! I wonder where they found a sword though?’

Ygraine’s expression turned introspective, betraying a hint of the internal conflict she felt. “I met Uthyr only once, but he impressed me as an honorable man. I even found him…,” she trailed off, unwilling or unable to finish the thought. Shaking her head as if to dispel the tangled web of her emotions, she added, “But why would he do this? It does not seem worthy of him.”

“Men are like two tom cats on the same farm,” Magra interjected. “It matters little if there is room enough for both; each thinks they own the whole of it!” Shaking her head in revulsion, she added, “And those two need no more reason to fight than to be around each other. Gorloys will probably find him and raise a fuss. If this Uthyr is as honorable as you believe, then he will back down.”

“For my part, I hope Gorloys does not find him,” Ygraine replied. “He also travels to the port at the mouth of the Tamar River in the south to retrieve the brimstone Merlin said is required to make dragon’s breath.”

As Marilyn had seen many times before, Ygraine struck a mocking pose, hands on hips with her chest poked out, and lowered her voice as she repeated her husband's words: “Perhaps I will run across that fool and remove his tongue to remind everyone that Cornwall is a free land, not subject to his rule.”

Marilyn snickered at the sudden levity, causing Ygraine to giggle and Magra to guffaw, then responded, “Gorloys made no claims that Uthyr harmed anyone. At that meeting, Uthyr demanded your husband’s loyalty, which Gorloys gave, however begrudgingly. Perhaps Uthyr only seeks to test the limits of that loyalty?”

"I hope that is all, Merlin," Ygraine replied, clasping her hands worriedly. She stood and paced the short span in front of the hearth. "Gorloys has decided to take our daughter, Morghais, with him!" she added, her voice laden with concern. "Why now of all times? She has seen only eight winters. She is too young!"

Magra, who had gotten up to stir and poke at the logs on the hearth, chimed in with her own insights, her voice carrying a blend of concern and pragmatism. "Gorloys will keep Morghais safe, Ygraine. I may not care for the man, but even I can see he is more than capable, nor is he a fool," she assured Ygraine, her confidence seeming to offer the woman a small measure of comfort.

Marilyn looked down at Morgan, feeling a change in the rhythm of the infant's suckling. She yawned a tiny yawn, bringing a smile to Marilyn's mouth. Seeing her, Magra instructed, "You need to burp the child, or she will spit up. Babies swallow a great deal of air when they feed." The distraction pulled Ygraine from her thoughts as she came over to help Marilyn in her new responsibilities. But Marilyn's own thoughts remained at the forefront of her mind now that the next step of her plan was in motion; the mention of Gorloys' imminent departure to retrieve brimstone so she could make dragon's breath for him – a task she had no intention of fulfilling - only adding to the urgency of her situation. 'If Uthyr doesn't come through,' she thought worriedly, 'we are all screwed!'

CHAPTER 23

Clay and Fire

In the cool, mist-laden morning that draped over the mainland village, Morghais, cloaked in a blend of excitement and trepidation, stood at the edge of a large, fenced paddock. Her small hands clutched the wooden fence, her knuckles white with anticipation. This was a day unlike any other, a day she had dreamt of yet scarcely believed would come to pass. Her father, Gorloys, stood in the center of the enclosure, surrounded by twenty of his men, his presence commanding and formidable.

Morghais shifted uncomfortably, acutely aware of the foreign feeling of trousers against her legs, a stark contrast from the soft flow of dresses to which she was accustomed. Yesterday morning, her father had performed an odd ritual as he came to her room and commanded her to stand. She remembered the sudden fear she had felt as he unsheathed his sword, quickly replaced by confusion as he stood it beside her, appraised her with a piercing look, then departed with her shoes in silence.

She had finally understood when he returned at dusk bearing gifts that would forever alter her world: boots, trousers, a shirt, tunic, and coat, mirroring his own attire. It was then she realized he had used his sword to measure her height and taken her shoes to give to the village cordwainer. The surprise and delight that surged through her as he explained the reason had been overwhelming, manifesting in an uncharacteristic embrace she threw around his neck.

His brief smile, quickly masked by a stern facade, was a rare treasure. “Be ready in the morning," he had said, his voice a mix of stern command and an undercurrent of something softer, before turning away abruptly. She had lain awake long into the night, restless and thinking about the adventure to come, about the opportunity it represented, about her father - a man who, though he was never cruel to her, had always been cold and distant. She knew he wanted a boy. "I will show him, I can be just as good as any boy!" she resolved finally as she allowed sleep to take her.

Now, watching the men prepare for their journey, she could not help but fidget impatiently. The sleeves of her shirt and coat fell to her palms, a result of the shoulders having been cut too wide for her. So, she preoccupied herself with rolling them up while she waited.

Her attention snapped to her father when his voice, loud and commanding, shattered the morning calm. "No! No! No! Not the dun, you fool! That horse is much too large for her." The stable hand mumbled a response, too quiet for Morghais to catch, and swept his hand across the yard, signaling toward other choices.

Her father’s tone softened to a calm yet authoritative command. "Saddle the grey there," he directed, pointing towards a more suitable mount. Moments later, he approached her, leading a gentle grey mare now adorned in tack. "It is time," he announced, as one of his men who had been trailing, stepped up beside him.

With a mixture of nervousness and determination, Morghais reached out to pet the horse’s nose. The softness of its muzzle and the warmth of its breath against her hand melted away her apprehensions. "He is handsome!" she said, her voice filled with wonder, then inquired, "What is his name?"

"He… is a she. Smaller and easier to handle," he corrected with a smirk. "Her name is ‘horse’," he added with a hint of disdain, as if he found the thought of naming an animal silly. Morghais did not like his other comment at all though and felt kind of insulted by it. "She is pretty! And I think she will do as well as any boy horse!" she said proudly, a hint of challenge as she emphasized 'she' and 'boy'.

"Indeed?" her father replied, arching his eyebrow and smirking. " She looks like the morning mist," Morghais continued, inspired by the mare's smooth grey coat. "May I call her Mist, Father?"

"As you wish," he conceded, still smirking at her. But, then his tone turned serious. "While we journey… Mist… is your responsibility to feed, water, and curry. You are still too small to tack up or dress down a horse, so Garel here will see to that." He gestured to a man beside him, clarifying his role in their journey. "I will show you the rest when the time comes."

"Yes, Father," Morghais replied solemnly, embracing her new responsibilities.

It was then Garel offered, "I will help the Penâvorow mount her horse, Pen Gorloys."

Surprised yet pleased by the title, Morghais mulled over its meaning – chief after tomorrow. Gorloys, however, quickly dismissed the formal address. "Do not call her that! We are Cornwall, not those fool Franks! A title must be earned, not bestowed by some accident of birth." Seeing Morghais's disappointment, he softened, offering an alternative, "If you insist on formalities, then call her… Kinsa-mowes, or simply Mowes."

Though slightly deflated, Morghais found solace in her new title, "Kinsa-mowes," which distinguished her as the first girl, especially now that she had a younger sister. "Kinsa-mowes, please Father," she requested, embracing the name that set her apart.

Gorloys acknowledged with a speculative gaze, "Very well… Kinsa-mowes Morghais…"

As Garel moved to pick her up, Morghais stepped out of reach. "I can do it myself!" she declared, tossing the man a reproachful look. Her father was there watching! She was not going to allow this "poopie head" to deny her the opportunity to show him she could do things herself! As she glanced over, Garel's grin mocked her and strengthened her resolve as she stuck her chin out. As she looked up however, her father arched an amused eyebrow and nodded at Garel to stand down.

At first, she struggled to mount Mist in the traditional manner, her foot barely reaching the stirrup, her grip on the saddle insufficient. But she was not about to give up that easily! Not with her father watching. Looking around quickly, she led Mist to the fence, climbed it, and put her foot in the stirrup. As she successfully swung her leg over the saddle and settled atop Mist, she beamed a satisfied grin, earning an approving nod from Gorloys.

"You will ride beside me while I teach you to lead the horse by her reins," Gorloys instructed, grabbing Mist's reins and taking the lead as his men lined up to leave the paddock and begin their journey.

"Where are we going, father?" she finally asked, as they started away from the village up the trodden path ahead. She listened intently as he explained their destination, imagining ships and ports and what a "city" must be like, hanging on to his every word.

In the dwindling light of the evening, Gorloys watched Morghais as she diligently curried Mist, her movements gentle yet determined. Lost in thought, he admired her dutifulness, her eager desire to please, and the resilience she had shown since their departure. He remembered the first night they made camp, noticing the stiffness in her gait as she dismounted, surely saddle sore from the day's ride. He braced himself for complaints that never came.

Now, on their third evening, as Morghais watched one of the men hack at reeds to gather kindling, a curious expression formed on her face. Turning to Gorloys, she pointed to the sword at his hip.

"Will I get a sword, Father?" she asked, a mixture of innocence and earnestness in her voice.

Gorloys couldn’t help but feel both shocked and amused. "Girls do not play with swords, Morghais. Why do you want a sword?"

"To fight?" she shrugged, her brow furrowed in thought. "Mother says fighting is bad, though. But I want to be like you! You have a sword! So, I want one as well."

Still amused, yet touched by her admiration, Gorloys replied, "A sword must be earned, Kinsa-mowes."

The use of her title brought a fleeting smile to Morghais’s face, but Gorloys could see the light of hope in her eyes dim with his words. Observing her deflated spirits, a moment of introspection washed over him. ‘There is so much she does not know about how to survive, and yet, the child wants a sword?’ he mused, his gaze lingering on her determined yet crestfallen face. The request seemed naive, almost amusing at first, but it sparked a deeper train of thought within him.

As he watched her, Gorloys found himself considering the vast expanse of knowledge and skills she lacked, skills that were second nature to him but foreign to her. ‘What if she were left alone in this world?’ The thought, unsettling as it was, ignited a sense of urgency in him. Morghais was strong-willed and bright, yet unprepared for the harsh realities beyond the safety of their home and his protection.

This realization led to an epiphany. Teaching her, guiding her through the lessons of survival, could serve a dual purpose – it would prepare her for the unforeseeable and allow her to earn the privilege of carrying a weapon. More than that, it would be a chance to forge a stronger bond between them, an opportunity to pass on his knowledge and, perhaps, understand his daughter better.

With newfound resolve, Gorloys softened, his mind alight with the possibilities this path offered. “I will make a deal with you,” he began, capturing Morghais’s attention with the serious, contemplative tone in his voice. He gave a moment’s consideration to the skills he wanted her to learn and pared the list down to five items. There were other, more martial skills he would have taught a son. But he decided he would work with the clay he had. And in the process of molding her, he realized, perhaps in some small way, she would reshape him as well. "Complete five tasks – lessons you will learn from me while we travel," he finally said. "Do this, and you will earn a sword of your own."

Morghais's eyes lit up at his words, anticipation mingled with impatience and curiosity. 'Good,' he thought. 'She is eager.' He smiled as she finally burst out, unable to contain her youthful energy. "Really, Father? What are the tasks? When do we start?"

Gorloys couldn't help but admire her fervor. It was clear that he had succeeded in turning the prospect of earning a sword into more than a simple desire; it was a challenge she would embrace as a way to prove herself to him. And perhaps along the way, she may prove her worth herself, but more importantly, to him.

"We begin this evening when we stop to break camp," he said, watching her reaction closely. "Your first lesson will be in making a fire – a skill essential not just for warmth and cooking, but for survival itself."

Gorloys spent the remainder of the day pointing out sources for fuel and kindling as she rode beside him. He found himself pleased by her inquisitiveness, especially when, having left some details unspoken, she asked pointed questions. "What if there is no dead wood, Father? Can you not cut limbs from the trees?" she inquired, her curiosity piqued.

"No," he replied with stern clarity. "Trees bleed too, though not like us. Their blood is called sap," he explained. "Sap causes the wood to burn up more quickly and would not last through the night. It also produces a great deal of smoke, which fills the camp and can sicken your men. But more importantly, smoke rises and can betray your position."

Morghais looked up at him, curiosity shadowed by a hint of confusion. "Why is that bad, Father?"

Gorloys hesitated, pondering how best to impart a harsh truth. "Morghais, you are too young to hear this, perhaps. But know this: the world is not a kind place, especially to girls. Revealing your position when alone can attract the attention of bad men who would do you harm. Do you understand?"

Morghais nodded sagely, her understanding dawning.

That evening, as they made camp, Gorloys invited Morghais to closely observe as he demonstrated the methodical process of building a fire. From the initial spark coaxed from kindling to the careful addition of twigs and branches, he guided each step. "Can you repeat what I have done?" he asked once the fire was established.

"Yes, Father," Morghais replied with a confidence that pleased him.

Handing her the flint and steel, he admonished, "Flint and steel are luxuries you might find yourself lacking. Tomorrow, I will show you how to make fire with a bow drill and fire board. For now, use these. Go and find your own wood and kindling and repeat what you have learned over there," he instructed, pointing to a spot a short distance away. "Do not return to the main camp until you have started your own fire."

Morghais accepted the tools solemnly. "Yes, Father," she acknowledged before heading towards the edge of the woods with a determined stride.

"Caradoc!" Gorloys called out, catching the attention of one of his men.

"Yes, Pen Gorloys?" Caradoc approached, awaiting orders.

Gorloys nodded towards his daughter's retreating figure. "Keep an eye on her. Ensure her safety."

"Yes, Pen Gorloys," Caradoc confirmed, turning to follow Morghais.

"From a distance, Caradoc. Do not let her see you," Gorloys instructed, emphasizing the need for discretion.

Caradoc slowed his pace, nodding over his shoulder in affirmation, "Yes, Pen Gorloys."

Later, as the sun drifted below the tree line and the late afternoon gave way to dusk, Gorloys looked on from his vantage point by the fireside as Morghais, off in the distance, worked with determination to make her own fire. Frustration eventually gave way to delight as dusk settled and a small flame appeared, lighting up her face.

He realized suddenly that he was smiling with pride at her small triumph as she stoked the tiny flame and added larger and larger kindling. Then, to his further surprise, rather than return to the safety of the main camp, she chose to assert her independence and heaved a hefty log – grappling with its weight – to feed her own fire, and settled down beside it for the night, wrapping herself in her blanket.

The next morning, he gently shook her awake and showed her how to seek out hot coals from among the ash and use them to rekindle a new fire. "You did well last night, Morghais," he said, offering praise.

Beaming up at him, Morghais asked assertively, "As good as any boy, right Father?"

Laughing at her assertive question, Gorloys conceded, "Yes, Morghais; as good as any boy." It was in this moment, he grasped what their pact meant to her, the depth of it. More than seeking his love and approval, she wanted to challenge his beliefs and expectations; she understood somehow that she needed to prove her worth beyond the limits of his preconceived notions.

Watching her gaze up at him, her eyes alight with a mixture of hope and devotion, respect and admiration, Gorloys felt an unexpected shift within him: a reflected admiration for Morghais – not just for her tenacity or courage, but for her, entirely – his daughter.

CHAPTER 24

Tryst and Escape

Fynn looked again at the crest of the horizon over which Pen Gorloys and his men had disappeared three days earlier, bemoaning his plight to have been left behind with this idiot Buwel. 'Well…not an idiot. But I do wish he would stop talking,' Fynn reconsidered, even as Buwel prattled on about the fish he planned to catch later in the Spring when the weather warmed, yet another banal topic of no interest to Fynn.

'Warmer tomorrow is not soon enough for me,' Fynn mused to himself, feeling a chill gust of wind sweep up from the sea to buffet the outcrop. This wind tugged insistently at his cloak, which he hastily drew tighter around himself, silently grateful for the small mercy of having remembered to bring it at all. Despite Buwel's ceaseless chatter, which grated on Fynn's already sullen mood, it was unfair for Fynn to blame the man entirely. After all, their post was known to be a dreary one, typically rotated among the men since no one favored it. Buwel, for his part, seemed to have found a distraction in mending a net he'd brought along, an activity that sparked a flicker of envy in Fynn for not having remembered to bring along a knife and a block of wood to whittle along with his cloak.

Devoid of such foresight, Fynn resorted to honing his skills with a sling, using a small pile of stones he had gathered for this very purpose. He also took to observing the activities in the bucolic mainland village from their vantage point atop the platform tower. This structure, perched on an outcrop of the headland, offered views across the narrow isthmus that ended at the base of the tower as well as a large portion of the mainland. It was a strategic point, allowing enough time for mainland villagers to evacuate to the headland, and archers and catapults to be mobilized from the fortress and headland village beyond at the heart of the promontory, well before any attacking force could make its way to the neck of the isthmus at the far end.

Yet, as the sun climbed higher in the sky, ushering in a crisp, cloudless morning, no such force materialized. Instead, Fynn watched with a certain moroseness as the villagers went about their tasks. Some were busy digging at the great trench Pen Gorloys had ordered, an effort to further fortify the neck of the isthmus, limiting access by potential invaders from the natural valley to the northeast. From his distant vantage point, the villagers seemed no more significant than ants on a mound, each absorbed in their duties with a kind of industrious zeal. With Spring's arrival, there was indeed much to be done: preparing for the season's first ships, getting the mainland farms ready for sowing, and thatching roofs from the winter's damage, among other tasks.

It was amidst this bustle of activity that a stranger emerged from a stable, pulling a horse behind him. The unexpected sight of the animal seemed out of place, drawing looks from the villagers as well as capturing Fynn's attention. Fynn watch as the man led the horse to a nearby trough, hitched it to a post there intended for the purpose, then proceeded to make his way on foot across the uneven ground of the isthmus, heading straight toward their post.

The stranger stood firm, breaking the tension with his words. "I have a message from Taran for his brother Jowan." Fynn, sword in hand, descended from the platform, positioning himself squarely before the stranger. Despite the potential threat, the man showed no sign of carrying weapons.

Buwel, eyebrows raised in suspicion, interjected. "We were not expecting any messengers?"

With a smirk and an arched eyebrow, the stranger retorted, "You want me to go back and tell Taran he should send a messenger to let you know to expect a messenger?" He then produced a parchment, its wax seal bearing Jowan's familiar five-point Celtic knot emblem. As Fynn reached out to take it, the stranger pulled it back, a playful challenge in his eyes. "I would not be worth my boots as a messenger if I allowed that now, would I? The message is private for Jowan."

By now, Buwel had joined them, nodding in recognition of the seal. "That looks like Jowan's sigil."

Fynn sneered, his patience thinning. "I do not recognize you and cannot let you pass. But I will take your letter to Jowan and tell him you presented his sigil."

The stranger, unfazed, questioned Fynn's literacy with a skeptical tone. "Do you know how to read? I know Jowan does not."

Caught off guard, Fynn exchanged a bewildered glance with Buwel, who could only offer a shrug and a shake of the head. "Tell me the message and I will see that he gets it," Fynn proposed, seeking a compromise.

The stranger clutched the sealed parchment. "Did I not say 'private'? Perhaps one of you can take me to him? Or go and get him and bring him here?"

"He cannot come here. He guards…" Buwel's words were abruptly cut short as Fynn drove an elbow into his ribs hard, forcing a gasp from him. 'Just share our dealings with a stranger?' Fynn thought, reassessing his earlier leniency. 'Perhaps he is an idiot after all!'

Fynn covered swiftly, asserting control over the situation. "Jowan guards an important prisoner and cannot come here, and we cannot leave our posts until dusk."

The stranger sighed, resigned yet teasing in his impatience. "Then one of you will take me to him? Very well, I will wait. Seems a great deal of trouble for such a trivial message."

Buwel's curiosity, undeterred by the physical reprimand, bubbled over. "You know what the message says?"

"Of course!" The stranger's response was quick, tinged with amusement. "Taran cannot write or read either; those skills are part of my job as a messenger. All this to bring news of the ingredients for some silly new grog. He said Pen Gorloys was keenly interested in it though."

"A new grog?" echoed Fynn, his interest momentarily overriding his suspicion.

Nodding, the stranger leaned in closer, sharing a secret. "Some kind of mead he called dragon's breath." The guards exchanged a look, their interest clearly piqued, but the stranger pressed on with a conspiratorial wink. "That is all I can tell you, and I should not have even said that. But if you ask me, he should just have my wife spit in a bottle when she wakes up in the morning. Her breath stinks so bad, she could burn a man's eyebrows off!"

The air, once thick with tension, now vibrated with laughter. Fynn couldn't help but let out a chuckle, the stranger's joke slicing through the lingering unease. Buwel, too, was overcome with mirth, his laughter a testament to the sudden shift in mood. For a fleeting moment, the stranger's jest and infectious smile, brimming with genuine amusement, had dissolved any remnants of suspicion, as if such caution had never been warranted.

Their laughter was abruptly cut short though as the Lady of Cornwall, Penêsek Ygraine, suddenly appeared among them as though conjured by the very air, her arrival as sudden as it was startling. Winded and disheveled, she fixed her gaze directly on the stranger. "You!" she exclaimed, her voice cutting through the merriment and anchoring Fynn and Buwel back into a state of heightened vigilance.

"I was on the terrace and saw you…" she began, her breaths coming in short, hurried gasps. With a swift turn, she pointed towards an outcrop above and to their right, part of the fortress's expanse, its parapet just visible from where they stood. "But I could not believe my eyes!" she confessed, her astonishment evident. The air, moments ago lightened by laughter, crackled again with renewed tension.

The stranger's eyes widened in recognition. "Ygraine!"

Fynn's protective instincts surged. He pressed his sword against the stranger's throat, his voice cold and firm. "That would be Penêsek Ygraine, dog. You will show proper respect." The stranger's hands went up in a gesture of peace, the sealed parchment still clutched in one.

Buwel, caught between his duty and the unfolding drama, asked, "You recognize this man, Penêsek Ygraine?"

Before Ygraine could respond, the stranger interjected, a note of desperation in his voice. "I am happy you saw poor old Cadfan, Penêsek Ygraine. I came to bring a message to Jowan, but these men," he said, attempting to nudge Fynn's sword away with a cautious touch, "are diligent in their duty and will not let me pass!"

Ygraine's confusion was palpable. "Cadfan? Jowan?"

"Yes, Cadfan!" the stranger exclaimed, his hope flickering. "Though I have grown the beard since last we met…at the Standing Stones of Scorhill?"

In a swift motion, Buwel snatched the parchment, drawing a look of protest from the stranger. Fynn, undeterred, reinforced the sword's threatening position. "It seems your troubles are at an end, friend. The Penêsek can both deliver and read the message to Jowan."

The stranger's plea was earnest. "Begging your pardon, Penêsek Ygraine," he implored. "But if I do not deliver the message myself, then those brothers will never again use me as messenger, and my reputation will suffer!"

Fynn's voice was a sharp warning. "Persist further, and your days as messenger can end here and now."

Ygraine's decision was swift. "It is all right, Fynn. I know this man. Let him pass. I will take him to Jowan."

Buwel's concern was evident. "Are you certain, Penêsek? At least let me accompany you!"

"No, it will be well. He is...a friend. We need no escort," Ygraine assured, turning to the stranger with a nod of recognition. "Welcome to Tintagel...Cadfan."

Fynn eased the pressure of his sword, stepping back as the tension visibly drained from the stranger. A grateful smile spread across the man's face, acknowledging the lowered weapon. Penêsek Ygraine, with a nod of authority, extended the parchment back to him. "Follow me," her voice carried the weight of command, as she pivoted on her heel to lead the ascent towards the fortress. The stranger, with a respectful glance towards Fynn and Buwel, quickly fell into step behind her, the parchment now securely in his grasp.

As they rounded a bend in the path, effectively obscuring them from the guards at the platform tower, Uthyr broke the silence with a hushed tone. "Thank you," he murmured. "You were not supposed to be here."

The mere sound of his deep, resonant voice was like a cool breeze on a warm summer day, sending a shiver though her body. She halted abruptly, spinning to face him, which made him stop and gaze down at her with a hint of surprise. "I am not supposed to be here?" she echoed incredulously, scoffing at the ridiculous irony of his statement. "Reports have you dancing around Cornwall causing my husband a good deal of grief." Shaking her head in disbelief, at his words or his very presence, she could not say with certainty. "I am not supposed to be here?" she repeated. "This is my home," she reaffirmed, arching a challenging eyebrow at him.

His response was a smile, disarmingly handsome and boyish, igniting a warmth in her cheeks. "Merely a ruse...to lure Gorloys and his men away...so I could rescue Merlin," he explained, his eyebrow arching inquisitively. Ygraine was not fooled. Clearly, Uthyr was fishing for a sign of her awareness, testing the waters, unsure of how much she knew. "If my presence displeases you, I could depart and send another in my stead," he offered with a playful smile, his tone teasing. "Truly, the journey was worth every step, if only for this encounter."

Caught off guard by his charm, Ygraine found herself struggling to maintain her usual reserve. "Hmm. Blue," she finally managed, turning away to hide the flush on her face.

"Blue?" Uthyr's voice carried a note of confusion as he followed her.

"I have heard they exist, but I have never seen blue eyes," she replied, her voice carrying a mix of wonder and curiosity. "They are uncommon in Dumnonia and Cornwall; perhaps all of Briton."

"Oh," Uthyr responded, a hint of concern in his voice. "You do not like blue eyes?"

"I did not say that," she countered, a playful defiance in her tone. "When last we met, I was not allowed close enough to notice." She allowed herself a brief glance over her shoulder, meeting his gaze. "They are lovely," she conceded, allowing a small, coy smile to escape. "I do not like the beard though," she added. "You have a strong face and should not hide it behind all that hair. Beards are for older men… like my husband," she concluded, her voice trailing off with a frown.

As they reached the grand doors of the main house, she led him inside, navigating the great hall's sparse elegance to a more secluded corridor. Her choice to turn right, towards her own chambers, was deliberate.

"Where are we? Where is Merlin?" Uthyr's confusion was evident as they entered the intimate space of her sleeping chambers.

Inside, Ygraine faced the door, taking a moment to collect her thoughts, her back to Uthyr. "I have brought you here to wait," she stated, her voice steady yet imbued with an undercurrent of emotion. "Merlin should be forewarned of your arrival, and I… I need to say my goodbyes."

She hesitated, the weight of the moment pressing down on her. "Merlin and I have become friends," she continued, then turned to face him, her expression fraught with conflict. "Or so I had thought," she gasped quietly, her eyes widening as they landed on the sharp dagger now in Uthyr's hand.

Her initial shock gave way to surprise as Uthyr, with a flourish, flipped the dagger, catching it by the blade and offering the handle to her with a mischievous grin. "My lady dislikes the beard," he quipped, his eyes twinkling with humor. "Perhaps she would like to remove it?"

Caught off guard by the sudden shift from alarm to amusement, Ygraine realized she was simply standing there, likely looking a fool, momentarily lost in a whirlwind of emotions battling for dominance. Attraction and fascination warred with confusion and shame. She found everything about him appealing – his youth, virility, and boyish charm mingled perfectly with his rugged good looks and a masculine boldness and dominating presence she found difficult to ignore. This sudden brazen act of trust in her only added to that appeal.

Quickly turning away to hide her flushed cheeks, she closed the door behind them, allowing herself a few deep breaths to collect herself. As a child, her mother had told her fanciful tales of love and romance, often describing the sensation of having one's breath stolen away by someone's mere presence. Such a silly notion was meant to spark the imagination of little girls. Yet, here she was, experiencing just that with Uthyr.

Regaining her composure, she faced him once more, accepting the dagger with a determined air. "Sit by the terrace entry," she directed, pointing to a chair near her reflection pool. "The light there is better."

Uthyr walked over and lifted the chair with purpose, navigating across the room to place it directly in front of the open terrace doors. Morning light flooded in as he sat down, illuminating him against the backdrop of the sea visible through the doorway. The terrace, lined with a parapet holding vats of newly sprouting spring buds, offered a vibrant contrast to the serene indoors. Bees busied themselves among the early blossoms, their activity adding to the scene's tranquil yet lively ambiance.

Meanwhile, Ygraine, attempting subtlety yet feeling an unfamiliar flutter of nerves, moved to her wash basin. She filled a cup with a powder Magra had given her for the purpose, adding water before stirring it into a foamy mixture with a bristle of horsehair. Despite her efforts at discretion, she caught Uthyr's gaze fixed on her, his interest apparent in every deliberate move she made.

Ygraine reached Uthyr and, with a cautious yet deliberate motion, gently lifted his chin to tilt his head back. She was grateful for the task at hand, something that demanded her focus and care, a welcome diversion from the whirlwind of emotions swirling within her. As she began to spread the foamy mixture across his beard, the scent of his skin filled her senses–a pleasant, earthy musk reminiscent of bathing in lakes and nights spent by the fireside under open skies. But despite her best efforts to concentrate on the task, the brush of her fingers against his skin, the intensity of his gaze that never wavered from her face, all sparked a fire within her, igniting notions and secret desires she would scarcely admit to herself, even in the solitude of her thoughts.

Halfway through the careful task of shaving him, Uthyr's hand gently found its way to the back of her leg, resting there with a featherlight touch. The contact sent a surge of excitement through Ygraine, her reaction a mix of timidity and exhilaration as she drew in a quick, sharp breath. Uthyr's voice, soft yet earnest, broke the silence. "Since our first meeting, I have thought of no other than you, Ygraine," he confessed, his gaze dropping to his hand as it tenderly stroked her skin, an action filled with longing and reverence. "My heart has longed for this touch, though my head says it is forbidden," he continued, lifting his eyes to meet hers, a world of feelings conveyed in that look.

"I will take my hand away if it offends you," he offered, his words an assurance of honor, both a confession and a testament to his respect for her. Ygraine, her breath catching in her throat, could only shake her head in silent response, eyes closed and lips tight with restrained pleasure, giving her consent. His touch persisted, a comforting presence as she resumed her task. The world around them seemed to narrow down to this single point of connection, every stroke of the blade, every shared breath weaving a more complex tapestry of emotion and desire within her.

As his hand continued its gentle stroking along the back of her thigh, Ygraine was vividly reminded of her hurried dressing earlier. In her haste to respond to the unexpected sight of him from her terrace, Ygraine had thrown on the first garments she could find, neglecting undergarments in her rush. Now, as Uthyr's hand lingered gently on her thigh, the reality of her scant attire pressed upon her with a new intensity. The fabric of her dress, thin and barely a barrier, allowed every touch to resonate, the warmth in his gentle fingers bleeding through the fabric, almost as though her leg was bare. Despite the cool spring breeze that whispered in from the sea, with the fabric offering little protection from its cool embrace, a warmth spread through her, a flush of heat that seemed at odds with the day's chill. Yet, she carried on with her task, her focus unwavering, as though she were unaffected by the torrent of sensations threatening to overwhelm her.

Turning his chin to address the other side of his neck, she became acutely aware of his breath against her chest. The sensation was a whisper against the fabric, stirring a rush of warmth that spread through her. Unbidden, blood rushed into breasts, suddenly defining hard contours in her dress that she was beyond caring to conceal.

She started with the remainder of his mustache, quickly scraping it away with practiced ease. She had performed this task countless times before on Gorloys, a man whose response to accidental nicks varied between a casual lack of concern and cruel intolerance, depending on his mood. As she stole furtive glances into Uthyr's eyes, she remarked internally how different this experience was, marked by intimacy and closeness rather than duty and fear. The thought brought a demure smile to her lips.

As she finished with Uthyr's chin and bent over to better reach his neck, he moved his hand up her thigh, venturing with a gentleness that crossed into realms reserved only for intimate moments between lovers, his fingertips softly exploring the silhouette of her form beneath the thin fabric of her dress. His other hand, with equal boldness, reached up to tenderly caress the curve of her breast. His actions, though unexpected, were careful, a timid exploration hopeful for unchallenged discovery.

The surprise of his touch caused her hand to slip, nicking his neck with the dagger. Uthyr's reaction was one of complete calm, his gaze not leaving hers, a silent communication of trust. She glanced at the nick, where a small bead of blood welled, her mind racing. Attempting to retreat, caught between a reflex to preserve her modesty and the magnetic pull of their connection, she faltered. Reading her actions, he drew away slightly, continuing to caress her leg, but no longer attempting to negotiate more private territory.

"Uthyr, I…" she began. The words evaporated as her eyes unwittingly met the undeniable evidence of his desire, the contours of his arousal pressing against the confines of his trousers. Embarrassed, she diverted her gaze back to the minor wound, her voice barely a whisper, "I have cut you! Let me…," her breath catching with the effort to maintain composure.

"Ygraine…" his voice carried a gentle tone, yet still demanding her attention. She looked into his eyes and felt lost in them, adrift in that sea of blue that was at once so calm, and yet so stormy. "I have done worse to myself. If you have scraped away enough beard to see my lips, then kiss me," he pleaded.

In a moment of profound uncertainty, Ygraine hesitated, the tension between them almost palpable. Then, with a resolve that seemed to come from the very depths of her being, she let the dagger fall to the floor, its clatter a final punctuation to her indecision. She surged into Uthyr's embrace as he rose to meet her, their mutual desire igniting a passion that felt both ancient and newly discovered.

As they embraced, Ygraine experienced a reawakening, her senses heightened as if exploring passion for the very first time. Hands and lips roamed with a fervor that spoke of long-suppressed yearnings, their clothes discarded in a trail that led the short distance to her bed, a soft landscape of furs and wool.

Ygraine had spent the last year without intimacy, at first due to Gorloys avoiding her because of the shame he felt at the way he cruelly and forcefully took her the night of the parley among the stones at Scorhill, then because she avoided him for a time. The pretended pregnancy, cloistered away in Magra's apartment these last months, only lengthened that time.

As she lay here now with Uthyr, her mind could not help but draw a comparison between that night and this moment. Then, she had cried out in pain as her husband asserted his dominance over her – a cruel display of his manhood to Uthyr, who lay across the valley in his own camp, audience to her every outcry.

Now, as Uthyr began making love to her, his touch assured yet gentle, an explosion of ecstasy she had never felt with Gorloys burst forth from her loins, suffusing her entire body. Her outcries were those of passion, release, and unmitigated pleasure, rather than pain. As Uthyr's motions became more urgent, she caressed his back and hips, feeling his muscles strain as he echoed her outcries in a deep, sonorous voice. Eventually, urgency gave way to absolution as Uthyr reached the pinnacle of his passion and called out her name in exultation and triumphant release. As the warmth of his seed burst forth into her, she felt a second explosion of pleasure, topping the first, forcing an echoing outcry of his name from her own lips in a breathless climax, outcries of affirmation that crescendoed in a symphony of shared pleasure.

In the quiet aftermath of their shared passion, Ygraine and Uthyr found themselves wrapped in a silence that spoke volumes. Lingering touches and shared glances filled the space between words, each keenly aware that the reality of Uthyr's mission could not be ignored forever. Despite the deep connection they had just forged, duty and destiny called him elsewhere, though neither could deny the significance of their tryst.

As they stood and began to redress, a palpable sense of completion enveloped them, tempered by the unspoken acknowledgment of the complexities that lay ahead. Ygraine guided Uthyr back to the chair, her hands steady as she resumed the task of shaving his beard, a symbolic gesture of returning to the world from which they had briefly escaped.

Their conversation, once silent, now ventured into the uncertain future that lay before them. Uthyr broke the contemplative quiet, "What do we do now?"

Ygraine, her smile tinged with both sadness and fondness, responded, "There is nothing to do. Let us just enjoy this moment. What was it you said to me earlier? 'The journey here was worth every step'." Her gentle reminder of his earlier words served as a balm, even as the reality of their situation loomed large.

Uthyr, his voice heavy with emotion, offered, "Say the word, Ygraine, and I will widow you and marry you, all in the same day!"

"Do not say such foolish words, Uthyr!" Ygraine swiftly rebuked him, her voice a blend of affection and pragmatism. "Your passion has won my heart. Do not lose your kingdom for it."

Before Uthyr could protest, Ygraine continued, "No! Listen to me, please Uthyr! The Cornish are a proud people. If you destroy Gorloys over the rule of a kingdom, you will earn their ire for a time. Yet, I suspect you are a just and noble king; they would eventually forgive you. But if you destroy the man and take his wife, you will have earned their enmity forever. Then where is your hope for a united kingdom?"

Uthyr sighed and nodded, his face drooping in resignation, as Ygraine's words sank in.

Ygraine lifted his chin gently to meet his gaze and offered a final piece of herself, "This vessel may belong to him, but my heart now belongs to you, Uthyr. I will remember this day fondly…always. And who knows? Maybe we will see each other again one day. Now…I must go and speak with Merlin. Wait here for my return."

Closing the door softly behind her, Ygraine made her way down the long corridor, the weight of her talk with Uthyr pressing heavily on her heart. As she rounded the bend towards Magra's door, she found Jowan standing guard, his presence a sharp reminder of the world outside her fleeting moments of intimacy.

"Penêsek," Jowan greeted her with a slight bow and a friendly smile. "Did you have a good nap? Your baby has been quiet."

"Yes, thank you for asking, Jowan. I suspect she will soon be hungry though," Ygraine replied, attempting to navigate the sudden shift back to her role as a mother and a wife amidst the tumult of her emotions.

Jowan nodded, his grin broadening salaciously as he stepped aside to let her knock on Magra's door. Ignoring his crudeness and announcing herself, she entered to find Magra gently rocking Morgan in her cradle, while Merlin sat scooping something from a bowl hungrily.

As Ygraine stepped into the room, her gaze immediately fixed upon Merlin. There was an intensity in her stare, a mixture of accusation and hurt that seemed to fill the space between them. Merlin, for her part, was initially oblivious to the shift in atmosphere, her attention momentarily caught up in the simple act of eating. However, the quiet of the room, the stillness of Magra's comforting rocking motion, and the palpable tension emanating from Ygraine eventually drew her attention away from her meal.

Merlin looked up, finally noticing the accusatory eyes fixed upon her. The bowl of food, once a point of focus, now seemed trivial in comparison to the weight of Ygraine's stare.

"What? Why are you looking at me like that?" Merlin's confusion was palpable.

"I thought we were friends, Merlin. I thought you trusted me," Ygraine couldn't hide the hurt lacing her words, her eyes searching Merlin's for an explanation.

"We are friends, Ygraine! What is this about?" Merlin's protest was sincere, her concern for Ygraine evident.

"Uthyr. He sits waiting in my bed chamber, waiting to come and rescue you," Ygraine revealed, her statement hanging heavy in the air.

Merlin's reaction was a whirlwind of emotions. "Oh!" she exclaimed, the excitement quickly giving way to understanding as she repeated more solemnly, "Oh." She took a deep, sighing breath and continued, facing Ygraine's withering stare. "Ygraine, I withheld my plans for escape to keep you safe from Gorloys' retribution. Please understand," Merlin implored as she sat aside the bowl and began preparations to leave, her movements and actions suddenly taking on new urgency.

Magra interjected with her usual no-nonsense wisdom, "Phaw! The more ears that hear, the more mouths that can talk. You know that, girl!"

Merlin paused, the weight of Ygraine's stare pressing down on her. "Though I expected Uthyr to send another man, not come himself. That was…a daring choice," she finally admitted, her voice tinged with a mix of admiration and concern for the unexpected turn their plan had taken.

Ygraine, grappling with the revelations, couldn't hide her surprise. "So, you have known all along that his plan was to draw Gorloys and his men away from Tintagel?" The pieces of the puzzle were beginning to fall into place, yet the implications were staggering.

Merlin nodded, her expression one of chagrin. "It was my plan he executes," she confessed, meeting Ygraine's aghast look with a plea for understanding. "Ygraine, listen! I have no desire for bloodshed on my account. If I can avoid it, I will!" Her earnestness was palpable as she elaborated on the necessity of their strategy. "And you well know that the only way I could possibly do that and affect my escape was to ensure this place had as few men to prevent my escape as possible when my rescuer came."

The room fell silent for a moment, the gravity of Merlin's admission hanging heavily between them. Her plan, borne of desperation and a deep-seated aversion to violence, had set in motion events that could not be easily undone. Yet, her intention to minimize harm and ensure the safety of all involved, especially Ygraine, underscored the complexity of their predicament. Merlin's plan, Ygraine had to admit, was as brilliant as it was devious.

Ygraine sulkily acknowledged the brilliance of Merlin's plan, yet she could not help but worry about the aftermath. "What of Magra?" she inquired with concern. "When Gorloys returns and finds you gone, she may suffer for it." With the very question, Ygraine realized she had accepted a role in their shared plot. Her tone, previously one of hurt and accusation, was now one of excitement and intrigue.

Merlin smiled, picking up on Ygraine's change in demeanor as Magra scoffed, her disdain for the threat she might face evident in her dismissal. "What is he going to do to a little old woman, easily subdued and tied up? Phaw!" She waved off the concern with a rugged chuckle. "It is not my duty to guard Merlin! That duty belongs to Jowan out there."

Ygraine, her mind already moving towards solutions, nodded with resolve. "Speaking of which, I will handle Jowan," she declared, a thoughtful look crossing her features as she considered the implications. "Or rather, I will ensure Uthyr causes him no lasting harm. Jowan is a good man."

"Agreed," Merlin quickly added, seeming appreciative of the care Ygraine showed in keeping to Merlin's goal of preventing bloodshed if possible.

The air in the room seemed to thicken with tension as Ygraine broached the next topic with care. "As for Morgan, I will love her as my own until you can return to claim her," she promised, her voice laden with solemnity and warmth, and offering a mother's assurance knowing that no matter how she presented it, the notion would be met with stiff resistance.

As Ygraine expected, Merlin's immediate response was one of visceral rejection, the idea of parting from her daughter sparking a raw, protective instinct. "What? No! Ygraine, I appreciate all your help! But I am not giving up my daughter! Morgan is coming with me!" Her outburst, a blend of desperation and determination, echoed painfully in the confines of the room.

"Do not be foolish, Merlin," Magra interjected softly with a grandmother's kindness. "Until you can return to your realm, the baby must remain here for her own safety."

Merlin began to shake her head in stubborn protest when Ygraine laid a hand on her arm to draw her attention. "If you escape alone, Gorloys will not seek you out. Admitting to your capture would be an embarrassment he would not care to face under Uthyr's scrutiny. But if you escape and take his daughter? Or so he believes…" Ygraine quickly added as outrage flashed in Merlin's eyes. "Unless you can spirit Morgan away with you to your realm, and beyond his reach, Gorloys will hunt you to the ends of the earth."

Merlin scoffed at the notion, her defiance tinged with a hint of denial. "He cares nothing for daughters. You said so yourself! Just say she died while he was away, and…What?"

Ygraine shook her head, her sadness palpable, as Magra joined in, underscoring the cultural customs that bound their hands. "It will not work, Merlin. Whatever he may feel about daughters, Cornish custom requires him to burn the body of his child to usher her spirit on to Annwn."

"And whatever may have been true in the past," Ygraine added, her voice soft but firm, "he is out there now, hunting Uthyr with his eldest daughter in tow, trying… finally… to be a father to her."

In a moment of raw vulnerability, Merlin snatched Morgan from her cradle, her actions driven by a maternal instinct as primal as it was profound. Clutching her daughter close, she sobbed, the reality of the situation crashing down around her. "But…" she sniffled, the question that followed as much a plea as it was a concern, "She is only five days old! Who will nurse her? How can she survive?"

Magra's response came softly, imbued with the wisdom of age and experience. "Goat's milk, girl. When a mother dies too soon, their babes are nursed by a wet nurse, another mother who is nursing, if one can be found. If not, then the child is fed goat's milk. It has been done that way in our world since farmers had goats to raise. What is good for a kid is good enough for your baby!" Her words, meant to comfort, carried the weight of centuries of tradition and necessity.

A small chuckle broke through Merlin's tears, a brief respite in the midst of her turmoil. Her tender hold on Morgan did not waver as she found a sliver of humor in their grim situation.

"What is funny?" Ygraine asked, puzzled by the sudden shift.

Merlin wiped her eyes, the ghost of a smile lingering as she explained, "What Magra said. 'Kid' in my native language is the same word and means the same thing – a baby goat. But the word is also commonly used to refer to one's children in my language as well." The bittersweet realization that words could bridge worlds, even in the darkest of times, offered a fleeting sense of connection.

Ygraine, ever perceptive, sensed a deeper current running beneath Merlin's words. "How had you planned to tell Uthyr in any event? Does he not believe you to be a man, as Gorloys did? As the rest of the world does?" Her question, gentle yet pointed, probed at the heart of Merlin's secret.

Merlin's admission came with a heavy sigh, her gaze dropping to the precious bundle in her arms. "If I am honest, I had not thought that far ahead. I had hoped to escape before Morgan came into the world." The confession laid bare the depth of her desperation, the lengths to which she had been willing to go to protect her child, and herself, from a world not yet ready to understand her truth.

Magra's voice carried a note of finality, her words a gentle but firm reminder of the reality Merlin faced. "If you wish to maintain that ruse for now, then you have yet more reason for Morgan to stay with Ygraine. She is a good mother, Merlin. She will love the child as her own until you can come and take her. Morgan will be safe here. But out there? On the run? Even in the best of circumstances, it is a harsh world, filled with danger for you and for the little one you seek to protect."

In the silence that followed, the air was thick with unspoken emotions. Ygraine's heart ached for Merlin, witnessing the tumultuous storm of love, anger, shame, hope, desperation, and heartbreak that played across her face. With a gentle resolve, Ygraine stepped forward, her voice soft but imbued with a strength born of understanding and empathy. "Merlin, when you are ready, I will return Morgan to you. I promise." She stooped to comfort Merlin, her presence a solid reassurance in the midst of chaos. "I understand a mother's bond, a mother's love. But if Morgan is ever to see her real mother again, then you must let her go for now."

As Merlin nodded, her resolve mingled with sorrow, Ygraine saw the depth of her struggle reflected in the interaction with her daughter. Merlin, amidst her tears, focused on Morgan, who, in her innocence, remained a light in the shadow of parting. Ygraine watched as Merlin tenderly played with Morgan, each giggle and touch a testament to the love that bound them. It was a poignant scene that spoke volumes to Ygraine, witnessing the strength of Merlin's love, tempered by the harsh reality of their circumstances.

To Ygraine, this moment underscored the gravity of their situation, not just as a matter of safety, but of emotional sacrifice. The resolve in Merlin's eyes, even as they filled with tears, told Ygraine more about her character and the lengths she would go to protect her child than words ever could. In the gentle, yet heart-wrenching, interactions between mother and daughter, Ygraine found a renewed sense of commitment to protect and care for Morgan in Merlin's stead, holding onto hope for a future where Merlin could reclaim her role without fear or danger.

Ygraine's voice was gentle, yet firm, as she addressed Merlin, offering a solution borne of necessity and compassion. "Allow me to take her for now, Merlin. She should not be in this room when Uthyr arrives should violence break out."

The desperation in Merlin's voice was palpable, her request a whisper of hope in a moment filled with despair. "Allow me to feed her one last time?"

Ygraine nodded sympathetically, granting her assent without hesitation. She retreated to the hearth, giving Merlin the privacy and dignity this final act of motherhood deserved. In the quiet of the room, Ygraine could hear the soft murmur of Merlin's voice, a lullaby of love and farewell, as she nursed Morgan for the last time. Tears glimmered in Merlin's eyes, each one a silent testament to the depth of her love and the pain of her sacrifice.

When the moment came to an end, and Morgan returned to a slumbering state, Ygraine approached to take the baby and help her burp. "What was the last thing you said to her?" she asked, her voice soft, seeking to understand the final words shared between mother and daughter.

Merlin looked up, her eyes reflecting a mix of pride and sorrow. "I said 'Your mother loves you' in my own tongue."

Ygraine's response was heartfelt, her words intended to offer comfort and affirmation. "You are making the right choice for her, Merlin," she said reassuringly. "So… I suppose this is good-bye for now."

Merlin's nod was filled with pain, her silence a heavy cloak around her. Yet, Ygraine felt compelled to express her gratitude for their unlikely friendship. "Merlin? I am glad we are friends," she admitted, her departure heavy with the weight of what was left unsaid.

As Ygraine left Magra's apartment, Morgan cradled securely in her arms, the sound of Merlin's grief followed her–a keening wail that pierced the heart. Glancing back, she caught a fleeting glimpse of Magra comforting Merlin with an embrace, a final image of solidarity and love before the door closed behind her.

Outside, Jowan's questioning gaze met hers. Without revealing the truth, Ygraine offered a plausible explanation for the sound of sorrow. "Magra just found out her son, Branok, is dead," she shrugged, a lie easier to bear than the truth of their parting.

Jowan's understanding nod, accompanied by a solemn shake of his head, was a silent expression of sympathy. In that moment, Ygraine felt the full weight of their collective sacrifices, each person playing their part in a story of loss, love, and resilience.

In the aftermath of their daring escape, Marilyn remained vigilant, scanning the shoreline for any sign of pursuit while Uthyr skillfully navigated their small craft away from the danger they had just left behind.

As they cleared the sheltered waters of the inlet, Uthyr transitioned from rowing to sailing, pulling the oars into the boat with a fluid efficiency that spoke of his familiarity with the sea.

"There!" Marilyn's sharp eye caught movement on the terrace from which they had descended a short time ago. Two figures, quickly joined by Ygraine cradling Morgan, pointed and shouted down at them, drawing Uthyr's attention away from setting the sail.

"Perfect!" Uthyr exclaimed, the satisfaction evident in his grin as he caught sight of their audience.

"Perfect?" Marilyn echoed, her tone laced with incredulity. "They could send more men to hunt us!"

Uthyr shook his head, his grin unwavering. "I came to the mainland village last night and removed the shoes from the only horse I saw in the whole village," he confessed with a hint of mischief. "And I threw all the blacksmith's fuel into the quenching barrel early this morning. It will be half a day before those men could even think of hunting us. And by then, we will be with my men!"

As their small boat ventured further into the open waters, Marilyn's gaze lingered on the receding terrace, an adjunct of the chambers shared by Ygraine and her husband. The rope she and Uthyr had used to descend the steep, craggy incline below still remained tied haphazardly around one of the merlons of the low parapet edging the terrace. In their scramble to escape, Marilyn had spotted and grabbed her shock staff as well. Of immense value to her, she could not believe it lay so carelessly discarded in a corner recess of the room, as if of no consequence to Gorloys beyond denying her of its possession.

She watched as the men had vanished, but Ygraine remained, a solitary figure amongst the vats of spring flowers lining the parapet's crenellations, holding Morgan close. As Ygraine waved a final goodbye, Marilyn returned the gesture, a silent acknowledgment of the bond forged amidst the tumult of their shared ordeal.

Uthyr, noticing the exchange, turned back to Marilyn with a contemplative look. "We will get her back, Merlin. I promise," he said, his voice carrying a weight of solemnity.

"What?!" Marilyn's shock was palpable, her mind racing to grasp the implications of his words.

"Your daughter. Morgan. Or Morgana…Ygraine was not quite clear on the child's name. Whichever, we will get her back," Uthyr reiterated, his statement simple yet loaded with conviction.

Marilyn struggled for words, her thoughts a whirlwind of confusion and disbelief. "Uthyr, I…"

Uthyr cut her off, his hand raised in a gesture of peace. "Peace, Merlin! I have suspected for a long time. But when she presented the baby to me, I knew."

Marilyn attempted to clarify, "Uthyr, the child is hers. I…"

Uthyr's grin broadened, his tone playful yet revealing. "Is she now? Ygraine certainly did not feel like she had birthed a child only days ago while I was with her. And I did not taste a mother's milk when her breast was in my mouth…"

Marilyn's astonishment rendered her speechless, her emotions a tangled web of indignation, embarrassment, and outrage. 'The gall of this man!' she thought. 'How could he?' Aghast and unable to find words in his language strong enough, all she could do was blubber. "I cannot believe…! I… You…! But…!"

Uthyr laughed heartily, his amusement clear. "Peace, Merlin! You were not the only reason I came to Tintagel. Though I hoped Ygraine would be there, I did not know for certain. But I admit, you were not my first stop during my visit." Uthyr's eyes glazed over as his mouth donned a lecherous smirk.

Marilyn's initial shock gave way to a realization of Uthyr's deeper motives, her earlier outrage compounded by them. "You dirty, rotten, stinking…!" she burst out, unable to mask the mixture of disbelief and anger in her voice, but not familiar with enough bad names in his tongue to bring anything to mind. Then, her mind found a word. "You scoundrel!" she blurted out finally as Uthyr sat there grinning like a fool. "You seduced that poor girl to rescue me?!" Marilyn accused.

Uthyr's laughter, full of both confession and pride, echoed through the air. "Oh, no! No, you have me all wrong, my friend. My affection for Ygraine began the day we met, long before you returned to this land from your cave. And as it happens, she shared that infatuation."

Marilyn, her face a portrait of mixed emotions, responded with a tone that wove together reproach and inquiry. "And that matters how, Uthyr? You are young, handsome, a king! How many villages and towns have you visited where women fawn over you? I imagine many were no less beautiful! Why her? Why Ygraine, the wife of a man who despises you? Is that why? Because of him?"

Uthyr's jovial mood shifted abruptly to solemnity as he commanded, "Enough, Merlin!" His outburst hung in the air, leaving Marilyn to speculate on the depth of emotions beneath his stern exterior. After a moment of charged silence, Uthyr sighed, a gesture of weary resignation. "Let me tell you of the day we first met. Then maybe you will understand my feelings."

As Uthyr recounted the tale of his and Ygraine's first meeting, Marilyn listened, her earlier indignation softening as she absorbed the sincerity and depth of his affection.

When Uthyr finished, he awaited Marilyn's response. She sighed, acknowledging the complexity of their situation. "Uthyr, I was imprisoned there for months. I was witness to some of the struggles in their marriage. But she is still a married woman! You invade land that is…what is the word…sacred."

Uthyr's reaction was sharp, his voice tinged with bitterness. "Ygraine is a kept woman, not a married woman! She is a possession to Gorloys to do with as he pleases, not his wife!" He then softened, adding, "I ask you this. If Ygraine was happy in her marriage, do you not think our coming together this morning would never have happened, no matter my affections?"

Marilyn pondered his words, then nodded. "Perhaps, Uthyr, but…"

"No! No more objection!" Uthyr's insistence cut through the air. "Hear my words. Am I handsome to you?"

Marilyn was taken aback, flustered by the unexpected question. "What has that to do with anything?"

"Answer the question! Do you find me handsome? Do you see in me the things other women do?" Uthyr pressed.

Feeling awkward now that her secret was known, Marilyn admitted, "I… I suppose, Uthyr, but…"

"And yet you have never once cast your eyes at me as Ygraine has. Your bond with your baby's father is strong, yes?" Uthyr's question drove home his point.

"Yes," Marilyn nodded, finally understanding the depth of Uthyr's feelings. "I think I understand, Uthyr. But surely you see that nothing more can come of your affections?"

Uthyr's demeanor became pensive then, his voice taking on a tone of dejection as he responded thoughtfully. "Ygraine said much the same thing," he began, casting his gaze back toward Tintagel, now too distant to see. Marilyn watched as he seemed lost in reverie, perhaps recalling earnest words between the two that she would never hear. Yet the emotions that played across Uthyr's face bore a silent testament to the depth of his feelings.

Pulling himself back to the present, Uthyr concluded with a heavy heart, "We must be satisfied with this day." His words, spoken with a sense of resignation, seemed to carry the weight of unfulfilled dreams and the acceptance of a reality dictated by duty and circumstance.

The weight of Uthyr's admission and Marilyn's subsequent reflection softened the atmosphere between them. "Forgive me, Uthyr. My friendship with Ygraine, the trust I placed in her to help me while imprisoned, was at times strained. That may not have been so had I known any of this. But you have never spoken of her," Marilyn observed, signaling a newfound understanding and empathy towards Uthyr's situation.

Uthyr's reply was tinged with mystery. "I have spoken to no one about a great many things," he noted, acknowledging the secrets they both kept, subtly hinting that that same discretion carried Marilyn's secrets as well.

Marilyn accepted his assurance with gratitude. "Thank you," she said, a simple acknowledgment of the bond they shared and the trust between them.

Uthyr nodded. "Truth be told, I had not actually given much thought to whether Ygraine was a new mother," he admitted. "She did not give up your secret. But those did," he grinned again, pointing at Marilyn's chest. Caught off guard, Marilyn looked down to see evidence of lactation leaking through her clothing, a physical reminder of her recent motherhood. "If you wish your secrets to remain your own, I suggest you find some way to deal with that," he offered.

"Christ!" Marilyn exclaimed, hastily covering herself with her backpack.

Uthyr's teasing continued, his curiosity unabated. "What do you expect the Jesus god to do about it?"

Marilyn's blush deepened, her response a mix of embarrassment and admonishment. "Nothing! Just…stop looking at me! Steer the boat."

Their conversation quieted with a final snicker from Uthyr. But after a few moments, he spoke up again. "I have been meaning to ask you something," he stated, his tone one of puzzlement.

"What?" Marilyn's curiosity was piqued.

"I cannot make any sense of the message you had me read to Jowan," he replied, confusion evident. "Why should he care about the comfort of his birds?"

Marilyn's laughter rang out, the absurdity of the situation and her clever ruse bringing a moment of levity to their escape. 'Your cock is cold,' she thought, amused by the play on words. "A bit of a joke," she explained. "In my tongue, when someone is knocked senseless, they are said to have been cold-cocked. Thank you for not killing him."

Uthyr's amusement was infectious as he repeated the phrase, "Cold-cocked?" Their laughter echoed over the waters, a shared moment of laughter as they sailed on, the afternoon sun at their backs. She was free and under an open sky again. 'Maybe the team has found a way to return me and Morgan home,' she mused with hope. 'Perhaps a little prayer would not be such a bad thing after all.'

CHAPTER 25

Bargain

Gorloys watched as Morghais stooped low and blew gently at the dark ember until a familiar orange glow emerged from its darkened heart. "Now, add a little kindling and blow on the ember until it lights the kindling for you," he instructed. "Good," he continued, offering praise as her compliance met with success. "Now build that into a proper fire as you did last night. I must go and help my men. I will return shortly."

"Yes, Father," Morghais beamed up at him, then proceeded to follow his instructions. He nodded, satisfied, and turned to go.

He returned a short time later as the fire crackled to life, a testament to Morghais's quick learning and determination. When he approached, her face lit up as brightly as her burgeoning fire. "Spot-nose!" she called out gleefully, recognizing the rabbit he carried - one of several from the hutch back home. Gorloys sighed inwardly. 'This lesson will be difficult for her,' he thought bitterly.

Gorloys handed her the rabbit, his expression blank, feeling the weight of the moment as she took the creature hesitantly, her joy turning to confusion. "Father, what are you…" she began as she stroked it gently between its ears.

"Morghais, last night you began your part in meeting our bargain and learned your first lesson," Gorloys interrupted, his voice firm. "Most of it at least; I must still teach you how to make fire without flint and steel. But that is for another time. This morning you will learn your second lesson – perhaps the most difficult one of all."

He watched Morghais's expression turn from confusion to concern as he held out a small knife, extending the handle in her direction. "Take it," he ordered when she stepped back apprehensively.

Morghais reached out and grabbed the handle timidly at first. Then Gorloys reminded her sternly, "Is that how you plan to handle the sword you want so badly?" His mild rebuke had the intended effect as her gaze stiffened defiantly and she took the knife with a firm hand.

"Morghais, the world can be a cruel place. To survive in it, you must learn to kill when the need arises, without hesitation. We must kill to have meat for the table. Goats, chickens," he paused, nodding toward the rabbit nestled in the crook of her arm, "Even rabbits," he added. "And sometimes we must kill to defend ourselves, our family, our land, from those who would take by force."

"But father, I do not know how," Morghais said, her voice barely above a whisper, her eyes locked on the rabbit that had suddenly become more than just a favored pet.

"Take the rabbit by the ears and dangle it with its feet away from you so it cannot kick at you. Then cut across its throat with the knife as deeply as you can," Gorloys instructed, his voice unwavering.

Gorloys watched intently as Morghais's expression twisted into one of horror as she adjusted her grip on the rabbit and it began to squeal, sensing its peril. She hesitated, the knife raised, but her resolve was waning. "I... I cannot," she finally whispered, her voice breaking as tears welled up in her eyes.

Anger momentarily welled within him at the sign of his daughter's weakness. 'She is so eager to prove herself better than a boy?' he thought callously, a slight smile tugging at the corners of his mouth, hidden from her view. But in that moment, recalling his own childhood and the cost of the harsh lessons he had learned himself as a boy, he realized he likely held the same frighteningly stern look his father had held. 'I can do better than that bastard,' he thought bitterly and softened his face.

It was a test, all of it. A test for him as a father. And for Morghais? A test of will, of courage, of the resolve he knew lay within her, just waiting for the right nudge to surface. He sighed heavily, allowing a tone of sullen disappointment to lace his words, a calculated move to ignite the fire he knew burned inside her. "Ah well. You are only a girl. I should not have expected this much of you," he said, his words heavy with challenge, aimed like an arrow at her pride.

He could see that the remark stung, igniting a look of fierce determination within Morghais. Her grip on the rabbit tightened, and without another word, she ended its life with a swift motion, more decisive than he had anticipated. The rabbit's squeals ceased, and for a moment, the only sound was the crackling of the campfire and the low murmur of men and horses as they continued preparations for the day's journey. Gorloys watched, a complex mix of emotions churning within him, a reflection of those he could see in her eyes. Pride, for her courage to overcome her hesitancy, and sorrow, for the innocence lost in the act. Yet the lesson was not at an end.

"Because of your hesitation, it suffered before death, Morghais. Next time, do it swiftly. It is a mercy for both you and the rabbit," Gorloys said softly as the rabbit's last weak kicks ceased, acknowledging the difficulty of the lesson. "Do you understand?" he inquired.

Morghais nodded, her expression solemn, a mix of resolve and sadness in her eyes. "Yes, Father," she said, her voice steadier. Gorloys put a hand on her shoulder and continued, his voice firm yet not without compassion, a deliberate effort to bridge the gap his earlier callousness had created. "Life demands much from us, Morghais. Often, it demands the hardest things. But it is how we meet those demands that defines us."

Morghais wiped the wetness from her eyes – remnants of unshed tears – and nodded, straightening her face. "Good," Gorloys replied, acknowledging her resolve. "Now we must skin and dress it. This lesson is about more than having the courage to kill when necessary," he continued, his demeanor shifting to that of a teacher as he began to show her how to skin and dress the rabbit. Each movement was deliberate, meant to teach and to preserve. "This same technique applies to all animals with fur. And many have more to offer than just meat and fur," he explained as they worked together. "We clean and dry the rabbit's entrails, for example, to use as stitching for wounds."

After they ate and set out for the day, Gorloys spent the morning casting furtive glances in Morghais's direction, watching as she rode in solemn silence. 'Perhaps I demand too much,' he thought for a moment, then chastised himself for such musings. 'No! Her mother coddles her and shields her from the world. I will not do the same!' Still, he could not help but feel a modicum of sympathy, knowing that his lessons foist a heavy burden of expectation on her shoulders. 'But that was the bargain,' he reasoned. 'I would have expected no less of a son.'

That evening marked a change; as they stopped to make camp, Morghais took charge of the fire, building it with a skill that earned the praise of several of the men. Gorloys observed quietly as she swelled with pride at each complement, reflecting the swell of pride that rose within him as well. 'What a clever girl,' he mused, amazed at how quickly she had mastered the skill with flint and steel.

Recalling his earlier promise, he waited until she was done currying her horse, then called Morghais over to him. "Go and find as straight a stick as you can; two fingers thick and about this long," he ordered, holding out his hands.

When she returned, he handed her the knife used that morning to slay and skin the rabbit, but this time, still sheathed. "This is now yours. You have earned it," he stated. "It is a tool, Morghais, not a weapon. Do you understand?" he added, inquiring.

"Yes, Father," she replied seriously, taking the knife with a sense of reverence. He spent the next hour showing her how to sharpen the stick and start a fire using the hand drill and fire board method should she find herself without flint and steel.

Later, as they all sat around the campfire, sharing rabbit stew, Gorloys could tell that Morghais knew where the meat had come from by the tentative way that she took each bite, as though each morsel bore the guilt-laden mark of her hand in the creature's demise. But as the evening wore on and she saw everyone eating, saw Gorloys watching her, her demeanor slowly began to change. Hesitancy gave way to recognition of the truth he had needed her to learn. She had killed this day so that Gorloys, herself, and all the men eating stew around the campfire could live.

Twilight soon gave way to night and a blanket of stars covered the sky as everyone began to turn in for the night. Rather than sleeping separately though, Morghais made her bed near Gorloys so that the two lay with their heads together. As he lay there, Gorloys pondered what lesson to teach her next. 'Perhaps navigating by the sun and stars,' he thought as he stared up at the night sky. 'In the meantime,' he decided, 'if her resolve holds, she will need to know how to handle the sword she wants so badly.' Decision made, he told her, "Rest well, daughter. Tomorrow, you begin sword training." He lay there for a long moment, hearing no response, wondering if exhaustion had already taken her, when finally, she replied, "Thank you, Father…"

The days that followed were a blend of physical exertion and mental expansion for Morghais. Each morning began with the clashing of wooden swords, Garel meticulously guiding her through the motions as Gorloys watched, her frame accumulating bruises as tangible proof of her unyielding spirit. Yet, as the sun dipped below the horizon, their focus shifted from the earth beneath their feet to the vast expanse above.

Having taught her to use shadows cast by the sun as a guide, he put her to the test each day. "Morghais, draw the day's path," Gorloys would instruct, watching as she etched a compass into the dirt with a stick, marking the sun's journey from dawn till dusk. But it was the night sky that offered the deepest lessons. Lying side by side, Gorloys pointed towards the heavens, introducing her to the celestial guides of their ancestors.

"Do you see that bright star there?" Gorloys asked one evening, his finger tracing a line towards a steadfast light amidst the constellational drift.

"Unlike any other star, which travels across the sky with the moon, that star holds steady in the night sky. We call it Arawn's Eye, for Arawn, god of the night and the underworld, watches over us in our travels and guides us through the darkness," he explained, his voice a blend of reverence and instruction.

Morghais followed his gaze, her eyes locking onto the constant star. "Arawn's Eye," she repeated, the name rolling off her tongue as she committed it to memory alongside the patterns of the Great Bear and the Hunter.

These sessions under the stars became a time for reflection and connection, a counterbalance to the physical demands of the day. Gorloys observed Morghais's growing understanding of the world around her, not just the land they trod upon but also the celestial sphere that guided their nights. Her bruises from sword training found a counterpoint in her keen insights into the workings of the sky, each observation a step towards mastering her environment.

On the third day, Morghais approached Gorloys, her frustration palpable in her every move. "Garel's reach is longer than mine! He is so much larger than I, Father! Look at me! I sit here bruised from head to foot and he has not a single mark on him," she sulked, her voice thick with vexation and the sting of perceived injustice.

Gorloys looked at her, taking in the bruises that painted her skin, the physical testament to her tenacity. "I remember once watching you in the hen yard," he began, his voice even, aiming to guide her thoughts to a valuable lesson. "Your mother had sent you out there to catch a chicken."

"I remember," she responded, the edge of her frustration softening with the memory.

"Yes, I remember you laughing with glee. You would spend a great deal of time trying to catch the chicken, only to let it go and start over again," Gorloys continued, a hint of a smile touching his lips at the memory.

Morghais's expression turned a bit sad, the innocence of those moments now shadowed by the realities she faced. "Now that I know why Mother sent me, the game is no longer fun. What has that to do with anything though, Father?"

"Why was it so difficult for you to catch the chicken?" Gorloys asked, steering her towards the realization he intended her to reach.

"The chicken is small and quick," she admitted, the light of understanding beginning to dawn in her eyes.

"And yet you have the longer legs," Gorloys pointed out, watching as the pensive look on her face gave way to a grin of comprehension.

"Learn to fight with your own strengths, not Garel's," he advised, the lesson clear.

The next day, Gorloys' eyes followed Morghais as she practiced again with Garel, this time with a different strategy. She dodged and rolled as he jabbed and swiped, using her agility to her advantage. When she rolled under a swiping attack and caught him in a vulnerable spot, Garel dropped his practice sword and sank to his knees, cradling his groin. The men around the camp chuckled, a mixture of amusement and respect in their laughter.

Gorloys looked on, his emotions a blend of amusement and pride for her clever adaptation and newfound understanding, all muddled together with a burgeoning respect for the person Morghais was becoming – resilient, intelligent, and unyielding. With each challenge she overcame and each lesson she absorbed, his confidence in her ability to face future trials with the same tenacity and courage she had demonstrated grew.

Over the days that followed, having instilled in her the basics of navigation, Gorloys guided Morghais through the wilderness's silent language. They identified animal trails, scat, dens, and nests that bespoke of game, both large and small. Their afternoons were spent mastering the art of setting snares and understanding the hunt's subtleties, from wind direction to the prey's scent, drawing upon Gorloys' own years of experience. Watching Morghais, he saw her initial hesitations fade, replaced by a keen focus and a rapidly growing confidence as she adeptly mirrored his teachings.

As their days transitioned to evening, Morghais's routine shifted from the survivalist to the warrior. After completing her camp chores and as the sun began its descent, she would meet Garel for sword practice. This evening was no different. The nearby tree line cast long shadows across the open area where Morghais faced off with her opponent. The intermittent clacking of their wooden swords played counterpoint to the burgeoning call of cicadas in the late afternoon as the sun dipped below the tree line.

Gorloys observed from the sidelines, noting the sweat on Garel's brow – a testament to Morghais's progress and intensity. "She has come so far," he thought proudly. The days had been long, but worthwhile. She had absorbed every lesson he taught, surpassing his expectations, embodying a resilience and intelligence he had not expected of her, and in doing so, gained both his respect and affection. He chuckled to himself quietly, thinking back to each lesson. 'As good as any boy,' he muttered, smiling at the affirmation she sought repeatedly with each challenge met.

His reverie was broken as one of his men, Duryk, rode up and leapt from his horse with excitement, bearing a parcel wrapped in cloth, the contents of which elicited excitement within Gorloys. He took the parcel from the man, inquiring, "The blacksmith was good?"

"Better than good, Pen Gorloys!" Duryk replied. "When I told him who the weapon was for, he worked all through the night with two apprentices to craft it!"

Gorloys unwrapped the short sword - a weapon sized for his daughter - and unsheathed it. It was indeed a finely made weapon, polished to a dull shine, and sharpened with a keen edge. "Look here on the pommel," Duryk added. "The blacksmith added the sigil of Cornwall to the pommel." Gorloys smiled and nodded as he sheathed the sword and rewrapped it in the cloth. "It is fine work, Duryk. Say nothing more of this to anyone for now."

Twilight soon descended upon the camp, casting a soft, golden hue over the clearing. The day's training had yielded to an evening of communal reprieve. The campfire, central to this night's gathering, crackled and popped, its warm glow illuminating the faces of those gathered around it. The pleasing aroma of an animal flank being roasted on a spit wafted through the air, inviting the men to occasionally rise, either to cut a slice of the succulent meat for themselves or to rotate the spit for even cooking. Another took up the task of basting, ensuring every bite would be as flavorful as the last.

Amidst this scene of camaraderie and simple pleasures, Gorloys and Morghais found themselves seated together, sharing their evening meal. The tranquil moment, however, was pierced by the sudden sound of wolves growling and yipping in the darkness, not too far from where they sat. Gorloys saw Morghais tense up at the unfamiliar and close cries. Having been sheltered within the confines of Tintagel her whole life, he understood she had never encountered wolves, much less heard their eerie calls so nearby. "What was that?" she asked, a hint of fear in her voice.

Seeing her apprehension, Gorloys smiled gently and offered a reassuring explanation. "They are only wolves, Morghais. Like a wild dog, only they are larger and hunt in packs," he explained, his voice imbued with a calm certainty meant to ease her fears. He gestured towards the spit over the fire. "They can be fierce, but fear fire and will choose a free meal over one they must fight for," he continued, indicating the pragmatic approach they took to coexist with the wilderness. "We leave the animal entrails in the woods for them, and they leave us alone. You need not worry."

As Gorloys explained, he watched Morghais's reaction, noticing how her initial alarm gradually gave way to curiosity and then understanding. It was another silent testament to her ability to learn and adapt, qualities he had come to admire deeply in her. When she nodded, he knew she had grasped yet another facet of the complex dance of survival. Her attention then returned to the fire and the meal before them, a moment of learning woven seamlessly into the fabric of their daily life.

He sat quietly for a time, gnawing on a bit of the meat from the fire. Beside him lay the parcel, meticulously wrapped, its contents hidden yet unmistakably significant – the sword forged for Morghais. Its presence exuded a force, as if inciting a nervous energy within him, marking both an end and a beginning of their journey together. Watching the flames reflect in Morghais's eyes, he felt a surge of anticipation mixed with a profound sense of responsibility. The time had come to acknowledge her growth and the strides she had made.

"I was watching you with Garel earlier," he began, breaking the silence, his voice tinged with a mixture of amusement and pride. "You actually made the man sweat! Your sword training is coming along well, Morghais." He paused, searching for the right words, the pride in his chest threatening to overwhelm him. "I… I just wanted to say… I am proud of you."

Morghais looked up, a glint of gratitude in her eyes. "Thank you, father," she murmured, her voice steadier than Gorloys expected. It was a simple yet significant moment between them, less about the emotional depth and more a testament to their journey's tangible progress.

Gorloys, feeling a surge of pride, instinctively tightened his grip on the parcel beside him. "You deserve praise, daughter. As agreed, you have learned all five lessons I wished to teach you. And you have become proficient enough with the sword that tomorrow morning, before the whole camp, I will gift you the sword that was the prize of our agreement."

Her eyes shone with a mixture of pride and something else – anticipation, perhaps. "Is there not a final test, Father?" she asked, tilting her head slightly, a trace of challenge in her voice.

Gorloys felt a twinge of discomfort. "Who said anything about a final trial? That was not a part of our agreement."

"It was something Garel said," Morghais pressed, her gaze steady. "One day, he spoke of the things you have been teaching me, Father. He said these things reminded him of the lessons his father gave him as a boy to prepare him for his test of manhood."

Gorloys sighed, realizing the expectation he had inadvertently set. "Ah, I see. Yes, Morghais, usually a weapon is given as a reward for completing a final test – this test of manhood Garel mentioned. It is a rite of passage, one that most boys do not face until they are older, and whiskers begin to appear on their chin and beneath their noses."

"What is the test?" she asked, a spark of determination in her eyes.

"You have observed the men, going out to hunt, returning each day with wild game to sustain us all?" Gorloys explained. "A boy coming of age would face such a test – to go out alone and return only when he has succeeded in the hunt."

"Then I will do the same," Morghais declared, her voice firm.

"No, Morghais," Gorloys countered, his voice heavy with a mix of frustration and fear for her safety. "Such a test is dangerous for a girl…or even a boy of your age," he added quickly, seeing her affronted expression.

Morghais's face hardened, her disappointment turning to controlled anger. "Then I do not want it. Keep your sword," she retorted, her pride wounded.

"Do not take that tone with me, girl!" Gorloys' voice rose, his own emotions getting the better of him.

Morghais, undeterred and boiling with a quiet rage, stood and faced him. Almost eye to eye, she still stared down at him with a smoldering intensity he recognized in himself. "Father, when we made our bargain, you said 'A sword must be earned, Kinsa-mowes.' Garel calls me Kinsa-mowes and not Penâvorow because of what you told him – that the title must be earned, not given as the Franks do. You would not give me a title I have not earned then. I will not now take a sword I have been given, a sword that I have not truly earned," she said, each word slicing through the air with the sharpness of a blade.

With that, she turned and stalked off, leaving Gorloys sitting in stunned silence, his own words thrown back at him with a clarity and conviction that left him grappling with a mix of admiration, surprise, and a simmering anger – at himself, at her, he couldn't quite tell.

They went to sleep in silence that night, Morghais making her own fire and camping alone. 'I have no time for this! Let her sulk,' Gorloys thought bitterly as he rolled over, trying to find sleep amidst his turmoil.

Morning came all too soon, and with it, panic at the realization that his daughter was gone, the spot where she had chosen to camp bereft of everything but the cold remains of a small fire. A frantic search of the camp and nearby terrain revealed only one certainty so far as Gorloys was concerned – that stubborn child had stolen away in the night, determined to prove herself, to earn the sword and title in her own right, leaving Gorloys to confront the day with a complicated blend of fear for her wellbeing, pride in her bravery, respect for her tenacity, and anger for her insolence.

CHAPTER 26

Divine Mandate

Marilyn trailed behind Uthyr, her boots echoing softly on the wooden planks leading away from the wharf at Bearda Market – a port now familiar to her in her travels. Though their initial arrival had been unremarked, Marilyn surmised that her enigmatic appearance in camouflage fatigues, black trench coat, and military boots drew some of the curious glances and hushed whispers that began as the two of them made their way along the road from the wharf toward the great house that was a favorite of Uthyr's. Even had she been dressed in the local attire though, Uthyr strutted along before her with all the pride and arrogance of a returning king.

As recognition began to kindle in the eyes of the onlookers, whispers became murmurs and gossip, passing from one clump of residents to another, racing ahead of them as a crowd began to form. Marilyn could hear 'King Uthyr' bandied about as often as references to her as 'Merlin the Sage' or 'Merlin the Healer', depending on the tale being told. Uthyr, ever the charismatic leader, acknowledged the growing adulation with gracious smiles and nods, his demeanor that of a king beloved by his people. Marilyn, for her part, was caught between amusement and a modest desire to blend into the background, unaccustomed as she was to such public attention.

Yet, as they progressed, she couldn't help but be swept up in the moment's energy, a smile tugging at her lips despite herself. 'The first paparazzi, indeed,' she mused silently, watching as Uthyr basked in the glow of the crowd's admiration. His charm was not just a veneer but a testament to the bond he shared with the people he ruled, a bond forged not just in admiration, but in trust as well.

Marilyn pondered the strangeness of it all, recalling a famous Shakespeare quote: 'Some are born great, some achieve greatness, and some have greatness thrust upon 'em.' As she watched him interact with the crowd, she had no doubt he had done much to achieve greatness. But she could not help feeling that Shakespeare's observations fell short of the reality of it all. Greatness, or at least fame, seemed to have as much to do with the admirers as the one being admired. 'The English monarchy still lives to this day,' she pondered, reflecting upon the state of affairs in her own time. 'Perhaps it's in our nature to seek out paragons…a beacon on a hill…a lighthouse that promises safety.'

By the time they reached the main doors of the great house, the crowd had burgeoned, their voices uniting in a tumultuous welcome. Unlike her previous visits, which held no such fanfare, rather than open the doors and proceed inside, this time Uthyr paused and turned to face the crowd with a flourish. His eyes sparkled mischievously as he surveyed them with a wide toothy grin. 'He looks like a politician about to kiss babies and hug grandmothers!' Marilyn thought, smiling.

Instead, with a dramatic gesture, he beckoned for silence, and the crowd complied, their anticipation palpable in the hushed air. "My friends," he began, his voice resonant with the gravity of the moment, yet underscored by an unmistakable warmth. As he spoke, his gaze lingered on each face, as if committing each one to memory. Then, with a showman's flair, he raised his arms, presenting Marilyn as if she were a prize beyond measure. "Merlin the Wise has returned to us!"

His declaration, bold and triumphant, reverberated through the market, a signal fire igniting the spirits of all who heard as a wave of cheers and applause erupted, leaving Marilyn aghast, reddening with embarrassment at the sudden attention. Thinking quicky, she flicked the power on to her shock staff and held it up, drawing gasps of awe as the crowd quieted.

"And now…" she began loudly, signaling the crowd to greater silence. "Now I will use my powers to swell your king's head even more!" she announced, waving the sparkling tip vaguely in Uthyr's direction. Gasps turned to guffaws and mirth-filled chuckles as Uthyr raised his hands in conciliatory mock surrender without missing a beat. "Perhaps later, my friends!" he quickly added. "For now, we have …larger… matters demanding Merlin's attention." His delayed emphasis on the word 'larger' elicited more laughter as he opened the doors for Marilyn to step inside and the crowd, sensing the end of the moment, began to disperse.

Stepping over the threshold into the great house once again, Marilyn was greeted by a scene markedly different from her prior nocturnal visits. The grandeur of the feast hall was the same, a sprawling testament to ancient craftsmanship with its hefty hewn timbers, yet the atmosphere was transformed by the morning light and the tasks of a new day.

Gone was the dim, firelit ambiance that had lent the hall a mystical air. In its stead, the room buzzed with the industry of morning chores, the air fresh and vibrant with the scent of spring rather than the woody smell of warmth protecting against a winter chill. The enormous fire pit, the centerpiece of her memories, now lay dormant, its ashes being carefully cleaned out by diligent hands preparing for the evening's cookfire.

As Marilyn's eyes adjusted to the environment, which was brighter than before though still more dimly lit than outside, she noticed a cook stationed at a hearth she hadn't observed before. The cook was busy transforming the remnants of the previous night's feast – roast and vegetables – into a hearty stew. The aroma, rich and inviting, spoke of practicality and the seamless transition from one meal to the next, a continuation of hospitality that knew no bounds.

The innkeeper, a portly figure whose presence commanded the space as much as it did before, was engaged in a task Marilyn had not witnessed on her last visit. With a long pole in hand, he moved with purpose, unhooking and lifting tarps that had been draped over the upper rafters. As each tarp was lifted, shafts of morning light spilled into the hall, chasing away shadows and filling the room with a warm, golden glow. The action not only brightened the space but invited in a breath of fresh air, stirring the banners and tapestries that adorned the walls.

The transformation was profound. Where evening had been a time for revelry and closeness, the morning brought openness and renewal. The beds along the walls, meant to offer rest to weary revelers, were now neatly made, waiting for the night to come again. The barrels of mead, fuel for each night's festivities, stood sentinel, their contents undisturbed in the calm of the morning.

As Marilyn and Uthyr moved deeper into the hall, she took in the sight of the men who saw and recognized their king. Many stood and greeted him as he came near or passed by, acknowledging joy for his safe return to them. Others assisted with the chores, lending their strength to the tasks at hand, while still others simply waved as they shared quiet conversations over bowls of steaming stew.

Occasionally, when Uthyr would stop to speak with a cluster of men, Marilyn would participate briefly and offhandedly ask after a man named Taran. Eventually, one of the respondents pointed to a pair of men sitting at a table across the room, eating stew and talking quietly with each other. "The one on the right. That is Taran," the man said. Uthyr thanked him and followed Marilyn over to their table.

Taran and his meal-time companion, engrossed in conversation as they were, had paid no attention to the king's arrival before. But now, as Marilyn stepped up to the table, the two stopped mid-conversation and looked up. Catching Uthyr's stern expression, the man sitting opposite Taran inquired "King Uthyr?"

For answer, Marilyn quietly reached into a pocket of her trench coat and fished the emblem she had stolen from an unconscious Jowan the day of her rescue, placing it on the table in front of Taran. "Go," Uthyr commanded of his companion, then turned to Taran while the man scrambled to depart. Once alone, Uthyr locked eyes with Taran. "I have a message for Jowan," he began quietly. "Tell him that he lives because Merlin bid me to be merciful and allow it," Uthyr stated with quiet menace. "Tell him also that his brother Taran lives to greet him, also at Merlin's behest. Do you understand?"

Taran picked up the emblem and nodded in fear. "You would do well to never return, Taran," Marilyn added as the man stood. With a quick final glance for the two of them, he ran for the door and was gone.

As Taran's form vanished through the doorway, Marilyn and Uthyr exchanged a glance, a brief interlude of shared satisfaction that needed no words. Uthyr, his eyes twinkling with mirthful light, leaned closer and inquired, "How do you suppose Jowan will take it when Taran tells him who sent the message?"

"And he learns that King Uthyr himself walked right into Tintagel, knocked him senseless, and escaped with his prisoner?" Marilyn inquired in return. "If he has any good sense at all, he and Taran will never tell another soul. Gorloys would have his head on a pike!"

Still staring at the exit, she pondered for a moment whether Jowan would indeed remain silent, as well as the potential consequences to Ygraine – and to Morgan – if he did not. It was she, after all, who had helped Uthyr gain entry to Tintagel. Sighing at the futility of such worries, she sat them aside and was about to turn away when a familiar face came through the door Taran had just exited.

Brother Dubric appeared, the telltale signs of travel upon him, yet carrying an air of determined purpose. At his side was another figure, clad in vestments that were the telltale sign of travelling clergy but unfamiliar to Marilyn. Eager to greet an old friend and intrigued by the newcomer, which frankly made her worry at the absence of Brother Cadfan, she moved toward them, momentarily setting aside her banter with Uthyr.

"Brother Dubric!" she exclaimed, her voice rich with both surprise and warmth. "It is good to behold a familiar face within these walls once more."

The light in Brother Dubric's eyes brightened at the sight of Merlin, his smile widening as though her presence was the very news he had hoped to encounter. "Merlin! God be praised! In His mercy, you are delivered as King Uthyr promised," he declared, his tone infused with genuine happiness.

"You have a new companion," she replied. "I hope this does not bode ill for Brother Cadfan?" she added, her voice laced with concern.

"Rest easy, Merlin!" Dubric replied with a smile. "He is well and still grows the flock in Glouvum. This is Brother Marcus. He arrived in Execaer from Rome with the first ship of spring."

He motioned toward the man accompanying him who stepped forward and bowed congenially. So far as Marilyn was concerned, he fulfilled every trope she could imagine of a native Roman – an olive-skinned man of average height, with curly, shoulder-length, black hair, and piercing eyes the color of amber, framed by a face sporting the shadow of a beard that was groomed regularly. He even had a prominent nose and jawline that lent a rugged handsomeness to his appearance rather than detracting from his looks.

"He is a new missionary to the land and does not yet know its languages, but speaks Latin," Dubric offered. "So, I am his interpreter and guide for now. When word of your captivity reached us, I insisted he accompany us. I wanted him to meet you."

"Ah," Marilyn replied, then turned to Brother Marcus and pressed her palms together as if in prayer, "In nomine Patris, et Filii, et Spiritus Sancti." She spoke the Latin catechism reverently, hoping to indicate that she shared in his beliefs and faith. "Regnet in aeternum," Marcus replied cordially, smiling.

Dubric's eyebrows rose. "You know the Latin tongue?" he inquired with shock, bringing a grin to Marilyn's face.

"I studied it for a time in my youth Dubric, but no," Marilyn replied. "I remember some words and phrases, and could perhaps follow bits of a conversation," she explained. "But I could not hold a conversation. I know what I said to Marcus. But what he said to me is a mystery."

"May he rule forever," Uthyr offered up, surprising them both as they looked at him. "Rome may no longer rule the land, but her influence lingers," he added, shrugging. "My father had me learn to both speak and write Latin."

Dubric shook his head in wonder. "You surprise me each day, King Uthyr." Then he turned to Marilyn. "Merlin, I last saw you leaving this very hall last Summer with Sinbad," he said. "Were you not leaving this realm, never to return? How is it that you came into Gorloys' captivity?"

"That is a tale to be told while sharing food and drink around a table; not standing about!" Uthyr proclaimed. "Come." He led them over to an unoccupied table near his men and flagged a servant down to bring some bowls of the stew simmering in the hearth and something to drink.

As they settled at the table, the rich aroma of hearty stew wafted through the air, a welcome contrast to Marilyn's recent fare of dried jerky and stale water. What caught her by surprise, however, was not the meal itself but the cold sweat beading on her wooden cup. Taking a sip, she expected the warmth of mead but was instead greeted by the crisp, refreshing taste of a chilled spiced cider. Delight sparkled in her eyes as she turned to Uthyr. "My drink is cold! How is this possible?" she marveled.

Uthyr grinned. "Now you know why this is my favorite town to visit," he offered. "The innkeeper, Ieuan, purchased an ancient quarry east of here. Not far. You could walk to it in an afternoon. In winter, he freezes blocks of ice and stows them there underground." He took a deep draught from his own cup, a gesture of satisfaction clear upon his face. "In the warmer months, he brings the ice to the inn, storing it in a cellar below, ensuring our drinks remain cool. Refreshing, is it not?"

Marilyn's smile, though touched by nostalgia for modern conveniences, showed her appreciation for the ingenuity before her. Her thoughts briefly wandered to the simple luxuries of her own time. 'What I wouldn't give for an ice-cold soda and a hot shower!' she mused. "Now that we all have some food in us," Dubric interrupted, pulling her from her reverie, "you were going to share with us how you came to be Gorloys' prisoner?"

Marilyn nodded, setting her cup down "As he had promised, Uthyr gave me a crew of men," she began, then stopped when she heard Dubric murmuring quietly to Marcus in Latin. Locking eyes with her, he blushed. "Forgive me, Merlin. I am translating so Marcus can understand the tale as well. Is that acceptable?" he pleaded.

"Yes, of course!" she replied, though now she knew she must be more mindful of the secrets she kept and what should remain in confidence. Marilyn began her tale again, this time her words measured and deliberate, weaving the story of her journey and capture, while being mindful of her audience.

"As he had promised, Uthyr gave me the crew of men and tools that I needed to free my…" she began again, then paused, looking at Marcus. "…ship…" she continued hesitantly, a term that seemed too mundane for the marvel it represented. "...from the cave where it was trapped. As you said before, Dubric, I left here with that crew the morning after Gorloys swore fealty to Uthyr, and arrived at the cave to find Sinbad and his men were still there."

Uthyr, with a hint of amusement coloring his tone, chimed in, "Yes, some of those men returned telling tales of a cave of glass shards and a window to another world with strange sights to behold. That I have seen it for myself makes the tales no less incredible. Still...your 'ship'?"

The question hung in the air, a playful challenge to the terminology Marilyn had chosen. Her annoyance was palpable yet tinged with the understanding of the necessity of Dubric's translations. "Dubric is repeating in Latin every word I say so that Brother Marcus can follow along. Do you have a better word?" she asked, her gaze fixed on Uthyr with a mix of irritation and jest.

Uthyr, sensing the moment's gravity and the potential for misunderstanding, raised his hands in a gesture of quiet concession, signaling his willingness to let the matter rest.

"Perhaps he is right, Brother Dubric. It would be better perhaps to describe the thing as my 'door between worlds' and let Brother Marcus make of it what he will," Marilyn mused, softening as she considered the implications of her words and the broader understanding they sought to convey.

Dubric's smile was one of admiration and slight bemusement at the unfolding conversation. "As you wish," he agreed. "He should not be surprised. He has already heard tales of you spread across the land. In fact, stories of your deeds reached all the way to Rome! You are why he is here!" he revealed, turning to Marcus to share this insight while Marilyn absorbed the weight of her reputation's reach.

When Dubric was done, and Marilyn saw a look of what she took to be comprehension cross Marcus's face, she continued. "In the end, we freed my door, but it was damaged," Marilyn continued, her tone shifting to one of reflection. "So, we traveled by ship to the port at Abona, where I thought to bring the door to Execaer until I could determine how to repair it. But Gorloys found me and took me captive in the wilderness between," Marilyn concluded.

Brother Marcus, now engrossed in the tale, spoke up in Latin shifting his gaze equally between Marilyn and Dubric. Dubric smiled and nodded, then translated. "He asks how the king helped you escape? Surely Gorloys would not simply give you up."

Before Marilyn could reply though, Uthyr interjected. "That part of the tale is for me to tell, Merlin!" he proclaimed, the mischievous grin of the boy she had met so long ago resurfacing on his face. Interest piqued, Marilyn nodded her consent quietly, then set back to listen as Uthyr continued the story.

Uthyr started by explaining Lynok's visit to Execaer, adding, "Even as a prisoner within the walls of Tintagel, Merlin sought allies and hatched plans!" As he shot a grin in her direction, she realized what he was doing. By pulling attention away from her and her imprisonment at Tintagel, he cunningly steered the conversation away from matters that were private for both of them.

Even so, he was careful not to mention Lynok by name referring to him only as a "mysterious messenger" in his tale. 'What a ham!' Marilyn thought amusedly as he stood to continue his oration. Yet, she had to concede his clever thinking. Though Taran was rooted out, there was no way to tell loyal subject from spy among the remaining occupants of the hall. Looking around, she saw more and more men becoming quiet and turning to listen. Uthyr was indeed a charismatic orator, drawing in others like moths to a flame.

As he continued his tale, detailing his journey to the lake upon Merlin's instructions, relayed to him by "the mysterious stranger", everyone was drawn in. Even the innkeeper had stopped in his duties to lend an ear, and the boys cleaning the ash from the central fire pit sat motionless and enraptured, ignoring their duties to listen to Uthyr's story. As he spoke, Marilyn listened intently, each word drawing a vivid picture in her mind.

"On Merlin's instructions, told to me by the mysterious stranger, I was led to a distant lake. The location was exactly as he described. As my men and I drew closer, we saw a light proceeding forth from beneath the surface at the edge of the lake. The shimmering glow of the water might have cast eerie shadows into the surrounding woods, but it was not so!"

Uthyr paused for effect, looking around at each face and allowing Dubric to finish translating, then continued. "For shadows could find no life there! As we drew nearer, the magic of the place began to move even the heavens above us, the day and night racing by in mere moments, the sun and moon changing places after a few paces only to change places again after a few paces more in a furious dance between day and night. The sky rushed between light and dark, giving shadows no chance for purchase."

Marilyn felt captivated and entranced by his story. Though she knew and understood the principle behind the time dilation effect he was describing, she had never experienced its effects within the confines of the cave. Listening to Uthyr – a man of this ancient time – spin his tale, she could easily see how magic and mystery wove itself into the fabric and culture of his world, his views and perspective colored by the limits of his knowledge and understanding.

"The faint light drew me in, shimmering just above the lake's surface. As I approached the water's edge, I saw what gave it life - a massive, round... stone." Marilyn noted the momentary pause as Uthyr decided on the right word to describe her artifact. Seemingly satisfied with his choice, he went on.

"Beneath the water's surface lay the massive stone, smooth as the finest glass, yet holding a vision of another world within its depths, blurred slightly by the ripples in the water." Uthyr grinned as gasps of awe emanated from several in the growing crowd. When Dubric finished translating for Marcus, even Marcus's eyes grew larger.

"I stepped from the edge of the shore and walked upon its smooth surface, looking down into that other world, bathed in the light that came from within. I stood atop it, struck to silence, wondering why I and the water around me should not fall into those depths like a stone into a well. Yet the stone remained solid beneath my feet! All the while, the heavens raced above me, the sun and moon chasing each other's tails, marking days in moments. A few of my men who were there later told me I looked like the Jesus god that Brother Dubric speaks of, walking on water!"

A few chuckles broke out as Uthyr paused, grinning at Brother Dubric who simply grinned back, not taking the bait at his jest. Nonetheless, the room hung on his every word as Uthyr continued and a glint of wonder shone in his eyes as he recounted the next part. "And then, through this window of stone, I saw her. A maiden with hair like woven silver and eyes as blue as a cloudless sky. A beauty I had never witnessed in all my days. She seemed as surprised to see me as I her!"

"I shall be sure to inform her of your unbridled admiration," Marilyn teased. Recognizing the description, her mind clearly picturing the woman from Uthyr's tale, she continued, a small smile touching her lips, a feeling of homesickness washing over her, "Her name is Naomi."

"Nimmue," Uthyr tried, struggling with the unfamiliar name. 'Close enough,' Marilyn thought, grinning at the irony of his difficulty with the pronunciation, given how common it was in modern England. "Thank you, Merlin," he said, blushing at her taunt. "Now hush and let me tell my tale," Uthyr chided, nonplussed.

"We could not hear each other, but Merlin, in his wisdom, had even prepared for that! I carried with me parchments, upon which were written his words, and I showed these to the lady in the lake. She understood and then signaled to me with her hands like this…"

Uthyr held his palm out before him in a gesture that Marilyn was fairly certain would span a universe of time and language barriers meaning wait, stop, or hold.

"I waited as the sun and moon traveled the sky repeatedly. Then, after what felt like ages, she returned bearing a sword and cloth with this sigil," Uthyr's voice was filled with reverence as he spoke of the moment. From within a pocket of his cloak, he withdrew a piece of cloth Marilyn immediately recognized – a crude duplicate of the Gryffindor scarf from her office back in the present.

Even Marilyn was shocked at the revelation. She had left simple clues in her message, alluding to use of a decoy to distract Gorloys and his men away from Tintagel. Though her instructions and plans had been laid out in detail to Lynok, who in turn shared them with Uthyr, she had no idea what her team in the present would do to assist with the sparse clues she had left. The scarf was a rather brilliant stroke, offering a symbol for men to easily recognize and follow. 'But where the hell did Naomi get a sword?' she wondered.

"The Lady of the Lake thrust the sword up through stone and water as though the surface upon which I stood was not even there, offering up the sword to be freed from the stone," Uthyr continued.

Marilyn's eyes widened at the title he gave Naomi – the Lady of the Lake, but then grew even more when she caught the translation of Uthyr's final words into Latin as Dubric repeated the story to Marcus; one phrase in particular: 'ex calce libera,' Latin for 'freed from the stone'. It reminded her suddenly of the time she was in, the part in history and legend she had chosen to play. She knew almost nothing of the Arthurian legends, but even she had, at some point in her life, heard of the legendary wizard named Merlin linked to an equally legendary sword.

Interrupting Uthyr's tale, unable to contain her excitement, " A fitting phrase you've used, Uthyr – 'freed from the stone'."

Uther acknowledged her repetition with a nod and replied "Yes. So?"

"In my land, all great swords of story and legend have a name," she replied. "The sword… Nimmue… gave you is perhaps one such sword." A sense of wonder at the legend she was in the middle of creating spread across her face. "Your turn of phrase is ironic in its Latin translation – 'ex calce libera' – since the sword you were given could very well be 'Excalibur' – a weapon whose reputation is legendary in my world – a sword of kings. The Lady of the Lake may have given you a great gift indeed! Where is it now?" she inquired.

Uthyr looked at her, a flicker of realization passing through his eyes. The weight of the sword's legacy, paired with its new name, seemed to settle on his shoulders. The room was hushed, the only sound being the sporadic pop from the embers beneath the kettle nearby and the soft whistle of wind in the rafters above. "Why, it is with King Uthyr, who even now is leading Gorloys on a merry chase across the countryside, his beastly sigil waving proudly as he wields the shining blade of Excalibur, bringing swift justice to the land!"

Uthyr danced around waving the bit of cloth over his head, pretending to ride a horse and slay invisible foes with an invisible sword in a mock play. The crowd burst into laughter at the jest, several of his men knowing the truth of his ruse, and all of them knowing the real Uthyr sat right there before them acting a fool. Marilyn noticed a few men slip quietly from the hall though, and she shared a glance with Uthyr who nodded in acknowledgement – more of Gorloys' spies.

As the laughter died down, Uthyr sat once again and finished his tale more quietly. "With Gorloys and his men leaving Tintagel all but abandoned to chase after the man he believes is me, I was able to sneak into Tintagel as a messenger and rescue Merlin without so much as a drop of blood spilled. A guard there woke up with a sore hear, but no worse."

Marcus nodded in appreciation as Dubric finished translating, then asked Dubric another question. Dubric's eyes sparkled with sudden inspiration as he turned to Marilyn and inquired, "This Nimmue. Is she a follower of Christ in your land, Merlin?"

Taken aback, Marilyn nodded, "Yes, I believe she is. I recall the room where she sleeps adorned with a crucifix." Although Dubric had also misspoken Naomi's name, using Uthyr's revision instead, she saw no reason to correct him now.

Brother Dubric's eyes gleamed with fervor. Standing tall, he addressed Uthyr. "Can you not see, Uthyr? The Lady of the Lake – this Nimmue – a chosen servant of the Almighty, has bestowed upon you a sword of legend. Such a gift should not be treated idly! It signals that you are chosen by divine decree, meant to rule these lands with the grace and will of God!"

Uthyr, usually so unshakeable, was taken aback. Marilyn hid a smirk behind her hand, completely surprised by Dubric's audacity. The young man would use anything and everything he could to convince Uthyr to become a Christian, including it seemed, framing even the most tenuous connection as a bedrock of proof in his faith.

Dubric, pressing his advantage, moved closer. "The crucifix Merlin mentioned is our symbol of the Christ! God has ordained your path, Uthyr. Even now, one in four of your men follow the faith! Look!" Turning to the room, Dubric announced loudly, "Followers of Christ, fear not and approach your king!"

Uthyr watch quietly as several men stood and came forward. Marilyn took a quick survey and decided Dubric was right. Though not quite one in four, he had certainly been busy in his missionary efforts among Uthyr's men.

"I would desire that all in your kingdom follow you in faith, King Uthyr!" Dubric continued. "They will if you take the lead! Embrace His guidance, and your reign will be just, marked by fortitude, honor, and unwavering compassion." He then placed a gentle hand upon Uthyr's shoulder and stared into his eyes earnestly. "Will you not pledge to govern with God's benevolence and grace, solidifying your reign's divine foundation?"

Uthyr hesitated, the weight of the decision pressing down upon him. He glanced around the room, taking in the faces of his men and of Marilyn, whom he knew also to be Christian. In that moment, she could see in his eyes that Dubric had finally broken through. She was about to bear witness to the birth of this land's first Christian king.

Finally, with a determined look, he nodded. "I will," he declared, his voice resonant and unwavering. "I pledge my allegiance to your Christ, and I will lead my kingdom under His watchful eye. Let all who follow me do the same!"

Dubric, sensing the magnitude of the moment, retrieved a small vial of holy water from within a pocket of his robes. "In the world of men, let every knee bend before you. But to wear the mantle of God's chosen ruler, you must kneel in humility and devotion before Him." Uthyr, understanding the gravity of the request, stood, then slowly began to kneel. The hall became a sanctuary, the ground beneath them transformed into sacred soil.

Dubric carefully uncorked the vial's cap. "Allow me to baptize you," he intoned, "and bestow upon you the blessing of the Father, the Son, and the Holy Spirit, that you might govern with the divine right and grace granted by our Lord." With gentle precision, he sprinkled the holy water onto Uthyr's forehead, marking him in the sign of the cross.

In that hallowed moment, Marilyn was enveloped by a profound swell of emotion. She was acutely aware of the ritual's deep significance, witnessing the very threads of history being woven before her eyes. This was no ordinary ceremony; it was the confluence of destiny, faith, and human resolve – a rare alignment where the currents of time seemed to pause, acknowledging the gravity of what was unfolding.

The room itself appeared to hold its breath as the weight of history's gaze settled upon them. The solemnity of Uthyr's vow, his voice resonating with a newfound resolve, seemed to resonate in the very stones of the hall. As Dubric consecrated this pledge with holy water, a tangible sense of gravitas rippled through the gathered men.

It was as though the very air had shifted, charged with an unspoken understanding of the duty, honor, and faith converging upon this singular moment. Those among the men who had already embraced the faith instinctively knelt, a unified gesture of solidarity and devotion to their king and his path forward. Their movement, silent yet powerful, was a beacon, compelling others to follow suit.

Witnessing their king kneel in humble submission to a higher calling, and seeing the first to echo his action, a wave of collective conviction swept through the room. One by one, moved by a shared sense of duty and reverence, even those who might have harbored doubts found themselves lowering onto their knees. It was as if Uthyr's personal act of faith ignited a chain reaction, binding the fate of all present to his fate, and to that of the land they served.

Marcus, standing beside Dubric, lent his voice to the chorus of blessings, his Latin refrains weaving through the air, lending an ancient solemnity to the proceedings. The language of the Roman Church, imbued with centuries of tradition and authority, underscored the monumental shift occurring within this room.

Marilyn, watching the scene unfold, felt the immense weight of the moment. It was a vivid testament to the enduring strength of belief, the capacity of leadership to inspire change, and the indomitable spirit of those who dared to follow where faith led. This wasn't merely the baptism of a king; it was the birth of a new era, one where duty, honor, faith, and devotion converged under the banner of a divinely sanctioned reign.

As every man in the room, including Ieuan the innkeeper, accepted the blessings, a profound sense of unity filled the space. Dubric's face, alight with satisfaction and triumph, reflected not just the personal victory of witnessing Uthyr's conversion, but the broader implication he knew was to come – that all under Uthyr's rule were now likely to follow their king in his newfound faith.

CHAPTER 27

Hunter

In the muted glow of the moon, Morghais moved with a stealth that belied her age, dismantling her makeshift camp with swift, quiet efficiency, her hands steady despite the adrenaline coursing through her veins. The fabric of her shelter whispered against the forest floor as she folded it away, her movements deliberate, born of a rebellion simmering within. The camp behind her, immersed in sleep's deep embrace, remained oblivious to her departure.

Her father's words from their last confrontation replayed in her mind, igniting a fierce blaze of defiance within her. 'Such a test is dangerous for a girl…' The memory of his voice, laced with authority and concern in equal measure, yet undercut by doubt, spurred her forward. 'I will not accept a sword I have not truly earned,' she reminded herself, her resolve hardening with each step into the darkness.

With her pack secure, Morghais moved like a shadow to the edge of camp where the dim light of the night sentry's fire mocked her efforts. Beyond them was the outer darkness, an unexplored wilderness beyond the security of the camp and the protection the sentries offered. Quelling a sudden stab of fear, she allowed her resentment and determination to steel her resolve as she fixed her gaze on the dense trees ahead.

Slipping past the watchful eyes of the camp's guards was easier than she had anticipated. Their attention was lax, their conversations a low murmur lost to the night, their vigilance dulled by the late hour. Once enveloped by the forest's dense embrace, Morghais paused, her breath a mist in the cool air, as she looked back at the dimly lit clearing to see if her movements had raised any alarm. But the night remained still, the camp oblivious to her departure. Satisfied, she turned once again to the forest.

Her every sense felt heightened, every sound amplified in the quiet of the night. The distant hoot of an owl, the rustle of small creatures scurrying in the underbrush – these were the sounds of her complicity, her allies in this moment of escape. She allowed herself a brief moment to feel the weight of her actions. She was alone now, propelled by a need to prove her worth beyond the confines of her father's expectations. The darkness around her felt alive, an ally in her quest for validation.

As the trees welcomed her into their midst, swallowing her form, Morghais couldn't help but smirk at the thought of her father's reaction come morning. 'Let him worry,' she mused, the edge of her anger sharpened by the anticipation of the challenge ahead. 'I will return with my prize, earned, not given.'

She picked her way quietly forward, the moon's light her only guide, as the campfire's glow dimmed behind her, but the fire within her burned brighter with each step. Ahead lay uncertainty, danger, and the wild – but also freedom, a chance to prove her mettle, to earn her sword and title not as a gift but as a right. The forest floor, littered with fallen leaves and pine needles, muffled her footsteps, conspiring with her in this act of silent rebellion.

For a time, Morghais delved deeper into the woods, occasionally looking back over her shoulder for signs of campfires until she could see none. She needed a light source and knew that if she lit a torch while able to see the fires back in her father's camp, then the keen eye of a camp sentry might spot her own fire and come investigate. So, even though she saw no campfires, she waited a little longer and travelled a little further before stopping. Satisfied, she stooped down to fish the torch and ember box she had prepared earlier that evening from her pack. Soon, she had a torch flickering softly in the night breeze and held it over her head as she went on to prevent night blindness.

She lost track of time as she trudged on, the light of her torch beating back the darkness to help her pick a sure-footed path forward until dawn teased the edges of the night. Even then, aware that she could not have travelled far, Morghais, veiled by the last shadows of darkness, pressed deeper into the wilderness, knowing that soon, her absence would be discovered. Fortunately, her journey thus far had been silent, a solitary passage marked only by the soft crush of leaf and twig beneath her boots. The dense canopy above whispered of a world awakening, yet her mind was on the distance she'd put between herself and the camp she'd fled.

Finally, as her torch guttered and it was clear that dawn had arrived and the torch was no longer needed, Morghais snuffed it out, then buried it in some dirt and covered the spot with pine needles. Feeling a mix of exhaustion and urgency, she decided to gauge her progress. With practiced agility, she found a sturdy tree, its branches a ladder to the vantage she sought. The climb was swift, each limb and bough familiar obstacles she'd conquered in countless days of play and exploration.

From atop the canopy, Morghais surveyed the awakening world – a vast expanse of green illuminated by the nascent light of dawn. She scanned the forest until she found what she was looking for, a scar in the vast lumpy sea of green and brown marking a clearing. Plumes of smoke billowed from the scar to dissipate just above the treetops as the morning breeze broke them apart, marking the location of her father's encampment. A brief swell of pride filled her at the thought of having traversed such a distance under the cover of night, potentially outpacing the risk of immediate pursuit.

However, the comfort derived from this observation was short-lived. As she nestled against the tree's sturdy trunk, seeking a moment's rest in her elevated sanctuary, the sound of voices pierced the stillness below. Two men from the camp, their figures small and indistinct among the trees but unmistakably part of her father's contingent, moved with purpose beneath her.

Their presence, so close and yet unaware of her perch above, served as a stark reminder of her vulnerability. The smoke that had seemed a marker of her success now mocked her; distance was a deceptive ally. The realization that she had not ventured as far from her father's reach as she had hoped washed over her, sharpening her resolve.

"Pen Gorloys is furious," one muttered, the concern in his voice painting a vivid picture of her father's wrath.

"The girl has spirit," the other replied, a note of admiration undercut with a dismissive chuckle. "But what does she hope to prove? That she can catch some fish? Snare a few rabbits?"

As the sounds of their conversation faded with them into the distance, Morghais's grip on the branch tightened, their words both a balm and a blade to her pride. "I do not hope for anything!" she muttered to herself acidly. 'I WILL prove my worth,' she vowed silently, her resolve crystallizing with their every word. But the two men had a point. If she returned to camp with fish or rabbits, no matter how many, then she will not have proven anything! She needed a prize whose worth was beyond reproach. 'But what?' she pondered.

Lost in thought, she nearly missed the subtle rustle of leaves below – a sound not of human trespass but of cautious, wild movement. Her eyes, trained to spot the slightest anomaly, caught the flicker of movement at the forest's edge. There, emerging from the shadows, was the figure of a young wolf. Its coat, a blend of grays and browns, made it almost invisible against the forest floor, save for the cautious grace with which it moved.

As Morghais watched the young wolf navigate the underbrush, its youthful curiosity mirrored in its cautious steps. Like her, it seemed to be hunting, perhaps even for the first time alone. Not yet fully grown but beyond the helplessness of a pup, the wolf posed no real threat to her. It seemed more inclined to avoid her than to attack, its survival instincts prioritizing discretion over confrontation.

The wolf paused, lifting its nose to the air. It sampled the scents carried by the breeze – first in the direction the men had taken, then down an alternate path. Its decision-making process was deliberate, weighing options with the seriousness of a seasoned hunter. Eventually, it chose the path leading away from both the men and Morghais's father's camp, slipping silently into the shadows of the forest.

Morghais observed the young wolf's departure, noting the intelligence and caution in its actions. It moved with a purposeful grace that spoke of innate wildness and a keen understanding of the world it inhabited. The way it had analyzed its options and chosen its path resonated with her, a silent echo of her own choices made under the cover of the previous night.

The idea to follow the wolf sprang from a place of instinct and intuition. This young hunter, on its quest, might unwittingly guide her to the prize she sought – a testament to her worth that would silence any doubts. Morghais set off after the wolf, her movements calculated and silent, a shadow amongst the foliage.

She descended from her perch in the tree and followed down the trail the wolf had taken as quickly and silently as she could. Using the skills her father had taught her these past weeks to track game on the run, she followed the wolf, keeping her distance yet never losing sight, or when she did, reading the wilderness for the telltale signs of its passage, until she spotted it once again.

As their journey continued, Morghais found herself venturing into unfamiliar territory. The wolf led her away from the well-trodden paths and into areas of the forest marked by the wild and unknown. When the wolf finally halted, it was in a clearing that had all the signs of an animal den. The evidence of a wild boar was unmistakable here – the deep imprints of hooves in the earth, the scoring on tree bark, the remnants of foraging. This was no simple prey, but a beast to challenge the skills of any hunter! This was what she had been searching for, the challenge that would prove her mettle.

In that moment, Morghais felt a profound connection to the young wolf. It was more than a silent acknowledgment of their shared journey. It was a realization that, for a time, she had bonded with nature itself and, in so doing, discovered a new way to harness the wilderness - a method discovered on her own and apart from her father's teachings. Feeling a profound sense that the forest had given up a secret for her alone, she vowed to keep it a secret, to remain hers alone. She watched as the young wolf moved away, perhaps sensing her presence or perhaps simply deciding that the prey it had found would pose too great a challenge. But not so for Morghais. She resolved as she watched it scurry away through the undergrowth, that what had deterred the wolf would not deter her.

She reached edge of the clearing with wary steps. Mindful of her lack of defenses should the boar unexpectedly appear, she withdrew her knife from its holster, but stalked between trees she could swiftly climb if needed. She skirted the edge of the small clearing, examining the wallow in its midst - a mud-lined puddle of black still water that mirrored the sky peeking through the encroaching forest canopy overhead. Tracks were everywhere in the mud and grime. Seeing bark stripped away from trees all around the clearing - places where the boar had rubbed its tusks to mark its territory, she decided that, while it must be out foraging or seeking a mate, it would be back.

Having completed her survey of the clearing and with the adrenaline of the night's events gradually fading, Morghais recognized the toll exerted on her body. It was still mid-morning, and she had been propelled by sheer determination since the night before. She understood that rest was crucial if she was to face the boar effectively.

She found an ideal spot for rest not too far up – a convergence of branches forming a natural nook within the tree. It was perfectly positioned: high enough to escape notice, but low enough that the branches were broad and robust, offering a semblance of shelter. Carefully, she climbed up, weaving herself into this makeshift cradle. To prevent any chance of falling during her sleep, Morghais took the leather strap from her pack, securely tying her arm to one of the sturdier branches. She positioned her pack under her head as a makeshift pillow, its contents soft enough to cushion her, yet firm enough to support.

Finally settled, exhaustion enveloped her swiftly in this precarious nest. Despite the forest's symphony and the shade that the forest's canopy offered from the mid-day sun, Morghais slipped into a deep, fitful sleep, her body and mind yielding to the pressing need for rest.

Pulled from dreams where she chased rabbits through fields ablaze with flowers, Morghais ran alongside a yipping young wolf, their joy shared in the freedom of the hunt. At times, she felt herself become the wolf, moving with a grace and wildness that felt as natural as breathing. But the dream shifted, the playful yips turning to a low growl, resonating with a deep, primal warning.

The growl blended into a physical sensation – a vibration and a subtle knocking that traveled up the tree to where she lay. As the borders between dream and wakefulness blurred, Morghais slowly surfaced to consciousness, the growl transforming into the guttural oinking and snorting of the boar below. Peering through the leaves, her heart quickened as she spotted the boar rubbing its tusks against her tree, the force sending tremors through her makeshift bed.

She remembered her father's words about the keen sense of smell boars possess, realizing the boar was likely marking its territory, agitated by her scent yet unaware of her exact location. With every snort and rub against the tree, the boar declared its dominion, even as Morghais watched from above, a silent intruder to its territory.

As the boar ceased its agitated marking, it sauntered towards the center of the clearing, its broad-shouldered form, still lean from the sparse offerings of winter, easing into the mud of the wallow. The sight of it, momentarily at peace in its natural habitat, offered Morghais a contrast to the tense vigil she had kept. Despite the danger below, a sense of calm enveloped her as she watched, her mind turning over possibilities.

Quietly, she delved into her pack, pulling out a piece of dried meat. As she chewed thoughtfully, her gaze never left the boar. She had initially considered setting a snare, but quickly dismissed the idea. The boar was too strong, too fierce, and she lacked the weight and strength to construct a trap it couldn't easily destroy.

Finishing her meager meal, she tossed the remnants idly towards a gap between two trees on the clearing's fringe. The boar's reaction was immediate and revealing. Its head snapped up, nostrils flaring as it caught the scent. With surprising speed, it charged, leaping over a fallen log that lay in its path between the two trees.

Moments later, the boar returned, satisfied that its territory remained defended. Morghais let go a breath she hadn't realized she was holding. Never had she suspected such a display of speed, power, and agility from the lumbering beast that even now resumed its wallowing. But in witnessing it, clarity dawned with the force of revelation. She couldn't outmuscle the boar, but she could outwit it. That leap over the log, a moment of airborne vulnerability, illuminated her strategy. No need for ropes and weights; leverage and timing would harness the boar's momentum against it.

Morghais chose her ambush spot with care, positioning herself behind the sturdy log the boar had leapt over the day before. Nestled between two trees in a break in the dense thicket, the clearing funneled the boar toward her chosen path – a narrow trail from which her only escape, should her plans fail, lie in a crude vine rope dangling from one of the trees, providing a quick escape to its lower branches. Satisfied with her quick survey, she placed two sharpened branches – too thick to be called spears – behind the log, their tips pointed forward, ready for use.

Hours passed as she waited, the stillness of the forest a stark contrast to the turmoil of anticipation churning within her. The golden light filtering through the canopy gradually dimmed as late afternoon settled in, casting the wallow ahead in muted hues. Though her faith in her plan never wavered, the lulling quiet of the scene gnawed at her patience as she began to worry that the boar might not return before dusk. But as resignation of the inevitable began to take root, the underbrush stirred at the edge of the clearing, and the boar emerged, its massive form materializing like a shadow, returning to claim its domain.

Morghais's heart leapt – now facing it on the ground, the boar appeared even larger than it had from the canopy the day before, easily half again her own weight. If she succeeded in this hunt, a new struggle would await her in cleaning, dressing, and transporting the carcass. If she failed, though, none of that would matter.

This was the moment for which her entire day had been poised. She took a deep, calming breath to steady her nerves, then clacked the spear-like branches together loudly to draw the boar's attention, the sharp sound slicing through the ambient forest noise. As its head swiveled toward the noise, she rustled a nearby branch violently and stood, ensuring her presence was unmistakable – a direct challenge to provoke its charge.

The boar's gaze snapped toward her, and with a guttural snort, it charged. Morghais crouched behind the log but remained visible to keep the beast focused on her presence. The ground trembled as the boar thundered forward, eyes burning with primal fury, fixed on the intruder behind the log.

Time seemed to slow, and her muscles coiled tight as the boar barreled closer, tusks aimed to gore. In the final moment, as the boar leapt the log, Morghais shifted her spear-like branches up and into the beast's path. The boar's momentum transformed into a lethal trajectory, driving one of the weapons into its neck and the other deep into its chest. Morghais ducked with a scream, feeling the rush of air and hearing the boar's wild squeal as it sailed over her, impaled. Like palisade stakes, the sharpened branches, anchored by the weight of the beast, dug their butts into the ground, arcing its entire body overhead mere inches from her. The boar crashed to the ground with a heavy thud, roaring in pain and fury.

Terror gripped her as the boar thrashed wildly. She scrambled back on her heels and elbows, breathless, barely aware she'd fallen onto her back. Unable to take her eyes off the enraged creature, her hands somehow found the vine she'd placed earlier. Frantically pulling herself up, she sat on the lowest limb and watched as the boar roared in pain and frustration.

Though the spear in its neck had come free, leaving a gaping wound from which blood freely flowed, the one piercing its chest had broken, lodging itself deeply in the beast's flesh. But with each futile attempt to pull the broken shaft free, the boar only drove the splinter deeper. Blood leaked steadily from its wounds as a bloody froth formed along its jowls, spewing crimson droplets everywhere with its exceedingly labored breaths.

Finally, realizing the end was near, it gave up and stumbled ungraciously back over the log, seeking the final comfort of its wallow. As it moved away, Morghais cautiously lowered herself from the tree limb and picked up the still intact spear, her eyes never leaving the beast even as it collapsed in the mud just shy of its wallow.

Recalling her father's admonishment to kill swiftly so that the animal did not suffer, she stepped gingerly toward the beast, then stabbed at its belly with the spear as hard as she could. Too weak now to stand and fight, it squealed weakly in pain and terror, its eyes rolling toward her. Tears streamed down her face as Morghais whispered desperate apologies, her voice breaking into wailing sobs as each thrust filled her with a mixture of horror and guilt, mortified at the feeling of how easily the point slid into living flesh, and agonizing at the beast's feeble cries. Then she remembered another thing her father said about gut wounds and quickly dropped the spear to pull out her belt knife. As she drew a deep gash across the creature's throat, blood poured from the wound, silencing the boar's cries as it gave a final shudder and lay still.

For a long moment, the forest seemed frozen in time, the echo of the struggle still hanging in the air. Slowly, Morghais rose, her breath coming in ragged gasps, tears still slipping down her cheeks. Exhausted, yet filled with exhilaration, confronting the reality of what she had just achieved. The boar lay still, the fight gone from its body, and in that instant, Morghais knew she had proven her worth – not to her father, but to herself.

CHAPTER 28

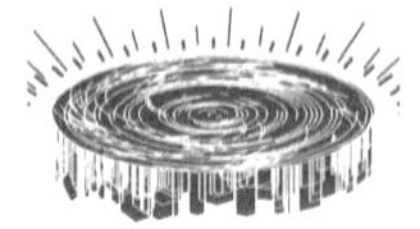

Keys to the Future

"Here's the coffee you wanted, Flip." Takashi's voice cut through the cavern's quiet like a sudden crack of thunder, pulling Philip away from his intense watch over the artifact, anxious for any sign, any news of his wife-to-be. Absorbed in his vigil, Philip hadn't heard him approach and was startled by the interruption, having completely forgotten about the request. He shook his head to clear it, taking the Styrofoam cup from Takashi's outstretched hand.

'God bless him,' Philip thought but chided aloud with a half-smile, "Don't sneak up on a man like that!"

"She'll be alright," Takashi reassured, reading Philip's furrowed brow as he accepted the coffee. "The boss is tough as nails, Flip. And that fellow Uthyr looked like a man who could handle trouble."

"Thanks, Tak," Philip replied, taking a cautious sip. "Apparently, Naomi's handed off her crush on Sinbad to Ayesha. She's set her sights on Uthyr now."

Takashi chuckled, his light-hearted banter cutting through the tension. "As if either of them could land one of those men. They're just trying to keep the mood light."

Philip nodded, grateful for the momentary distraction. "Still, look at it, Tak," he gestured toward the artifact. Now that the thing had been turned over in the past, smooth side down, and the jagged protrusions of its crystalline belly faced the sky, small fish and water bugs flitted through the shallow water where it remained submerged, dancing about through the glass-like maze where algae and mud had begun to collect in the crevices, an idyllic display that belied the frenetic pace of the world beyond. "Every minute we stand here, three days pass over there. Shouldn't we have heard something by now?"

"Flip, we don't know exactly what's happening on her end," Takashi said, a soothing tone in his voice. "But if the lieutenant colonel is really the inspiration for the stories of Merlin, then trust me, her story doesn't end here. She will be back." He glanced at his watch. "You've been here less than ten minutes," he continued. "And at least some of that time was spent with Uthyr getting beyond the influence of the time dilation."

Philip nodded gratefully. What Takashi said made perfect sense, but it did little to quell his own worries. "How are Doctor Okun and Avery doing with the translation?" he asked, hoping to distract himself from his gnawing anxiety.

"Um, about that," Takashi hesitated, then quickly added at Philip's alarmed look, "It's not bad news!"

He walked over to the workstation and started typing. The mesmerizing screen saver that Ayesha had set earlier was replaced by icons of pages from the alien notebook. Selecting one, a page filled with a diagram and alien script appeared.

"See this diagram here?" Takashi asked rhetorically. It depicted a figure eight lying on its side, the infinity symbol, but with a distinctive alteration. A vertical line cut through each loop precisely in its center. Between these lines, the infinity symbol was rendered with a solid, assertive stroke, suggesting a specific area of function or importance. But outside the lines, the loops were drawn more faintly in a dashed stroke, giving the impression of virtually closed loops in some technical diagram. "We think this represents an additional part or component – something made of the same material as the artifact. Doctor Okun's still working on the translation, but Avery already suspects what it is."

"Well?" Philip pressed, eager for more.

"As you know, the beam keeping the portal open is proton-based, not like a laser that uses light," Takashi explained. "A beam of protons can't be diverted with a mirror – at least not any kind of mirror we know how to make. You usually need a strong magnetic field to influence it."

Philip stared impatiently and swept his hand around vaguely toward all the technology surrounding them. The collider did that very thing.

"Right. Sorry, Flip," Takashi replied abashed. "But you can also use a technique called crystal channeling to deflect the beam." He pointed to the huge device beside the workstation currently deflecting the collider's beam into the artifact's surface. "We think the artifact uses crystal channeling, but on a much more advanced scale than we are capable of achieving."

Realization began to dawn on Philip as he stared at the diagram. "I think I get what Avery is thinking," he said, tracing his finger around the figure eight. "It's some sort of parabolic crystal channeling device that forms a closed loop. Sort of like completing a circuit."

"Exactly," Takashi confirmed. "Not a mirror, but the next best thing. He thinks its purpose is to redirect the beam back through the artifact from the other side. If he's right, it might just be the key to getting the lieutenant colonel back home."

Philip's growing excitement was suddenly disrupted by a loud banging from the control room window overlooking the cavern and catwalk, drawing the attention of both men. Naomi stood at the window, pointing to the nearby workstation, and cupping her ears.

Philip's hands trembled with an anxious energy as he fumbled with his earpiece, nearly dropping it in his haste. His heart pounded in his chest, each beat echoing his mounting apprehension. Beside him, Takashi donned his earpiece with a steadier grip, eyes locked on the water-laden view on the other side of the artifact that now served as their only lifeline to Marilyn.

The moment his earpiece was secure, Philip was met with an auditory enigma; Marilyn's voice stretched and distorted as if time itself was struggling to relay her words through the vast distance. It started as an elongated groan, "Lllllloooooo-ttt-eh-eh-eh-eh-eh-nnnnn-aaaa-nnnn-ttt...," slowly gaining pace, a haunting chorus that seemed to drag like an old jukebox that had lost power and was powering back up in painfully slow motion.

Philip's instinct was to respond immediately. "Mare! Can you hear me? Over," he blurted into the headset. However, Naomi's voice intercepted, her tone firm yet controlled. "She's close but still too far away, sir. Whatever you say now, it'll sound like chipmunk squeaks to her. Give her a moment to get closer."

Restless, Philip started pacing along the catwalk in front of the artifact, the distorted call sign of his fiancée a constant presence in his ear. "Lllllieeeeeu-ten-nnn-an-nttt c-ol-o-nelll... Ma-ri-lyynnn Morrr-gannnn..." The sounds were coalescing, merging into a more recognizable pattern, still not right but getting closer with each torturous second.

"Running comms through Doppler processing, Flip. Try now," Naomi's voice came again.

The words began to take proper shape, a little sluggish but understandable, "...Marilyn Morgan, United States Air Force, reporting in. Do you read me? Over."

"We read you, Mare! Over. Get closer to the artifact!" Philip urged, gripping the catwalk's guard rail as if by sheer will, he could pull her voice into perfect clarity.

Marilyn's voice crackled through the headset, relief palpable in her tone. "Flip? Oh, thank God! We're coming up on it now. Let the team know I am okay."

A wave of cheers and messages of welcome erupted over the comms from the team, their collective relief echoing through the cavernous space.

"Time has washed away the markers I could use to find the artifact. I know we're close, but I need a beacon, Flip."

"We?" Philip queried, a note of surprise in his voice.

"Explanations later, Flip. Beacon now," Marilyn insisted urgently.

"Hold on, Mare," Philip responded, signaling to Takashi. Together, they quickly maneuvered the big screen back in front of the portal, switching it to a plain white screen to serve as a makeshift beacon.

"Spotted! Thank you, Flip. It's about 20 yards away," Marilyn's voice came through more clearly now. "Listen, Uthyr sent a small army to protect me this time while we retrieve the artifact. While I have some men fish it out of the water, I need you to send people down to the mess hall and bring back as much raw fruit as you can find – crates of it if they have it. And send someone to the commissary to buy all the candy bars and protein bars you can find."

Philip furrowed his brow, concern edging his voice. "Okay, now you have me worried, Mare. Why all the food?"

Marilyn chuckled, a weary sound tinged with relief. "I made these men accompany me here straight away, without stopping to hunt or forage. We've been traveling for two days, and I promised them food to delight their senses when we arrived. And frankly, right now, I'd kill for a banana…or a Snickers® bar!"

Marilyn's horse plodded along the cart path, slowing as the village of Glestinga came into view to the north – a beacon atop a hill amidst the surrounding marshlands. The world just yards beyond the entourage of men following her began to accelerate, like an old film reel played too fast.

The sky above soon raced by, casting shifting shadows that danced across the landscape in a slow strobe of light and dark, every ten seconds morphing the world into night and back into day. Distant trees shivered violently yet lost no leaves, their branches a blur of motion. In a nearby clearing, wildflowers bloomed and wilted in rapid succession, their life cycles exploding like little fireworks of fleeting glory. Uthyr had described many of these phenomena when recounting his tale of visiting the artifact on her behalf. So, she knew to expect them, yet found that no words could truly do justice to experiencing it firsthand.

Amidst this disorienting display, Marilyn heard the worried murmurs of the men and the restless nickering of horses. She scanned her surroundings, searching for the beacon of light that marked the window to her world. The alternating light made it difficult to focus, but she persisted, knowing what she needed to find. Finally spotting it, she beckoned the men to follow.

Vibrant light shimmered through ripples where the artifact lay immersed in shallow water, casting a show of dancing light through the surrounding trees. Knowing how awed she felt, she imagined the fear and anxiety the men around her must be experiencing. She could do nothing to alter the world around her, but she could at least diminish the watery spectacle before her. "Okay, Flip, you can cut the light show now," she spoke clearly into the headset, her tone balancing command and diplomacy.

Once the unnatural light subsided, Marilyn addressed the group of warriors gathered around her, their faces etched with curiosity and caution. "The large round stone there in the water is what we came to retrieve," she stated plainly, pointing towards the artifact submerged just offshore.

She quickly singled out six of the warriors. "You three, wade in from the left," she directed, pointing to the first group. Turning to the others, she commanded, "And you three from the right."

One of the men hesitated, his eyes measuring the artifact's significant size. "But Merlin, surely we will need more men? The size of it..."

Marilyn cut him off, her voice firm yet reassuring, "This is no ordinary stone. It weighs much less than it appears." Trusting in her assurance, the men followed her instructions and waded into the water. As they positioned themselves around the artifact and prepared to lift, their initial skepticism turned to astonishment. The artifact, despite its formidable appearance, was indeed deceptively light. They exchanged surprised glances as they easily lifted it out of the water, their previous doubts washed away by the unexpected ease of their task.

Meanwhile, over the headset, Marilyn listened as Philip coordinated the team's movements from the cavern's catwalk. He relayed instructions for Naomi to call Doctor Bennett to the catwalk before she and Ayesha headed to the mess hall for supplies. Amidst these directives, Takashi's voice cut through, eager and clear, "Flip, I'll run to the commissary and get those candy bars the boss wanted."

As one, Marilyn and Philip both responded with grateful synchronicity, "Thanks, Tak!" Their voices overlapped, a small echo of unity across the vast distance. Marilyn then added, with a note of earnestness in her voice, "And remember the Snickers® bars, Tak. Avery's estimate is holding – three days pass here for every minute you experience. We need to stay efficient and on task. Those bars are not just a treat; they're a quick source of energy for us while we move."

"Understood, ma'am. I'll grab those first," Takashi replied, his tone matching the seriousness of their situation. "Anything else?"

"Yes, juice boxes if they have them," Marilyn said, thinking ahead. "But only if you can get a few dozen."

"You got it!" Takashi confirmed before cutting his comms.

As the men emerged from the water, Marilyn directed them to lean the artifact on its side against the cart they had brought for transport. As they carried it toward the cart, Philip's voice came through the headset, marked by suspicion and worry. "Mare, you said Uthyr sent men to protect you. Why would you need their protection? What's going on?" he pressed, seeking clarity amid his concerns.

Keeping her eyes on the men as they positioned the artifact against the cart, Marilyn responded, her voice revealing the stress of watching the sky flicker the days by. "Given the circumstances, we don't have time for more than a brief explanation, Flip. But suffice to say that I got caught up in a political struggle between two factions," she explained, her tone measured. "Uthyr promised aid in extracting the artifact from the sea cave if I helped him subdue his rival, Gorloys. After our success, Gorloys set spies on me and eventually captured me in the wilderness. The men are here to prevent that from happening again."

While she was explaining, Doctor Bennett arrived at the workstation in the cavern. His expression turned to one of deep concern as he took in Marilyn's appearance through the portal. "Marilyn, it's good to see you," he started, his voice filled with warmth yet tinged with worry. "How are you feeling? You look... well, it's been quite a time for you, hasn't it?"

Marilyn managed a small smile, appreciating his gentle approach. "I'm holding up, Doctor Bennett. Really, I'm fine," she reassured him, though the quick pace of her response betrayed her tension.

His brow furrowed slightly, reflecting his years of medical experience. "You've been through a lot recently. I just want to make sure you're truly okay," he continued, his voice filled with genuine concern. "It is not at all uncommon for first-time mothers to experience difficulties under far less stressful conditions than yours –"

Before Doctor Bennett could continue, Philip, struck by the sudden reminder, blurted out, "Oh my God, I am such an idiot!" Smacking his forehead, he exclaimed, "Mare, I'm sorry! It's only been a month over here!" His words tumbled out in a rush, "I barely even got used to the idea... What, Mare?"

Revealing the amused blush she had been hiding with the back of her hand, Marilyn chortled softly, shaking her head at the two of them. "Our daughter... Morgan... is fine!" she announced, her voice firm yet filled with a warmth that hadn't been there moments before.

Both men's emotions flipped from somberness to surprise, then quickly to elation. A flurry of questions followed, the two men speaking over each other in their shock and excitement. "Has it really been that long? When was she born? Where is she?"

"Both of you, calm down," Marilyn interjected, raising her hands for emphasis. "I'll explain as much as I can." Just then, through the fragmented visage presented by the artifact, she noticed men marching down the catwalk, arms laden with bags and boxes of fruits and vegetables. "But first things first. Let's get the men with me fed and resupplied," she said, nodding toward the approaching figures to draw attention to them.

Marilyn watched, wary of the days passing around them, as the next ten minutes were filled with a flurry of activity. The men around her, initially fearful and timid of the parcels mysteriously emerging through the crystalline stone, soon settled into an uneasy rhythm. Accepting the boxes and bags that protruded from the forest of broken shards, each of them continued to watch, wary of the shattered visage of the world from which the food came.

As they worked, Marilyn showed Philip a Polaroid she had snapped of their little girl lying swaddled in a crib in Magra's apartment. They shared an unspoken but tender moment, a brief escape from the chaos of their current predicament that was soon interrupted by the return of the rest of the team, including Avery, who had been briefed on Marilyn's safe return. With Takashi and Avery both present, conversation quickly shifted to the artifact and the insights gleaned from the alien notes.

Marilyn took a candy bar from the bag Takashi had tossed through the portal, nodding gratefully in his direction. Peeling off the wrapper with practiced ease, she tore off a bite of the chocolate-covered, nutty caramel confection and closed her eyes, relishing the moment. "Been a while?" came Takashi's voice over the comms, a smirk audible in his tone.

"Right now? Better than sex, Tak," she replied seriously, drawing laughter from several of the crew and an exclamation of "Preach!" from Ayesha. "Hang on a moment. Now that the foodstuffs are here, I want to turn this thing around so I can see you clearly," she told her team through the headset, then walked over to the gathering of warriors.

Instructing a couple of men to adjust the artifact for a clear view, she had them turn it around, revealing the lab clearly through its flat surface. The men around her marveled at the seamless window into another world, pointing and murmuring in awe. To redirect their attention and lessen their apprehension, she demonstrated how to peel a banana and an orange, revealing the bright, juicy interiors. She then carefully unwrapped a chocolate bar, breaking it into squares. Handing them out, she watched the men's faces light up with delight as they tasted chocolate for the first time, their expressions filled with wonder at the bittersweet, rich flavors.

Once the initial excitement had settled and the men were contentedly munching on their new treats, Marilyn returned to the artifact. She resumed her conversation with the team, her gaze now fixed on the clear diagram displayed on the big screen. The detailed illustration of the alien technology came into sharp focus.

"Goddammit," Marilyn exclaimed with a sigh, her frustration evident as she listened to their descriptions. "What?" Philip inquired, his alarm rising in response to her tone.

"The figure you are describing there – I have it...had it...It was in my possession. But I hid it to keep it from being stolen," Marilyn replied, her voice tinged with a mix of regret and resolve. "I can get it back. But it's going to take a while."

"Well, that's not necessarily a bad thing, lieutenant colonel," Avery interjected. "Even if we had it – and the fact that you know what it is and where to get it is a blessing in itself, by the way – even if we had it, we don't yet know how to make use of it."

"The notes don't tell you that?" Marilyn inquired, her eyebrows arching in concern.

"I'm sure they do," Avery replied. "But we've only had a couple of weeks plus to work on the translation when the artifact portal was closed. Math may be a universal language, but it still took us a week just to figure out that these aliens did math in base eight! I am guessing they had eight fingers rather than ten."

Marilyn nodded, her mind racing as she tried to recall memories of the alien corpses from the sea cave. Turning back to Philip, she said, "I'll need at least a month, maybe more, to move the artifact to a safe location, secure the chalice, and retrieve Morgan. Can you figure it out in that time?"

"We'll make it happen, Mare. We are going to get you home," Philip replied, his voice firm, projecting confidence. Yet, despite his reassuring words, Marilyn could see the subtle worry in his eyes as he cast quick, concerned glances at Avery.

Unaware of Philip's silent exchange with Marilyn, Avery chimed in with his own perspective, emphasizing the challenge they faced. "Doctor Okun is brilliant, ma'am. But we're still struggling to make sense of the math, much less their language. It's like showing differential equations homework written in some ancient language to a fifth-grader. We see structures and patterns that we will eventually figure out, but we need at least... two months... to get anywhere meaningful."

Marilyn noted the hesitation in Avery's voice, recognizing his attempt at optimism while understanding he wanted more time. Anxious to get herself and her new baby back home to the modern world, she sighed, her gaze shifting between Philip and Avery. Her shoulders slumped slightly as she accepted the timeline with resigned patience. "Alright, we'll turn off the artifact for two months. That should give both sides enough time to sort things out. Let's plan to reestablish contact then."

As the team nodded in agreement and began to disperse, Philip lingered, his expression serious. "Mare, can we talk a moment? Just you and me," he asked, motioning for the others to give them some space.

Naomi piped in before cutting her comms, "Twenty-one minutes and counting, boss. Just be aware…"

Once they were alone, Philip's concern was palpable. "Mare… You are my world," he began, then shook his head. "You...and our new baby...are my world. If...if we can't get you back..." His voice faltered, laden with worry.

Marilyn, perceiving the direction of Philip's thoughts even before he finished speaking, felt a surge of both anger and fear. While she cherished his devotion, she recognized in his words the shadow of Don Quixote, a man lost in heroic fantasies that bore no resemblance to their harsh realities. This misguided gallantry was not just a distraction; it was a dangerous dance along the edge of surrender that stirred in her a visceral ire.

"How dare you even think like that, Philip!" she snapped sharply, her voice rising with both anger and fear. Philip tried to interject, his face registering surprise at her intensity, but Marilyn overrode him. "You will not fail us! You cannot! I refuse to raise our child in this barbaric world! You must find the answers, by God! You have no idea what it's like here! Everywhere I turn, death is waiting in one form or another! And if the people don't kill you, then disease, famine, and bad dental hygiene are waiting in line!"

Philip's initial shock at Marilyn's outburst morphed into a matching intensity. "Do you think this has been any easier for me? I'm a worrier, Mare! You know that!" he retorted, his frustration boiling over. He gripped the catwalk's railing, his knuckles whitening as he stared intensely at her through the short space between them that spanned the vastness of time and space. "I have hardly slept, worrying about you, feeling powerless to do anything more than send you care packages through this goddamn portal!" he continued as he waved a dismissive hand toward the artifact and the world she inhabited on the other side. "And now we have a baby to consider!" he added.

Somewhat drained after her initial outburst, but still seething, Marilyn shot back, "I can take care of Morgan!" Suddenly realizing the callousness of her retort, she wished with all her heart she could take the words back, seeing the sudden shock and hurt in his eyes. "Philip, I am sorry," she said, sighing. "But you mustn't give up! You can't! Please!"

She watched him as he closed his eyes and took a deep, calming breath. He let go of the catwalk railing, and began to pace briefly, his voice thick with emotion. "When I first joined the Army, I served my first tour in Kandahar with a lot of guys who watched their babies grow up in pictures. Their wives, despite love and good intentions, grew cold and distant. Do you think I want to be one of those guys? All their families wanted was their presence, and all those men could offer for solace was their paycheck. I'm doing everything I can to get you and our baby back to me. But I am also a realist. If… IF… it proves impossible, I WILL be joining you."

The intensity of their exchange hung in the air, a testament to the desperation and determination that had come to define their situation. Both were silent for a moment, allowing the magnitude of their words to sink in. Finally, Marilyn shook her head, a mixture of admiration and exasperation coloring her tone. "Don't be daft, Flip! I love you and miss you terribly, and I don't want you to have to watch your daughter grow up in pictures! But I wouldn't wish this backward world on my worst enemy. Besides, things are looking up! Five minutes ago, you had no idea what that diagram was. Now you know what it is and that we can get our hands on it! 'We' are in this together, and that is where 'we' are," she responded, emphasizing the shared pronoun.

Philip's face tightened, the words "But Mare…" starting to form.

She cut him off with a firm, soldierly poise, "Just…stop," she commanded, then softened. "Let's cross that bridge if we come to it. For now, focus on what you need to do there, and I'll do what I must here. We'll make this work. I don't want to be here, nor raise our daughter here, any more than you do." Her voice, though resolute, carried an undercurrent of warmth, bridging the gap between them with her steadfast resolve and love.

Philip lowered his head and nodded, then raised his chin, resolve firming in his visage. "Of course. Of course, you're right, Mare. We'll get you home."

"I know," she replied warmly. "I keep reminding you I am usually right. Just remember that from now on and you'll save us both a great deal of time," she quipped, smirking. "I love you. Now go!"

"I love you too!" Philip replied, then stepped over to the workstation controlling the proton beam. "Sixty days," he said, and she nodded. He manipulated something at the controls, and she watched as the vision of her world dimmed to darkness.

CHAPTER 29

Affirmation

Morghais made her way slowly along the deer run. As narrow as it was, it was the clearest path back to the encampment, weaving through the dense underbrush that blanketed the forest floor. Though the occasional limb still managed to snag an arm or a leg, impeding her progress, she plodded forward with steady resolve, and was soon rewarded with the faint sounds of her destination. Her breath came in labored pulls, each a mixture of dust and determination. The murmurs of camp, once muffled, grew clearer with every step she took through the dense underbrush.

Strapped across her chest, her pack – barely more than a collection of essential survival tools – pressed against her in a feeble attempt to balance the grotesque heft of the gutted boar carcass draped over her back like some morbid cloak. It had been too heavy, even after gutting and dressing, for her to carry. So, she had cut away most of the rib cage as well. The result was an even more macabre scene with the broken stumps of what ribs remained draping her shoulders like grotesque pauldrons, lending extra support. Its forelegs, secured about her neck by a bit of leather cord mirrored the macabre belt of its hind legs, secured in similar fashion around her waist. Completing the ensemble, the boar's head rested upon her own, its tusked jowls lining her forehead in a grim parody of a crown. 'I must look a sight,' she mused idly as a fresh trickle of blood found its way from somewhere in the recesses of the boar's head to join other now dried streaks marking her face and neck.

As she came nearer to the clearing, the tree canopy above her thinned, and the morning light seeped through in a large patch, casting her shadow before her – a fearsome beast from a storyteller's tale. The silhouette of the spear-turned-walking staff she carried for support stood out starkly beside the beast's shadow. The sight coaxed a smile from her as she glanced up at her staff, its tip encrusted with the dried blood that bore testament to her triumph over the beast that was her burden. She would carry that testament to her journey's end, she resolved, and lay it before her father's feet.

Her steps finally carried her out of the woods as the forest and foliage gave way and she emerged along the clearing's edge and gazed upon the encampment. At first, no one noticed her presence as men went about various mundane tasks of camp life. But as she trudged forward, her movements caught the eye of one of the nearby men who let go with a shout of fear. Smiling, she mused again on her earlier thought and muttered to herself, "Yes, I must be a like a walking nightmare.

As Morghais drew nearer the camp fell into an eerie tableau at the sight of her. Initial fear turned to recognition and a slow ripple of shock and awe travelled through the camp as men pointed and murmured. Men paused, mid-motion, tools hanging forgotten in their hands, stunned expressions washing over the faces as her presence unfurled across the clearing.

She recognized two of the men from the first morning of her hunt. She had evaded them as they passed below in their search while she hid within the canopy of a tree overhead. They were pointing in the direction from which she had come, muttering in fear, but not at her. Then she understood – her father could be… unforgiving… of failure. But their inability to find her was not their fault. 'No one would think to look to the trees when tracking a deer,' she thought. Approaching them, she said, "I heard and saw you the first day and hid. You are not to blame. I will tell him." Looks of gratitude passed between her and the men as they nodded, and she moved on.

With each step forward, the world seemed to narrow, focusing solely on the path before her and the figure of her father standing at the heart of the camp. As the commotion she had caused reached him and claimed his attention, Gorloys turned and spotted her. He stood frozen, his shock as palpable as the silence that befell the camp at her approach. The whispers of the forest behind her, the nickering of horses, the distant calls of birds, even the shuffle of feet – all faded to mere echoes in the background. The eyes of all in the camp were upon her, but it was his gaze she sought, his approval for which she yearned despite everything.

Morghais stopped before him, the distance between them an arm's reach away, yet as wide as a river. Her father finally broke the silence of the moment as she stared up at him from beneath her gruesome crown. "I sent men in every direction looking for you," he offered quietly, concerned lacing his words.

"I know," she replied. "I hid from them in the trees while they passed beneath me. They are blameless for their failure." With a deliberate motion, she reached for the knife in a pouch of the pack on her chest, the blade glinting briefly as she severed the cords that bound the boar carcass' legs about her neck and waist. Its bulk hit the ground with a dull thud, its descent to the earth a release of more than just physical weight.

She tossed the spear at her father's feet next. "As good as any boy," she declared, her statement heavy with both pride and rebuke, each word a challenge, each word a plea. Her proclamation carried the weight of all she had learned, all she had endured. More than a testament to her triumph, it was a defiant demand for her father's acknowledgment.

The camp held its breath, a collective heart paused mid-beat. His eyes, wide with a storm of emotions, glanced down at the spear as it lay in the dirt, then finally met hers. A moment passed, a shared eternity in a glance, as Gorloys, momentarily lost for words, closed his eyes, murmuring a silent prayer or perhaps an apology known only to himself, then lowered himself before her, one knee to the ground, so that they faced each other at eye level.

"I have held onto this since the morning you vanished, Morghais," he said, holding up an item wrapped in brown cloth that he had been holding with a white knuckled grip since she had entered the clearing. Unwrapping the brown cloth, he revealed a sword still in its scabbard, shorter than usual, yet longer than a dagger, sized to fit her. "It was to be a gift in recognition of all you learned, the prize of our original agreement – a sword of your own."

He presented it to her with both hands, an altar which held the reward for all her sacrifice. "But it is a gift no more, my daughter," he continued. "My gift is my apology. The sword…You have earned it, Penâvorow Morghais."

Morghais stood momentarily shocked. The change of title from "Kinsa-mowes – 'First Daughter', to Penâvorow – 'Chief of Tomorrow' was an honor she recognized as profound in her father's eyes. Her hand trembled as she took the sword and unsheathed it, the weight of it in her grasp a tangible link to her father, to the respect she had earned in his eyes and those of the camp. Lifting it high, she let out a breath she hadn't realized she'd been holding, a sigh of relief, of victory, of coming into her own.

The camp exploded into cheers, a cacophony of joy and celebration for their Penâvorow, the girl who had ventured into the wilds and returned not just with a prize, but with her place among them, unequivocally claimed and forever changed. That night, as the fire crackled and cast its warm glow over the faces of the men gathered around, Morghais sat quietly, the weight of the sword by her side a comforting presence. She listened intently as stories of the day's events were passed around like prized possessions, each retelling adding another layer to her legend. Amid the murmurs, the phrase "The Boar of Cornwall" surfaced repeatedly, each mention drawing nods and wide-eyed expressions of respect. It took her a moment to realize they were speaking of her – her courage, her cunning, her triumph now woven into the fabric of camp lore.

Glancing towards her father, she caught him watching her, a contented smile playing across his lips as he shared in the telling. His eyes met hers, and in that exchange, she felt not just the pride of her father but the acceptance of her people. As the night deepened and the tales grew taller, her heart swelled with a newfound sense of belonging and purpose.

She pondered the new label the men had begun to use in their stories – ”The Boar of Cornwall” – and what the animal symbolized. Recalling discussions she had overheard between her father and his scouts, she knew her father was hunting a man named Uthyr, who bore a family crest featuring a golden beast on a field of red – a dragon, the men said, invoking images of fire-breathing creatures from her mother's tales. The thought lingered in her mind, 'Perhaps our family, too, should claim a crest.' The idea of a boar, strong and resolute as she had been this day, seemed fitting. As drowsiness pulled at her consciousness, drawing her toward her pallet, the notion of her own legacy, symbolized by the steadfast boar, nestled firmly in her thoughts.

Gorloys sat back in his chair at the long table, watching as the gray-haired farmer shuffled out of the tent. As the two guardsmen, their helms and green tabards immaculate and identical, held open the flaps for him to exit, the fleeting look of satisfaction on the man's face was replaced by a cowed expression, taken aback by the formality. It was a stark contrast to the usual, more informal state of the encampment. But when scouts reported that a village elder was on his way, he quickly had the usually stowed pavilion tent erected, setting an appropriate stage for the man's arrival.

The village itself was a nondescript dot to the north, hardly worth noting on any map – a mere gathering of modest farmsteads that could scarcely boast wealth or strategic importance. Gorloys' gaze lingered on the swaybacked mare waiting outside, likely the best the farmer could muster. It underscored the village's humble means and reinforced his disdain for Uthyr's tactics. To harass such an insignificant place was either an act of desperation or a deliberate provocation. Either way, it confirmed his worst assessments of Uthyr: contemptible, untrustworthy, and unabashedly eager to claim dominion over lands that were not rightfully his.

Gorloys turned his attention back to Morghais, who sat at the opposite end of the table, quietly finishing her breakfast. He and his men had visited several towns and villages over the last days, chasing rumors and sightings of Uthyr, but none quite so small as the little hamlet from which the elder came. Still, wherever they went, his men would often seek out the local public house or gathering area to drink and gossip with the locals, looking for news of the world beyond the confines of their camp.

It pleased him to discover that some of these rumors had outpaced him. Villages and towns were becoming aware that he and his company were in the field, protecting his domain from outsiders. But somehow, it pleased him even more that rumors had begun to spread of Morghais's exploits. Parents had begun to point her out to their children, whispering "The Boar of Cornwall."

At first, Morghais was embarrassed by the attention. But eventually, she learned to walk with her head held high, each whisper of "The Boar of Cornwall" transforming her initial discomfort into a sense of responsibility and pride. He could see she was becoming more than just the daughter of Pen Gorloys. As young as she was, she had begun to build her own legacy – a mantle she was beginning to embrace, shaping her into a symbol of resilience and strength that others would point to their own children and say to them, 'See her? That could be you!' The thought made Gorloys beam with pride. Still smiling, Gorloys pulled himself from his reverie and focused again on her. "Were you paying attention?" he asked, a test as much as a question.

"Yes," Morghais replied, wiping her mouth on her sleeve, a gesture unbecoming the formality of their setting. Gorloys could not help but grin inwardly, thinking to himself, 'As good as any boy? As bad as any boy too, I see,' while maintaining his composure.

"Mother always says, 'Paying attention costs nothing, but gains much,'" she added, mimicking her mother's admonishing tone, which only solidified his amusement, transforming his inward grin into an open smirk. "But I do not understand why you had all of this set up just to see that old man?" she continued, her spoon waving vaguely around the pavilion tent, drawing his attention.

Gorloys leaned forward, his gaze encompassing the tent as he mimicked his daughter's earlier gesture. "Morghais, this…" he gestured broadly around them, "is a stage; nothing more." He paused, letting the words sink in before continuing. "My father often said that what is real means little; people see what they want to see."

He watched Morghais, gauging her reaction as she pondered his father's words of wisdom. "That man," he nodded towards the path the elder had taken, "wants to feel safe; he wants his village to feel safe. For that, he needs to believe there is some sense of order in the world, and that when that order is disrupted, there is someone who can restore it."

Morghais tilted her head, absorbing his words. Her voice was thoughtful, yet uncertain. "And he finds that order... here?"

Gorloys leaned in slightly, choosing his next words with care. "Do you remember last spring when you were stung by a bee while playing in the flowers?"

"Yes?" Morghais answered, a flicker of memory crossing her expression.

"You were in pain, hurt, and scared. You ran to your mother because she made you feel safe. You trusted her to make things right again – to restore order. She, in turn, went to Magra when your hand swelled because Magra makes her feel safe. When things go wrong, your mother trusts me or Magra to make them right again, depending on what is wrong."

Morghais nodded slowly, the pieces coming together in her mind. "So, he came to you because you make him feel safe?"

"Yes, exactly," Gorloys affirmed, pleased with her understanding. "When he comes here and sees this tent, the guards, the men and horses under my command, he sees a man capable of restoring order. He sees a leader." The concept seemed to take root, and Gorloys pressed on, "And because of that, because I make him feel safe, he will follow."

He leaned back, his expression thoughtful. "Leaders do not lead by strength alone," he mused aloud. "They lead by shaping how others see them."

Morghais, her brow furrowed in thought, looked up at her father. "Is that the difference between you and the man you hunt, father? This 'Uthyr Pendragon' who calls himself a king? Does a king not make people feel safe? Is that the difference between a Pen and a King?"

Gorloys considered her question for a moment, his gaze distant as he formulated his response. "It is more than just that," he finally said. "Kings tax the people and make those who cannot pay suffer for it. A king believes people should serve him, regardless of whether he does anything to deserve it. A Pen, on the other hand, serves his people, and in so doing, is compensated by his people for his efforts." He gestured expansively, encompassing the lands beyond their tent. "The people of Cornwall send young men from each town or village to serve and protect the land under my leadership. The villages and towns that cannot do so will spare crops and livestock as they can. The village elder there did not come empty-handed. He brought two laying hens and a cock to help feed the men coming to protect his home and family."

Just then, Duryk – the scout who had escorted the village elder to the encampment – returned, drawing Gorloys' attention. He raised a questioning eyebrow, having expected Duryk to escort the man home again.

"Apologies, Pen Gorloys," Duryk began with a conciliatory bow. "The old man said he may have needed help to find our camp, but he could find his own way home." He bent and grabbed the small of his back, in mockery of old age and mimicked a croaky voice, "I been hunting in these woods my whole life, boy," drawing a giggle from Morghais.

Gorloys shot a look at Morghais, then focused his attention back on Duryk. "If I want theatrics, I will pay for a fool," he said sternly, reasserting order.

"Yes, Pen Gorloys," Duryk replied with remorse, straightening his posture.

Gorloys then stood and beckoned Duryk to the table. "Are scouts tracking him?" he inquired.

Duryk quickly pulled a small map from a leather pouch at his waist and walked over to the table, laying it out for both to see. "We are here," he pointed to a dot on the map. "And the elder's village here, next to a ford in a small river running through the Whitemoor. Uthyr and his men left the village following the river southwest through the Whitemoor."

"How far?" Gorloys inquired, weighing the implications. By this time, Morghais had gotten up and joined them, looking at the map herself with interest, which pleased him though he said nothing.

"Perhaps three mille'roma to the south," Duryk replied speculatively, using the local term that echoed ancient Roman measurements still present in their own vernacular even after generations. "Ferys is following Uthyr's trail and will return when Uthyr makes camp again."

"Good," Gorloys replied, satisfied. "Go find Garel and send him in." With the pavilion tent having been set up for the visit from the village elder, plans to break down the camp for travel for the day had been paused. But now that Uthyr was near, he wanted to keep pace with the man and not lose him.

Just as Duryk nodded and turned to leave, Morghais's small voice came from beside him, "Are you going to kill Uthyr, Father?"

The question caught Gorloys off-guard. His first impulse was to snap – a leader's decisions were not to be questioned, especially not by a child. Yet as he turned to face her, seeing the earnest curiosity mixed with a hint of fear in her eyes, his irritation softened. She is here to learn, not just to watch, he reminded himself.

"I do not know, Morghais," he said, his tone more gentle than he initially intended. "Killing Uthyr is not the goal, but if it comes to that to protect our lands and our people, then I must be prepared." He saw her absorb this, her brow furrowing slightly, a thoughtful, slightly overwhelmed look crossing her face. "Leaders must make hard choices sometimes, not because they want to, but because they must ensure the safety of many."

He placed a hand on her shoulder, feeling the significance of the moment. "You must understand, it is never as simple as just deciding to kill a man. It is about protecting our home, our way of life." He paused, his gaze intense as he searched her face for signs of comprehension. "In this instance, this man Uthyr has decided to set himself against me – to make me his enemy. How should I respond?"

Morghais shrugged with uncertainty, the fear and discomfort he had witnessed when he asked her to slaughter a rabbit returning to her face.

Gorloys shook his head slightly and sighed. "Morghais, do you remember the rabbit? Taking a life is never a decision to be made lightly, but when it is done, it must serve a purpose. And once decided, it should be carried out swiftly and with certainty. If you hesitate, it may be your life that is taken. Do you understand?"

Morghais nodded, her voice barely above a whisper, "I think so, Father."

Gorloys watched her, his heart a mix of pride and a deep, poignant regret. He had wanted her to learn about leadership, about the difficult decisions one must face, but at what cost to what remained of her innocence? It was a burden he hoped she would not have to bear any time soon.

By the time the camp was broken down and moved to the edge of the little village to the south, most of the day had passed. As they rode, rain began to fall, casting a dreary pall over the landscape. Now, while the men busied themselves trying to erect tents to protect against the downpour, Gorloys and Morghais stood drying themselves within the confines of the village elder's hovel.

Dafydd, whose name Gorloys had only just recalled from their earlier meeting, stoked the fire in the middle of the room and threw a couple of logs into the pit. "I have some chicken stew in the pot I could heat if you are hungry, sire?" the elder offered, his voice echoing slightly in the humble space.

"Thank you, but no, Dafydd. Shelter and warmth from the rain are enough," Gorloys replied, glancing around the modest hovel. After a moment's contemplation, he added, "On second thought, Dafydd, my privacy is of great importance to me. Would you be able to stay with someone for the night and allow me the use of your cottage?"

Dafydd beamed, his eyes crinkling with delight. "My home is yours, sire!" he exclaimed, then offering Morghais a mischievous wink, he added, "I've been looking for a reason to pay a visit to Widow Ennor!" Grabbing an old leather hide from a peg on the wall, he draped it over his head and stepped out into the rain, leaving Gorloys and Morghais to the flickering warmth of the fire.

As the afternoon wore on and the rain ceased, leaving the sky a heavy grey that began to darken with the coming dusk, Ferys arrived at the village elder's cottage, wet but resolute, to report on Uthyr's movements. Gorloys watched as Ferys, squatting at the fire pit to warm his hands, cast furtive glances around the hovel, seemingly searching for some hidden nook or an additional room not easily noticed from the exterior.

Gorloys, noting Ferys' cautious behavior, reassured him with a firm nod. "You may speak freely; we are alone. The man who lives here stays elsewhere for the night."

Satisfied, Ferys stood and turned to him. "Uthyr followed the river. He stopped early because of the rain and is now camped along a bend, a half day's ride to the southwest," Ferys reported.

"How many men does he have? How are they armed?" Gorloys questioned, his voice low and urgent as he strategized their next move.

Ferys pulled a dagger from the pommel at his waist and began to scratch a crude map into the hovel's packed dirt floor, using ash from the fire pit on the tip of his blade to strengthen the lines.

The two men poured over the map as Ferys answered his questions, adding details such as where the horse picket lines were located and where Uthyr's tent could be found. Morghais, seemingly not content to remain a mere observer, stepped closer, her hand resting confidently on the hilt of her newly earned sword. "I can fight too. I've trained for this," she asserted, her eyes burning with fierce determination to prove her mettle.

Gorloys turned towards her, catching her determined look, a surge of both pride and apprehension washing over him. He admired her courage but feared for her safety should the confrontation escalate into violence – a likely outcome given the tensions. "Morghais, facing a man one-on-one is an entirely different matter than what could potentially become a battle. If that happens, I cannot ensure your safety. In fact, I would be in more danger trying to focus on protecting you rather than myself."

Ferys, having overheard their exchange, chimed in with a strategic suggestion. "Sire, I observed Uthyr's encampment from a hill across the river here." He pointed to a spot on the dirt map opposite where Uthyr's camp was marked. "Perhaps if we cross the ford here in the village as Uthyr did, and the Penâvorow mirrors our movement from the other side, she could observe from that hill and... warn us of any ambush from the opposite bank."

Grateful for Ferris's quick thinking – a ploy to make Morghais not only feel included but also participate in an important way – Gorloys turned to his daughter. "Is that acceptable? Or you may wait here in the village for our return?"

Morghais, with a resolute nod, responded, "Yes, father. I will scout the other side of the river."

Gorloys nodded and turned back to Ferys. "Let the men know we ride out at dawn," he commanded.

CHAPTER 30

Vengeance

As dawn broke, a chill breeze seeped through the gaps in the hovel's crude walls. Gorloys pulled on his chainmail coat, feeling the familiar weight settle over his shoulders, a grounding reminder of the morning's somber reality. He then picked up the studded leather bracers, offering them to Morghais. "Could you help with the lacing?" he asked, a simple request that bridged the gap between leader and father.

The camp outside stirred, the sounds of men preparing for the day's march filling the air with a low murmur. Inside, the hovel was quieter, but the tension was just as palpable. Gorloys felt it – a tightness in his chest as he readied himself not just for battle, but for the uncertainties it brought.

As Morghais carefully laced the bracers, her fingers deft and assured, he draped a green tabard over his chainmail, the fabric's color merging with the early light. He was about to reach for his helm when Morghais's voice, soft yet laden with concern, stopped him. "Father?"

He turned to find her stepping forward, the last lace tied, her eyes searching his. Before he could offer words of reassurance, she closed the distance between them and wrapped her arms around him in a fierce embrace. The unexpected warmth against his chainmail startled him, but only for a moment.

Gorloys' arms came around her slowly, the initial stiffness giving way as he returned the hug with equal intensity. His hand came up to the back of her head, gently pressing her closer. "It will be well," he murmured, though whether the words were more for her benefit or his, he could not say.

He stood there with his daughter, both clinging to the moment. Finally, Gorloys gently disentangled himself, placing his hands on her shoulders and fixing her with a steady, earnest look. "Keep pace with us from your side of the river and watch from the hill," he instructed, his voice carrying the weight of command tinged with a father's concern. "I will come find you when it is over."

The final implied reassurance of his survival and return seemed to calm her. Morghais took a deep, shuddering breath and nodded, stepping back as Gorloys picked up his helm and positioned it under his arm. With one last look at her, a silent promise hanging between them, they turned and stepped out of the hovel into the dim morning and headed for the horse lines.

Gorloys rode in silence through the forest along the river, its quiet murmur blending with the soft rustle of leaves stirred by a gentle breeze. Flanked by a four-man escort – his most trusted warriors – dressed to match him in the formal green tabards and helms of their rank, they formed a solemn procession through the mist-laden woods. Their presence invoked memories of his last confrontation with Uthyr, where he had stood alone and humiliated. 'That will not happen again,' he vowed silently, shifting his gaze back to the men trailing behind. The heavy grey skies matched their somber mood, their faces set in grim determination, knowing the stakes of the engagement ahead.

A morning fog clung to the ground, obscuring the forest floor and muffling the sounds of their passage, making the world seem smaller, more intimate and immediate. Gorloys considered the weather and terrain – slick, rain-soaked earth that could betray a man in the heat of battle. But he trusted his men; this was his land, their land, and Uthyr was the outsider – a maxim that lent him a quiet confidence. Yet, uncertainty gnawed at him; he cast a furtive glance toward the river he knew was there, but could not see, hoping Morghais was keeping pace on the other side.

As the sun climbed and the fog dissipated, its last remnants clinging to the river's surface, heard the clear sounds of a chough, a bird call all too familiar to he and his men, prompting Gorloys to raise his fist, signaling a halt. The company froze, a tense silence enveloping them as his escort readied their bows, arrows nocked but not drawn.

He sat staring intensely into the foliage of the forest before him, when Duryk and Ferys, his best scouts, resolved from their hiding places like spirits of the woods, easily within deadly arrow range, though he and his men had seen no evidence of the passing.

Once recognized as their own, the two men approached Gorloys horse. "Sire, the encampment is just ahead perhaps three stone throws," Duryk began. "The fog forced us closer than intended, but the camp remains quiet – for now."

"I may have been seen," Ferys added, his tone apologetic. "I tried to move closer to confirm their numbers. Forgive me, Pen Gorloys."

Gorloys waved away the apology, his mind already racing with tactical considerations. "Did you linger to see if they raised an alarm?"

"Yes, sire. That is why I cannot be certain. For now, they seem unaware of our presence or approach," Ferys reported, relief evident in his voice.

Gorloys nodded, satisfied. "Is there a clear path through the forest to flank them and charge from the west, pinning them against the riverbank?" he queried, his mind already tracing routes on an internal map of the terrain.

"I scouted a path to approach the clearing from the west, sire," Duryk replied, stepping forward. "But the undergrowth is too dense for a mounted charge. The river's edge offers the clearest approach for that."

Nodding, Gorloys considered the strategic implications. His forces, numbering around a hundred, outnumbered Uthyr's by twenty men or more if yesterday's reports were accurate. Turning to Duryk and Ferys, he commanded, "Take forty of our best archers and approach on foot from the west, then lead the charge with a volley of arrows. Loose a second volley, then I will lead the mounted charge from the north while your men storm the field from the west."

As the two men hurried away to execute his orders, Gorloys turned his mount toward the river, trying to spot Morghais through the thinning mist. Garel, sensing his concern, reassured him softly, "Be at ease, Pen Gorloys. The Penâvorow knows what she is about." Motioning toward the other three escorts, who all turned and nodded, he added, "You…we…trained her well."

Gorloys straightened his composure, angry with himself for showing any sign of weakness or worry. "Stay alert," he commanded his escort, his voice low and tense. "Follow my lead and be ready to strike hard and fast."

The forest canopy thinned with each step as his mounts pushed through the underbrush, approaching the edge of the forest. When Uthyr's camp began to resolve between the trees, they were spotted, and shouts of alarm went up around the camp just as a volley of arrows rained down from the west on the unsuspecting camp. Shouts of alarm turned to a chaotic milieu of rage and pain as a second volley hit the camp, felling men who failed to seek cover in time.

Gorloys smiled at the thought of an arrow impaling Uthyr before the battle had even truly begun, then urged his mount forward in a rush, raising his sword in a shout, signaling his men to follow. As they burst into the clearing, the rumble of over fifty hooves thundering like an approaching storm, the field revealed itself – a tapestry of violence and quick movements.

Several of Uthyr's men lay fallen, struck down by the arrows. Others had managed to arm bows and fire a return volley, felling several men on the western front, left behind as the rest rushed the field on foot, closing the gap for melee combat. Though Duryk continued to lead the charge, Ferys was among the fallen, having taken an arrow to the leg. If the man survived this day, he would limp for the remainder of his life.

As his mounts collided with the camp in blood and chaos, fresh screams of rage and pain erupted when pikes and bills appeared unexpectedly, impaling riders and horses alike as their whinnies of protest joined the cacophony of battle sounds. But the charge had been effective, felling twice as many of Uthyr's men.

Men leapt into the foray, abandoning their horses to fight on foot in the confined space of the camp. Three of his escort surrounded him on foot, fighting off attacks while Gorloys remained mounted, scanning the field for the man he sought most. His fourth man, Garel had either fallen or was drawn away in the chaos.

As the western front closed the gap to join the fray, he heard someone calling his name and looked over to see Ferys in the distance trying to get his attention. "The horse lines!" the man yelled, pointing at the camp's line of unsaddled mounts, then slashed across his waist with a free hand. Realization suddenly dawned as Gorloys thought, 'There are too few!'

On the heels of his realization, a large assembly of perhaps thirty of Uthyr's men thundered into the clearing from the south, crashing into his men from behind. Ill-prepared for the flanking attack, his men were decimated before they had ever reached the main encampment.

"I have lost," Gorloys thought morosely as the prize he sought finally appeared, wielding the shining sword, and wearing the dragon-emblazoned tabard – the signs of which he had heard so often. 'I am sorry, Morghais,' he thought. 'I will die this day.' Dismounting amidst his men, he whispered to himself with newfound determination, "But I can kill that whelp of a diseased whore, so you never have to deal with him," a promise to his daughter he would give his life to fulfill.

Blood and sweat permeated the air as he joined the fray, making his way toward Uthyr, cutting down anyone in his path. His escort, now down to two men – Jory and Garel, who had somehow returned –

followed, protecting his flank. Men fought, screamed, and died all around them, sometimes by his own sword, as he made his way across the camp toward his target.

"Uthyr! Uthyr Pendragon!" he called out as the gap between them closed. The man turned and Gorloys stopped in his tracks, shocked to his core. "You are not Uthyr," he uttered in stunned disbelief, his voice laced with shock and confusion. The man had the same height and build as Uthyr, and a familiar look to him that gnawed at Gorloys' like a memory that would not come to mind.

"No, I am not Uthyr," the stranger replied. "But I will be the man to bring your death." The blade the man wielded flashed, gleaming with unnatural brightness like nothing Gorloys had ever witnessed before, as the man struck with a ferocity and speed that he would not have thought possible. The man's sword was longer and should have been too heavy to allow such a sudden onslaught. Yet, Gorloys barely managed to parry the blow as his opponent's blade notched deeply into his own, sending a jarring shock of pain up his arm.

"Where is Uthyr?" Gorloys demanded, breathing heavily as he stepped back out of range of the longer blade and spared a glance over his shoulder. Garel and Jory were holding off men at his flank against staggering odds of two to three opponents each. But their opponents seemed more content to keep them preoccupied from joining his own fight, neither seeking to help his opponent, nor hinder him in this standoff.

"Uthyr is probably at Tintagel now, giving it to that pretty wife of yours," the stranger taunted. "At the very least, he rescues Merlin," he added. "The secret of dragon fire will never belong to Cornwall."

Enraged, Gorloys took the offensive, swinging and thrusting his sword with all the martial skill he could muster. The younger man lithely danced aside from each thrust, using his sword to parry Gorloys' slashing attacks, and countering with his own nimble use of the obviously lighter weapon. This man was undoubtedly younger than he and wielded a superior weapon. The only advantage Gorloys could see to his advantage was his experience and skill. But the light swiftness of the shining blade all but negated that advantage. Stepping back once again, Gorloys spared a glance for his own blade, and saw that it was chipped and notched all along its length where the superior weapon had bitten into its iron edge. Whatever its make, it was sturdier than iron as well.

"Why do you seem familiar? Who are you!? I have no quarrel with you!" Gorloys spat, trying to catch his breath.

"I am Lynok – younger brother of Branok, executed by your hand for cowardice," the young man replied. "But you face no coward today, Gorloys," Lynok added, then twisted the sword in his hand, catching the morning sun and reflecting it into Gorloys' eyes.

Instinctively, Gorloys raised his sword to parry the blow he knew was coming but could not see, blinded by the sudden reflection as he was. A shock of pain shot up his arm once again as Gorloys stumbled back, staring stunned at the shattered stump where his blade had been, apparently struck from the side, and weakened by the notches on its edge.

In his hesitation, the useless weapon went flying as he took a boot to the chest, knocking him to the ground. From behind him, he heard Garel exclaim, "Pen Gorloys!" followed by the sounds of both men dying in gasps of anguish, suddenly overwhelmed by the host that had held them at bay.

Lynok stood over him, the shining sword at his throat, staring down. "If it is of any solace, Uthyr leant me this pretty weapon to kill you," he stated matter-of-factly, pausing to admire the shining blade for a moment, then pointed the tip at Gorloys' throat, forcing him against the ground.

"I have a daughter!" Gorloys pleaded, reaching out in a last plea for mercy.

"And I had a brother!" Lynok retorted angrily, savagely shoving the blade into Gorloys' throat and through his neck. Blood pulsing from the wound, the sensation of drowning took over as he stared up and convulsed. "Perhaps she will avenge your death someday as I have avenged his," he heard Lynok declare as the light faded, and the darkness crept in.

His last thoughts before the darkness took him were for his daughter and the world he had left for her, one no better than before. 'I am sorry, Morghais,' he thought finally, a final regret ushering him into oblivion.

Morghais sat her mount as she watched her father and his men traverse the river through the shallow ford by the village. The horse's hooves kicked up mud and silt, forming slurries that were quickly swept away by the swift current. When the last man among them disappeared into the trees, she turned her mount and headed toward the forest's edge on her side of the river. As she entered the forest's domain, she looked over to her right with fretfulness. The thick morning fog obscured her view, creating a curtain of mist that made it impossible to see the opposite bank and the forest beyond.

Anxiety gnawed at her – each obscured sound and shadow in the fog could have been her father's men, or she might have outpaced them without realizing. Then her horse stumbled on the uneven terrain, forcing her to look down and guide the mare along a more level path. It was just as possible that her father and his men had outpaced her! This side of the river seemed to be more rugged from what little she could tell in this thick fog, hampering her travel.

Before long, the morning sun began to rise and burn off the fog. Seeing more clearly, she realized that her assessment of the ground was more accurate than she had anticipated. On her side of the river, the fog had already melted away from the higher, more hilly terrain, while the river itself and the forest along the other side remained shrouded in mystery.

Arriving at the hilltop across from Uthyr's encampment earlier than expected, she found herself alone with her thoughts, the fog across the river beginning to lift in the warming light of the sun. From her concealed position, she tried to pierce the veil of mist with her gaze, searching for any sign of her father and his men. The quiet was unsettling, and she wrapped her cloak tighter against the chill, her mind racing with the possibilities of what might be coming. Her father was a stern, proud man who was quick to anger – a combination that she felt surely would result in conflict rather than the peaceful resolution she earnestly hoped for.

As the fog dissipated and the world across the river slowly came into focus, Morghais's heart pounded with a mix of anticipation and fear. From her concealed position, she intently watched Uthyr's encampment, where men hurried about like ants tending to their mound. Their tasks, at first mundane and ordinary, took on a sudden urgency as several men broke away and scurried to the horse lines, saddling horses and riding into the woods to the south. Her stomach churned; something was amiss. She gripped the hilt of her sword, feeling the cold metal beneath her fingers, and forced herself to breathe, preparing herself for what might come next.

As the encampment stirred into alertness, Morghais's unease deepened. She felt powerless yet desperate to do something, her mind racing for a way to warn her father of the hidden danger to the south.

Forming a desperate plan, she slid off her horse and retrieved her small bow from the saddlebag. Her hands trembled slightly as she strung it. From a small pouch, she pulled out the green sash given to her in a formal ceremony the night she had earned her sword and the title of Penâvorow – a night when the entire camp had celebrated her victory, feasting on the boar she had brought back. She tied the sash around the shaft of her lightest arrow, her movements accompanied by a silent prayer. If only she could signal him, let him know of the trap that awaited.

With a deep breath, she notched the arrow, aimed high into the sky toward the edge of the wood north of the encampment, and let it fly, hoping her father would find it before it was too late. The arrow arched beautifully, catching the light as it soared, but as it reached its zenith, Morghais's heart sank. It fell far short, splashing into the river with a faint, distant plop, swallowed by the swift currents. She watched helplessly as it disappeared, a potent reminder of her isolation and helplessness.

Tears pricked her eyes as she realized the futility of her attempt. She was alone, unable to change the tide of what was to come, and the weight of that realization settled heavily on her young shoulders. Turning back to the encampment, she could only wait and watch as the men continued their preparations, unaware of her desperate attempt to alert her father of the danger toward which he rode.

From her vantage point on the hilltop, Morghais watched in a mix of awe and apprehension as the battle unfolded across the river. At first, there was a deceptive lull—then suddenly, her father's archers burst from the western woods, loosing volleys of arrows on the unsuspecting camp. The initial chaos that erupted in the camp gave her a flicker of hope, her heart swelling with pride as, a moment later, she saw her father at the forefront of a thundering charge of men on horse, his green tabard, and those of his closest warriors, vivid in the morning sun.

The battle seemed to tilt in their favor as the encampment reeled under the surprise attack. Morghais found herself on the edge of her seat, hands clenched tightly around her bow, her breath catching with each clash of metal and shout of war. But the tide turned quickly and drastically. As if in answer to her father's initial onslaught, those of Uthyr's horsemen that had disappeared into the southern woods earlier flowed from those same woods back into the clearing, charging into the fray and cutting through her father's archers with devastating efficiency, their swords flashing mercilessly in the morning light.

Morghais's excitement turned to dread as the battle degraded into a chaotic cluster of skirmishes. The air was filled with the sounds of battle, the clang of swords, and the cries of the fallen. She could do nothing but watch as the situation grew increasingly dire.

Her father dismounted and pushed forward, moving with a grim determination toward a man who had appeared suddenly from one of the tents, standing out starkly against the chaos – a lone figure clad in a dark red tabard with a glaring yellow beast emblazoned across it. The man's sword shone with an unnatural brilliance in the sunlight, catching her eye even from a distance. This could only be Uthyr Pendragon, the man her father sought, the thorn in Cornwall's side, the man who dared proclaim dominion over her father's lands.

The two men on the field, unmolested as the battle raged around them, red against green. The clash was fierce and brutal. Her father fought valiantly, matching his opponent blow for blow, but it soon became apparent her father was outmatched against this younger man with a seemingly superior weapon. She watched the truth of that belief with horror as Uthyr, with a forceful swing that followed a heated exchange, broke her father's sword in twain.

Obviously stunned, her father stumbled back, his weapon useless. Her breath caught in her throat as Uthyr kicked her father in the chest, sending the useless sword flying as her father, caught off guard, fell to the ground. Morghais felt her world tilt as Uthyr stood over him, his sword poised for a final blow. Though she could not hear their final words, the dreadful finality was clear as her father reached up in a desperate plea, and Uthyr, in response, drove his sword through her father's throat. As his head sunk back and his hand fell back to the earth, Morghais buried her face in her hands and wept.

Hours passed as she watched, gazing morosely as Uthyr's men tended their wounded and, with dispassionate efficiency, dispatched those of her father's men who, though mortally wounded, still lived. Though horrified, she considered it a small mercy to end their suffering, saved from the horror of having the carrion birds, that had begun to circle overhead, peck and tear at their flesh as they lay dying. She winced as Garel, one of the last, was stabbed through the heart with a pike, his back arching in a spasm of death before his lifeless body collapsed.

By mid-afternoon, Uthyr and his entourage had broken camp and headed back south along the river, leaving the corpses of the fallen on the field. Even from her vantage atop the hill, she could see the lifeless body of her father, left lying where he had fallen. That his body lay discarded like refuse, ill-regarded and disrespected, was more than she could stand.

Mounting her horse, she travelled upriver for a time, then urged her horse into the water, dismounting as the water reached her knees. She swam across, leading her horse by the reins, as the current carried them gently downstream to emerge from the river just past the clearing where the battle had occurred. As if a message from beyond the grave, she spotted the arrow she had shot earlier, the bit of green ribbon her father had given her still tied too it, bobbing gently in the mud.

As she made her way back upstream along the river's edge, she began to gather whatever dry bits of wood she could find. The rains from the previous day had made picking scarce, but she soon had a sizable bundle harnessed to her saddle with a leather thong.

By the time she reached her father's body, the carrion birds were out in force, swooping down to squabble with each other over one set of remains or another, though there was plenty to go around. She shooed away a few of the birds who had gotten too close, and they squawked in protest before flying away to find easier fare. Looking down at her father, her stomach lurched as she took in the scene, repulsed by the gaping hole of the final thrust through the neck that had ended his life.

She turned away and quickly began to pile the wood she had collected, forming a makeshift pyre around and over her father, Garel, and Jory. They deserved better, but she knew, from her father's lessons, that the carrion birds would soon attract other predators, eager to partake in an easy meal. She used her flint and steel to ignite kindling and set the pyre ablaze, crying as she recalled yet another lesson her father had taught her. As the small fire spread and the pyre began to burn in earnest, she mounted her horse and watched for a time, until the fire grew into an all-consuming blaze whose blackened smoke carried the spirits of the fallen into the sky.

"I will avenge you, father," she declared quietly, then turned her mount northeast toward home.

Four days later, Morghais stumbled through the gates of Tintagel, her body on the brink of collapse, her clothes muddied and torn. The guards, Buwel and Fynn, barely recognized the gaunt figure approaching. As she dismounted with difficulty, she said in a hollow voice, "I must see my mother," her tone devoid of emotion but carrying an undertone of urgency.

Bewildered yet concerned, the guards supported her by the elbows, flanking her as she shuffled toward her mother's chamber. She shrugged off their hands with a weak but determined gesture, her gaze locked on the path ahead.

Entering the room, she found her mother in a tender scene, nursing her newborn sister with a bladder of goat's milk. The contrast struck Morghais sharply; here was life, so gentle and fragile, in the lap of the woman who had taught her strength. Her mother's eyes widened in shock, her expression frozen as she struggled to reconcile the image of her eldest daughter, no longer a child in a dress but a warrior marked by battle, a bow slung over her shoulder and a sword at her waist.

Before a word could pass her mother's lips, Morghais spoke with a voice that seemed to carry the weight of her father's fate, "Father is dead." The words hung heavy in the air, a somber declaration that echoed mournfully in the suddenly too-quiet room.

As the finality of her statement settled, Morghais felt the room spin, the edges of her vision blurring as darkness crept in. Her legs buckled, and she collapsed to the floor, her strength finally failing her as she succumbed to exhaustion and grief.

CHAPTER 31

Legacy and Destiny

As the sun began its descent toward the distant hills, Marilyn rode alongside a guard of men, their path winding around the vast marshes that skirted Glestinga. The heavy cart laden with the artifact creaked and groaned, its contents overhanging the edges with a precarious grace. Not for the first time, she was thankful that the object was much lighter than it appeared. Despite its diameter, exceeding ten feet, only four men were needed to lift it and secure it atop the horse-drawn cart. Yet, the journey toward Mêlotir was slow; the men often dismounted to clear a path with their swords through the tangled heathland and around the dense moorland forests that stood as silent sentinels in the wild countryside.

Days ago, when they had arrived at the artifact, lying submerged at the edge of the marsh north of Glestinga, spring had barely begun, with the nights still cold and crisp, and the days offering a comfortable warmth if it wasn't raining. But months had passed beyond the artifact's influence while she visited with her team and resupplied her party.

Now, a sweltering mid-summer heat drew sweat from every pore and seemed to sap the strength from everyone, making the journey feel that much longer as they traversed the land from one water source to another. Kynan seemed to know where he was going though, despite Marilyn's inability to discern one hill, moor, or tract of forest from another. By the end of each day, they would break for camp beside some stream running through a valley or near a pool of cool, inviting water in some hidden dale. Wiping sweat from her brow, she glanced over at the late afternoon sun, making its slow march toward the horizon, and knew they would be stopping somewhere soon.

'Christ! I could use a break,' she thought, feeling the sweat trickle and itch between her swollen breasts. She had wrapped them in extra cloth to prevent leakage into her clothes, an otherwise dead giveaway of her gender that she would rather keep secret. But that was when it was spring. Now, in this summer heat, she had begun to argue with herself whether revealing her secret would be so bad – anything to relieve herself in this damnable heat! Her better senses would return though later in the evening as the men sat around the campfire and bragged of their exploits and conquests with the opposite sex. A single female alone in the wilderness amongst all these men? No, she would be fine letting them think she was some enigmatic, other-worldly figure, not to be trifled with, thank you.

As the party exited into a clearing through a break in the scrub barely wide enough for the cart, the wooden cartwheels began to clatter, as if rolling over stone rather than softer terrain, drawing her from languid daydreams where her thoughts had been drifting aimlessly like wisps of clouds in the azure sky above. Still leading the way, Kynan looked over his shoulder at everyone and waved a hand, turning left. "This way," he proclaimed.

Marilyn reined in her horse, stunned. Before her stretched a wide berth of what could only be described as an ancient highway built of close-knit, flat stones. It stretched in both directions to the horizon as far as she could see, straight as a ruler. The road's broad, paved expanse cut through the landscape with an undeniable sense of purpose and permanence, its smooth, worn stones glistening in the sunlight.

Having realized she had stopped, the men with her followed suit and Kynan looked back once again, drawn by the commotion. "What is this…" she began, then realized she had no word in this ancient Welsh tongue to which she had become accustomed to speaking. In all her time in the past, she had never come across such a significant path. She knew the words for path and road, but this was so much more imposing than either. "I do not know the word in your tongue Kynan," she continued. "The word 'road' seems too small to describe something so grand. I have been many places in Britannia but have never seen it's like!"

Kynan smiled, looking up and down the expanse as she had moments before. "My father once told me that his grandfather's grandfather had helped build this when the Romans ruled the land," Kynan informed her. "My father said it is called the 'Fossa Via.' That is its name in the Roman tongue – the 'ditch road.' According to his story, it was once a ditch the Romans had dug to try and drain the upland marshes. But when it did not work, they filled the ditch in and built this road."

She marveled at the engineering prowess of a civilization long gone, their legacy etched indelibly into the earth beneath her feet. The road seemed to speak of an era of order and ambition, its presence a stark contrast to the wild, untamed world that had begun to reclaim it. This ancient artery, a lifeline of connectivity and commerce, now lay silent, a monument to human ingenuity and the relentless march of history. Marilyn felt a profound sense of awe and respect, the weight of centuries pressing upon her, as she stood at the threshold of this monumental relic of the past. "How long is the road?" she asked, curious.

"It runs from the River Exe to a distant land in the north called Llyndon," Kynan replied, then turned and continued down the paved road toward the northeast. The men and cart resumed following him as Marilyn trailed behind, pondering why she had never noticed the road's beginnings while at Execaer.

As they advanced along the ancient Roman road, the pace of travel quickened, the smooth stones beneath their feet facilitating a swifter journey than the wilder paths they had trodden before. Marilyn, feeling a surge of energy from the change, decided to walk at the front of the column alongside Kynan. They had just passed a farmer going in the opposite direction, his hay fork clutched tightly and his eyes darting between the cart and the travelers, a mix of suspicion and curiosity in his gaze.

The further they traveled, the more signs of habitation appeared. Farmers trudging back from their fields, people with carts or beasts of burden either headed to or coming from a market. Many gave Marilyn and her entourage curious stares, but some showed signs of recognition, offering respectful nods or a short greeting. It was becoming clear that her reputation had traveled faster and further than she had.

"A fine day to you, Merlin," greeted a passing farmer, tipping his cap with a blend of respect and wonder. Another, a woman cradling a baby in her arms, approached the column hesitantly. Her eyes, wide with a mix of reverence and desperation, met Marilyn's. "If it pleases you, Merlin," she implored, stepping forward. "Cast a ward to keep my child safe from sickness!" The woman's belief in her powers – a testament to the rumors that swirled around Marilyn's mysterious persona – was palpable.

Marilyn paused, the weight of the woman's expectation settling on her shoulders. Hesitantly, she laid a gentle hand on the child's brow, trying to think of some words of wisdom. "An apple a day keeps the doctor away," she finally murmured softly in English, more for the mother's comfort than from any belief in mystical powers, knowing the woman would not understand the little nursery rhyme spoken in her own tongue. Still, science had proven time and again the power of the placebo effect. Belief, she knew, is a powerful thing – often the key ingredient to ensuring a desired outcome.

The encounter left Marilyn feeling more grounded than pleased. As she continued to walk at the front of the column, her thoughts drifted to the peculiar nature of her fame. It was not just a shield warding off potential threats; it was also a mantle heavy with responsibilities she had never sought. Her identity as Merlin – once just a role assumed for survival – had grown into a persona imbued with divine-like expectations. Each respectful nod from passing locals, each whispered plea for magical aid, was a reminder of how deeply her new identity had woven itself into the local lore.

This mystique was both a boon and a burden, complicating her interactions and coloring the expectations placed upon her. She felt a profound sense of humility, aware that the line between the person she truly was and the legend she had become was blurring in the eyes of those around her.

"We are close," Kynan announced, pulling her from her reflections as they approached a cairn of stones on the roadside. The cairn was marked by an engraving of Roman numerals, LXVI – the number 66 – clearly chiseled into the stone, a relic pointing to the measured precision with which the Romans once dominated this landscape.

"King Uthyr will be eager to see you. But we will camp here for the night," Kynan declared, directing the column off the road and down a small hill to a stream. The area bore the scars of numerous past encampments; flattened grass, remains of old fires, and the comforting sound of flowing water welcomed them as they prepared to settle for the evening.

As tents went up and the horses were tended to, Marilyn's thoughts inevitably drifted to her own child. The brief encounter with the woman and her baby earlier had stirred a deep longing and concern for Morgan. Sitting quietly alone, she pulled the Polaroid shot of her child from her pack and stared at it, smiling. How was Morgan faring under Ygraine's care? Would she be able to reclaim her daughter without arousing Gorloys' suspicions? Such worries nagged at her, but as the cool night air replaced the day's sweltering heat, she found herself pushing these thoughts aside. "Worries for another day," she thought, yawning as she stowed the picture away again and settled back under the deepening sky, the first stars appearing in its indigo canvas. Tonight, she needed rest, to gather strength for the challenges that awaited.

The morning sun was just above the horizon, and already the summer heat was beginning to make itself felt as Marilyn and her entourage neared Mêlotir. The massive hill, its flat summit like a plateau, rose ahead of them, framed by a dense tract of forest through which a narrow lane had been cleared. This lane was the only breach in the unbroken expanse of trees that circled the hill's formidable base.

As they approached the foot of the hill, a series of switchbacks became visible, tracing a path up two sides of the hill, lined with remnants of ancient stone walls, now crumbled and weather-worn, and making them stand out prominently along the hillside. Despite their dilapidated state, these walls still served to remind Marilyn of the ancient history of the land. This hill was likely a place of some strategic importance in the past.

Beyond the forest, sprawling farmland stretched out, dotted with hovels where farmers were already busy with their morning tasks, largely oblivious to the massive sentinel towering over them. The wide, clear path leading to the hill – an offshoot from the Fossa Via – was bustling with activity. Carts laden with supplies, messengers on horseback, and laborers moved back and forth, contributing to the hive of industry at the hill's base and all along the path leading to the plateau at the summit.

As they drew closer, Marilyn could see a tent-riddled campsite atop the plateau, and along the path, clusters of workers were busy repairing the stone buttresses along the path. The sounds of construction echoed down the switchbacks, blending with the morning chorus of birds from the surrounding forest.

They cleared a rise, revealing a previously unseen vale that lay between the rise and the tract of forest surrounding the hill. The vale, home to a large village of thatch-covered, wattle-and-daub hovels nestled beside a stream, was doubtless home to many of the farmers and shepherds going about their chores in the fields under the shadow of the hill.

Kynan signaled to one of the men as they approached the village. "Go tell King Uthyr we have arrived," he commanded, heightening Marilyn's anticipation. The warrior quickly spurred his horse forward, galloping up the switchbacks to notify Uthyr of their imminent arrival.

Marilyn paused for a moment, taking in the vibrant scene, wondering why Uthyr chose for her to bring the artifact here of all places.

Despite its apparent strategic history, and her sense that it was fairly isolated from the world beyond, there was still a significant population here, many of which eyed the enormous, tarped object lying atop the horse cart with curiosity. One man even had the courage to ask what it was. "A gift for King Uthyr," Marilyn replied quickly, then turned away and rode on before the man could question further. She had thought Uthyr would choose a location secluded from others so as not to have the artifact's relativistic effects when activated adversely affect anyone nearby.

A gentle breeze greeted them as they cleared the forest canopy, offering a respite from the burgeoning heat of the day as they climbed the egress of switchbacks toward the summit. The surrounding countryside spread out beneath them – a vast panorama of rolling fields and scattered woodlands, with the Fossa Via cutting through the landscape like a deliberate scar. Marilyn's sense of awe deepened, reflecting on the enduring legacy and the commanding presence of Mêlotir.

Upon reaching the plateau, they were met not just with a temporary encampment but a thriving village of mixed structures. Tents stood alongside more permanent wattle-and-daub houses, and a building of stone and logs was under construction at the far end of the plateau, indicating the settlement's growing permanence. Crews of men were busily engaged with a pulley system, heaving huge logs up the backside of the hill from the forest below. Another crew was busily hewing the logs, while another used the finished product to add to an enormous parapet, walling off the burgeoning structure from the rest of the settlement.

Amidst this lively scene, Uthyr awaited, his presence as commanding as the hill they stood upon. Yet, as always, he had the same boyish grin he wore the day they met when he was actually little more than a boy. His eyes twinkled mischievously, bringing a smile to Marilyn's face, despite her weariness from the journey now behind her.

"Welcome back, Merlin," he said, his voice resonating with genuine affection. "It has been long!"

"Thank you, Uthyr. It is good to be back," she replied, offering a tired but sincere smile. "How long?" she inquired, curious. For her and the men with her, the trip had taken twelve days, most of which was spent getting to the artifact and then transporting it here.

"Three moons, almost four," Uthyr replied. 'Nearly four months,' Marilyn thought disparagingly, keenly feeling her absence from her child. Uthyr shifted his gaze from her to the artifact lying on the cart, then glanced at the sky. "The door is closed for now then. Good," he added, then turned to Kynan.

"You have witnessed its power when Merlin's door is open?" Uthyr asked. Kynan nodded, as did several of the men with him. "Then you know that others must be kept clear of it. Take it and put it in the building over there," he instructed, pointing to the unfinished stone and wood building at the far end of the plateau. "Then post men to keep guard at the perimeter wall being built around it so that no one gets close."

Marilyn admired Uthyr's prudence as she surveyed the perimeter wall once again – more than fifty yards from the main structure, ensuring no one would feel its temporal affects when the artifact was activated. "If anyone asks," she chimed in, "tell them it is nothing more than a huge round table meant for King Uthyr's great hall once finished – a gift from Merlin."

Kynan and his men left to execute Uthyr's orders while he motioned her to walk with him. "I have news!" he began excitedly. "Much has happened while you were away. But first a surprise. Come!"

Marilyn took in the sights and sounds of industry as they walked, marveling at the level of activity despite the seemingly remote location. "It is easy to lose your sense of where you are here among the marshes, forests, and hills," she mused aloud. "Why here, Uthyr? Where are we?"

"We are mid-way between Execaer and Glouvum," he replied. "As for why, this is the highest vantage in the area. The Romans once had a fortress built here, long ago." His eyes took on a speculative look as he cast his gaze around the hilltop for a moment, as though trying to envision ghosts of a long gone past whose distant imprint were all that remained. "We needed a place to keep your door safe, but nearby, so I thought of Mêlotir," he added, shrugging. "It is remote enough that the magic of your door can be kept at bay yet remain close enough to guard. So, I plan to rebuild the fortress." He pointed toward the unfinished stone and wood building at the far end of the plateau, and added, "Beginning with the great hall where your magical door will be secured away from the rest."

Marilyn nodded, satisfied with the explanation. "Mêlotir; that sounds familiar," Marilyn mused. "Like many words mashed together to form one?"

Uthyr nodded. "You have a keen ear, Merlin. The name Mêlotir comes from 'the honey of the land' in my tongue. The best beekeepers in all of Britannia reside in this area. Hence the name." She smiled, amused by his earnest attempt to clarify. To her, he had essentially repeated the name again one syllable at a time, adding articles – '(the) mêl o' (the) tir', still speaking in his own tongue.

"So, when you rebuild the fortress, you will call it 'Caer Mêlotir'?" she inquired.

"I have not given it much thought," he replied idly. "I suppose so. Why?" he asked in return.

Marilyn smirked, embracing her role in the legends with which she was now a part. "It sounds like a mouthful to me. Perhaps you could mash that together a bit; call your fortress Caermêlot?"

Uthyr paused, contemplating the suggestion. "Caermêlot? Hmm. Yes, it does roll off the tongue rather nicely."

They continued their walk, discussing the future plans for the fortress as he pointed toward one spot or another, explaining what this work crew or that was doing. But soon they were standing before a large pavilion tent where he turned toward her. "Are you ready for your surprise?" he asked excitedly.

"Ready as I will ever be," she replied, a mix of curiosity and caution in her voice. There was a palpable tension, the kind that preceded revelations, and Marilyn braced herself. The flap of the large pavilion tent was pulled aside, and Uthyr gestured for her to enter ahead of him.

Inside, the tent was surprisingly airy and bright, illuminated by shafts of light piercing through small gaps at the top. The interior was simple yet arranged with an air of temporary comfort: rugs on the ground, maps, and various instruments scattered around, and at the center, a large table covered with scrolls and plans.

But it was not the decor that caught her attention. Standing beside the table, her back turned, was a figure that made Marilyn's heart skip a beat. As the figure turned around, Marilyn's eyes widened in disbelief. It was Ygraine, cradling Morgan in her arms.

Without a moment's hesitation, Marilyn rushed forward, her face alight with joy and disbelief. "Morgan!" she exclaimed, her voice choked with emotion.

Ygraine, smiling warmly, stepped forward to meet her, gently transferring the infant into Marilyn's eager arms. "She has been waiting for you," Ygraine said softly, her eyes twinkling with happiness.

Cradling Morgan close, Marilyn felt a surge of overwhelming love and relief. The tiny weight in her arms, so fragile and yet so incredibly vital, anchored her to the moment, to the reality that her daughter was here, in her arms, after what felt like an eternity.

"How...?" Marilyn began, her eyes flicking between Morgan and Ygraine, a flood of questions ready to spill forth.

"We'll have time for all your questions," Uthyr interjected gently, observing the reunion with a fond expression. "For now, just enjoy this moment, Merlin."

Marilyn nodded, her gaze softening as she looked down at Morgan, who gurgled contentedly in her arms. The questions could wait. Right now, nothing mattered more than the tiny heartbeat against her chest, the warm presence of her daughter reassuring her that some miracles were indeed real.

They spent the next few moments in silence, Marilyn slowly rocking Morgan, absorbing the peace that filled the tent. Outside, the world continued its hustle, but inside, time seemed to pause - a mother and her child reunited at last. Then, Uthyr excused himself, claiming he had important matters to attend. "I will leave the two of you to talk," he announced as he stepped out of the tent and let the flap fall behind him.

"She will be wanting to nurse soon," Ygraine said, looking at Morgan. "Are you still with succor?" she asked Marilyn matter-of-factly.

"Yes, but I feel gross and likely taste of sweat," Marilyn replied. "Do we have privacy and a wash basin?"

"Yes, to both questions," Ygraine replied, grinning. "Hand her to me," she said, then reached out and took Morgan back. "There is a bowl of clean water and fresh cloths over in the corner there. I can have a kettle of hot water fetched from the firepit outside if you need it."

"This will be enough, thank you," Marilyn replied as she removed her shirt and began unwrapping the makeshift brassiere from around her swollen breasts. Soon she was clean and had Morgan back in her arms, her baby latched on and suckling gently with a blanket thrown around the two of them for a bit of modesty.

"How is this possible?" Marilyn finally asked, turning to Ygraine as Morgan suckled contentedly.

Ygraine took a deep breath, her expression solemn. "Well...the first thing I suppose you should know...is that Gorloys is dead," she replied, the words coming out in a rush as if it took some courage to utter them.

Marilyn's eyes widened in shock, the words tumbling out before she could stop them. "Uthyr did not!...?" she started, too stunned to complete her question.

"No! No, not Uthyr," Ygraine hurried to clarify, her voice a mix of urgency and reassurance. "In fact, when Uthyr found out, he rushed to Tintagel to tell me. But I already knew. Morghais was witness to his death and told me." She paused, a shadow crossing her face. "But she refuses to talk about it."

"So, you do not know how? Where is Morghais? Perhaps I can speak with her and convince her," Marilyn proposed, a hint of determination creeping into her voice despite the shock.

"It was Magra's son, Lynok, Merlin." Ygraine's voice was low, carrying a weight of sadness. "He said nothing to us, but when he agreed to help in your escape, it was with a mind toward revenge for his brother's death, for whom he apparently blamed Gorloys. Uthyr told me this." She sighed, her gaze distant. "As for Morghais, she refused to join me when I chose to return here with Uthyr. She would not say why, though. Magra told me to leave her be, and that she would look after Morghais."

Marilyn let out a deep sigh, her mind racing to process the revelations. "At least Uthyr did not do the deed himself. Well...now that Morgan is returned to me, you will be going back to Tintagel I suppose?"

Ygraine shook her head, her expression somber. "Well...no. There is more you do not know, Merlin."

Marilyn's eyes narrowed slightly, sensing another layer of complication about to unfold. "If this is about the afternoon the two of you spent together the day I was rescued from Tintagel, I already know, Ygraine. Uthyr confessed it to me. But your husband is barely gone, and your daughter is in pain. You cannot possibly be thinking to just take up with Uthyr?!"

Ygraine reached down and instinctively rubbed her belly, her eyes meeting Marilyn's with a mixture of defiance and resignation. "I have little choice, Merlin," she whispered, her voice barely audible. "I am carrying his child."

Marilyn stared at Ygraine, words failing her as the full implications of Ygraine's news sank in. The tent seemed to close in around her, the weight of each revelation heavier than the last. She stood speechless, the tangled web of personal and political intrigues suddenly binding her tighter than she had ever anticipated, all started a year ago by a seemingly simple agreement she had made while seeking help to return home to her own time.

Marilyn's thoughts shifted, focusing on the immediate needs that tied all these revelations together. "Where is Lynok now?" she asked abruptly, her voice steady despite the turmoil inside her. She needed him to retrieve the chalice – the key item that would allow her to return home with Morgan. And he was the only person who knew precisely where it was hidden. Although she knew it was somewhere in the crevices of the caves beneath Tintagel, without his guidance, finding it could be an impossible task that might take years.

Ygraine's expression turned somber as she answered, "Uthyr sent him to the northern border of his kingdom to help with a problem his cousin Vortigern is having with Pictish and Scotti raiders until things settle down here."

Marilyn frowned, absorbing this new obstacle. Lynok's absence was not just inconvenient; it was a significant complication. "How long will he be gone?" she pressed, her mind racing through the various scenarios and their implications.

Ygraine shrugged slightly, her uncertainty evident. "I do not know, Merlin. You will have to ask Uthyr what is happening there that he sent Lynok to aid."

Marilyn nodded, the weight of the situation settling on her shoulders. "I will speak with Uthyr," she resolved quietly, her mind already turning to the necessary conversations. "Do you recall the strange cup I had him hide for me? I need it back if I am to return home. Only Lynok knows where it is."

Ygraine met Marilyn's gaze, her eyes filled with understanding. "Uthyr will make sure you get it back, Merlin. He knows how badly you wish to return to your home – not just for you but for Morgan as well now."

"Thank you, Ygraine," Marilyn said, offering a weary smile as she gently rocked Morgan in her arms. "For now, I suppose we wait and make the best of things as they are."

As Ygraine nodded and stepped out of the tent, Marilyn sat back, allowing herself a moment to breathe and take in the enormity of her journey thus far. Outside, the sounds of the bustling settlement continued, a constant reminder of the world crafted by the choices she had made, and the silent burden of responsibility for those choices that weighed on her, affecting the lives and deaths of people whose fate might have been entirely different but for her presence, the ripple effects, both good and bad, leaving an indelible mark on history.

The soft sounds of Morgan's breathing next to her provided a counterbalance to her tumultuous thoughts, anchoring her in the moment and grounding her amid the swirling uncertainties of time and fate as she looked out of the tent's entrance at the fading light.

Tomorrow's challenges would come soon enough, and she would meet them with the determination that had brought her this far. The weight of her choices was immense, but so too was her resolve to ensure a future for herself and her daughter, not in the world she found herself in now, but in the world where she belonged, with Philip. Tonight, though, was for peace, for stillness, and for the soft, comforting weight of Morgan in her arms.

The twilight deepened, drawing a curtain over the day, and setting the stage for the night's quiet vigil. Marilyn settled more comfortably, her gaze lingering on the stars beginning to peek through the darkening sky. They were the same stars under which her other life unfolded, worlds and times away, yet here they also watched over her, timeless and steadfast. With a deep, steadying breath, she whispered an oath to the quiet around her, "We'll find our way back, Morgan. I promise."

-- END OF BOOK ONE --

www.ingramcontent.com/pod-product-compliance
Lightning Source LLC
Chambersburg PA
CBHW020616310726
48979CB00008B/1514/J

* 9 7 9 8 9 9 1 8 0 4 5 0 9 *